Ida M. Tarbell

A Short Life of Napoleon Bonaparte

Ida M. Tarbell

A Short Life of Napoleon Bonaparte

ISBN/EAN: 9783337350437

Printed in Europe, USA, Canada, Australia, Japan

Cover: Foto ©Raphael Reischuk / pixelio.de

More available books at **www.hansebooks.com**

A SHORT LIFE

OF

NAPOLEON BONAPARTE

By IDA M. TARBELL

WITH 250 ILLUSTRATIONS

FROM THE HON. GARDINER G. HUBBARD'S
COLLECTION OF NAPOLEON ENGRAVINGS,
SUPPLEMENTED BY PICTURES FROM THE
COLLECTIONS OF PRINCE VICTOR NAPOLEON,
PRINCE ROLAND BONAPARTE, BARON LARREY
AND OTHERS

NEW YORK
S. S. McCLURE, LIMITED
30 LAFAYETTE PLACE
1895

Press of J. J. Little & Co.
Astor Place, New York

PREFACE.

THE chief source of illustration for this volume, as in the case of the Napoleon papers in McCLURE'S MAGAZINE, is the great collection of engravings of Mr. Gardiner G. Hubbard, which has been generously placed at the service of the publishers. In order to make the illustration still more comprehensive, a representative of McCLURE'S MAGAZINE and an authorized agent of Mr. Hubbard visited Paris, to seek there whatever it might be desirable to have in the way of additional pictures which were not within the scope of Mr. Hubbard's splendid collection. They secured the assistance of M. Armand Dayot, *Inspecteur des Beaux-Arts*, who possessed rare qualifications for the task. His official position he owed to his familiarity with the great art collections, both public and private, of France, and his official duties made him especially familiar with the great paintings relating to French history. Besides, he was a specialist in Napoleonic iconography. On account of his qualifications and special knowledge, he had been selected by the great house of Hachette et Cie. to edit their book on *Napoléon raconté par l'Image*, which was the first attempt to bring together in one volume the most important pictures relating to the military, political, and private life of Napoleon. M. Dayot had just completed this task, and was fresh from his studies of Napoleonic pictures, when his aid was secured by the publishers of McCLURE'S MAGAZINE, in supplementing the Hubbard collection.

The work was prosecuted with the one aim of omitting no important picture. When great paintings indispensable to a complete pictorial life of Napoleon were found, which had never been either etched or engraved, photographs were obtained, many of these photographs being made especially for our use.

A generous selection of pictures was made from the works of Raffet and Charlet. M. Dayot was able also to add a number of pictures—not less than a score—of unique value, through his personal relations with the owners of the great private Napoleonic collections. Thus were obtained hitherto unpublished pictures, of the highest value, from the collections of Monseigneur Duc d'Aumale ; of H. I. H., Prince Victor Napoleon ; of Prince Roland ; of Baron Larrey, the son of the chief surgeon of the army of Napoleon ; of the Duke of Bassano, son of the minister and confidant of the emperor ; of Monsieur Edmond Taigny, the friend and biographer of Isabey ; of Monsieur Albert Christophle, Governor-General of the *Crédit-Foncier* of France ; of Monsieur Paul le Roux, who has perhaps the richest of the Napoleonic collections ; and of Monsieur le Marquis de Girardin, son-in-law of the Duc de Gaëte, the faithful Minister of Finance of Napoleon I. It will be easily understood that no doubt can be raised as to the authenticity of documents borrowed from such sources.

The following letter explains fully the plan on which Mr. Hubbard's collection is arranged, and shows as well its admirable completeness. It gives, too, a classification of the pictures into periods, which will be useful to the reader.

WASHINGTON, *October*, 1894.

S. S. McCLURE, Esq.

Dear Sir :—It is about fourteen years since I became interested in engravings, and I have since that time made a collection, including many portraits, generally painted and engraved during the life of the personage. I have from two hundred to three hundred prints relating to Napoleon, his family, and his generals. The earliest of these is a portrait of Napoleon painted in 1791, when he was twenty-two years old ; the next in date was engraved in 1796. There are many in each subsequent year, and four prints of drawings made immediately after his death.

There are few men whose characters at different periods of life are so distinctly marked as Napoleon's, as will appear by an examination of these prints. There are four of these periods : First Period, 1796–

1797, Napoleon the General ; Second Period, 1801-1804, Napoleon the Statesman and Lawgiver ; Third Period, 1804-1812, Napoleon the Emperor ; Fourth Period, the Decline and Fall of Napoleon, including Waterloo and St. Helena. Most of these prints are contemporaneous with the periods described. The portraits include copies of the portraits painted by the greatest painters and engraved by the best engravers of that age. There are four engravings of the paintings by Meissonier—" 1807," " Napoleon," " Napoleon Reconnoitring," and " 1814."

FIRST PERIOD, 1796-1797, *Napoleon the General.*—In these the Italian spelling of the name, " Buonaparte," is generally adopted. At this period there were many French and other artists in Italy, and it would seem as if all were desirous of painting the young general. A French writer in a late number of the " Gazette des Beaux-Arts " is uncertain whether Gros, Appiani, or Cossia was the first to obtain a sitting from General Bonaparte. It does not matter to your readers, as portraits by each of these artists are included in this collection.

There must have been other portraits or busts of Bonaparte executed before 1796, besides the one by Greuze given in this collection. These may be found, but there are no others in my collection. Of the portraits of Napoleon belonging to this period eight were engraved before 1798, one in 1800. All have the long hair falling below the ears and over the forehead and shoulders ; while all portraits subsequent to Napoleon's expedition to Egypt have short hair. The length of the hair affords an indication of the date of the portrait.

SECOND PERIOD, 1801-1804, *Napoleon the Statesman and Lawgiver.*—During this period many English artists visited Paris, and painted or engraved portraits of Napoleon. In these the Italian spelling " Buonaparte " is adopted, while in the French engravings of this period he is called " Bonaparte " or " General Bonaparte." Especially noteworthy among them is " The Review at the Tuileries," regarded by Masson as the best likeness of Napoleon " when thirty years old and in his best estate." The portrait painted by Gérard in 1803, and engraved by Richomme, is by others considered the best of this period. There is already a marked change from the long and thin face in earlier portraits to the round and full face of this period. In some of these prints the Code Napoléon is introduced as an accessory.

THIRD PERIOD, 1804-1812, *Napoleon the Emperor.*—He is now styled " Napoleon," " Napoléon le Grand," or " L'Empereur." His chief painters in this period are Léfevre, Gérard, Isabey, Lupton, and David (with Raphael-Morghen, Longhi, Desnoyers, engravers)—artists of greater merit than those of the earlier periods. The full-length portrait by David has been copied oftener and is better known than any other.

It has been said that we cannot in the portraits of this period, executed by Gérard, Isabey, and David, find a true likeness of Napoleon. His ministers thought " it was necessary that the sovereign should have a serene expression, with a beauty almost more than human, like the deified Cæsars or the gods of whom they were the image." " Advise the painters," Napoleon wrote to Duroc, September 15, 1807, " to make the countenance more gracious (*plutôt gracieuses*)." Again, " Advise the painters to seek less a perfect resemblance than to give the beau ideal in preserving certain features and in making the likeness more agreeable (*plutôt agréable*)."

FOURTH PERIOD, 1812-1815, *Decline and Fall of Napoleon.*—We have probably in the front and side face made by Girodet, and published in England, a true likeness of Napoleon. It was drawn by Girodet in the Chapel of the Tuileries, March 8, 1812, while Napoleon was attending mass. It is believed to be a more truthful likeness than that by David, made the same year ; the change in his appearance to greater fulness than in the portraits of 1801-1804 is here more plainly marked. He has now become corpulent, and his face is round and full. Two portraits taken in 1815 show it even more clearly. One of these was taken immediately before the battle of Waterloo, and the other, by J. Eastlake, immediately after. Mr. Eastlake, then an art student, was staying at Plymouth when the " Bellerophon " put in. He watched Napoleon for several days, taking sketches from which he afterwards made a full-length portrait.

The collection concludes with three notable prints : the first of the mask made by Dr. Antommarchi the day of his death, and engraved by Calamatta in 1834 ; another of a drawing " made immediately after death by Captain Ibbetson, R. N.;" and the third of a drawing by Captain Crockatt, made fourteen hours after the death of Napoleon, and published in London July 18, 1821. These show in a remarkable manner the head of this wonderful man.

The larger part of these prints was purchased through Messrs. Wunderlich & Co., and Messrs. Keppel of New York, some at auctions in Berlin, London, Amsterdam, and Stuttgart ; very few in Paris.

GARDINER G. HUBBARD.

The historical and critical notes which accompany the illustrations in this volume have been furnished by Mr. Hubbard as a rule, though those signed A. D. come from the pen of M. Armand Dayot.

TABLE OF CONTENTS.

CHAPTER. PAGE.

I. Youth and Early Surroundings.—School Days at Brienne .   1

II. In Paris.—Lieutenant of Artillery.—Literary Work.—The Revolution   7

III. Robespierre.—Out of Work.—First Success   16

IV. Courtship and Marriage.—Devotion to Josephine .   21

V. Italian Campaign.—Rules of War   26

VI. Return to Paris.—Egyptian Campaign.—The 18th Brumaire   44

VII. Statesman and Lawgiver.—The Finances.—The Industries.—The Public Works .   52

VIII. Return of the Émigrés.—The Concordat.—Legion of Honor.—Code Napoleon.   64

IX. Opposition to the Centralization of the Government.—Prosperity of France   75

X. Preparations for War with England.—Flotilla at Boulogne.—Sale of Louisiana .   81

XI. Emperor of the French People—King of Italy   88

XII. Campaigns of 1805, 1806, 1807.—Peace of Tilsit   104

XIII. Extension of Napoleon's Empire.—Family Affairs   126

XIV. Berlin Decree.—Peninsular War.—The Bonapartes on the Spanish Throne .   138

XV. Disasters in Spain.—Erfurt Meeting.—Napoleon at Madrid   149

XVI. Talleyrand's Treachery.—Campaign of 1809 .   156

XVII. Divorce of Josephine.—Marriage with Marie Louise.—Birth of the King of Rome   164

TABLE OF CONTENTS.

Chapter.		Page.
XVIII.	Trouble with the Pope.—The Conscription.—The Tilsit Agreement Broken	173
XIX.	Russian Campaign.—Burning of Moscow.—A New Army	183
XX.	Campaign of 1813.—Campaign of 1814.—Abdication	192
XXI.	Elba.—The Hundred Days.—The Second Abdication	202
XXII.	Surrender to English.—St. Helena.—Death	213
XXIII.	The Second Funeral	226
	Table of the Bonaparte Family	244
	Chronology of the Life of Napoleon Bonaparte	246

THE LIFE OF NAPOLEON.

CHAPTER I.

NAPOLEON'S YOUTH AND EARLY SURROUNDINGS.—HIS SCHOOL DAYS AT BRIENNE.

"IF I were not convinced that his family is as old and as good as my own," said the Emperor of Austria when he married Marie Louise to Napoleon Bonaparte, "I would not give him my daughter." The remark is sufficient recognition of the nobility of the father of Napoleon, Charles Marie de Bonaparte, a gentleman of Ajaccio, Corsica, whose family, of Tuscan origin, had settled there in the sixteenth century, and who, in 1765, had married a young girl of the island, Lætitia Ramolino.

BONAPARTE AT BRIENNE.

The original of this statue is in the gallery of Versailles. It dates from 1851, and is by Louis Rochet, one of the pupils of David d'Angers.

Monsieur de Bonaparte gave his wife a noble name, but little else. He was an indolent, pleasure-loving, chimerical man, who had inherited a lawsuit, and whose time was absorbed in the hopeless task of recovering an estate of which the Church had taken possession. Madame Bonaparte brought her husband no great name, but she did bring him health, beauty, and remarkable qualities. Tall and imposing, Mademoiselle Lætitia Ramolino had a superb carriage, which she never lost, and a face which attracted attention particularly by the accentuation and perfection of its features. She was reserved, but of ceaseless energy and will, and though but fifteen when married, she conducted her family affairs with such good sense and firmness that she was able to bring up decently the eight children spared her from the thirteen she bore. The habits of order and economy formed in her years of struggle became so firmly rooted in her character that later, when she became *mater regum*, the " Madame Mère " of an imperial court, she could not put them aside, but saved from the generous income at her disposal, " for those of my children who are not yet settled," she said. Throughout her life she showed the truth of her son's characterization: " A man's head on a woman's body."

The first years after their marriage were stormy ones for the Bonapartes. The Corsicans, led by the patriot Pascal Paoli, were in revolt against the French, at that time masters of the island. Among Paoli's followers was Charles Bonaparte. He shared the fortunes of his chief to the end of the struggle of 1769, and when, finally, Paoli was hopelessly defeated, took to the mountains. In all the dangers and miseries of this war and flight, Charles Bonaparte was accompanied by his wife, who, vigorous of body and brave of heart, suffered privations, dangers, and fatigues without complaint. When the Corsicans submitted, the Bonapartes went back to Ajaccio. Six weeks later Madame Bonaparte gave birth to her fourth child, Napoleon.

" I was born," said Napoleon, " when my country was perishing. Thirty thousand Frenchmen were vomited upon our soil.

CHARLES BONAPARTE, FATHER OF NAPOLEON. BORN 1746; DIED 1785.

Cries of the wounded, sighs of the oppressed, and tears of despair surrounded my cradle at my birth."

Young Bonaparte learned to hate with the fierceness peculiar to Corsican blood the idea of oppression, to revere Paoli, and, with a boy's contempt of necessity, even to despise his father's submission. It was not strange. His mother had little time for her children's training. His father gave them no attention; and Napoleon, "obstinate and curious," domineering over his brothers and companions, fearing no one, ran wild on the beach with the sailors or over the mountains with the herdsmen, listening to their tales of the Corsican rebellion and of fights on sea and land, imbibing their contempt for submission, their love for liberty.

At nine years of age he was a shy, proud, wilful child, unkempt and untrained, little, pale, and nervous, almost without instruction, and yet already enamored of a soldier's life and conscious of a certain superiority over his comrades. Then it was that he was suddenly transplanted from his free life to an environment foreign in its language, artificial in its etiquette, and severe in its regulations.

It was as a dependant, a species of charity pupil, that he went into this new atmosphere. Charles Bonaparte had become, in

the nine years since he had abandoned the cause of Paoli, a thorough parasite. Like all the poor nobility of the country to which he had attached himself, and even like many of the rich in that day, he begged favors of every description from the government in return for his support. To aid in securing them, he humbled himself before the French Governor-General of Corsica, the Count de Marbœuf, and made frequent trips, which he could ill afford, back and forth to Versailles. The free education of his children, a good office with its salary and honors, the maintenance of his claims against the Jesuits, were among the favors which he sought.

By dint of solicitation he had secured a place among the free pupils of the college at Autun for his son Joseph, the oldest of the family, and one for Napoleon at the military school at Brienne.

To enter the school at Brienne, it was necessary to be able to read and write French, and to pass a preliminary examination in that language. This young Napoleon could not do; indeed, he could scarcely have done as much in his native Italian. A preparatory school was neces-

sary, then, for a time. The place settled on was Autun, where Joseph was to enter college, and there in January, 1779, Charles Bonaparte arrived with the two boys.

Napoleon was nine and a half years old when he entered the school at Autun. He remained three months, and in that time made sufficient progress to fulfil the requirements at Brienne. The principal record of the boy's conduct at Autun comes from Abbé Chardon, who was at the head of the primary department. He says of his pupil:

" Napoleon brought to Autun a sombre, thoughtful character. He was interested in no one, and found his amusements by himself. He rarely had a companion in his walks. He was quick to learn, and quick of apprehension in all ways. When I gave him a lesson, he fixed his eyes upon me with parted lips; but if I recapitulated anything I had said, his interest was gone, as he plainly showed by his manner. When reproved for this, he would answer coldly, I might almost say with an imperious air, ' I know it already, sir.' "

AT SCHOOL AT BRIENNE.

When he went to Brienne, Napoleon left his brother Joseph behind at Autun. The boy had not now one familiar feature in his life. The school at Brienne was made up of about one hundred and twenty pupils, half of whom were supported by the government. They were sons of nobles, who, generally, had little but their great names, and whose rule for getting on in the world was the rule of the old *régime*—secure a powerful patron, and, by flattery and servile attentions, continue in his train. Young Bonaparte heard little but boasting, and saw little but vanity. His first lessons in French society were the doubtful ones of the parasite and courtier. The motto which he saw everywhere practised was, "The end justifies the means." His teachers were not strong enough men to counteract this influence. The military schools of France were at this time in the hands of religious orders, and the Minim Brothers, who had charge of Brienne, were principally celebrated for their ignorance. They cer-

PORTRAIT OF BONAPARTE, DONE IN CRAYON, BY ONE OF HIS SCHOOLFELLOWS.

This sketch, which used to figure in the *Musée des Souverains*, became afterwards the property of Monsieur de Beaudicourt, who lately presented it to the Louvre. It possesses an exceptional interest. Executed at Brienne by one of the schoolfellows of the future Cæsar, it may be considered as the first portrait of Bonaparte taken from life. Under it are these words written in pencil:

"*Mio caro amico Buonaparte. Pontormini del 1785 Tournone.*"

tainly could not change the arrogant and false notions of their aristocratic young pupils.

It was a dangerous experiment to place in such surroundings a boy like the young Napoleon, proud, ambitious, jealous ; lacking any healthful moral training ; possessing an Italian indifference to truth and the rights of others ; already conscious that he had his own way to make in the world, and inspired by a determination to do it.

From the first the atmosphere at Brienne was hateful to the boy. His comrades were French, and it was the French who had subdued Corsica. They taunted him with it sometimes, and he told them that had there been but four to one, Corsica would never have been conquered, but that the French came ten to one. When they said : "But your father submitted," he said bitterly : "I shall never forgive him for it." As for Paoli, he told them, proudly, "He is a good man. I wish I could be like him."

He had trouble with the new language. They jeered at him because of it. His name was strange ; *la paille au nez* was the nickname they made from Napoleon.

He was poor ; they were rich. The contemptuous treatment he received because of his poverty was such that he begged to be taken home.

"My father [he wrote], if you or my protectors cannot give me the means of sustaining myself more honorably in the house where I am, please let me return home as soon as possible. I am tired of poverty and of the jeers of insolent scholars who are superior to me only in their fortune, for there is not one among them who feels one hundredth part of the noble sentiment which animates me. Must your son, sir, continually be the butt of these boobies, who, vain of the luxuries which they enjoy, insult me by their laughter at the privations which I am forced to endure ? No, father, no ! If fortune refuses to smile upon me, take me from Brienne, and make me, if you will, a mechanic. From these words you may judge of my despair. This letter, sir, please believe, is not dictated by a vain desire to enjoy extravagant amusements. I have no such wish. I feel simply that it is necessary to show my companions that I can procure them as well as they, if I wish to do so.

"Your respectful and affectionate son,
"BONAPARTE."

Charles Bonaparte, always in pursuit of pleasure and his inheritance, could not help his son. Napoleon made other attempts to escape, even offering himself, it is said, to the British Admiralty as a sailor, and once, at least, begging Monsieur de Marbœuf, the Governor-General of Corsica, who had aided Charles Bonaparte in securing places for both boys, to withdraw his protection. The incident which led to this was characteristic of the school. The supercilious young nobles taunted him with his father's position ; it was nothing but that of a poor tipstaff, they said. Young Bonaparte, stung by what he thought an insult, attacked his tormentors, and, being caught in the act, was shut up. He immediately wrote to the Count de Marbœuf a letter of remarkable qualities in so young a boy and in such circumstances. After explaining the incident he said :

"Now, Monsieur le Comte, if I am guilty, if my liberty has been taken from me justly, have the goodness to add to the kindnesses which you have shown me one thing more—take me from Brienne and withdraw your protection ; it would be robbery on my part to keep it any longer from one who deserves it more than I do. I shall never, sir, be worthier of it than I am now. I shall never cure myself of an impetuosity which is all the more dangerous because I believe its motive is sacred. Whatever idea of self-interest influences me, I shall never have control enough to see my father, an honorable man, dragged in the mud. I shall always, Monsieur le Comte, feel too deeply in these circumstances to limit myself to complaining to my superior. I shall always feel that a good son ought not to allow another to avenge such an outrage. As for the benefits which you have rained upon me, they will never be forgotten. I shall say I had gained an honorable protection, but Heaven denied me the virtues which were necessary in order to profit by it."

In the end Napoleon saw that there was no way for him but to remain at Brienne, galled by poverty and formalism.

It would be unreasonable to suppose that there was no relief to this sombre life. The boy won recognition more than once from his companions by his bravery and skill in defending his rights. He was not only valorous ; he was generous, and "preferred going to prison himself to denouncing his comrades who had done wrong." Young Napoleon found, soon, that if there were things for which he was ridiculed, there were others for which he was applauded.

He made friends, particularly among his teachers ; and to one of his comrades, Bourrienne, he remained attached for years. "You never laugh at me ; you like me," he said to his friend. Those who found him morose and surly, did not realize that beneath the reserved, sullen exterior of the little Corsican boy there was a proud and passionate heart aching for love and recognition; that it was sensitiveness rather than arrogance which drove him away from his mates.

At the end of five and one-half years Napoleon was promoted to the military school at Paris. The choice of pupils for this school was made by an inspector, at this time one Chevalier de Kéralio, an amiable old man, who was fond of playing with the boys as well as examining them. He was particularly pleased with Napoleon, and named him for promotion in spite of his being strong in nothing but mathematics, and not yet being of the age required by the regulations. The teachers protested, but De Kéralio insisted.

"I know what I am doing," he said. "If I put the rules aside in this case, it is not to do his family a favor—I do not know them. It is because of the child himself. I have seen a spark here which cannot be too carefully cultivated."

De Kéralio died before the nominations were made, but his wishes in regard to young Bonaparte were carried out. The recommendation which sent him up is curious. The notes read :

"Monsieur de Bonaparte ; height four feet, ten inches and ten lines ; he has passed his fourth examination ; good constitution, excellent health ; submissive character, frank and grateful ; regular in conduct ; has distinguished himself by his application to mathematics ; is passably well up in history and geography ; is behindhand in his Latin. Will make an excellent sailor. Deserves to be sent to the school in Paris."

 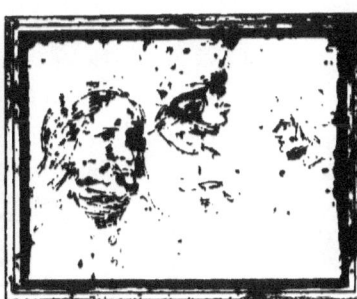 

PENCIL SKETCHES BY DAVID, REPRESENTING BONAPARTE AT BRIENNE, BONAPARTE GENERAL OF THE ARMY OF ITALY, BONAPARTE AS EMPEROR.

CHAPTER II.

NAPOLEON IN PARIS.—LIEUTENANT OF ARTILLERY.—LITERARY WORK.—NAPOLEON AND THE REVOLUTION.

It was in October, 1784, that Napoleon was placed in the École Militaire at Paris, the same school which still faces the Champ de Mars. He was fifteen years old at the time, a thin-faced, awkward, countrified boy, who stared open-mouthed at the Paris street sights and seemed singularly out of place to those who saw him in the capital for the first time.

Napoleon found his new associates even more distasteful than those at Brienne had been. The pupils of the École Militaire were sons of soldiers and provincial gentlemen, educated gratuitously, and rich young men who paid for their privileges. The practices of the school were luxurious. There was a large staff of servants, costly stables, several courses at meals. Those who were rich spent freely ; most of those who were poor ran in debt. Napoleon could not pay his share in the lunches and gifts which his mates offered now and then to teachers and fellows. He saw his sister Eliza, who was at Madame de Maintenon's school at St. Cyr, weep one day for the same reason. He would not borrow. "My mother has already too many expenses, and I have no business to increase them by extravagances which are simply imposed upon me by the stupid folly of my comrades." But he did complain loudly to his friends. The Permons, a Corsican family living on the Quai Conti, who made Napoleon thoroughly at home with them, even holding a room at his disposal, frequently discussed these complaints. Was it vanity and envy,

132

or a wounded pride and just indignation? The latter, said Monsieur Permon. This feeling was so profound with Napoleon, that, with his natural instinct for regulating whatever was displeasing to him, he prepared a memorial to the government, full of good, practical sense, on the useless luxury of the pupils.

A year in Paris finished Napoleon's military education, and in October, 1785, when sixteen years old, he received his appointment as second lieutenant of the artillery in a regiment stationed at Valence. Out of the fifty-eight pupils entitled that year to the promotion of second lieutenant, but six went to the artillery; of these six, Napoleon was one. His examiner said of him:

" Reserved and studious, he prefers study to any amusement, and enjoys reading the best authors; applies himself earnestly to the abstract sciences; cares little for anything else. He is silent and loves solitude. He is capricious, haughty, and excessively egotistical; talks little, but is quick and energetic in his replies, prompt and severe in his repartees; has great pride and ambitions, aspiring to anything. The young man is worthy of patronage."

LIEUTENANT OF ARTILLERY.

He left Paris at once, on money borrowed from a cloth merchant whom his father had patronized, not sorry, probably, that his schooldays were over, though it is certain that all of those who had been friendly to him in this period he never forgot in the future. Several of his old teachers at Brienne received pensions; one was made rector of the School of Fine Arts established at Compiègne, another librarian at Malmaison, where the porter was the former porter of Brienne. The professors of the École Militaire were equally well taken care of, as well as many of his schoolmates. During the Consulate, learning that Madame de Montesson, wife of the Duke of Orleans, was still living, he sent for her to come to the Tuileries, and asked what he could do for her. " But, General," protested Madame de Montesson, " I have no claim upon you."

"You do not know, then," replied the First Consul, "that I received my first crown from you. You went to Brienne with the Duke of Orleans to distribute the prizes, and in placing a laurel wreath on my head, you said: 'May it bring you happiness.' They say I am a fatalist, Madame, so it is quite plain that I could not forget what you no longer remember;" and the First Consul caused the sixty thousand francs of yearly income left Madame de Montesson by the Duke of Orleans, but confiscated in the Revolution, to be returned. Later, at her request, he raised one of her relatives to the rank of senator. In 1805, when emperor, Napoleon gave a life pension of six thousand francs to the son of his former protector, the Count de Marbœuf, and with it went his assurance of interest and good will in all the circumstances of the young man's life. Generous, forbearing, even tender remembrance of all who had been associated with him in his early years,

NAPOLEON AT THE TUILERIES, AUGUST 10, 1792

After a lithograph by Charlet. Lieutenant Bonaparte on the terrace of the Tuileries, watching the crowd of rioters who were hastening to the massacre of the Swiss Guards.

was one of Napoleon's marked characteristics.

His new position at Valence was not brilliant. He had an annual income of two hundred and twenty-four dollars, and there was much hard work. It was independence, however, and life opened gayly to the young officer. He made many acquaintances, and for the first time saw something of society and women. Madame Colombier, whose *salon* was the leading one of the town, received him, introduced him to powerful friends, and, indeed, prophesied a great future for him.

The sixteen-year-old officer, in spite of his shabby clothes and big boots, became a favorite. He talked brilliantly and freely, began to find that he could please, and, for the first time, made love a little—to Mademoiselle Colombier—a frolicking boy-and-girl love, the object of whose stolen rendezvous was to eat cherries together. Mademoiselle Mion-Desplaces, a pretty Corsican girl in Valence, also received some attention from him. Encouraged by his good beginning, and ambitious for future success, he even began to take dancing lessons.

Had there been no one but himself to think of, everything would have gone easily, but the care of his family was upon him. His father had died a few months before, February, 1785, and left his affairs in a sad tangle. Joseph, now nearly eighteen years of age, who had gone to Autun in 1779 with Napoleon, had remained there until 1785. The intention was to make him a priest; suddenly he declared that he would not be anything but a soldier. It was to undo all that had been done for him; but his father made an effort to get him into a military school. Before the arrangements were complete Charles Bonaparte died, and Joseph was obliged to return to Corsica, where he was powerless to do anything for his mother and for the four young children at home: Louis, aged nine; Pauline, seven; Caroline, five; Jerome, three.

Lucien, now nearly eleven years old, was at Brienne, refusing to become a soldier, as his family desired, and giving his time to literature; but he was not a free pupil, and the six hundred francs a year needful for him was a heavy tax. Eliza alone was provided for. She had entered St. Cyr in 1784 as one of the two hundred and fifty pupils supported there by his Majesty, and to be a *demoiselle de St. Cyr* was to be fed, taught, and clothed from seven to twenty, and, on leaving, to receive a dowry of three thousand francs, a *trousseau*, and one hundred and fifty francs for travelling expenses home.

Napoleon regarded his family's situation more seriously than did his brothers. In-

deed, when at Brienne he had shown an interest, a sense of responsibility, and a good judgment about the future of his brothers and sisters, quite amazing in so young a boy. When he was fifteen years old, he wrote a letter to his uncle, which, for its keen analysis, would do credit to the father of a family. The subject was his brother Joseph's desire to abandon the Church and go into the king's service. Napoleon is summing up the pros and cons:

" First. As father says, he has not the courage to face the perils of an action ; his health is feeble, and will not allow him to support the fatigues of a campaign ; and my brother looks on the military profession only from a garrison point of view. He would make a good garrison officer. He is well made, light-minded, knows how to pay compliments, and with these talents he will always get on well in society.

Second. He has received an ecclesiastical education, and it is very late to undo that. Monseignor the Bishop of Autun would have given him a fat living, and he would have been sure to become a bishop. What an advantage for the family ! Monseignor of Autun has done all he could to encourage him to persevere, promising that he should never repent. Should he persist in wishing to be a soldier, I must praise him, provided he has a decided taste for his profession, the finest of all, and the great motive power of human affairs. . . . He wishes to be a military man. That is all very well ; but in what corps ? Is it the marine ? First : He knows nothing of mathematics ; it would take him two years to learn. Second : His health is incompatible with the sea. Is it the engineers ? He would require four or five years to learn what is necessary, and at the end of that time he would be only a cadet. Besides, working all day long would not suit him. The same reasons which apply to the engineers apply to the artillery, with this exception ; that he would have to work eighteen months to become a cadet, and eighteen months more to become an officer. . . . No doubt he wishes to join the infantry. . . . And what is the slender artillery officer ? Three-fourths of the time a scapegrace. . . . A last effort will be made to persuade him to enter the Church, in default of which, father will take him to Corsica, where he will be under his eye."

It was not strange that Charles Bonaparte considered the advice of a son who could write so clear-headed a letter as the one just quoted, nor that the boy's uncle Lucien said, before dying : " Remember, that if Joseph is the older, Napoleon is the real head of the house."

Now that young Bonaparte was in an independent position, he felt still more keenly his responsibility, and it was for this reason, as well as because of ill-health, that he left his regiment in February, 1787, on a leave which he extended to nearly fifteen months, and which he spent in energetic efforts to better his family's situation, working to reestablish salt works and a mulberry plantation in which they were concerned, to secure the nomination of Lucien to the college at Aix, and to place Louis at a French military school.

LITERARY WORK.

When he went back to his regiment, now stationed at Auxonne, he denied himself to send money home, and spent his leisure in desperate work, sleeping but six hours, eating but one meal a day, dressing once in the week. Like all the young men of the country who had been animated by the philosophers and encyclopedists, he had attempted literature, and at this moment was finishing a history of Corsica, a portion of which he had written at Valence and submitted to the Abbé Raynal, who had encouraged him to go on. The manuscript was completed and ready for publication in 1788, and the author made heroic efforts to find some one who would accept a dedication, as well as some one who would publish it. Before he had succeeded, events had crowded the work out of sight, and other ambitions occupied his forces. Napoleon had many literary projects on hand at this time. He

had been a prodigious reader, and was never so happy as when he could save a few cents with which to buy second-hand books. From everything he read he made long extracts, and kept a book 'of "thoughts." Most curious are some of these fragments, reflections on the beginning of society, on love, on nature. They show that he was passionately absorbed in forming ideas on the great questions of life and its relations.

Besides his history of Corsica, he had already written several fragments, among them a romance, an historical drama called the "Count of Essex," and a story, the "Masque Prophète." He undertook, too, to write a sentimental journey in the style of Sterne, describing a trip from Valence to Mont-Cenis. Later he competed for a prize offered by the Academy of Lyons on the subject : "To determine what truths and feelings should be inculcated in men for their happiness." He failed in the contest ; indeed, the essay was severely criticised for its incoherency and poor style.

The Revolution of 1789 turned Napoleon's mind to an ambition greater than that of writing the history of Corsica—he would free Corsica. The National Assem-

BONAPARTE'S FIRST BATTLE.

From a lithograph by Raffet. Bonaparte first took up arms in Sardinia, and even received there a slight wound in the leg. In the beginning of 1793 he took part in an expedition against the island ; with two Corsican battalions he gained possession of the fort of St. Etienne and the islands of La Madeleine. This was his first military success. But the naval division charged to disembark troops for his support was dispersed by a storm ; the expedition ended in failure, and the young Bonaparte received orders to abandon his conquest and return to Corsica. I have been unable to find any other picture consecrated to this feat of arms.—A. D.

BONAPARTE AT THE SIEGE OF TOULON.

This reproduction of the original water color is of particular interest. It was executed during the siege, that is, in 1793, by a Toulonese artist named Grégoire. One may say that it is the unique original picture dating from that period. It was not till after Arcola that artists began going back to the siege of Toulon, and even to the Sardinian campaign, to paint Bonaparte's brilliant actions. In Grégoire's fine sepia the young officer is observing, from the parapet of the fort, the English fleet.

bly had lifted the island from its inferior relation and made it a department of France, but sentiment was much divided, and the ferment was similar to that which agitated France. Napoleon, deeply interested in the progress of the new liberal ideas, and seeing, too, the opportunity for a soldier and an agitator among his countrymen, hastened home, where he spent some twenty-five months out of the next two and a half years. That the young officer spent five-sixths of his time in Corsica, instead of in service, and that he in more than one instance pleaded reasons for leaves of absence which one would have to be exceedingly unsophisticated not to see were trumped up for the occasion, cannot be attributed merely to duplicity of character and contempt for authority. He was doing only what he had learned to do at the military schools of Brienne and Paris, and what he saw practised about him in the army. Indeed, the whole French army at that period made a business of shirking duty. Every minister of war in the period complains of the incessant desertions among the common soldiers. Among the officers it was no better. True, they did not desert; they held their places and—did nothing. "Those who were rich and well born had no need to work," says the Marshal Duc de Broglie. "They were promoted by favoritism. Those who were poor and from the provinces had no need to work either. It did them no good if they did, for, not having patronage, they could not advance." The Comte de Saint-Germain said in regard to the officers: "There is not one who is in active service; they one and all amuse themselves and look out for their own affairs."

Napoleon, tormented by the desire to help his family, goaded by his ambition and that imperative need of action and achievement with which he had been born, still divided in his allegiance between France and Corsica, could not have been expected, in his environment, to take nothing more than the leaves allowed by law.

PRIVATION AND ECONOMIES.

Revolutionary agitation did not absorb all the time he was in Corsica. Never did he work harder for his family. The portion of this two and a half years which he

LIEUTENANT-COLONEL BONAPARTE OF THE CORSICAN VOLUNTEERS.
Engraved by Edwards. After Philippoteaux.

spent in France, he was accompanied by Louis, whose tutor he had become, and he suffered every deprivation to help him. Napoleon's income at that time was sixty-five cents a day. This meant that he must live in wretched rooms, prepare himself the broth on which he and his brother dined, never go to a *café*, brush his own clothes, give Louis lessons. He did it bravely. "I breakfasted off dry bread, but I bolted my door on my poverty," he said once to a young officer complaining of the economies he must make on two hundred dollars a month.

Economy and privation were always more supportable to him than borrowing. He detested irregularities in financial matters. "Your finances are deplorably conducted, apparently on metaphysical principles. Believe me, money is a very physical thing," he once said to Joseph, when the latter, as King of Naples, could not make both ends meet. He put Jerome to sea largely to stop his reckless expenditures. (At fifteen that young man paid three thousand two hundred dollars for a shaving case "containing everything except the beard to enable its owner to use it.") Some of the most furious scenes which occurred between Napoleon and Josephine were because she was continually in debt. After the divorce he frequently cautioned her to be watchful of her money. "Think what a bad opinion I should have of you if I knew you were in debt with an income of six hundred thousand dollars a year," he wrote her in 1813.

The methodical habits of Marie Louise were a constant satisfaction to Napoleon. "She settles all her accounts once a week, deprives herself of new gowns if necessary, and imposes privations upon herself in order to keep out of debt," he said proudly. A bill of sixty-two francs and thirty-two centimes was once sent to him for window blinds placed in the *salon* of the Princess Borghese. "As I did not order this expenditure, which ought not to be charged to my budget, the princess will pay it," he wrote on the margin.

It was not parsimony. It was the man's sense of order. No one was more generous in gifts, pensions, salaries; but it irritated him to see money wasted or managed carelessly.

NAPOLEON AND THE REVOLUTION.

Through his long absence in Corsica, and the complaints which the conservatives of the island had made to the French government of the way he had handled his battalion of National Guards in a riot at Ajaccio, Napoleon lost his place in the French army. He came to Paris in the spring of 1792, hoping to regain it. But in the confused condition of public affairs little attention was given to such cases, and he was obliged to wait.

Almost penniless, he dined on six-cent dishes in cheap restaurants, pawned his watch, and with Bourrienne devised schemes for making a fortune. One was to rent some new houses going up in the city and to sub-let them. While he waited he saw the famous days of the "Second Revolution"—the 20th of June, when the mob surrounded the Tuileries, overran the palace, put the *bonnet rouge* on Louis XVI.'s head, did everything but strike, as the agitators had intended. Napoleon and Bourrienne, loitering on the outskirts, saw the outrages, and he said, in disgust:

"*Che coglione*, why did they allow these brutes to come in? They ought to have shot down five or six hundred of them with cannon, and the rest would soon have run."

He saw the 10th of August, when the king was deposed.

He was still in Paris when the horrible September massacres began—those massacres in which, to "save the country," the fanatical and terrified populace resolved to put "rivers of blood" between Paris and the *émigrés*. All these excesses filled him with disgust. He began to understand that the Revolution he admired so much needed a head.

In August Napoleon was restored to the army. The following June found him with his regiment in the south of France. In the interval spent in Corsica, he had abandoned Paoli and the cause of Corsican independence. His old hero had been dragged, in spite of himself, into a move-

BONAPARTE, LIEUTENANT OF ARTILLERY.

From a water color in the collection of Baron Larrey. In spite of many efforts, I have been unable to discover the name of the author of this charming picture, or the date of its execution. This is the first time it has been reproduced.— A. D.

ment for separating the island from France. Napoleon had taken the position that the French government, whatever its excesses, was the only advocate in Europe of liberty and equality, and that Corsica would better remain with France rather than seek English aid, as it must if it revolted. But he and his party were defeated, and he with his family was obliged to flee.

The Corsican period of his life was over; the French opened. He began it as a thorough republican. The evolution of his enthusiasm for the Revolution had been natural enough. He had been a devoted believer in Rousseau's principles. The year 1789 had struck down the abuses which galled him in French society and government. After the flight of the king in 1791 he had taken the oath:

"I swear to employ the arms placed in my hands for the defence of the country, and to maintain against all her enemies, both from within and from without, the Constitution as declared by the National Assembly; to die rather than to suffer the invasion of the French territory by foreign troops, and to obey orders given in accordance with the decree of the National Assembly."

"The nation is now the paramount object," he wrote; "my natural inclinations are now in harmony with my duties."

The efforts of the court and the *émigrés* to overthrow the new government had increased his devotion to France. "My southern blood leaps in my veins with the rapidity of the Rhone," he said, when the question of the preservation of the Constitution was brought up. The months spent at Paris in 1792 had only intensified his radical notions. Now that he had abandoned his country, rather than assist it to fight the Revolution, he was better prepared than ever to become a Frenchman. It seemed the only way to repair his and his family's fortune.

JOSEPHINE (MARIE JOSEPHINE ROSE) TASCHER DE LA PAGERIE.
After an unpublished miniature, by Rocher, in the collection of the Marquis de Girardin. It must have been shortly after Josephine's arrival in France (in 1778), and some months after her marriage, that this delicate painting was done from life. It is the only one known to me representing Josephine as a very young woman.—A. D.

The condition of the Bonapartes on arriving in France after their expulsion from Corsica was abject. Their property "pillaged, sacked, and burned," they had escaped penniless—were, in fact, refugees dependent upon French bounty. They wandered from place to place, and soon found a good friend in Monsieur Clary of Marseilles, a soap-boiler, with two pretty daughters, Julie and Désirée, and Joseph and Napoleon became inmates of his house.

It was not as a soldier but as a writer that Napoleon first distinguished himself in this new period of his life. An insurrection against the government had arisen in Marseilles. In an imaginary conversation called *le souper de Beaucaire*, Napoleon discussed the situation so clearly and justly that Salicetti, Gasparin, and Robespierre the younger, the deputies who were looking after the South, ordered the paper published at public expense, and distributed it as a campaign document. More, they promised to favor the author when they had an opportunity.

It soon came. Toulon had opened its doors to the English and joined Marseilles in a counter-revolution. Napoleon was in the force sent against the town, and he was soon promoted to the command of the Second Regiment of artillery. His energy and skill won him favorable attention. He saw at once that the important point was not besieging the town, as the general in command was doing and the Convention had ordered, but in forcing the allied fleet from the harbor, when the town must fall of itself. But the commander-in-chief was slow, and it was not until the command was changed and an officer of experience and wisdom put in charge that Napoleon's plans were listened to. The new general saw at once their value, and hastened to carry them out. The result was the withdrawal of the allies in December, 1793, and the fall of Toulon. Bonaparte was mentioned by the general-in-chief as "one of those who have most distinguished themselves in aiding me," and in February, 1794, was made general of brigade.

It is interesting to note that it was at Toulon that Napoleon first came in contact with the English. Here he made the acquaintance of Junot, Marmont, and Duroc. Barras, too, had his attention drawn to him at this time.

The circumstances which brought Junot and Napoleon together at Toulon were especially heroic. Some one was needed to carry an order to an exposed point. Napoleon asked for an under officer, audacious and intelligent. Junot, then a sergeant, was sent. "Take off your uniform and carry this order there," said Napoleon, indicating the point.

Junot blushed and his eyes flashed. "I am not a spy," he answered; "find some one beside me to execute such an order."

"You refuse to obey?" said Napoleon.

"I am ready to obey," answered Junot, "but I will go in my uniform or not go at all. It is honor enough then for these —— Englishmen."

The officer smiled and let him go, but he took pains to find out his name.

A few days later Napoleon called for some one in the ranks who wrote a good hand to come to him. Junot offered himself, and sat down close to the battery to write the letter. He had scarcely finished when a bomb thrown by the English burst near by and covered him and his letter with earth.

"Good," said Junot, laughing, "I shall not need any sand to dry the ink.".

Bonaparte looked at the young man, who had not even trembled at the danger. From that time the young sergeant remained with the commander of artillery.

CHAPTER III.

NAPOLEON AND ROBESPIERRE.—OUT OF WORK.—GENERAL-IN-CHIEF OF THE ARMY OF THE INTERIOR.

THE favors granted Napoleon for his services at Toulon were extended to his family. Madame Bonaparte was helped by the municipality of Marseilles. Joseph was made commissioner of war. Lucien was joined to the Army of Italy, and in the town where he was stationed became famous as a popular orator—"little Robespierre," they called him. He began, too, here to make love to his landlord's daughter, Christine Boyer, afterwards his wife.

The outlook for the refugees seemed very good, and it was made still brighter by the very particular friendship of the younger Robespierre for Napoleon. This friendship was soon increased by the part Napoleon played in a campaign of a month with the Army of Italy, when, largely by his genius, the seaboard from Nice to Genoa was put into French power. If this victory was much for the army and for Robespierre, it was more for Napoleon. He looked from the Tende, and saw for the first time that in Italy there was "a land for a conqueror." Robespierre wrote to his brother, the real head of the government at the moment, that Napoleon possessed "transcendent merit." He engaged

him to draw up a plan for a campaign against Piedmont, and sent him on a secret mission to Genoa. The relations between the two young men were, in fact, very close, and, considering the position of Robespierre the elder, the outlook for Bonaparte was good.

That Bonaparte admired the powers of the elder Robespierre, is unquestionable. He was sure that if he had "remained in power, he would have reëstablished order and law; the result would have been attained without any shocks, because it would have come through the quiet exercise of power." Nevertheless, it is certain that the young general was unwilling to come into close contact with the Terrorist leader, as his refusal of an offer to go to Paris to take the command of the garrison of the city shows. No doubt his refusal was partly due to his ambition—he thought the opening better where he was—and partly due, too, to his dislike of the excesses which the government was practising. That he never favored the policy of the Terrorists, all those who knew him testify, and there are many stories of his efforts at this time to save *émigrés* and suspects from the violence of the rabid patriots; even to save the English imprisoned at Toulon. He al-

ROBESPIERRE, MAXIMILIEN (1758-1794).

Robespierre was born at Arras, and educated in Paris for the law. He was admitted to the bar in 1781, and returned to Arras to practice, where he soon became known as a successful and conscientious advocate. In 1783 he was admitted to the academy of the town, and he competed for prizes offered by provincial academies, though without success. In 1789 he was elected a deputy of the *Tiers États* to the States-General, and afterwards to the Constituent Assembly. He obtained great influence over the people of Paris ; and when the Constituent Assembly dissolved in 1791 he was crowned with Pétion an "incorruptible patriot." The Girondins accused him of aspiring to the dictatorship, and a war between him and that party was waged until their expulsion from the Convention, May 31, 1793. On July 27, 1793, he was elected to the Committee of Public Safety—the real executive government of France at the moment—and he has been credited with being the inventor of the Reign of Terror which that committee inaugurated. On July 26, 1794, Robespierre declared in the Convention that the Terror ought to be ended and deputies who had exceeded their powers punished. His enemies used his speech to arouse a revolt against him, and the next day, 9th Thermidor, he was arrested. His friends rescued him and took him to the Hôtel de Ville. where he was again arrested. In the arrest he was horribly wounded. The next day (28th July) he was executed with twenty-one of his followers ways remembered Robespierre the younger with kindness, and when he was in power gave Charlotte Robespierre a pension.

Things had begun to go well for Bonaparte. His poverty passed. If his plan for an Italian campaign succeeded, he might even aspire to the command of the army. His brothers received good positions. Joseph was betrothed to Julie Clary, and life went gayly at Nice and Marseilles, where Napoleon had about him many of his friends—Robespierre and his sister ; his own two pretty sisters ; Marmont, and Junot, who was deeply in love with Pauline. Suddenly all this hope and happiness were shattered. On the 9th Thermidor Robespierre fell, and all who had favored him were suspected, Napoleon among the rest. His secret mission to Genoa gave a pretext for his arrest, and for thirteen days, in August, 1794, he was a prisoner, but through his friends was liberated.

Soon after his release, came an appointment to join an expedition against Corsica. He set out, but the undertaking was a failure, and the spring found him again without a place.

OUT OF WORK.

In April, 1795, Napoleon received orders to join the Army of the West. When he reached Paris he found that it was the infantry to which he was assigned. Such a change was considered a disgrace in the army. He refused to go. " A great many officers could command a brigade better than I could," he wrote a friend, " but few could command the artillery so well. I retire, satisfied that the injustice done to the service will be sufficiently felt by those who know how to appreciate matters." But though he might call himself " satisfied," his retirement was a most serious affair for him. It was the collapse of what seemed to be a career, the shutting of the gate he had worked so fiercely to open.

He must begin again, and he did not see how. A sort of despair settled over him. " He declaimed against fate," says the Duchess d'Abrantès. " I was idle and discontented," he says of himself. He went to the theatre and sat sullen and inattentive through the gayest of plays. " He had moments of fierce hilarity," says Bourrienne.

A pathetic distaste of effort came over him at times ; he wanted to settle. " If I could have that house," he said one day to Bourrienne, pointing to an empty house near by, " with my friends and a cabriolet,

I should be the happiest of men." He clung to his friends with a sort of desperation, and his letters to Joseph are touching in the extreme.

Love as well as failure caused his melancholy. All about him, indeed, turned his thoughts to marriage. Joseph was now married, and his happiness made him envious. " What a lucky rascal Joseph is ! " he said. Junot, madly in love with Pauline, was with him. The two young men wandered through the alleys of the Jardin des Plantes and discussed Junot's passion. In listening to his friend, Napoleon thought of himself. He had been touched by Désirée Clary, Joseph's sister-in-law. Why not try to win her ? And he began to demand news of her from Joseph. Désirée had asked for his portrait, and he wrote : " I shall have it taken for her ; you must give it to her, if she still wants it ; if not, keep it yourself." He was melancholy when he did not have news of her, accused Joseph of purposely omitting her name from his letters, and Désirée herself of forgetting him. At last he consulted Joseph : " If I remain here, it is just possible that I might feel inclined to commit the folly of marrying. I should be glad of a line from you on the subject. You might perhaps speak to Eugénie's [Désirée's] brother, and let me know what he says, and then it will be settled." He waited the answer to his overtures " with impatience " ; urged his brother to arrange things so that nothing " may prevent that which I long for." But Désirée was obdurate. Later she married Bernadotte and became Queen of Sweden.

Yet in all these varying moods he was never idle. As three years before, he and Bourrienne indulged in financial speculations ; he tried to persuade Joseph to invest his wife's *dot* in the property of the *émigrés.* He prepared memorials on the political disorders of the times and on military questions, and he pushed his brothers as if he had no personal ambition. He did not neglect to make friends either. The most important of those whom he cultivated was Paul Barras, revolutionist, conventionalist, member of the Directory, and one of the most influential men in Paris at that moment. He had known Napoleon at Toulon, and showed himself disposed to be friendly. " I attached myself to Barras," said Napoleon later, " because I knew no one else. Robespierre was dead ; Barras was playing a *rôle :* I had to attach myself to somebody and something." One of his plans for himself was to go to Turkey. For two or three years, in fact, Napoleon had thought of the Orient as a possible field for his genius, and his mother had often worried lest he should go. Just now it happened that the Sultan of Turkey asked the French for aid in reorganizing his artillery and perfecting the defences of his forts, and Napoleon asked to be allowed to undertake the work. While pushing all his plans with extraordinary enthusiasm, even writing Joseph almost daily letters about what he would do for him when he was settled in the Orient, he was called to do a piece of work which was to be of importance in his future.

The war committee needed plans for an Italian campaign ; the head of the committee was in great perplexity. Nobody knew anything about the condition of things in the South. By chance, one day, one of Napoleon's acquaintances heard of the difficulties and recommended the young general. The memorial he prepared was so excellent that he was invited into the topographical bureau of the Committee of Public Safety. His knowledge, sense, energy, fire, were so remarkable that he made strong friends, and he became an important personage.

Such was the impression he made, that when, in October, 1795, the government was threatened by the revolting sections, Barras, the nominal head of the defence, asked Napoleon to command the forces which protected the Tuileries, where the Convention had gone into permanent session. He hesitated for a moment. He had much sympathy for the sections. His sagacity conquered. The Convention stood for the republic ; an overthrow now meant another proscription, more of the Terror, perhaps a royalist succession, an English invasion.

"I accept," he said to Barras ; "but I warn you that once my sword is out of the scabbard I shall not replace it till I have established order."

It was on the night of 12th Vendémiaire that Napoleon was appointed. With incredible rapidity he massed the men and cannon he could secure at the openings into the palace and at the points of approach. He armed even the members of the Convention as a reserve. When the sections marched their men into the streets and upon the bridges leading to the Tuileries, they were met by a fire which scattered

NAPOLEON IN PRISON.

After a lithograph by Motte. Bonaparte, master of Toulon, had already attained fame when the events of Thermidor imposed a sudden check on his career. His relations with the younger Robespierre laid him open to suspicion ; he was suspended from his functions and put under arrest by the deputies of the Convention.

them at once. That night Paris was quiet. The next day Napoleon was made general of division. On October 26th he was appointed general-in-chief of the Army of the Interior.

GENERAL-IN-CHIEF OF THE ARMY OF THE INTERIOR.

At last the opportunity he had sought so long and so eagerly had come. It was a proud position for a young man of twenty-six, and one may well stop and ask how he had obtained it. The answer is not difficult for one who, dismissing the prejudice and superstitions which have long enveloped his name, studies his story as he would that of an unknown individual. He had won his place as any poor and ambitious boy in any country and in any age must win his—by hard work, by grasping at every opportunity, by constant self-denial, by courage in every failure, by springing to his feet after every fall.

He succeeded because he knew every detail of his business (" There is nothing I cannot do for myself. If there is no one to make powder for the cannon I can do it "); because neither ridicule nor coldness nor even the black discouragement which made him write once to Joseph, " If this state of things continues I shall end by not turning out of my path when a carriage passes," could stop him; because he had profound faith in himself. " Do these people imagine that I want their help to rise? They will be too glad some day to accept mine. My sword is at my side, and I will go far with it." That he had misrepresented conditions more than once to secure favor, is true; but in doing this he had done simply what he saw done all about him, what he had learned from his father, what the oblique morality of the day justified. That he had shifted opinions and allegiance, is equally true; but he who in the French Revolution did not shift opinion was he who regarded " not

what is, but what might be." Certainly in no respect had he been worse than his environment, and in many respects he had been far above it. He had struggled for place, not that he might have ease, but that he might have an opportunity for action ; not that he might amuse himself, but that he might achieve glory. Nor did he seek honors merely for himself; it was that he might share them with others.

The first use Bonaparte made of his power after he was appointed general-in-chief of the Army of the Interior, was for his family and friends. Fifty or sixty thousand francs, *assignats*, and dresses go to his mother and sisters ; Joseph is to have a consulship ; "a roof, a table, and carriage" are at his disposal in Paris ; Louis is made a lieutenant and his aide-de-camp ; Lucien, commissioner of war ; Junot and Marmont are put on his staff. He forgets nobody. The very day after the 13th Vendémiaire, when his cares and excitements were numerous and intense, he was at the Permons', where Monsieur Permon had just died. " He was like a son, a brother." This relation he soon tried to change, seeking to marry the beautiful widow Permon. When she laughed merrily at the idea, for she was many years his senior, he replied that the age of his wife was a matter of indifference to him so long as she did not *look over thirty*.

The change in Bonaparte himself was great. Up to this time he had gone about

PEN PORTRAIT OF BONAPARTE IN PROFILE. LOUVRE.

By Gros. This drawing, which I discovered among the portfolios of the Louvre, is one of the most precious documents of Napoleonic portraiture. It was the gift of Monsieur Delestre, the pupil and biographer of Gros. In this clear profile we see already all that *characteristic expression* sought for by Gros above everything, and superbly rendered by him soon after in the portrait of *Bonaparte at Arcola*. I imagine that this pen sketch was preparatory to a finished portrait.   A. D.

Paris " in an awkward and ungainly manner, with a shabby round hat thrust down over his eyes, and with curls (known at that time as *oreilles des chiens*) badly powdered and badly combed, and falling over the collar of the iron-gray coat which has since become so celebrated; his hands, long, thin, and black, without gloves, because, he said, they were an unnecessary expense; wearing ill-made and ill-cleaned boots." The majority of people saw in him only what Monsieur de Pontécoulant,

who took him into the War Office, had seen at their first interview: "A young man with a wan and livid complexion, bowed shoulders, and a weak and sickly appearance."

But now, installed in an elegant *hôtel*, driving his own carriage, careful of his person, received in every *salon* where he cared to go, the young general-in-chief is a changed man. Success has had much to do with this; love has perhaps had more.

CHAPTER IV.

NAPOLEON'S COURTSHIP AND MARRIAGE.—HIS DEVOTION TO JOSEPHINE.

In the five months spent in Paris before the 13th Vendémiaire, Bonaparte saw something of society. One interesting company which he often joined, was that gathered about Madame Permon at a hotel in the Rue des Filles Saint-Thomas. This Madame Permon was the same with whom he had taken refuge frequently in the days when he was in the military school of Paris, and whom he had visited later, in 1792, when lingering in town with the hope of recovering his place in the army. On this latter occasion he had even exposed himself to aid her and her husband to escape the fury of the Terrorists and to fly from the city. Madame Permon had returned to Paris in the spring of 1795 for a few weeks, and numbers of her old friends had gathered about her as before the Terror, among them, Bonaparte.

Another house—and one of very different character—at which he was received, was that of Barras. The 9th Thermidor, as the fall of Robespierre is called, released Paris from a strain of terror so great that, in reaction, she plunged for a time into violent excess. In this period of decadence Barras was sovereign. Epicurean by nature, possessing the tastes, culture, and vices of the old *régime*, he was better fitted than any man in the government to create and direct a dissolute and luxurious society. Into this set Napoleon was introduced, and more than once he expressed his astonishment to Joseph at the turn things had taken in Paris.

" The pleasure-seekers have reappeared, and forget, or, rather, remember only as a dream, that they ever ceased to shine. Libraries are open, and lectures on history, chemistry, astronomy, etc., succeed each other. Everything is done to amuse and make life agreeable. One has no time to think; and how can one be gloomy in this busy whirlwind? Women are everywhere—at the theatres, on the promenades, in the libraries. In the study of the *savant* you meet some that are charming. Here alone, of all places in the world, they deserve to hold the helm. The men are mad over them, think only of them, live only by and for them. A woman need not stay more than six months in Paris to learn what is due her and what is her empire. . . . This great nation has given itself up to pleasure, dancing, and theatres, and women have become the principal occupation. Ease, luxury, and *bon ton* have recovered their throne; the Terror is remembered only as a dream."

Bonaparte took his part in the gayeties of his new friends, and was soon on easy terms with most of the women who frequented the *salon* of Barras, even with the most influential of them all, the famous Madame Tallien, the great beauty of the Directory.

JOSEPHINE DE BEAUHARNAIS.

Among the women whom he met in the *salon* of Madame Tallien and at Barras's own house, was the Viscountess de Beauharnais (*née* Tascher de la Pagerie), widow of the Marquis de Beauharnais, guillotined on the 5th Thermidor, 1794. At the time of the marquis's death his wife was a prisoner. She owed her release to Madame Tallien, with whom she since had been on intimate terms. All Madame Tallien's circle had, indeed, become attached to Josephine de Beauharnais, and with Barras she was on terms of intimacy which led to a great amount of gossip. Without fortune, hav-

"ROSE JOSÉPHINE BONAPARTE, NÉE DE LA PAGERIE."

Companion piece to portrait on page 23, and executed at same time and place—Milan, 1796.

ing two children to support, still trembling at the memory of her imprisonment, indolent and vain, it is not remarkable that Josephine yielded to the pleasures of the society which had saved her from prison and which now opened its arms to her, nor that she accepted the protection of the powerful Director Barras. She was certainly one of the regular *habitués* of his house, and every week kept court for him at her little home at Croissy, a few miles from Paris. The Baron Pasquier, afterwards one of the members of Napoleon's Council of State, was at that moment living in poverty at Croissy—and was a neighbor of Josephine. In his "Memoirs" he has left a paragraph on the gay little outings taken there by Barras and his friends.

"Her house was next to ours," says Pasquier. "She did not come out often at

"BONAPARTE, GÉNÉRAL EN CHEF DE L'ARMÉE D'ITALIE."

"Designed after nature, and engraved at Milan in 1796." This is supposed to be the first engraving
of Napoleon ever made. Below the print runs the legend:

Cui laurus æternis honores,
Italico peperit triumphi.
— Horatii, 4 Libr. 2.

that time, rarely more than once a week, to receive Barras and the troop which always followed him. From early in the morning we saw the hampers coming. Then mounted *gendarmes* began to circulate on the route from Nanterre to Croissy, for the young Director came usually on horseback.

"Madame de Beauharnais's house had, as is often the case among creoles, an appearance of luxury; but, the superfluous aside, the most necessary things were lacking.

Birds, game, rare fruits, were piled up in the kitchen (this was the time of our greatest famine), and there was such a want of stewing-pans, glasses, and plates, that they had to come and borrow from our poor stock."

There was much about Josephine de Beauharnais to win the favor of such a man as Barras. A creole past the freshness of youth—Josephine was thirty-two years old in 1795—she had a grace, a sweetness, a charm, that made one forget that she was not beautiful, even when she was beside such brilliant women as Madame Tallien and Madame Récamier. It was never possible to surprise her in an attitude that was not graceful. She was never ruffled nor irritable. By nature she was the perfection of ease and repose.

Artist enough to dress in clinging stuffs made simply, which harmonized perfectly with her style, and skilful enough to use the arts of the toilet to conceal defects which care and age had brought, the Viscountess de Beauharnais was altogether one of the most fascinating women in Madame Tallien's circle.

The goodness of Josephine's heart undoubtedly won her as many friends as her grace. Everybody who came to know her at all well, declared her gentle, sympathetic, and helpful. Everybody except, perhaps, the Bonaparte family, who never cared for her, and whom she never tried to win. Lucien, indeed, draws a picture of her in his "Memoirs" which, if it could be regarded as unprejudiced, would take much of her charm from her:

"Josephine was not disagreeable, or perhaps I better say, *everybody declared that she was very good;* but it was especially when goodness cost her no sacrifice. . . . She had very little wit, and no beauty at all; but there was a certain creole suppleness about her form. She had lost all natural freshness of complexion, but that the arts of the toilet remedied by candle-light. . . . In the brilliant companies of the Directory, to which Barras did me the honor of admitting me, she scarcely attracted my attention, so old did she seem to me, and so inferior to the other beauties which ordinarily formed the court of the voluptuous Directors, and among whom the beautiful Tallien was the true Calypso."

NAPOLEON ATTRACTED FROM THE FIRST.

But if Lucien was not attracted to Josephine, Napoleon was from the first; and when, one day, Madame de Beauharnais said some flattering things to him about his military talent, he was fairly intoxicated by her praise, followed her everywhere, and fell wildly in love with her; but by her station, her elegance, her influence, she seemed inaccessible to him, and then, too, he was looking elsewhere for a wife. When he first knew her, he was thinking of Désirée Clary; and he had known Josephine some time when he sought the hand of the widow Permon.

Though he dared not tell her his love, all his circle knew of it, and Barras at last said to him, "You should marry Madame de Beauharnais. You have a position and talents which will secure advancement; but you are isolated, without fortune and without relations. You ought to marry; it gives weight," and he asked permission to negotiate the affair.

Josephine was distressed. Barras was her protector. She felt the wisdom of his advice, but Napoleon frightened and wearied her by the violence of his love. A letter of hers, written at this stage of the affair, shows admirably her feelings:

"'Do you like him?' you ask. No; I do not. 'You dislike him, then?' you say. Not at all; but I am in a lukewarm state that troubles me, and which in religion is considered more difficult to manage than unbelief itself, and that is why I need your advice, which will give strength to my feeble nature. To take any positive step has always seemed most fatiguing to my creole nonchalance. I have always found it far easier to yield to the wishes of others.

"I admire the courage of the General, the extent of his information (for he speaks equally well on all subjects), the vivacity of his wit, and the quick intelligence which enables him to grasp the thoughts of others almost before they are expressed; but I am terrified, I admit, at the empire he seems to exercise over all about him. His keen gaze has an inexplicable something which impresses even our Directors; judge, then, if he is not likely to intimidate a woman. In short, just that which ought to please me—the strength of a passion of which he speaks with an energy that permits no doubt of his sincerity—is precisely that which arrests the consent that often hovers on my lips.

"Having passed my *première jeunesse,* can I hope to preserve for any length of time this violent tenderness, which in the General amounts almost to delirium? If when we are married he should cease to love me, would he not reproach me for what I had allowed him to do? Would he not regret a more brilliant marriage that he might have made? What, then, could I say? What could I do? Nothing but weep. . . . . . .

"Barras declares that if I will marry the General he will certainly secure for him the command of the Army of Italy. Yesterday Bonaparte, in speaking of this favor, which has excited a murmur of discontent in his brother officers, even though not yet granted, said to me: 'Do they think that I need protection to rise? They will be glad enough some day if I grant them mine. My sword is at my side, and with it I can go far.'

"What do you say of this certainty of success? Is it not a proof of self-confidence that is almost ridiculous? A general of brigade protecting the heads of government! I feel that it is; and yet this preposterous assurance affects me to such a degree that I can believe everything may be possible to this man, and with his imagination, who can tell what he may be tempted to undertake?

"But for this marriage, which worries me, I should by very gay in spite of many other things; but until this is settled one way or another, I shall torment myself."

In spite of her doubts she yielded at last, and on the 9th of March, 1796, they were married. Shortly before, Napoleon had been appointed commander-in-chief of the Army of Italy, and two days later he left his wife for his post.

NAPOLEON'S LOVE FOR HIS WIFE.

From every station on his route he wrote her passionate letters:

"Every moment takes me farther from you, and every moment I feel less able to be away from you. You are ever in my thoughts; my fancy tires itself in trying to imagine what you are doing. If I picture you sad, my heart is wrung and my grief is increased. If you are happy and merry with your friends, I blame you for so soon forgetting the painful three days' separation; in that case you are frivolous and destitute of deep feeling. As you see, I am hard to please; but, my dear, it is very different when I fear your health is bad, or that you have any reasons for being sad; then I regret the speed with which I am being separated from my love. I am sure that you have no longer any kind feeling toward me, and I can only be satisfied when I have heard that all goes well with you. When any one asks me if I have slept well, I feel that I cannot answer until a messenger brings me word that you have rested well. The illnesses and anger of men affect me only so far as I think they may affect you. May my good genius, who has always protected me amid great perils, guard and protect you! I will gladly dispense with him. Ah! don't be happy, but be a little melancholy, and, above all, keep sorrow from your mind and illness from your body. You remember what Ossian says about that. Write to me, my pet, and a good long letter, and accept a thousand and one kisses from your best and most loving friend."

Arrived in Italy he wrote:

"I have received all your letters, but none has made such an impression on me as the last. How can you think, my dear love, of writing to me in such a way? Don't you believe my position is already cruel enough, without adding to my regrets and tormenting my soul? What a style! What feelings are those you describe! It's like fire; it burns my poor heart. My only Josephine, away from you there is no happiness; away from you, the world is a desert in which I stand alone, with no chance of tasting the delicious joy of pouring out my heart. You have robbed me of more than my soul; you are the sole thought of my life. If I am worn out by all the torments of events, and fear the issue, if men disgust me, if I am ready to curse life, I place my hand on my heart; your image is beating there. I look at it, and love is for me perfect happiness; and everything is smiling, except the time that I see myself absent from my love. By what art have you learned how to captivate all my faculties, to concentrate my whole being in yourself? To live for Josephine! That's the story of my life. I do everything to get to you; I am dying to join you. Fool! Do I not see that I am only going farther from you? How many lands and countries separate us! How long before you will read these words which express but feebly the emotions of the heart over which you reign! . . ."

"Don't be anxious; love me like your eyes—but that's not enough—like yourself; more than yourself, than your thoughts, your mind, your life, your all. But forgive me, I'm raving. Nature is weak when one loves . . ."

"I have received a letter which you interrupt to go, you say, into the country; and afterwards you pretend to be jealous of me, who am so worn out by work and fatigue. Oh, my dear! . . . Of course, I am in the wrong. In the early spring the country is beautiful; and then the nineteen-year-old lover was there, without a doubt. The idea of wasting another moment in writing to the man three hundred leagues away, who lives, moves, exists only in memory of you; who reads your letters as one devours one's favorite dishes after hunting for six hours!"

GENERAL BONAPARTE.

Medallion in terra-cotta. By Boizot. Collection of Monsieur Paul le Roux. All historians who have seriously studied the complex and mysterious iconography of Napoleon, agree in stating that the medallion of Boizot is one of the most faithful portraits of Bonaparte at the time of the Italian campaign. Boizot did not content himself with the few moments of pose accorded by the general, but, desirous of definitely executing his medallion, followed, observed, spied on him, and sketched at all angles the countenance of his glorious model. I have myself handled one or two of those precious little pencil-sketches.—A. D.

CHAPTER V.

But Napoleon had much to occupy him besides his separation from Josephine. Extraordinary difficulties surrounded his new post. Neither the generals nor the men knew anything of their future commander. "Who is this General Bonaparte? Where has he served? No one knows anything about him," wrote Junot's father when the latter at Toulon decided to follow his artillery commander.

In the Army of Italy they were asking the same questions, and the Directory could only answer as Junot had done : "As far as I can judge, he is one of those men of whom nature is avaricious, and that she permits upon the earth only from age to age."

He was to replace a commander-in-chief who had sneered at his plans for an Italian campaign and might be expected to put obstacles in his way. He was to take an army which was in the last stages of poverty and discouragement. Their garments were in rags. Even the officers were so nearly shoeless that when they reached Milan and one of them was invited to dine at the palace of a marquise, he was obliged to go in shoes without soles and tied on by cords carefully blacked. They had provisions for only a month, and half rations at that. The Piedmontese called them the "rag heroes."

Worse than their poverty was their inactivity. "For three years they had fired off their guns in Italy only because war was going on, and not for any especial object—only to satisfy their consciences." Discontent was such that counter-revolution gained ground daily. One company had even taken the name of "Dauphin," and royalist songs were heard in camp.

Napoleon saw at a glance all these difficulties, and set himself to conquer them. With his generals he was reserved and severe. "It was necessary," he explained afterward, "in order to command men so much older than myself." His look and bearing quelled insubordination, restrained familiarity, even inspired fear. "From his arrival," says Marmont, "his attitude was that of a man born for power. It was plain to the least clairvoyant eyes that he knew how to compel obedience, and scarcely was he in authority before the line of a cele-

brated poet might have been applied to him :

"'Des egaux? dès longtemps Mahomet n'en a plus.'"

General Decrès, who had known Napoleon well at Paris, hearing that he was going to pass through Toulon, where he was stationed, offered to present his comrades. "I run," he says, "full of eagerness and joy ; the *salon* opens ; I am about to spring forward, when the attitude, the look, the sound of his voice are sufficient to stop me. There was nothing rude about him, but it was enough. From that time I was never tempted to pass the line which had been drawn for me."

Lavalette says of his first interview with him : "He looked weak, but his regard was so firm and so fixed that I felt myself turning pale when he spoke to me." Augereau goes to see him at Albenga, full of contempt for this favorite of Barras who has never known an action, determined on insubordination. Bonaparte comes out, little, thin, round-shouldered, and gives Augereau, a giant among the generals, his orders. The big man backs out in a kind of terror. "He frightened me," he tells Masséna. "His first glance crushed me."

He quelled insubordination in the ranks by quick, severe punishment, but it was not long that he had insubordination. The army asked nothing but to act, and immediately they saw that they were to move. He had reached his post on March 22d ; nineteen days later operations began.

The theatre of action was along that portion of the maritime Alps which runs parallel with the sea. Bonaparte held the coast and the mountains; and north, in the foot-hills, stretched from the Tende to Genoa, were the Austrians and their Sardinian allies. If the French were fully ten thousand inferior in number, their position was the stronger, for the enemy was scattered in a hilly country where it was difficult to unite their divisions.

As Bonaparte faced his enemy, it was with a youthful zest and anticipation which explains much of what follows. "The two armies are in motion," he wrote Josephine, "each trying to outwit the other. The more skilful will succeed. I am much pleased with Beaulieu. He manœuvres very well, and is superior to his predecessor. I shall beat him, I hope, out of his boots."

SIX VICTORIES IN FIFTEEN DAYS.

The first step in the campaign was a skilful stratagem. He spread rumors which made Beaulieu suspect that he intended marching on Genoa, and he threw out his lines in that direction. The Austrian took the feint as a genuine movement, and marched his left to the sea to cut off the French advance. But Bonaparte was not marching to Genoa, and, rapidly collecting his forces, he fell on the Austrian army at Montenotte on April 12th, and defeated it. The right and left of the allies were divided, and the centre broken.

By a series of clever feints, Bonaparte prevented the various divisions of the enemy from reenforcing each other, and forced them separately to battle. At Millesimo, on the 14th, he defeated one section ; on the same day, at Dego, another ; the next morning, near Dego, another. The Austrians were now driven back, but their Sardinian allies were still at Ceva. To them Bonaparte now turned, and, driving them from their camp, defeated them at Mondovi on the 22d.

It was phenomenal in Italy. In ten days the "rag heroes," at whom they had been mocking for three years, had defeated two well-fed armies ten thousand stronger than themselves, and might at any moment march on Turin. The Sardinians sued for peace.

The victory was as bewildering to the French as it was terrifying to the enemy, and Napoleon used it to stir his army to new conquests.

BONAPARTE, GENERAL OF THE ARMY IN ITALY.

Profile in plaster. By David d'Angers. Collection of Monsieur Paul le Roux. This energetic profile presents considerable artistic and iconographic interest. It is the first rough cast of the face of Bonaparte on the pediment of the Pantheon at Paris. Some months ago, Baron Larrey told me an interesting anecdote regarding this statue. The Baron, son of the chief surgeon to Napoleon I., and himself ex-military surgeon to Napoleon III., happening to be with the emperor at the camp of Châlons conceived the noble idea of trying to save the pediment of the Pantheon, then about to be destroyed to satisfy the Archbishop of Paris, who regarded with lively displeasure the image of Voltaire figuring on the , façade of a building newly consecrated to religion. At the emperor's table, Baron H. Larrey adroitly turned the conversation to David, and informed the sovereign, to his surprise, that the proudest effigy of Napoleon was to be seen on this pediment. Bonaparte, in fact, is represented as seizing for himself the crowns distributed by the Fatherland, while the other personages receive them. On hearing this, Napoleon III. was silent ; but the next day the order was given to respect the pediment. The plaster cast I reproduce here is signed *J. David*. and dates from 1836. The Pantheon pediment was inaugurated in 1817.—A. D.

"Soldiers !" he said, "in fifteen days you have gained six victories, taken twenty-one stands of colors, fifty-five pieces of cannon, and several fortresses, and conquered the richest part of Piedmont. You have made fifteen hundred prisoners, and killed or wounded ten thousand men.

"Hitherto, however, you have been fighting for barren rocks, made memorable by your valor, but useless to the nation. Your exploits now equal those of the conquering armies of Holland and the Rhine. You were utterly destitute, and have supplied all your wants. You have gained battles without cannons, passed rivers without bridges, performed forced marches without shoes, bivouacked without brandy, and often without bread. None but republican phalanxes—soldiers of liberty—could have borne what you have endured. For this you have the thanks of your country.

" The two armies which lately attacked you in full confidence, now fly before you in consternation. . . . But, soldiers, it must not be concealed that you have done nothing, since there remains aught to do. Neither Turin nor Milan is ours. . . . The greatest difficulties are no doubt surmounted ; but you have still battles to fight, towns to take, rivers to cross. . . ."

Not less clever in diplomacy than in battle, Bonaparte, on his own responsibility, concluded an armistice with the Sardinians, which left him only the Austrians to fight, and at once set out to follow Beaulieu, who had fled beyond the Po.

As adroitly as he had made Beaulieu believe, three weeks before, that he was going to march on Genoa, he now deceives him as to the point where he proposes to cross the Po, leading him to believe it is at Valenza. When certain that Beaulieu had his eye on that point, Bonaparte marched rapidly down the river, and crossed at Placentia. If an unforeseen delay had not occurred in the passage, he would have been on the Austrian rear. As it was, Beaulieu took alarm, and withdrew the body of his army, after a slight resistance to the French advance, across the Adda, leaving but twelve thousand men at Lodi.

Bonaparte was jubilant. "We have crossed the Po," he wrote the Directory. " The second campaign has commenced. Beaulieu is disconcerted; he miscalculates, and continually falls into the snares I set for him. Perhaps he wishes to give battle, for he has both audacity and energy, but not genius. . . . Another victory, and we shall be masters of Italy."

Determined to leave no enemies behind him, Bonaparte now marched against the twelve thousand men at Lodi. The town, lying on the right bank of the Adda, was guarded by a small force of Austrians ; but the mass of the enemy was on the left bank, at the end of a bridge some three hundred and fifty feet in length, and commanded by a score or more of cannon.

Rushing into the town on May 10th the French drove out the guarding force, and arrived at the bridge before the Austrians had time to destroy it. The French grenadiers pressed forward in a solid mass, but, when half way over, the cannon at the opposite end poured such a storm of shot at them that the column wavered and fell back. Several generals in the ranks, Bonaparte at their head, rushed to the front of the force. The presence of the officers was enough to inspire the soldiers, and they swept across the bridge with such impetuosity that the Austrian line on the opposite bank al-

lowed its batteries to be taken, and in a few moments was in retreat. "Of all the actions in which the soldiers under my command have been engaged," wrote Bonaparte to the Directory, "none has equalled the tremendous passage of the bridge of Lodi. If we have lost but few soldiers, it was merely owing to the promptitude of our attacks and the effect produced on the enemy by the formidable fire from our invincible army. Were I to name all the officers who distinguished themselves in this affair, I should be obliged to enumerate every *carabinier* of the advanced guard, and almost every officer belonging to the staff."

The Austrians now withdrew beyond the Mincio, and on the 15th of May the French entered Milan. The populace greeted their conquerors as liberators, and for several days the army rejoiced in comforts which it had not known for years. While it was being *fêted*, Bonaparte was instituting the Lombard Republic, and trying to conciliate or outwit, as the case demanded, the nobles and clergy outraged at the introduction of French ideas. It was not until the end of May that Lombardy was in a situation to permit Bonaparte to follow the Austrians.

After Lodi, Beaulieu had led his army to the Mincio. As usual, his force was divided, the right being near Lake Garda, the left at Mantua, the centre about halfway between, at Valeggio. It was at this latter point that Bonaparte decided to attack them. Feigning to march on their right, he waited until his opponent had fallen into his trap, and then sprang on the weakened centre, broke it to pieces, and drove all but twelve thousand men, escaped to Mantua, into the Tyrol. In fifty days he had swept all but a remnant of the Austrians away from Italy. Two weeks later, having taken a strong position on the Adige, he began the siege of Mantua.

The French were victorious, but their position was precarious. Austria was preparing a new army. Between the victors and France lay a number of feeble Italian governments whose friendship could not be depended upon. The populace of these states favored the French, for they brought promises of liberal government, of equality and fraternity. The nobles and clergy hated them for the same reason. It was evident that a victory of the Austrians would set all these petty princes on Bonaparte's heels. The Papal States to the south were plotting. Naples was an ally of Austria. Venice was neutral, but she could not be trusted. The English were

"NAPOLEONE BUONAPARTE, GENERAL-IN-CHIEF OF THE ARMIES OF ITALY."

" From an original drawing in the possession of the Rev. J. Thomas," Epsom. Engraved by John Whessel.
Published November 4, 1797, by John Harris, Sweetings Alley, London.

off the coast, and might, at any moment, make an alliance which would place a formidable enemy on the French rear.

THE AUSTRIANS BRING A NEW ARMY INTO THE FIELD.

While waiting for the arrival of the new Austrian army, Bonaparte set himself to lessening these dangers. He concluded a peace with Naples. Two divisions of the army were sent south, one to Bologna, the other into Tuscany. The people received the French with such joy that Rome was glad to purchase peace. Leghorn was taken. The malcontents in Milan were silenced. By the time a fresh Austrian army

"BONAPARTE."

"Drawn from the life in Italy. Published in London, April 20, 1797, by Tomkins, No. 49 New Bond Street." This is probably the first engraving of Napoleon published in London.

ness, he fell on the enemy piecemeal. Wherever he could engage a division he did so, providing his own force was superior to that of the Austrians at the moment of the battle. Thus, on July 31st, at Lonato, he defeated Quasdanovich, though not so decisively but that the Austrian collected his division and returned towards the same place, hoping to unite there with Wurmser, who had foolishly divided his divisions, sending one to Lonato and another to Castiglione, while he himself went off to Mantua to relieve the garrison there. Bonaparte engaged the forces at Lonato and at Castiglione on the same day (August 3d), defeating them both, and then turned his whole army against the body of Austrians under Wurmser, who, by this time, had returned from his relief expedition at Mantua. On August 5th, at Castiglione, Wurmser was beaten, driven over the Mincio and into the Tyrol. In six days the campaign has been finished. "The Austrian army has vanished like a dream," Bonaparte wrote home.

of sixty thousand men, under a new general, Wurmser, was ready to fight, Italy had been effectually quieted.

The Austrians advanced against the French in three columns, one to the west of Lake Garda, under Quasdanovich, one on each side of the Adige, east of the lake, under Wurmser. Their plan was to attack the French outposts on each side of the lake simultaneously, and then envelop the army. The first movements were successful. The French on each side of the lake were driven back. Bonaparte's army was inferior to the one coming against him, but the skill with which he handled his forces and used the blunders of the enemy more than compensated for lack of numbers. Raising the siege of Mantua, he concentrated his forces at the south of the lake in such a way as to prevent the reunion of the Austrians. Then, with unparalleled swift-

It had vanished, true, but only for a day. Reënforcements were soon sent, and a new campaign started early in September. Leaving Davidovich in the Tyrol with twenty thousand men, Wurmser started down the Brenta with twenty-six thousand men, intending to fall on Bonaparte's rear, cut him to pieces, and relieve Mantua. But Bonaparte had a plan of his own this time, and, without waiting to find out where Wurmser was going, he started up the Adige, intending to attack the Austrians in the Tyrol, and join the army of the Rhine, then on the upper Danube. As it happened, Wurmser's plan was a happy one for Bonaparte. The French found less than half the Austrian army opposing them, and, after they had beaten it, discovered that they were actually on the rear of the other half. Of course Bonaparte did not lose the opportunity. He sped down the Brenta behind Wurmser, overtook him at Bassano on the 8th of September, and of course defeated him. The Austrians fled in terrible demoralization. Wurmser succeeded in reaching Mantua, where he united with the garrison. The sturdy old Austrian had the courage, in spite of his losses, to come out of Mantua and meet Bonaparte on the 15th, but he was defeated again, and obliged to take refuge in the fortress. If the Austrians had been beaten repeatedly, they had no idea of yielding, and, in fact, there was apparently every reason to continue the struggle. The French army was in a most desperate condition. Its number was reduced to barely forty thousand, and this number was poorly supplied, and many of them were ill. Though living in the richest of countries, the rapacity and dishonesty of the army contractors were such that food reached the men half spoiled and in insufficient quantities, while the clothing supplied was pure shoddy. Many officers were laid up by wounds or fatigue ; those who remained at their posts were discouraged, and threatening to resign. The Directory had tampered with Bonaparte's armistices and treaties until Naples and Rome were ready to spring upon the French; and Venice, if not openly hostile, was irritating the army in many ways.

Bonaparte, in face of these difficulties, was in genuine despair :

" Everything is being spoiled in Italy," he wrote the Directory. " The prestige of our forces is being lost. A policy which will give you friends among the princes as well as among the people, is necessary. Diminish your enemies. The influence of Rome is beyond calculation. It was a great mistake to quarrel with that power. Had I been consulted I should have delayed negotiations as I did with Genoa and Venice. Whenever your general in Italy is not the centre of everything, you will run great risks. This language is not that of ambition ; I have only too many honors, and my health is so impaired that I think I shall be forced to demand a successor. I can no longer get on horseback. My courage alone remains, and that is not sufficient in a position like this."

It was in such a situation that Bonaparte saw the Austrian force outside of Mantua, increased to fifty thousand men, and a new

commander-in-chief, Alvinzi, put at its head. The Austrians advanced in two divisions, one down the Adige, the other by the Brenta. The French divisions which met the enemy at Trent and Bassano were driven back. In spite of his best efforts, Bonaparte was obliged to retire with his main army to Verona. Things looked

JUNOT (1771–1813).

Junot, afterwards Duc d'Abrantès, was born at Bussy-le-Grand. He studied law, and in 1791 joined a company of volunteers. His comrades gave him the name of *The Tempest.* At Toulon, where he was sergeant, Napoleon took him for a secretary. Junot distinguished himself in the Italian campaign, particularly at Lonato, where he was severely wounded in the head. He went to Egypt, and there became General-in-Chief. In the battle of Nazareth he showed the most brilliant courage, breaking a column of ten thousand Turks with a body of three hundred horse. Junot was severely wounded in Egypt, in a duel that he fought on account of his General-in-Chief, to whom he was devoted. After the battle of Marengo he was named Commander of Paris, General of Division, and then Colonel-General (1804). He was sent as ambassador to the court of Lisbon from 1804-1805, was present at Austerlitz, was Governor of Paris in 1806, and in 1807 was given the command of the Army of Portugal. He conquered this kingdom in less than two months, a success which earned him the title of the Duc d'Abrantès, but was subsequently beaten by Wellington, and was obliged to evacuate the country in 1808. He showed himself incapable in the Russian campaign, and was appointed to a position in the government of the Illyrian provinces. His grief at this deranged him, and he was sent home to be cared for. In his insanity he threw himself from the window, suffering injuries from which he died some days afterward, July 29, 1813. Junot married Mademoiselle Permon, daughter of the Madame Permon who was so kind to Napoleon in his youth at Paris.

serious. Alvinzi was pressing close to Verona, and the army on the Adige was slowly driving back the French division sent to hold it in check. If Davidovich and Alvinzi united, Bonaparte was lost.

"Perhaps we are on the point of losing Italy," wrote Bonaparte to the Directory. "In a few days we shall make a last effort."

THE BATTLE OF ARCOLA.

On November 14th this last effort was made. Alvinzi was close upon Verona,

(AUGEREAU, 1757-1816.)

Engraved by Lefevre, after a design by Le Dru. Began his military career as a carbineer in the Neapolitan army. In 1792 joined the republican army. From the army of the Pyrenees he passed to that of Italy, where his intrepidity and military talents soon won him a first place. He distinguished himself at Lodi, Castiglione, and Arcola. After the death of Hoche he was sent to take his place in the army of the Rhine-and-Moselle. Augereau was a member of the Council of Five Hundred, and after the 18th Brumaire, received the command of the army of Holland. When Napoleon became emperor, Augereau was made marshal, was given the eagle of the Legion of Honor, and the title of Duke of Castiglione. On the Restoration, Augereau joined Louis XVIII.: but when Napoleon returned from Elba he tried to regain his good will. The Bourbons refused him after the Hundred Days. He died in 1816.

rowfully among themselves that Italy was lost. When far enough from Verona to escape the attention of the enemy, Bonaparte wheeled to the southeast. On the morning of the 15th he crossed the Adige, intending, if possible, to reach the defile by which alone Alvinzi could escape from his position. The country into which his army marched was a morass crossed by two causeways. The points which it was necessary to take to command the defile were the town of Arcola and a bridge over the rapid stream on which the town lay. The Austrians discovered the plan, and hastened out to dispute Arcola and the bridge. All day long the two armies fought desperately, Bonaparte and his generals putting themselves at the head of their columns and doing the work of common soldiers. But at night Arcola was not taken, and the French retired to the right bank of the Adige, only to return on the 16th to reëngage Alvinzi, who, fearful lest his retreat be cut off, had withdrawn his army from near Verona, and had taken a position at Arcola. For two days the French struggled with the Austrians, wrenching the victory from them before the close of the 17th, and sending them flying towards Bassano. Bonaparte and his army returned to Verona, but this time it was by the gate which the Austrians, three days before, were pointing out as the place where they should enter.

It was a month and a half before the Austrians could collect a fifth army to send against the French. Bonaparte, tormented on every side by threatened uprisings in Italy; opposed by the Directory, who wanted to make peace; and distressed by the condition of his army, worked incessantly to strengthen his relations, quiet his enemies, and restore his army. When the Austrians, some forty-five thousand strong, advanced in January, 1797, against him, he had a

holding a position shut in by rivers and mountains on every side, and from which there was but one exit, a narrow pass at his rear. The French were in Verona.

On the night of the 14th of November Bonaparte went quietly into camp. Early in the evening he gave orders to leave Verona, and took the road westward. It looked like a retreat. The French army believed it to be so, and began to say sor-

"BONAPARTE À LA BATAILLE D'ARCOLE, LE 27 BRUMAIRE, AN V."

Engraved at Milan by J. Longhi, 1798, after painting by Gros. The Count La Vallette, aide de-camp of Napoleon at this time, states the circumstances under which this portrait was painted : "It was during his (Napoleon's) short stay at Milan that the young painter Gros, since so celebrated, made the first portrait that we have of the General. He represented him on the bridge at Lodi at the moment when, flag in hand, he rushed forward to lead his troops. The painter could not obtain a moment's sitting. Madame Bonaparte took him on her knees after breakfast and held him some moments. I was present three times. The age of the couple, the modesty of the painter, and his enthusiasm for his subject excused this familiarity. The portrait was astonishingly like him at the time. Some copies have been made of it, but the original is in the hands of the Queen of Holland, Madame the Duchess of Saint Leu."—*Memoirs et Souvenirs du Comte La Vallette*, vol. i. p. 103.

force of about thirty-five thousand men ready to meet them. Some ten thousand of his army were watching Wurmser and the twenty thousand Austrians shut up at Mantua.

Alvinzi had planned his attack skilfully. Advancing with twenty-eight thousand men by the Adige, he sent seventeen thousand under Provera to approach Verona from the east. The two divisions were to approach secretly, and to strike simultaneously.

At first Bonaparte was uncertain of the position of the main body of the enemy. Sending out feelers in every direction, he became convinced that it must be that it approached Rivoli. Leaving a force at Verona to hold back Provera, he concentrated his army in a single night on the plateau of Rivoli, and on the morning of January 14th advanced to the attack. The struggle at Rivoli lasted two days. Nothing but Bonaparte's masterly tactics won it, for the odds were greatly against him. His victory, however, was complete. Of the twenty-eight thousand Austrians brought to the field, less than half escaped.

While this battle was waging, Bonaparte was also directing the fight with Provera, who was intent upon reaching Mantua and attacking the French besiegers on the rear, while Wurmser left the city and engaged them in front. The attack had begun, but Bonaparte had foreseen the move, and sent a division to the relief of his men. This battle, known as La Favorita, destroyed Provera's division of the Austrian army, and so discouraged Wurmser, whose army was terribly reduced by sickness and starvation, that he surrendered on February 2d.

The Austrians were driven utterly from Italy, but Bonaparte had no time to rest. The Papal States and the various aristocratic parties of southern Italy were threatening to rise against the French. The spirit of independence and revolt which the invaders were bringing into the country could not but weaken clerical and monarchical institutions. An active enemy to the south would have been a serious hindrance to Napoleon, and he marched into the Papal States. A fortnight was sufficient to silence the threats of his enemies, and on February 19, 1797, he signed with the Pope the treaty of Tolentino. The peace was no sooner made than he started again against the Austrians.

When Mantua fell, and Austria saw herself driven from Italy, she had called her ablest general, the Archduke Charles, from the Rhine, and given him an army of over one hundred thousand men to lead against Bonaparte. The French had been reënforced to some seventy thousand, and though twenty thousand were necessary to keep Italy quiet, Bonaparte had a fine army, and he led it confidently to meet the main body of the enemy, which had been sent south to protect Trieste. Early in March he crossed the Tagliamento, and in a series of contests, in which he was uniformly successful, he drove his opponent back, step by step, until Vienna itself was in sight, and in April an armistice was signed. In May the French took possession of Venice, which had refused a French alliance, and which was playing a perfidious part, in Bonaparte's judgment, and a republic on the French model was established.

Italy and Austria, worn out and discouraged by this "war of principle," as Napoleon called it, at last compromised, and on October 17th, one year, seven months, and seven days after he left Paris, Napoleon signed the treaty of Campo Formio. By this treaty France gained the frontier of the Rhine and the Low Countries to the mouth of the Scheldt. Austria was given Venice, and a republic called the Cisalpine was formed from Reggio, Modena, Lombardy, and part of the States of the Pope.

NAPOLEON'S RULES OF WAR.

The military genius that this twenty-seven-year-old commander had shown in the campaign in Italy bewildered his enemies and thrilled his friends.

"Things go on very badly," said an Austrian veteran taken at Lodi. "No one seems to know what he is about. The French general is a young blockhead who knows nothing of the regular rules of war. Sometimes he is on our right, at others on our left; now in front, and presently in our rear. This mode of warfare is contrary to all system, and utterly insufferable."

It is certain that if Napoleon's opponents never knew what he was going to do, if his generals themselves were frequently uncertain, it being his practice to hold his peace about his plans, he himself had definite rules of warfare. The most important of these were:

"Attacks should not be scattered, but should be concentrated."

"Always be superior to the enemy at the point of attack."

"Time is everything."

To these formulated rules he joined marvellous fertility in stratagem. The feint by which, at the beginning of the cam-

BATTLE OF RIVOLI, JANUARY 14, 1797.

By Philippoteaux. General Bonaparte, whose horse was killed under him, has mounted another, held by Bessières; in front of him Lasalle, Commander of the Hussars, points out the cannon taken from the enemy. In the background are the heights of Monte Baldo. This picture, exposed in the *Salon* of 1845, is now at Versailles.

"ITALIE."

From a lithograph by Raffet.

paign, he had enticed Beaulieu to march on Genoa, and that by which, a few days later, he had induced him to place his army near Valenza, were masterpieces in their way.

His quick-wittedness in emergency frequently saved him from disaster. Thus, on August 4th, in the midst of the excitement of the contest, Bonaparte went to Lonato to see what troops could be drawn from there. On entering he was greatly surprised to receive an Austrian *parlementaire*, who called on the commandant of Lonato to surrender, because the French were surrounded. Bonaparte saw at once that the Austrians could be nothing but a division which had been cut off and was seeking escape; but he was embarrassed, for there were only twelve hundred men at Lonato. Sending for the man, he had his eyes unbandaged, and told him that if his commander had the presumption to capture the general-in-chief of the army of Italy he might advance; that the Austrian division ought to have known that he was at Lonato with his whole army; and he added that if they did not lay down their arms in eight minutes he would not spare a man. This audacity saved Bonaparte, and won him four thousand prisoners with guns and cavalry.

His fertility in stratagem, his rapidity of action, his audacity in attack, bewildered and demoralized the enemy, but it raised the enthusiasm of his imaginative Southern troops to the highest pitch.

He insisted in this campaign on one other rule : "Unity of command is necessary to assure success." After his defeat of the Piedmontese, the Directory ordered him, May 7, 1796, to divide his command with Kellermann. Napoleon answered :

" I believe it most impolitic to divide the army of Italy in two parts. It is quite as much against the interests of the republic to place two different generals over it. . . .

" A single general is not only necessary, but also it is essential that nothing trouble him in his march and operations. I have conducted this campaign without consulting any one. I should have done nothing of value if I had been obliged to reconcile my plans with those of another. I have gained advantage over superior forces and when stripped of everything myself, because persuaded that your confidence was in me. My action has been as prompt as my thought.

" If you impose hindrances of all sorts upon me, if I must refer every step to government commissioners, if they have the right to change my movements, of taking from me or of sending me troops, expect no more of any value. If you enfeeble your means by dividing your forces, if you break the unity of military thought in Italy, I tell you sorrowfully you will lose the happiest opportunity of imposing laws on Italy.

" In the condition of the affairs of the republic in Italy, it is indispensable that you have a general that has your entire confidence. If it is not I, I am sorry for it, but I shall redouble my zeal to merit your esteem in the post you confide to me. Each one has his own way of carrying on war. General Keller-mann has more experience and will do it better than I, but both together will do it very badly.

" I can only render the services essential to the country when invested entirely and absolutely with your confidence."

He remained in charge, and throughout the rest of the campaign continued to act more and more independently of the Directory, even dictating terms of peace to please himself.

INFLUENCE OVER SOLDIERS AND GENERALS.

It was in this Italian campaign that the almost superstitious adoration which Napoleon's soldiers and most of his generals felt for him began. Brilliant generalship was not the only reason for this. It was due largely to his personal courage, which they had discovered at Lodi. A charge had been o r d e r e d across a wooden bridge swept by thirty pieces of cannon, and beyond was the Austrian army. The men hesitated. Napoleon sprang to their head and led them into the thickest of the fire. From that day he was k n o w n among them as the " Little Corporal." He had won them by the quality which appeals most deeply to a soldier in the ranks—contempt of death. Such was their devotion to him that they gladly exposed their lives if they saw him in danger. There were several

such cases in the battle of Arcola. The first day, when Bonaparte was exposing himself in an advance, his aide-de-camp, Colonel Muiron, saw that he was in imminent danger. Throwing himself before Bonaparte, the colonel covered him with his body, receiving the wound which was destined for the general. The brave fellow's blood spurted into Bonaparte's face. He literally gave his life to save his commander's. The same day, in a final effort to take Arcola, Bonaparte seized a flag, rushed on the bridge, and planted it there. His column reached the middle of the bridge, but there it was broken by the enemy's flanking fire. The grenadiers at the head, finding themselves deserted by the rear, were compelled to retreat ; but, critical as their position was, they refused to abandon their general. They seized him by his arms, by his clothes, and dragged him with them through shot and smoke. When one fell out wounded, another pressed to his place. Precipitated into the morass, Bonaparte sank. The enemy were surrounding him when the grenadiers perceived his danger. A cry was raised, " Forward, soldiers, to save the General!" and immediately they fell upon the Austrians with such fury that they drove them off, dragged out their hero, and bore him to a safe place.

His addresses never failed to stir them to action and enthusiasm. They were ora-

PORTRAIT OF RAFFET.

Drawn by himself in the costume worn by him during his travels in Southern Russia with Prince Demidoff, in 1837. This portrait, for which we are indebted to Monsieur Auguste Raffet, son of the illustrious artist, is one of the best likenesses of the latter. Raffet saw Napoleon only once. (This interesting fact was communicated to me also by Monsieur Auguste Raffet.) It was at the close of 1813, when Raffet was only about twelve years old ; but in spite of his youth, he retained, graven on his memory, an ineffaceable impression of the emperor's features. Yet he had but a momentary glimpse ; for the emperor was passing rapidly along the boulevards in a carriage, surrounded by a numerous escort. The emperor was already suffering from the malady which was to cause his death, and the apprehension of near and inevitable disaster gave to his deathly pale countenance a painful and tragic expression. This vision strongly impressed the child Raffet. He became, as it were, possessed by it ; and whether he is depicting 1796, 1810, 1812, 1814, or 1815, he shows us always a gloomy, careworn, tragic Bonaparte. It can hardly be said that among the numerous artists who painted Napoleon, Raffet is the one who respected most conscientiously the truth to life of his representation. It would have been difficult for him to do so, considering that he was barely thirteen years old when the emperor embarked for St. Helena, that he saw him only on one occasion, and that his young fingers did not even trace from life the outline of his features. But he has succeeded, with astonishing skill, in embodying, in his numerous paintings of Napoleon, the characteristic features of the different portraits which were taken from life ; and I will not hesitate to say that it is in the work of Raffet that future generations will delight to seek for the true image of Napoleon. And it is there they will find it, both legendary and true, but always heroic, such as they will have pictured it in their dreams. The emperor of Raffet and of Meissonier will remain the definite portrait of Napoleon ; and it must be added, to the glory of Raffet, that Meissonier's effigies of Napoleon were inspired entirely by his.—A. D.

BONAPARTE,

Engraved by Bartolozzi, R.A., an Italian engraver, resident of England, after the portrait by Appiani.

torical, prophetic, and abounded in phrases which the soldiers never forgot. Such was his address at Milan :

" Soldiers ! you have precipitated yourselves like a torrent from the summit of the Apennines ; you have driven back and dispersed all that opposed your march. Piedmont, liberated from Austrian tyranny, has yielded to her natural sentiments of peace and amity towards France. Milan is yours, and the Republican flag floats throughout Lombardy, while the Dukes of Modena and Parma owe their political existence solely to your generosity. The army which so haughtily menaced you, finds no barrier to secure it from your courage. The Po, the Ticino, and the Adda have been unable to arrest your courage for a single day. Those boasted ramparts of Italy proved insufficient. You have surmounted them as rapidly as you cleared the Apennines. So much success has diffused joy through the bosom of your country. Yes, soldiers, you have done well ; but is there nothing more for you to accomplish ? Shall it be said of us that we knew how to conquer, but knew not how to profit by victory ? Shall posterity reproach us with having found a Capua in Lombardy ? But I see you rush to arms ; unmanly repose wearies you, and the days lost to glory are lost to happiness.

"Let us set forward. We have still forced marches to perform, enemies to conquer, laurels to gather, and injuries to avenge. Let those tremble who have whetted the poniards of civil war in France; who have, like dastards, assassinated our ministers, and burned our ships in Toulon. The hour of vengeance is arrived, but let the people be tranquil. We are the friends of all nations, particularly the descendants of the Brutuses, the Scipios, and those illustrious persons we have chosen for our models. To restore the Capitol, replace with honor the statues of the heroes who rendered it renowned, and rouse the Roman people, become torpid by so many ages of slavery—shall, will, be the fruit of your victories. You will then return to your homes, and your fellow-citizens when pointing to you will say, '*He was of the army of Italy.*'"

Such was his address in March, before the final campaign against the Austrians:

"You have been victorious in fourteen pitched battles and sixty-six combats; you have taken one hundred thousand prisoners, five hundred pieces of large cannon and two thousand pieces of smaller, four equipages for bridge pontoons. The country has nourished you, paid you during your campaign, and you have beside that sent thirty millions from the public treasury to Paris. You have enriched the Museum of Paris with three hundred *chefs-d'œuvre* of ancient and modern Italy, which it has taken thirty ages to produce. You have conquered the most beautiful country of Europe. The French colors float for the first time upon the borders of the Adriatic. The kings of Sardinia and Naples, the Pope, the Duke of Parma have become allies. You have chased the English from Leghorn, Genoa, and Corsica. You have yet to march against the Emperor of Austria."

His approval was their greatest joy. Let him speak a word of praise to a regiment, and they embroidered it on their banners. "I was at ease, the Thirty-second was there," was on the flag of that regiment. Over the Fifty-seventh floated a name Napoleon had called them by, "The terrible Fifty-seventh."

His displeasure was a greater spur than his approval. He said to a corps which had retreated in disorder: "Soldiers, you have displeased me. You have shown neither courage nor constancy, but have yielded positions where a handful of men might have defied an army. You are no longer French soldiers. Let it be written on their colors, 'They no longer form part of the Army of Italy.'" A veteran pleaded that they be placed in the van, and during the rest of the campaign no regiment was more distinguished.

The effect of his genius was as great on his generals as on his troops. They were dazzled by his stratagems and manœuvres, inspired by his imagination. "*There was so much of the future in him,*" is Marmont's expressive explanation. They could believe anything of him. A remarkable set of men they were to have as followers and friends—Augereau, Masséna, Berthier, Marmont, Junot.

IMPRESSIONS OF THE ITALIAN CAMPAIGN IN PARIS.

The people and the government in Paris had begun to believe in him, as did the Army of Italy. He not only sent flags and reports of victory; he sent money and works of art. Impoverished as the Directory was, the sums which came from Italy were a reason for not interfering with the high hand the young general carried in his campaign and treaties.

"NAPOLEONE BUONAPARTE."

"Engraved by Henry Richter from the celebrated bust by Ceracchi, lately brought from Paris and now in his possession. Published June 1, 1801, by H. Richter. No. 26 Newman Street, Oxford Street." This bust was made in the Italian campaign by Ceracchi, a Corsican working in Rome. Ceracchi left Rome in 1799 to escape punishment for taking part in an insurrection in the city, and went to Paris, where he hoped to receive aid from the First Consul. He made the busts of several generals Berthier, Masséna, and Bernadotte but as orders did not multiply, and Napoleon did nothing for him, he became incensed against him, and took part in a plot to assassinate the First Consul at the opera, the 18th Brumaire, 1801. Arrested on his way to the *loge* in the opera, he was executed soon after.

BONAPARTE AT MALMAISON.

The title on the engraving reads: "Bonaparte, dédié à Madame Bonaparte." Engraved in 1803 by Godefroy, after Isabey. In 1798, after Josephine de Beauharnais had become Madame Bonaparte, she bought, for thirty-two thousand dollars, a property at Marly, eight miles from Paris, known as Malmaison. While Napoleon was in Egypt, Josephine spent most of her time here, gathering about her a circle of the *beaux esprits* of the day, including Bernardin de Saint-Pierre, Arnault, Chénier, Talma, Gérard, Girodet, Mesdames Tallien, Regnault de Saint Jean d'Angely, the Comtesse d'Houdetot, and Fanny de Beauharnais. When Napoleon returned from Egypt he found waiting him a powerful *salon*. After the 18th Brumaire, Malmaison was enlarged and beautified, becoming, in fact, another Trianon. Its park contained kiosks, a *hameau*, a temple of love, a theatre, fountains, lakes, and gardens, and the *château* a fine library and many valuable works of art. A few of the pictures brought to France as spoils of war were deposited at Malmaison, especially two superb Paul Potters. Napoleon is said to have always regretted, when he looked at them, that Josephine had taken them, as he wanted them for the Museum. Before the end of the consulate the Bonapartes left Malmaison for Saint Cloud, and after the Empire the place was almost entirely abandoned. When the divorce was pronounced in 1811 Josephine retired to Malmaison, where she died in 1814, three days after a visit from the Emperor Alexander, whose army had just invaded France. Napoleon visited Malmaison after his return from Elba, and spent five days there after Waterloo. Malmaison passed to Prince Eugène, who sold it to private parties in 1896. In 1861 the state bought it, and still owns it.

JOSEPHINE AT MALMAISON.

By Prud'hon. This charming portrait, which is one of Prud'hon's most successful works, and also one of the most graceful and faithful likenesses of Josephine, was doubtless executed at the same time as Isabey's picture of Napoleon wandering, a solitary dreamer, in the long alleys at Malmaison, (1798). (See opposite page.) Prud'hon shows us Josephine in the garden of the château she loved so well, and in which she spent the happiest moments of her life, before seeking it as a final refuge in her grief and despair. The empress presents a full-length portrait, turned to the left; she is seated on a stone bench amid the groves of the park, in an attitude of reverie, and wears a white *decolleté* robe embroidered in gold. A crimson shawl is draped round her.—A. D.

Never before had France received such letters from a general. Now he announces that he has sent "twenty first masters, from Correggio to Michael Angelo;" now, "a dozen millions of money;" now, two or three millions in jewels and diamonds to be sold in Paris. In return he asks only for men and officers "who have fire and a firm resolution not to make *learned retreats*."

The entry into Paris of the first art acquisitions made a profound impression on the people:

"The procession of enormous cars, drawn by richly caparisoned horses, was divided into four sections. First came trunks filled with books, manuscripts, . . . including the antiques of Josephus, on papyrus, with works in the handwriting of Galileo. . . . Then followed collections of mineral products. . . . For the occasion were added wagons laden with iron cages containing lions, tigers, panthers, over which waved enormous palm branches and all kinds of exotic shrubs. Afterwards rolled along chariots bearing pictures carefully packed, but with the names of the most important inscribed in large letters on the outside, as, The Transfiguration, by Raphael; The Christ, by Titian. The number was great, the value greater. When these trophies had passed, amid the applause of an excited crowd, a heavy rumbling announced the approach of massive carts bearing statues and marble groups: the Apollo Belvidere; the Nine Muses; the Laocoön. . . . The Venus de Medici was eventually added, decked with bouquets, crowns of flowers, flags taken from the enemy, and French, Italian, and Greek inscriptions. Detachments of cavalry and infantry, colors flying, drums beating, music playing, marched at intervals; the members of the newly established Institute fell into line; artists and savants; and the singers of the theatres made the air ring with national hymns. This procession marched through all Paris, and at the Champ de Mars defiled before the five members of the Directory, surrounded by their subordinate officers."

The practice of sending home works of art, begun in the Italian campaign, Napoleon continued throughout his military career, and the art of France owes much to the education thus given the artists of the first part of this century.

His agents ransacked Italy, Spain, Germany, and Flanders for *chefs-d'œuvre*. When entering a country one of the first things he did was to collect information about its chief art objects, in order to demand them in case of victory, for it was by treaty that they were usually obtained. Among the works of art which Napoleon sent to Paris were twenty-five Raphaels, twenty-three Titians, fifty-three Rubenses, thirty-three Van Dykes, thirty-one Rembrandts.

NAPOLEON'S STAR.

In Italy rose Napoleon's "star," that mysterious guide which he followed from Lodi to Waterloo. Here was born that faith in himself and his future, that belief that he "marched under the protection of the goddess of fortune and of war," that confidence that he was endowed with a "good genius."

He called Lodi the birthplace of this faith.

"Vendémiaire and even Montenotte did not make me believe myself a superior man. It was only after Lodi that it came into my head that I could become a decisive actor on our political field. Then was born the first spark of high ambition."

Trained in a religion full of mysticism, taught to believe in signs, guided by a "star," there is a tinge of superstition throughout his active, practical, hard-working life. Marmont tells that one day while in Italy the glass over the portrait of his wife, which he always wore, was broken.

"He turned frightfully pale, and the impression upon him was most sorrowful. 'Marmont,' he said, 'my wife is very ill or she is unfaithful.'" There are many similar anecdotes to show his dependence upon and confidence in omens.

"THE GENERAL OF THE GRAND ARMY."

This pencil portrait by David is nothing but a rapid sketch, but its iconographic interest is undeniable. David doubtless executed this design towards the end of 1797, after Bonaparte's return from Italy. It belongs to Monsieur Cheramy, a Paris lawyer.—A. D.

LOVE IN WAR.

In a campaign of such achievements as that in Italy there seems to be no time for love, and yet love was never more imperative, more absorbing, in Napoleon's life than during this period.

"Oh, my adorable wife," he wrote Josephine in April, " I do not know what fate awaits me, but if it keeps me longer from you, I shall not be able to endure it ; my courage will not hold out to that point. There was a time when I was proud of my courage ; and when I thought of the harm that men might do me, of the lot that my destiny might reserve for me, I looked at the most terrible misfortunes without a quiver, with no surprise.   But now, the thought that my Josephine may be in trouble, that she may be ill, and, above all, the cruel, fatal thought that she may love me less, inflicts torture in my soul, stops the beating of my heart, makes me sad and dejected, robs me of even the courage of fury and despair. I often used to say, ' Man can do no harm to one who is willing to die ; ' but now, to die without being loved by you, to die without this certainty, is the torture of hell ; it is the vivid and crushing image of total annihilation. It seems to me as if I were choking. My only companion, you who have been chosen by fate to make with me the painful journey of life, the day when I shall no longer possess your heart will be that when for me the world shall have lost all warmth and all its vegetation. . . . I will stop, my sweet pet ; my soul is sad. I am very tired, my mind is worn out, I am sick of men. I have good reason for hating them. They separate me from my love.'

Josephine was indifferent to this strong passion. " How queer Bonaparte is ! " she said coldly at the evidences of his affection which he poured upon her ; and when, after a few weeks' separation, he began to implore her to join him, she hesitated, made excuses, tried in every possible way to evade his wish. It was not strange that a woman of her indolent nature, loving flattery, having no passion but for amusement, reckless expenditure, and her own ease, should prefer life in Paris. There she shared with Madame Tallien the adoration which the Parisian world is always bestowing on some fair woman. At opera and ball she was the centre of attraction ; even in the street the people knew her. *Notre Dame des Victoires* was the name they gave her.

In desperation at her indifference, Napoleon finally wrote her, in June, from Tortona :

" My life is a perpetual nightmare. A black presentiment makes breathing difficult. I am no longer alive ; I have lost more than life, more than happiness, more than peace ; I am almost without hope. I am sending you a courier. He will stay only four hours in Paris, and then will bring me your answer. Write to me ten pages ; that is the only thing that can console me in the least. You are ill ; you love me ; I have distressed you ; you are with child ; and I do not see you. . . . I have treated you so ill that I do not know how to set myself right in your eyes. I have been blaming you for staying in Paris, and you have been ill there. Forgive me, my dear ; the love with which you have filled me has robbed me of my reason, and I shall never recover it. It is a malady from which there is no recovery. My forebodings are so gloomy that all I ask is to see you, to hold you in my arms for two hours, and that we may die together. Who is taking care of you ? I suppose that you have sent for Hortense ; I love the dear

child a thousand times better since I think that she may console you a little. As for me, I am without consolation, rest, and hope until I see again the messenger whom I am sending to you, and until you explain to me in a long letter just what is the matter with you, and how serious it is. If there were any danger, I warn you that I should start at once for Paris. . . . You ! you !—and the rest of the world will not exist for me any more than if it had been annihilated. I care for honor because you care for it ; for victory, because it brings you pleasure ; otherwise, I should abandon everything to throw myself at your feet."

After this letter Josephine consented to go to Italy, but she left Paris weeping as if going to her execution. Once at Milan, where she held almost a court, she recovered her gayety, and the two were very happy for a time. But it did not last. Napoleon, obliged to be on the march, would implore Josephine to come to him here and there, and once she narrowly escaped with her life when trying to get away from the army.

Wherever she was installed she had a circle of adorers about her, and as a result she neglected writing to her husband. Reproaches and entreaties filled his letters. He begged her for only a line, and he implored her that she be less cold.

" Your letters are as cold as fifty years of age ; one would think they had been written after we had been married fifteen years. They are full of the friendliness and feelings of life's winter. . . . What more can you do to distress me ? Stop loving me ? That you have already done. Hate me ? Well, I wish you would ; everything degrades me except hatred ; but indifference, with a calm pulse, fixed eyes, monotonous walk ! . . . A thousand kisses, tender, like my heart."

It was not merely indolence and indifference that caused Josephine's neglect. It was coquetry frequently, and Napoleon, informed by his couriers as to whom she received at Milan or Genoa, and of the pleasures she enjoyed, was jealous with all the force of his nature. More than one young officer who dared pay homage to Josephine in this campaign was banished " by order of the commander-in-chief." Reaching Milan once, unexpectedly, he found her gone. His disappointment was bitter.

" I reached Milan, rushed to your rooms, having thrown up everything to see you, to press you to my heart—you were not there ; you are travelling about from one town to another, amusing yourself with balls. . . . My unhappiness is inconceivable. . . . Don't put yourself out ; pursue your pleasure ; happiness is made for you."

It was between such extremes of triumphant love and black despair that Napoleon lived throughout the Italian campaign.

CHAPTER VI.

NAPOLEON'S RETURN TO PARIS.—THE EGYPTIAN CAMPAIGN.—THE 18TH BRUMAIRE.

IN December, 1797, he returned to Paris. His whole family were collected there, forming a "Bonaparte colony," as the Parisians called it. There were Joseph and his wife ; Lucien, now married to Christine Boyer, his old landlord's daughter, a marriage Napoleon never forgave ; Eliza, now Madame Bacciochi ; Pauline, now Madame Leclerc. Madame Letitia was in the city, with Caroline ; Louis and Jerome were still in school. Josephine had her daughter Hortense, a girl of thirteen, with her. Her son Eugène, though but fifteen years old, was away on a mission for Napoleon, who, in spite of the boy's youth, had already taken him into his confidence According to Napoleon's express desire, all the family lived in great simplicity.

The return to Paris of the commander-in-chief of the Army of Italy was the signal for a popular ovation. The Directory gave him every honor, changing the name of the street in which he lived to *rue de la Victoire*, and making him a member of the Institute ; but, conscious of its feebleness, and inspired by that suspicion which since the Revolution began had caused the ruin of so many men, it planned to get rid of him.

Of the coalition against France, formed in 1793, one member alone remained in arms—England. Napoleon was to be sent against her. An invasion of the island was first discussed, and he made an examination of the north coast. His report was adverse, and he substituted a plan for the invasion of Egypt—an old idea in the French government. The Directory gladly accepted the change, and Napoleon was made commander-in-chief of the Army of Egypt.

On the 4th of May he left Paris for Toulon.

To Napoleon this expedition was a merciful escape. He once said to Madame Rémusat :

" In Paris, and Paris is France, they never can take the smallest interest in things, if they do not take it in persons. . . . The great difficulty of the Directory was that no one cared about them, and that people began to care too much about me. This was why I conceived the happy idea of going to Egypt."

He was under the influence, too, of his imagination ; the Orient had always tempted him. It is certain that he went a w a y with gigantic projects—nothing less than to conquer the whole of the East, and to become its ruler and lawgiver.

"I d r e a m e d of all sorts of things, and I saw a way of carrying all my projects into practical execution. I would create a new religion. I saw myself in Asia, upon an elephant, wearing a turban, and holding in my hand a new Koran which I had myself composed. I would have united in my enterprise the experiences of two hemispheres, exploring for my benefit and instruction all history, attacking the power of England in the Indies, and renewing, by their conquest, my relations with old Europe. The time I passed in Egypt was the most delightful period of my life, for it was the most ideal."

His friends, watching his irritation during the days before the campaign had been decided upon, said : "A free flight in space is what such wings demand." He himself said : "Paris weighs on me like a leaden mantle."

BUST OF BONAPARTE.

Bust in terra cotta, occupying a place of honor in the Museum of Versailles. It is one of the best likenesses of Bonaparte. The original has been sought in vain ; the probability is that it no longer exists, and that the Versailles copy is the only one. As far as we know, this remarkable work has never before been reproduced, probably on account of the bad light in which it stands. It bears the following inscription : "*Le général Bonaparte en l'an 8. Fait par Corbet en l'an VIII.*" This bust was made in Egypt. A very beautiful marble copy of the Corbet bust, made by Iselin, is in the fine Napoleonic collection of Mr. Charles Bonaparte of Baltimore.

EXPEDITION IN EGYPT, 1798–1799.

Napoleon sailed from France on May 19, 1798 ; on June 9th he reached Malta,

VISCOUNT NELSON, DUKE OF BRONTE (1758-1805).

Engraved by Dick, after portrait by Knight. Nelson was born at Barnham, England. He entered the navy at twelve years of age. Was made a post-captain when twenty-one years old, and during the next few years was engaged actively in the American war. When war was declared between France and England in 1793, Nelson was given command of the "Agamemnon," and sent to the Mediterranean, where he took part in the sieges of Bastia and Cadiz. For his services in the winter of 1795-96 he was made commodore, and for his daring and skill in the engagement with the Spanish off Cape St. Vincent, February 13, 1797, he received the Order of the Bath and was made admiral. When Napoleon started for Egypt, Nelson was ordered to intercept him, but his squadron was crippled in a gale and Napoleon escaped. On August 1, 1798, he attacked the French fleet in the harbor of Aboukir, and destroyed all but two of the thirteen French ships. For the battle of the Nile, Nelson received a peerage. Nelson now went against Naples, where, after the French had been driven from Italy and an amnesty declared, he allowed the trial and sentence of Caraccioli, the admiral of the Neapolitan fleet a judicial murder similar to that of the Duc d'Enghien. In the spring of 1801 Nelson went to the Baltic. At Copenhagen he engaged the Danish and won the title of viscount. On the renewal of war between France and England in 1803, Nelson went to the Mediterranean, where for two years he kept the French shut in port at Toulon, while Napoleon was preparing for the invasion of England at Boulogne. In March, 1805, the French Admiral Villeneuve escaped. Nelson sought him in the Mediterranean, chased him across the Atlantic and back again, and finally, in September, 1805, found him at Cadiz. In October the French were forced to battle off Cape Trafalgar, where Nelson won a glorious victory, though at the cost of his life. His remains were interred in St. Paul's Cathedral on January 9, 1806.

NAPOLEON AS GENERAL-IN-CHIEF OF THE ARMY IN EGYPT.

DESAIX.

The portraits on pages 46, 47, 43, and 49, of the principal members of the Egyptian Commission and the principal generals of the Army of the East, are by Dutertre, and from the collection of Baron Larrey. Hitherto unpublished. They are of great importance on account of their unflinching reality. Dutertre, who took part in the expedition in the quality of official painter, was above all things a skilful draughtsman; his pencil was always well sharpened and his observation penetrating. Inaccessible to flattery, he never sought to idealize his models, or to represent them with Olympian features and in the attitude of demi-gods. His portraits, all taken from life, will live in history as most reliable documents.—A. D.

and won for France "the strongest place in Europe." July 2d he entered Alexandria. On July 3d he entered Cairo, after the famous battle of the Pyramids.

The French fleet had remained in Aboukir Bay after landing the army, and on August 1st was attacked by Nelson. Napoleon had not realized, before this battle, the power of the English on the sea. He knew nothing of Nelson's genius. The destruction of his fleet, and the consciousness that he and his army were prisoners in the Orient, opened his eyes to the greatest weakness of France.

The winter was spent in reorganizing the government of Egypt and in scientific work. Over one hundred scientists had been added to the Army of Egypt, including some of the most eminent men of the day: Monge, Geoffroy-St.-Hilaire, Berthollet, Fourier, and Denon. From their arrival every opportunity was given them to carry on their work. To stimulate them, Napoleon founded the Institute of Egypt, in which membership was granted as a reward for services.

These scientists went out in every direction, pushing their investigations up the Nile as far as Philœ, tracing the bed of the old canal from Suez to the Nile, unearthing ancient monuments, making collections of the flora and fauna, examining in detail the arts and industries of the people. Everything, from the inscription on the Rosetta Stone to the incubation of chickens, received their attention.

On the return of the expedition, their researches were published in a magnificent work called "Description de l'Egypte."

The information gathered by the French at this time gave a great impetus to the study of Egyptology, and their investigations on the old Suez canal led directly to the modern work.

The peaceful work of science and law-giving which Napoleon was conducting in Egypt was interrupted by the news that the Porte had declared war against France, and that two Turkish armies were on their way to Egypt. In March he set off to Syria to meet the first.

This Syrian expedition was a failure, ending in a retreat made horrible not only by the enemy in the rear, but by pestilence and heat.

The disaster was a terrible disillusion for Napoleon. It ended his dream of an Oriental realm for himself, of a kingdom embracing the whole Mediterranean for France. "I missed my fortune at St. Jean d'Acre," he told his brother Lucien afterward; and again, "I think my imagination died at St. Jean d'Acre." The words are those of the man whose discouragement at a failure was as profound as his hope at success was high.

As Napoleon entered Egypt from Syria, he learned that the second Turkish army was near the Bay of Aboukir. He turned against it and defeated it completely. In the exchange of prisoners made after the battle, a bundle of French papers fell into his hands. It was the first news he had had for ten months from France, and sad news it was: Italy lost, an invasion of Austrians and Russians threatening, the Directory discredited and tottering.

If the Oriental empire of his imagination

BERTHIER.

KLÉBER.

had fallen, might it not be that in Europe a kingdom awaited him? He decided to leave Egypt at once, and with the greatest secrecy prepared for his departure. The army was turned over to Kléber, and with four small vessels he sailed for France on the night of August 22, 1799. On October 16th he was in Paris.

THE 18TH BRUMAIRE.

For a long time nothing had been heard of Napoleon in France. The people said he had been exiled by the jealous Directory. His disappearance into the Orient had all the mystery and fascination of an Eastern tale. His sudden reappearance had something of the heroic in it. He came like a god from Olympus, unheralded, but at the critical instant.

The joy of the people, who at that day certainly preferred a hero to suffrage, was spontaneous and sincere. His journey from the coast to Paris was a triumphal march. *Le retour du héros* was the word in everybody's mouth. On every side the people cried : "You alone can save the country. It is perishing without you. Take the reins of government."

At Paris he found the government waiting to be overthrown. "A brain and a sword" was all that was needed to carry out a *coup d'état* organized while he was still in Africa. Everybody recognized him as the man for the hour. A large part of the military force in Paris was devoted to him. His two brothers, Lucien and Joseph, were in positions of influence, the former president of the Five Hundred, as one of the two chambers was called. All that was most distinguished in the political, military, legal, and artistic circles of Paris rallied to him. Among the men who supported him were Talleyrand, Sieyès, Chénier, Roederer, Monge, Cambacérès, Moreau, Berthier, Murat.

On the 18th Brumaire (the 9th of November), 1799, the plot culminated, and Napoleon was recognized as the temporary Dictator of France.

NAPOLEON AND JOSEPHINE.

The private sorrow to which Napoleon returned, was as great as the public glory. During the campaign in Egypt he had learned beyond a doubt that Josephine's coquetry had become open folly, and that a young officer, Hippolyte Charles, whom he had dismissed from the Army of Italy two years before, was installed at Malmaison. The *liaison* was so scandalous that Gohier, the president of the Directory, advised Josephine to get a divorce from Napoleon and marry Charles.

These rumors reached Egypt, and Napoleon, in despair, even talked them over with Eugène de Beauharnais. The boy defended his mother, and for a time succeeded in quieting Napoleon's resentment. At last, however, he learned in a talk with Junot that the gossip was true. He lost all control of himself, and declared he would have a divorce. The idea was abandoned, but the love and reverence he had given Josephine were dead. From that time she had no empire over his heart, no power to inspire him to action or to enthusiasm.

When he landed in France from Egypt, Josephine, foreseeing a storm, started out to meet him at Lyons. Unfortunately she took one road and Napoleon another, and when he reached Paris at six o'clock in the morning he found no one at home. When Josephine arrived Napoleon refused to see her, and it was three days before he relented. Then his forgiveness was due to

LANNES.

MURAT.

the intercession of Hortense and Eugène, to both of whom he was warmly attached.

But if he consented to pardon, he could never give again the passionate affection which he once had felt for her. He ceased to be a lover, and became a commonplace, tolerant, indulgent, *bourgeois* husband, upon whom his wife, in matters of importance, had no influence. Josephine was hereafter the suppliant, but she never regained the noble kingdom she had despised.

RETURN OF PEACE.

Napoleon's domestic sorrow weakened in no way his activity and vigor in public affairs.

He realized that, if he would keep his place in the hearts and confidence of the people, he must do something to show his strength, and peace was the gift he proposed to make to the nation.

When he returned he found a civil war raging in La Vendée. Before February he had ended it. All over France brigandage had made life and property uncertain. It was stopped by his new *régime*.

Two foreign enemies only remained at war with France—Austria and England. He offered them peace. It was refused. Nothing remained but to compel it. The Austrians were first engaged. They had two armies in the field ; one on the Rhine, against which Moreau was sent, the other in Italy—now lost to France—besieging the French shut up in Genoa.

Moreau conducted the campaign in the Rhine countries with skill, fighting two successful battles, and driving his opponent from Ulm.

Napoleon decided that he would himself carry on the Italian campaign, but of that he said nothing in Paris. His army was quietly brought together as a reserve force ; then suddenly, on May 6, 1800, he left Paris for Geneva. Immediately his plan became evident. It was nothing else than to cross the Alps and fall upon the rear of the Austrians, then besieging Genoa.

Such an undertaking was a veritable *coup de théâtre*. Its accomplishment was not less brilliant than its conception. Three principal passes lead from Switzerland into Italy : Mont Cenis, the Great Saint Bernard, and the Mount Saint Gothard. The last was already held by the Austrians. The first is the westernmost, and here Napoleon directed the attention of General Melas, the Austrian commander. The central, or Mount Saint Bernard, Pass was left almost defenceless, and here the French army was led across, a passage surrounded by enormous difficulties, particularly for the artillery, which had to be taken to pieces and carried or dragged by the men.

Save the delay which the enemy caused the French at Fort Bard, where five hundred men stopped the entire army, Napoleon met with no serious resistance in entering Italy. Indeed, the Austrians treated the force with contempt, declaring that it was not the First Consul who led it, but an adventurer, and that the army was not made up of French, but of refugee Italians. This rumor was soon known to be false. On June 2d Napoleon entered Milan. It was evident that a conflict was imminent, and to prepare his soldiers Bonaparte addressed them :

"Soldiers, one of our departments was in the power of the enemy ; consternation was in the south of France ; the greatest part of the Ligurian territory, the most faithful friends of the Republic, had been invaded. The Cisalpine Republic had again become the grotesque plaything of the feudal *régime*. Soldiers, you march,—and already the French territory is delivered ! Joy and hope have succeeded in your country to consternation and fear.

"You give back liberty and independence to the people of Genoa. You have delivered them from their eternal enemies. You are in the capital of the

JUNOT.

LARREY.

Cisalpine. The enemy, terrified, no longer hopes for anything, except to regain its frontiers. You have taken possession of its hospitals, its magazines, its resources.

"The first act of the campaign is terminated. Every day you hear millions of men thanking you for your deeds.

"But shall it be said that French territory has been violated with impunity? Shall we allow an army which has carried fear into our families to return to its firesides? Will you run with your arms? Very well, march to the battle; forbid their retreat; tear from them the laurels of which they have taken possession; and so teach the world that the curse of destiny is on the rash who dare insult the territory of the Great People. The result of all our efforts will be spotless glory, solid peace."

Melas, the Austrian commander, had lost much time; but finally convinced that it was really Bonaparte who had invaded Italy, and that he had actually reached Milan, he advanced into the plain of Marengo. He had with him an army of from fifty to sixty thousand men well supplied with artillery.

Bonaparte, ignorant that so large a force was at Marengo, advanced into the plain with only a portion of his army. On June 14th Melas attacked him. Before noon the French saw that they had to do with the entire Austrian army. For hours the battle was waged furiously, but with constant loss on the side of the French. In spite of the most intrepid fighting the army gave way. "At four o'clock in the afternoon," says a soldier who was present, "there remained in a radius of two leagues not over six thousand infantry, a thousand horse, and six pieces of cannon. A third of our army was not in condition for battle. The lack of carriages to transport the sick made another third necessary for this painful task. Hunger, thirst, fatigue, had forced a great number to withdraw. The sharp-shooters for the most part had lost the direction of their regiments.

"He who in these frightful circumstances would have said, 'In two hours we shall have gained the battle, made ten thousand prisoners, taken several generals, fifteen flags, forty cannons; the enemy shall have delivered to us eleven fortified places and all the territory of beautiful Italy; they will soon defile shamefaced before our ranks; an armistice will suspend the plague of war and bring back peace into our country,'— he, I say, who would have said that, would have seemed to insult our desperate situation."

The battle was won finally by the French, through the fortunate arrival of Desaix with reënforcements and the imperturbable courage of the commander-in-chief. Bonaparte's coolness was the marvel of those who surrounded him.

"At the moment when the dead and the dying covered the earth, the Consul was constantly braving death. He gave his orders with his accustomed coolness, and saw the storm approach without seeming to fear it. Those who saw him, forgetting the danger that menaced them, said : 'What if he should be killed? Why does he not go back?' It is said that General Berthier begged him to do so.

"Once General Berthier came to him to tell him that the army was giving way and that the retreat had commenced. Bonaparte said to him : 'General, you do not tell me that with sufficient coolness.' This greatness of soul, this firmness, did not leave him in the greatest dangers. When the Fifty-ninth Brigade reached the battle-field the action was the hottest. The First Consul advanced toward them and cried : 'Come, my brave soldiers, spread your banners; the moment has come to distinguish yourselves. I count on your courage to avenge your comrades.' At the moment that he pronounced these words, five men were struck down near him. He turned with a tranquil air towards the

NAPOLEON AT THE BATTLE OF THE PYRAMIDS, JULY 21, 1798.

Engraved by Vallot in 1838, after painting by Gros (1810). The moment chosen by the artist is that when Napoleon addressed to his soldiers that short and famous harangue, "Soldiers, from the summit of these Pyramids forty centuries look down upon you." In the General's escort are Murat, his head bare and his sword clasped tightly ; and after him, in order, Duroc, Sulkowski, Berthier, Junot, and Eugène de Beauharnais, then sub-lieutenant, all on horseback. On the right are Rampon, Desaix, Bertrand, and Lasalle. This picture was ordered for the Tuileries, and was exhibited first in 1810. Napoleon gave it to one of his generals, and it did not reappear in Paris until 1832. It is now in the gallery at Versailles. Gros regarded this picture as his best work, and himself chose Vallot to engrave it.

enemy, and said: 'Come, my friends, charge them.'

"I had curiosity enough to listen attentively to his voice, to examine his features. The most courageous man, the hero the most eager for glory, might have been overcome in his situation without any one blaming him. But he was not. In these frightful moments, when fortune seemed to desert him, he was still the Bonaparte of Arcola and Aboukir."

When Desaix came up with his division, Bonaparte took an hour to arrange for the final charge. During this time the Austrian artillery was thundering upon the army, each volley carrying away whole lines. The men received death without moving from their places, and the ranks closed over the bodies of their comrades. This deadly artillery even reached the cavalry, drawn up behind, as well as a large number of infantry who, encouraged by Desaix's arrival, had hastened back to the field of honor. In spite of the horror of this preparation Bonaparte did not falter. When he was ready he led his army in an impetuous charge which overwhelmed the Austrians completely, though it cost the French one of their bravest generals, Desaix. It was a frightful struggle, but the perfection with which the final attack was planned, won the battle of Marengo and drove the Austrians from Italy.

MEDALLION OF BONAPARTE.

The following inscription, written in French, by Dutertre, the official painter of the principal personages in the Egyptian expedition, appears on the reverse side of this medallion, which frames one of the most precious gems of Napoleonic iconography. "I, Dutertre, made this drawing of the general-in-chief from nature, on board the vessel 'L'Orient,' during the crossing of the expedition to Egypt in the year VII (sic) of the Republic." A short time ago the drawing came into the possession of the Versailles Museum.

The Parisians were dazzled by the campaign. Of the passage of the Alps they said, "It is an achievement greater than Hannibal's;" and they repeated how "the First Consul had pointed his finger at the frozen summits, and they had bowed their heads."

At the news of Marengo the streets were lit with "joy fires," and from wall to wall rang the cries of *Vive la république! Vive le premier consul! Vive l'armée!*

The campaign against the Austrians was finished December 3, 1800, by the battle of Hohenlinden, won by Moreau, and in February the treaty of Lunéville established peace. England was slower in coming to terms, it not being until March, 1802, that she signed the treaty of Amiens.

At last France was at peace with all the world. She hailed Napoleon as her savior, and ordered that the 18th Brumaire be celebrated throughout the republic as a solemn *fête* in his honor.

The country saw in him something greater than a peacemaker.

She was discovering that he was to be her lawgiver, for, while ending the wars, he had begun to bring order into the interior chaos which had so long tormented the French people, to reëstablish the finances, the laws, the industries, to restore public works, to encourage the arts and sciences, even to harmonize the interests of rich and poor, of church and state.

BONAPARTE CARING FOR THE PLAGUE-STRICKEN AT JAFFA.

Pencil sketch by Baron Gros. Collection of Baron Larrey. This is a sketch of the highest artistic and historical value. It has never before been published, and I owe the right of reproduction to the great kindness of Baron Larrey, ex-military-surgeon to Napoleon III., and son of Baron Larrey, surgeon-in-chief to the armies of Napoleon I. This drawing was presented to Baron Larrey by Gros himself. It was the first sketch, the *germ*. of the famous picture in the Louvre, also reproduced here. It seems that Baron Gros greatly modified his first design at the request of Denon, superintendent of the Beaux-Arts, who thought the picture too realistic, although heroic in idea and true to history. Thus it happened that in the final design Bonaparte is represented as merely touching with the tips of his fingers the tumor of one of the plague-stricken, while in the original drawing (here reproduced) he clasps the body of an unfortunate victim in his arms with a movement of rare energy. I cannot help regretting that the great painter should have felt obliged to yield to the counsels and entreaties of Denon.—A. D.

CHAPTER VII.

NAPOLEON AS STATESMAN AND LAWGIVER.—THE FINANCES.—THE INDUSTRIES.— THE PUBLIC WORKS.

THE NEW CONSTITUTION.

"Now we must rebuild, and, moreover, we must rebuild solidly," said Napoleon to his brother Lucien the day after the *coup a'état* which had overthrown the Directory and made him the temporary Dictator of France.

The first necessity was a new constitution. In ten years three constitutions had been framed and adopted, and now the third had, like its predecessors, been declared worthless. At Napoleon's side was a man who had the draft of a constitution ready in his pocket. It had been promised him that, if he would aid in the 18th Brumaire, this instrument should be adopted. This man was the Abbé Sieyès. He had been a prominent member of the Constituent Assembly, but, curiously enough, his fame there had been founded more on his silence and the air of mystery in which he enveloped himself than on anything he had done. The superstitious veneration which he had won, saved him even during the Terror, and he was accustomed to say laconically, when asked what he did in that period, "*I lived.*"

It was he who, when Napoleon was still in Egypt, had seen the necessity of

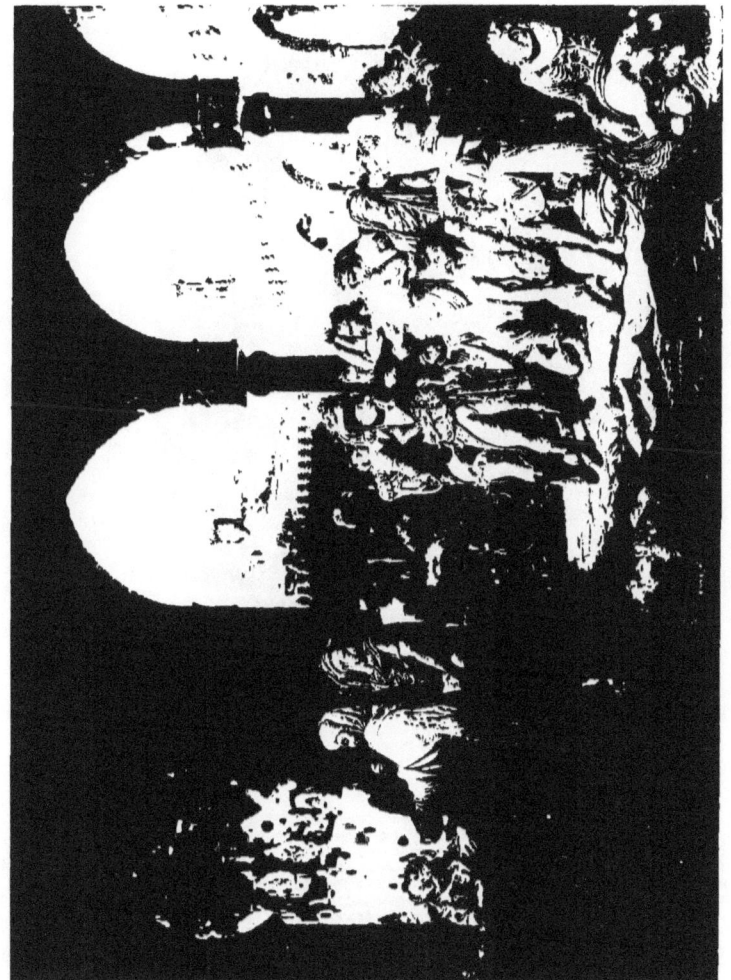

NAPOLEON IN THE MOSQUE AT JAFFA IN USE AS A PEST-HOUSE, MAY, 1799.

Engraved by Vallot, after painting by Gros. In 1801 Gros had undertaken to paint the battle of Nazareth and the brilliant action of Junot when he broke a column of ten thousand Turks with a body of three hundred horse. Napoleon stopped the artist, and bade him take as a subject the Pest at Jaffa. The canvas was exhibited in the *Salon* of 1804, and had an immense success. The state bought the picture for sixteen thousand francs.

KLÉBER, 1753 OR 1754-1800.

Engraved by G. Fiesinger, after portrait by Guérin. Jean-Baptist Kléber was born at Strasburg in 1754 (?). The son of a mason, he studied architecture for a time, but abandoned it to enter the military school of Munich, from which he went into the Austrian army. In 1783 he left the army to return to architecture. In 1792 he joined the revolutionary army, and served first on the Rhine, later in the Vendée, where he distinguished himself. Made general of division in the army of the North, Kléber won laurels at Fleurus, Mons, Louvain, and Maëstricht, and in the campaign of 1796. He was appointed commander-in-chief temporarily, but was recalled when about to enter Frankfort in 1797, the command being given to Hoche. Disappointed, he resigned from the army. When Napoleon went to Egypt, he asked for Kléber. In all the battles of the campaign he showed his bravery and skill ; and when Napoleon left for France he transferred his command to him. The situation of the French army in Egypt soon became desperate, and Kléber was trying to negotiate with the English and Turks an honorable retirement, when Admiral Keith ordered him to give up his army as prisoners of war. Kléber published the letter in the army, with the words, "Soldiers, such insolence can be answered but by victories ; prepare for combat." At Heliopolis, with eight thousand men. he met the Grand Vizir with eighty thousand, and completely conquered him. Soon after he put down a revolt in Cairo, and was beginning to reconquer and reorganize the country when he was assassinated. June 14, 1800.

"BUONAPARTE."

Ficsinger engraver, after Guérin. Published " 29 Vendémiaire, l'an VII." (1799.) It is of this portrait that Taine writes : " Look now at this portrait by Guérin, this lean body, these narrow shoulders in their uniform creased by his brusque motions, this neck enveloped in a high wrinkled cravat, these temples concealed by long hair falling straight over them, nothing to be seen but the face ; these hard features made prominent by strong contrasts of light and shade ; these cheeks as hollow as the interior angle of the eye ; these prominent cheek-bones ; this massive protruding chin ; these curving, mobile, attentive lips ; these great, clear eyes deeply set under the overarching eyebrows ; this fixed, incomprehensible look, sharp as a sword ; these two straight wrinkles which cross the forehead from the base of the nose like a furrow of continual anger and inflexible will."

"LUCIEN BONAPARTE, PRESIDENT OF THE COUNCIL OF THE FIVE HUNDRED,
18TH BRUMAIRE, 1799."

Lucien Bonaparte, born at Ajaccio, March 21, 1775, was educated in France, and returned to Corsica in 1792. Ardent revolutionist, he abandoned Paoli, and left Corsica for France. Obtaining a place at Saint Maximin, he became prominent as an agitator. Here he married Christine Hoyer, his landlord's daughter. In 1795 Lucien left Saint Maximin, and soon after was made commissary to the Army of the North, but resigned the next year. The two years following he passed in Corsica, but went to Paris in 1798, on being elected deputy to the Council of Five Hundred. He soon became prominent as a speaker, and his house was a centre for the best literary society of the capital. He was made president of the Council of Five Hundred after Napoleon's return from Egypt, and aided in the *coup d'état* of the 18th Brumaire. In the reorganization of the government Lucien was named Minister of the Interior, but he and Napoleon did not get on well, and he was sent as ambassador to Spain. Returning, he took an active part in the delicate work of the Concordat and Legion of Honor. Lucien was made senator after the Consulate for life was arranged, but he made a second marriage which displeased Napoleon. He left France, settling in Rome.

a military dictatorship, and had urged the Directory to order Napoleon home to help him reorganize the government—an order which was never received.

Soon after the 18th Brumaire, Sieyès presented his constitution. No more bungling and bizarre instrument for conducting the affairs of a nation was ever devised. Warned by the experience of the past ten years, he abandoned the ideas of 1789, and declared that the power must come from above, not the confidence from below. His system of voting took the suffrage from the people; his legislative body was composed of three sections, each of which was practically powerless. All the force of the government was centred in a senate of aged men. The Grand Elector, as the figure-

head which crowned the edifice was called, did nothing but live at Versailles and draw a princely salary.

Napoleon saw at once the weak points of the structure, but he saw how it could be rearranged to serve a dictator. He demanded that the Senate be stripped of its power, and that the Grand Elector be replaced by a First Consul, to whom the executive force should be confided. Sieyès consented, and Napoleon was named First Consul.

The whole machinery of the government was now centred in one man. "The state, it was I," said Napoleon at St. Helena. The new constitution was founded on principles the very opposite of those for which the Revolution had been made, but it was the only hope there was of dragging France from the slough of anarchy and despair into which she had fallen.

Napoleon undertook the work of reconstruction which awaited him, with courage, energy, and amazing audacity. He was forced to deal at once with all departments of the nation's life—with the finances, the industries, the *émigrés*, the Church, public education, the codification of the laws.

THE FINANCES.

The first question was one of money. The country was literally bankrupt in 1799. The treasury was empty, and the government practised all sorts of makeshifts to get money to pay those bills which could not be put off. One day, having to send out a special courier, it was obliged to give him the receipts of the opera to pay his expenses. And, again, it was in such a tight pinch that it was on the point of sending the gold coin in the Cabinet of Medals to the mint to be melted. Loans could not be negotiated; government paper was worthless; stocks were down to the lowest. One of the worst features of the situation was the condition of the taxes. The assessments were as arbitrary as before the Revolution, and they were collected with greater difficulty.

To select an honest, capable, and well-known financier was Napoleon's first act. The choice he made was wise—a Monsieur Gaudin, afterward the Duke de Gaëte, a quiet man, who had the confidence of the people. Under his management credit was restored, the government was able to make the loans necessary, and the department of finance was reorganized in a thorough fashion.

Napoleon's gratitude to Monsieur Gaudin

GENERAL BONAPARTE AT THE COUNCIL OF THE FIVE HUNDRED AT SAINT-CLOUD, NOVEMBER 10, 1799 (19TH BRUMAIRE).

By François Bouchot. On the 10th of November the *Anciens* assembled in the gallery of the château, and the Five Hundred in the orangery. Bonaparte presented himself first at the bar of the *Anciens*, and then betook himself to the Council of Five Hundred, presided over by his brother Lucien. He entered with bared head, accompanied by only four grenadiers. Hardly had he crossed the threshold when cries of "*hors de loi*" were heard. In vain he tried to speak; his bitterest enemies advanced against him with clinched fists and threatening looks, and covered him with insults. The grenadiers whom he had left at the door ran up, and, thrusting aside the deputies, seized him by the middle. Lucien quitted the chair, and coming to the side of his brother pronounced the dissolution of the Assembly. Soon after, the battalion of grenadiers, with fixed bayonets, advanced along the full width of the orangery, and so dispersed the deputies. Such was the famous scene which Bouchot has represented with conscientious regard for history in this superb canvas, now in the Versailles gallery.—A. D.

was lasting. Once when asked to change him for a more brilliant man, he said :

"I fully acknowledge all your *protégé* is worth ; but it might easily happen that, with all his intelligence, he would give me nothing but fresh water, whilst with my good Gaudin I can always rely on having good crown pieces."

The famous Bank of France dates from this time. It was founded under Napo-

"INSTALLATION OF THE COUNCIL OF STATE AT THE PALACE OF THE PETIT LUXEMBOURG, DECEMBER 29, 1799."

By Auguste Conder. The Councillors of State having assembled in the hall which had been arranged for the occasion, the First Consul opened the *séance* and heard the oath taken by the sectional presidents—Boulay de la Meurthe (legislation), Brune (war), Defermont (finances), Gantenume (marine), Roederer (interior). The First Consul crew up and signed two proclamations, to the French people and to the army. The Second Consul, Cambacérès, and the Third Consul, Lebrun, were present at the meeting. Locré, *secrétaire-général du Conseil d'État*, conducted the *procès-verbal*. This picture is at Versailles.

leon's personal direction, and he never ceased to watch over it jealously.

Most important of all the financial measures was the reorganization of the system of taxation. The First Consul insisted that the taxes must meet the whole expense of the nation, save war, which must pay for itself ; and he so ordered affairs that never after his administration was fairly begun was a deficit known or a loan made. This was done, too, without the people feeling the burden of taxation. Indeed, that burden was so much lighter under his administration than it had been under the old *régime*, that peasant and workman, in most cases, probably did not know they were being taxed.

" Before 1789," says Taine, " out of one hundred francs of net revenue, the w o r k m a n gave f o u r t e e n to his seignor, fourteen to the clergy, fifty-three to the state, and kept only eighteen or nineteen for h i m s e l f. Since 1800, from one hundred francs income he pays nothing to the seignor or the C h u r c h, and he pays to the state, the d e p a r t m e n t, and the commune but twenty-one francs, l e a v i n g seventy-nine in his pocket." And such was the method and care with w h i c h this s y s t e m was administered, that the state received more than twice as much as it had before. The enormous sums which the police and tax-collectors had appropriated now went to the state. Here is but one example of numbers which show how minutely Napoleon guarded this part of the finances. It is found in a letter to Fouché, the chief of police :

" What happens at Bordeaux happens at Turin, at Spa, at Marseilles, etc. The police commissioners derive immense profits from the gaming-tables. My intention is that the towns shall reap the benefit of the tables. I shall employ the two hundred thousand francs paid by the tables of Bordeaux in building a bridge or a canal. . . ."

BONAPARTE, FIRST CONSUL.

One of the best portraits of the First Consul—the *truest* of all, perhaps. Unlike Bouillon, Van Brée, Géhotte. Isabey, Boilly painted him in his real aspect, without any striving after the ideal. This is really the determined little Corsican, tormented by ambition and a thirst for conquest. This fine portrait has been admirably etched by Duplessis-Bertaux.—A. D.

A great improvement was that the taxes became fixed and regular. Napoleon wished that each man should know what he had to pay out each year. " True civil liberty depends on the safety of property," he told his Council of State. " There is none in a country where the rate of taxation is changed every year. A man who has three thousand francs income does not know how much he will have to live on the next year. His whole substance may be swallowed up by the taxes."

Nearly the whole revenue came from indirect taxes applied to a great number of articles. In case of a war which did not pay its way, Napoleon proposed to raise each of these a few centimes. The nation would surely prefer this, to paying it to the Russians or Austrians. When possible the taxes were reduced. " Better leave the money in the hands of the citizens than lock it up in a cellar, as they do in Prussia."

He was cautious that extra t a x e s should not come on the very poor, if it could be avoided. A suggestion to charge the vegetable and fish sellers for their stalls came before him. " T h e p u b l i c square, like water, ought to be free. It is quite enough that we tax salt and wine. . . . It would become the city of Paris much more to think of restoring the corn market."

An important part of his financial policy was the rigid economy which was insisted on in all departments. If a thing was bought, it must be worth what was paid for it. If a man held a position, he must do its duties. Neither purchases nor positions could be made unless reasonable and useful. This was in direct opposition to the old *régime*, of which waste, idleness, and parasites were the chief characteristics. The saving in expenditure was almost incredible. A trip to Fontainebleau, which cost Louis XVI. four hundred thousand dollars, Napoleon would make, in no less state, for thirty thousand dollars.

The expenses of the civil household, which amounted to five million dollars under the old *régime*, were now cut down to six hundred thousand dollars, though the elegance was no less.

THE INDUSTRIES.

A master who gave such strict attention to the prosperity of his kingdom would not, of course, overlook its industries. In fact, they were one of Napoleon's chief cares. His policy was one of protection. He would have France make everything she wanted, and sell to her neighbors, but never buy from them. To stimulate the manufactories, which in 1799 were as nearly bankrupt as the public treasury, he visited the factories himself to learn their needs. He gave liberal orders, and urged, even commanded, his associates to do the same. At one time, anxious to aid the batiste factories of Flanders, he tried to force Josephine to give up cotton goods and to set the fashion in favor of the batistes ; but she made such an outcry that he was obliged to abandon the idea. For the same reason he wrote to his sister Eliza : " I beg that you will allow your court to wear nothing but silks and cambrics, and that you will exclude all cottons and muslins, in order to favor French industry."

Frequently he would take goods on consignment, to help a struggling factory. Rather than allow a manufactory to be idle, he would advance a large sum of money, and a quantity of its products would be put under government control. After the battle of Eylau, Napoleon sent one million six hundred thousand francs to Paris, to be used in this way.

To introduce cotton-making into the country was one of his chief industrial ambitions. At the beginning of the century it was printed in all the factories of France, but nothing more. He proposed to the Council of State to prohibit the importation of cotton thread and the woven goods. There was a strong opposition, but he carried his point.

"As a result," said Napoleon to Las Cases complacently, "we possess the three branches, to the immense advantage of our population and to the detriment and sorrow of the English; which proves that, in administration as in war, one must exercise character. . . . I occupied myself no less in encouraging silks. As

Emperor, and King of Italy, I counted one hundred and twenty millions of income from the silk harvest."

In a similar way he encouraged agriculture; especially was he anxious that France should raise all her own articles of diet. He had Berthollet look into maple and turnip sugar, and he did at last succeed in persuading the people to use beet sugar ; though he never convinced them that Swiss tea equalled Chinese, or that chicory was as good as coffee.

PUBLIC WORKS.

The works he insisted should be carried on in regard to roads and public buildings were of great importance. There was need that something be done.

" It is impossible to conceive, if one had not been a witness of it before and after the 18th Brumaire [said the chancellor Pasquier], of the widespread ruin wrought by the Revolution. . . . There were hardly two or three main roads [in France] in a fit condition for traffic ; not a single one was there, perhaps, wherein was not found some obstacle that could not be surmounted without peril. With regard to the ways of internal communication, they had been indefinitely suspended. The navigation of rivers and canals was no longer feasible.

" In all directions, public buildings, and those monuments which represent the splendor of the state, were falling into decay. It must fain be admitted that if the work of destruction had been prodigious, that of restoration was no less so. Everything was taken hold of at one and the same time, and everything progressed with a like rapidity. Not only was it resolved to restore all that required restoring in various parts of the country, in all parts of the public service, but new, grand, beautiful and useful works were decided upon, and many were brought to a happy termination. This certainly constitutes one of the most brilliant sides of the consular and imperial *régime*."

In Paris alone vast improvements were made. Napoleon began the Rue de Rivoli, built the wing connecting the Tuileries and the Louvre, erected the triumphal arch of the Carrousel, the Arc de Triomphe at the head of the Champs Elysées, the Column Vendôme, the Madeleine, began the Bourse, built the Pont d'Austerlitz, and ordered, commenced, or finished, a number of minor works of great importance to the city. The markets interested him particularly. " Give all possible care to the construction of the markets and to their healthfulness, and to the beauty of the Halle-aux-blés and of the Halle-aux-vins. The people, too, must have their Louvre."

The works undertaken outside of Paris in France, and in the countries under her rule in the time that Napoleon was in power, were of a variety and extent which would be incredible, if every traveller in Europe did not have the evidence of them still before his eyes. The mere enumeration of these works and of the industrial achievements of Napoleon, made by Las Cases, reads like a fairy story. "You wish to know the treasures of Napoleon? They are immense, it is true, but they are all exposed to light. They are the noble harbors of Antwerp and Flushing, which are capable of containing the largest fleets, and of protecting them against the ice from the sea ; the hydraulic works at Dunkirk, Havre, and Nice ; the immense harbor of Cherbourg ; the maritime works at Venice ; the beautiful roads from Antwerp to Amsterdam, from Mayence to Metz, from Bordeaux to Bayonne ; the passes of the Simplon, of Mont Cenis, of Mount Genèvre, of the Corniche, which open a communication through the Alps in four different directions, and which exceed in grandeur, in boldness, and in skill of execution, all the works of the Romans (in that alone you will find eight hundred millions) ; the roads from the Pyrenees to the Alps, from Parma to Spezia, from Savona to Piedmont ; the bridges of Jena, Austerlitz, Des Arts, Sèvres, Tours, Roanne, Lyons, Turin ; of the Isère, of the Durance, of Bordeaux, of Rouen, etc. ; the canal which connects the Rhine with the Rhone by the Doubs, and thus unites the North Sea with the Medi-

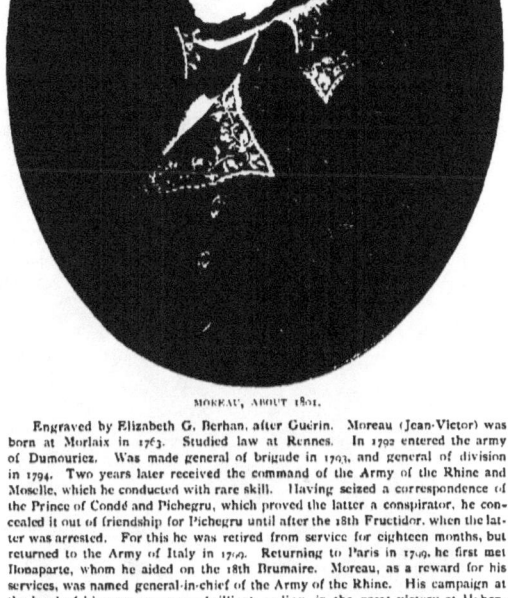

MOREAU, ABOUT 1801.

Engraved by Elizabeth G. Berhan, after Guérin. Moreau (Jean-Victor) was born at Morlaix in 1763. Studied law at Rennes. In 1792 entered the army of Dumouriez. Was made general of brigade in 1793, and general of division in 1794. Two years later received the command of the Army of the Rhine and Moselle, which he conducted with rare skill. Having seized a correspondence of the Prince of Condé and Pichegru, which proved the latter a conspirator, he concealed it out of friendship for Pichegru until after the 18th Fructidor, when the latter was arrested. For this he was retired from service for eighteen months, but returned to the Army of Italy in 1799. Returning to Paris in 1799, he first met Bonaparte, whom he aided on the 18th Brumaire. Moreau, as a reward for his services, was named general-in-chief of the Army of the Rhine. His campaign at the head of his new army was brilliant, ending in the great victory at Hohenlinden on December 3, 1800. Returning to Paris, he became the centre of a faction discontented with Bonaparte, and refused the title of marshal and the decoration of the Legion of Honor which the latter offered him. He was approached by agents of Louis XVIII., and was supposed to be connected indirectly with the Georges plot. Was arrested, tried, and exiled for two years. He retired to the United States, where at first he travelled extensively. Moreau settled in this country, leading a quiet life until 1813, when he was invited by the Emperor Alexander to return to Europe. With Bernadotte he prepared the plans of the campaign of 1813 and 1814, and it was by his advice that the allies refused to give general battle to Napoleon. At Dresden, on August 27, 1813, he was mortally wounded ; it is said, by a French bullet.

terranean; the canal which joins the Scheldt with the Somme, and thus joins Paris and Amsterdam ; the canal which unites the Rance to the Vilaine ; the canal of Arles ; that of Pavia, and the canal of the Rhine ; the draining of the marshes of Bourgoin, of the Cotentin, of Rochefort ; the rebuilding of the greater part of the churches destroyed by the Revolution ; the building of others; the institution of numerous establishments of industry for the suppression of mendicity ; the gallery at the Louvre ; the construction of public warehouses, of the Bank, of the canal of the Ourcq ; the distribution of water in the city of Paris ; of many hundreds of manufactories of cotton, for spinning and for weaving, which employ several millions of workmen ; funds accumulated to establish upwards of four hundred manufactories of sugar from

NAPOLEON CROSSING THE GREAT ST. BERNARD, 1800.

Engraved by François, after a picture by Delaroche, painted in 1848, published in 1852 by P. & D. Colnaghisco, London. " The Queen of England possesses at Osborne a reduction of this portrait made by Delaroche himself."

the numerous drains, the quays, the embellishments, and the monuments of that large capital ; the works for the embellishment of Rome ; the reëstablishment of the manufactures of Lyons ; the creation beet-root, for the consumption of part of France, and which would have furnished sugar at the same price as the West Indies, if they had continued to receive encouragement for only four years longer ; the sub-

NAPOLEON THE GREAT CROSSING THE MOUNT ST. BERNARD, MAY, 1800.

Engraved by Antonio Gilbert in 1809, under the direction of Longhi, after portrait painted by David in 1805. Dedicated to the Prince Eugène Napoleon of France, Viceroy of Italy. It was soon after his return from Marengo that Napoleon expressed a wish to be painted by David. The artist had long desired this work, and seized the opportunity eagerly. He asked the First Consul when he would pose for him.

"Pose!" said Bonaparte. "Do you suppose the great men of antiquity posed for their portraits?"

"But I paint you for your time, for men who have seen you. They would like to have it like you."

"Like me! It is not the perfection of the features, a pimple on the nose, which makes resemblance. It is the character of the face that should be represented. No one cares whether the portraits of great men look like them or not. It is enough that their genius shines from the picture."

"I have never considered it in that way. But you are right, Citizen Consul. You need not pose; I will paint you without that." David went to breakfast daily after this with Napoleon, in order to study his face, and the Consul put at his service all the garments he had worn at Marengo. It is told that David mounted Napoleon on a mule for this picture, but that the General demurred. He sprang upon his horse, and, making him rear, said to the artist, "Paint me thus" stitution of woad for indigo, which would have been at last brought to a state of perfection in France, and obtained as good and as cheap as the indigo from the colonies; numerous manufactories for all kinds of objects of art, etc.; fifty millions expended in repairing and beautifying the palaces belonging to the Crown; sixty millions in furniture for the palaces belonging to the Crown in France, in Holland, at Turin, and at Rome; sixty millions of diamonds for the Crown, all purchased with Napoleon's money; the *Regent* (the only diamond that was left belonging to the former diamonds of the Crown) withdrawn from the hands of the Jews at Berlin, in whose hands it had been left as a pledge for three millions. The Napoleon Museum, valued at upwards of four hundred millions, filled with objects legitimately acquired, either by moneys or by treaties of peace known to the whole world, by virtue of which the *chefs-d'œuvre* it contains were given in lieu of territory or of contributions. Several millions amassed to be applied to the encouragement of agriculture, which is the paramount consideration for the interest of France; the introduction into France of merino sheep, etc. These form a treasure of several thousand millions which will endure for ages."

Napoleon himself looked on these achievements as his most enduring monument. "The allied powers cannot take from me hereafter," he told O'Meara, "the great public works I have executed, the roads which I made over the Alps, and the seas which I have united. They cannot place their feet to improve where mine have not been before. They cannot take from me the code of laws which I formed, and which will go down to posterity."

CHAPTER VIII.

RETURN OF THE ÉMIGRÉS.—THE CONCORDAT.—LEGION OF HONOR.—CODE NAPOLÉON.

THE ÉMIGRÉS.

BUT there were wounds in the French nation more profound than those caused by lack of credit, by neglect and corruption. The body which in 1789 made up France had, in the last ten years, been violently and horribly wrenched asunder. One hundred and fifty thousand of the richest, most cultivated, and most capable of the population had been stripped of wealth and position, and had emigrated to foreign lands.

Napoleon saw that if the *émigrés* could be reconciled, he at once converted a powerful enemy into a zealous friend. In spite of the opposition of those who had made the Revolution and gained their positions through it, he accorded an amnesty to the *émigrés*, which included the whole one hundred and fifty thousand, with the exception of about one thousand, and this number, it was arranged, should be reduced to five hundred in the course of a year. More, he provided for their wants. Most of the smaller properties confiscated by the Revolution had been sold, and Napoleon insisted that those who had bought them from the state should be assured of their tenure; but in case a property had not been disposed of, he returned it to the family, though rarely in full. In case of forest lands, not over three hundred and seventy-five acres were given back. Gifts and positions were given to many *émigrés*, so that the majority were able to live in ease.

A valuable result of this policy of reconciliation was the amount of talent, experience, and culture which he gained for the government. France had been run for ten years by country lawyers, doctors, and pamphleteers, who, though they boasted civic virtue and eloquence, and though they knew their Plutarchs and Rousseaus by heart, had no practical sense, and little or no experience. The return of the *émigrés* gave France a body of trained diplomats, judges, and thinkers, many of whom were promptly admitted to the government.

THE CHURCH.

More serious than the amputation of the aristocracy had been that of the Church. The Revolution had torn it from the nation, had confiscated its property, turned its cathedrals into barracks, its convents and seminaries into town halls and prisons, sold its lands, closed its schools and hospitals. It had demanded an oath of the clergy which had divided the body, and caused thousands to emigrate. Not content with this, it had tried to supplant the old religion, first with a worship of the Goddess of Reason, afterwards with one of the Supreme Being.

But the people still loved the Catholic Church. The mass of them kept their the decade," said a workman once, " but we change our shirts on Sunday."

Napoleon understood the popular heart, and he proposed the reëstablishment of the Catholic Church. The Revolutionists, even

"NAPOLEONE BUONAPARTE, FIRST CONSUL OF FRANCE," 1800,

Painted by Masquerier, who visited Paris in 1800, where he made a portrait of Napoleon. "This, on being exhibited in England, where it was the first authentic portrait of the emperor, proved a source of considerable gain to the painter." The portrait was engraved, soon after his return to London, by C. Turner.

crucifixes in their houses, told their beads, observed fast days. No matter how severe a penalty was attached to the observance of Sunday instead of the day which had replaced it, called the "decade," at heart the people remembered it. "We rest on his warmest friends among the generals, opposed it. Infidelity was a cardinal point in the creed of the majority of the new *régime*. They not only rejected the Church, they ridiculed it. Rather than restore Catholicism, they advised Protestantism.

"But," declared Napoleon, "France is not Protestant ; she is Catholic."

In the Council of State, where the question was argued, he said : " My policy is to govern men as the greatest number wish to be governed. . . . I carried on the war of Vendée by becoming a Catholic ; I established myself in Egypt by becoming a Mussulman ; I won over the priests in Italy by becoming Ultramontane. If I governed Jews I should reëstablish the temple of Solomon. . . . It is thus, I think, that the sovereignty of the people should be understood."

Evidently this was a very different way of understanding that famous doctrine from that which had been in vogue, which consisted in forcing the people to accept what each idealist thought was best, without consulting their prejudices or feelings. In spite of opposition, Napoleon's will prevailed, and in the spring of 1802 the Concordat was signed. This treaty between the Pope and France is still in force in France. It makes the Catholic Church the state church, allows the government to name the bishops, compels it to pay the salaries of the clergy, and to furnish cathedrals and churches for public worship, which, however, remain national property. The Concordat provided for the absolution of the priests who had married in the Revolution, restored Sunday, and made legal holidays of certain *fête* days. This arrangement was not made at the price of intolerance towards other bodies. The French government protects and contributes towards the support of all religions within its bounds, Catholic, Protestant, Jew, or Mussulman.

The Concordat was ridiculed by many in the government and army, but undoubtedly it was one of the most statesmanlike measures carried out by Napoleon.

"The joy of the overwhelming majority of France silenced even the boldest malcontents," says Pasquier ; "it became evident that Napoleon, better than those who surrounded him, had seen into the depths of the nation's heart."

It is certain that in reëstablishing the Church Napoleon did not yield to any religious prejudice, although the Catholic Church was the one he preferred. It was purely a question of policy. In arranging the Concordat he might have secured more liberal measures—measures in which he believed—but he refused them.

" Do you wish me to manufacture a religion of caprice for my own special use, a religion that would be nobody's? I do not so understand matters. What I want is the old Catholic religion, the only one which is imbedded in every heart, and from which it has never been torn. This religion alone can conciliate hearts in my favor ; it alone can smooth away all obstacles."

"N. BONAPARTE, LUNÉVILLE, AN IX,"

Engraver signs U. P.

In discussing the subject at St. Helena he said to Las Cases :

" When I came to the head of affairs, I had already formed certain ideas on the great principles which hold society together. I had weighed all the importance of religion ; I was persuaded of it, and I had resolved to reëstablish it. You would scarcely believe in the difficulties that I had to restore Catholicism. I would have been followed much more willingly if I had unfurled the banner of Protestantism. . . . It is sure that in the disorder to which I succeeded, in the ruins where I found myself, I could choose between Catholicism and Protestantism. And it is true that at that moment the disposition was in favor of the latter. But outside the fact that I really clung to the religion in which I had been born, I had the highest motives to decide me. By proclaiming Protestantism, what would I have obtained ? I should have created in France two great parties about equal, when I wished there should be longer but one. I should have excited the fury of religious quarrels, when the enlightenment of the age and my desire was to make them disappear altogether. These two parties in tearing each other to pieces would have annihilated France and rendered her the slave of Europe, when I was ambitious of making her its mistress. With Catholicism I arrived much more surely at my great results. Within, at home, the great number would absorb the small, and I promised myself to treat with the latter so liberally that it would soon have no motive for knowing the difference.

"Without, Catholicism saved me the Pope; and with my influences and our forces in Italy I did not despair sooner or later, by one way or another, of finishing by ruling the Pope myself."

EDUCATION.

When the Church fell in France, the whole system of education went down with her. The Revolutionary governments tried to remedy the condition, but beyond many plans and speeches little had

VUE DE LA GRANDE PARADE PASSÉE PAR LE PREMIER CONSUL
dans la Cour du Palais des Tuilleries.

GRAND REVIEW BY THE FIRST CONSUL IN THE COURT OF THE TUILERIES.

been done. Napoleon allowed the religious bodies to reopen their schools, and thus primary instruction was soon provided again; and he founded a number of secondary and special schools. The greatest of his educational undertakings was the organization of the University. This institution was centralized in the head of the state as completely as every other Napoleonic institution. It exists to-day but little changed—a most efficient body, in spite of its rigid state control. This university did nothing for woman.

"I do not think we need trouble ourselves with any plan of instruction for young females," Napoleon told the Council. "They cannot be brought up better than by their mothers. Public education is not suitable for them, because they are never called upon to act in public. Manners are all in all to them, and marriage is all they look to. In times past the monastic life was open to women; they espoused God, and, though society gained little by that alliance, the parents gained by pocketing the dowry."

It was with the education of the daughters of soldiers, civil functionaries, and members of the Legion of Honor, who had died and left their children unprovided for, that he concerned himself, establishing schools of which the well-known one at St. Denis is a model. The rules were prepared by Napoleon himself, who insisted that the girls should be taught all kinds of housework and needlework—everything, in fact, which would make them good housekeepers and honest women.

The military schools were also reorganized at this time. Remembering his own experience at the *École Militaire*, Napoleon arranged that the severest economy should be practised in them, and that the pupils should learn to do everything for themselves. They even cleaned, bedded, and shod their own horses.

THE LEGION OF HONOR.

The destruction of the old system of privileges and honors left the government without any means of rewarding those who rendered it a service. Napoleon presented a law for a Legion of Honor, under control of the state, which should admit to its membership only those who had done something of use to the public. The service might be military, commercial, artistic, humanitarian; no limit was put on its nature; anything which helped France in any way was to be rewarded by membership in the proposed order. In fact, it was

"NAPOLEON REVIEWING THE CONSULAR GUARDS IN THE COURT OF THE TUILERIES." 1800.

Engraved in London, by C. Turner, after a painting by J. Masquerier, made during his visit to Paris in 1800. A similar picture, the *Revue du Decadi*, was painted by Isabey and Carle Vernet, and engraved by Mécou. Masson considers Napoleon's face finer at this time than at any other period.

the most democratic distinction possible, since the same reward was given for all classes of services and to all classes of people.

Now the Revolutionary spirit spurned all distinction; and as free discussion was allowed on the law, a severe arraignment of it was made. Nevertheless, it passed. It immediately became a power in the hands of the First Consul, and such it has remained until to-day in the government. Though it has been frequently abused, and never, perhaps, more flagrantly than by the present Republic, unquestionably the French "red button" is a decoration of which to be proud.

CODIFICATION OF THE LAWS.

The greatest civil achievement of Napoleon was the codification of the laws. Up to the Revolution, the laws of France had lieved justly that the greatest benefit he could render France would be to give her a complete and systematic code. He organized the force for this gigantic task, and pushed revision with unflagging energy.

NAPOLEON WHILE FIRST CONSUL OF FRANCE.

"Napoleon Bonaparte, Premier Consul de la République Française." Engraved by an English engraver, Dickinson, after a portrait by Gros. The original picture was given to the Second Consul, Cambacérès, by the First Consul, Bonaparte.

been in a misty, incoherent condition, feudal in their spirit, and by no means uniform in their application. The Constituent Assembly had ordered them revised, but the work had only been begun. Napoleon believed part in the work was interesting and important. After the laws had been well digested and arranged in preliminary bodies, they were submitted to the Council of State. It was in the discussion before this body that Napoleon took part. That a man of thirty-one, brought up as a soldier, and having no legal training, could follow the discussions of such a learned and serious body as Napoleon's Council of State always was, seems incredible. In fact, he prepared for each session as thoroughly as the law-makers themselves.

His habit was to talk over, beforehand generally, with Cambacérès and Portalis, two legislators of great learning and clearness of judgment, all the matters which were to come up.

"He examined each question by itself," says Roederer, "inquiring into all the authorities, times, experiences; demanding to know how it had been under ancient jurisprudence, under Louis XIV., or Frederick the Great. When a bill was presented to the First Consul, he rarely failed to ask these questions: Is this bill complete? Does it cover every case? Why have you not thought of this? Is that necessary? Is it right or useful? What is done nowadays and elsewhere?"

"NAPOLEON BUONAPARTE, FIRST CONSUL." 1802.

Painted in 1802 by T. Phillips, Esq., R.A. Engraved by C. Turner.

thus going directly to the practical sense of a thing, he frequently cleared up the ideas of the revisers themselves.

In framing the laws, he took care that they should be worded so that everybody could understand them. Thus, when a law relating to liquors was being prepared, he urged that *wholesale* and *retail* should be defined in such a way that they would be definite ideas to the people. "*Pot* and *pint* must be inserted," he said. "There is no objection to those words. An excise act isn't an epic poem."

Napoleon insisted on the greatest freedom of speech in the discussions on the laws, just as he did on "going straight to the point and not wasting time on idle talk." This clear-headedness, energy, and grasp of subject, exercised over a body of really remarkable men, developed the Council until its discussions became famous throughout Europe. One of its wisest members, Chancellor Pasquier, says of Napoleon's direction, that "it was of such a nature as to enlarge the sphere of one's ideas, and to give one's faculties all the development of which they were capable. The highest legislative, administrative, and sometimes even political matters were taken up in it (the Council). Did we not see, for two consecutive winters, the sons of foreign sovereigns come and complete their education in its midst?"

At night, after he had gone to bed, he would read or have read to him authorities on the subject. Such was his capacity for grasping an idea, that he would come to the Council with a perfectly clear notion of the subject to be treated, and a good idea of its historical development. Thus he could follow the most erudite and philosophical arguments, and could take part in them.

He stripped them at once of all conventional phrases and learned terms, and stated clearly what they meant. He had no use for anything but the plain meaning. By

It was the genius of the head of the state, however, which was the most impressive feature of the Council of State. De Molleville, a former minister of Louis XVI., said once to Las Cases:

THE FIRST CONSUL AND MADAME BONAPARTE VISITING THE MANUFACTORIES OF ROUEN, NOVEMBER, 1802.

Sepia sketch, measuring not less than sixty-six inches by forty-eight; one of the most important works of J. B. Isabey. The First Consul, accompanied by Madame Bonaparte, left Paris October 28, 1802, in order to visit the important factories of the department of Seine-Inférieure. In his journey to Normandy, Napoleon wished to inspect all the public establishments : the hospitals, workyards, wharves, and manufactories of all kinds. He left everywhere behind him marks of his kindness, generosity, and sense of justice. Isabey's beautiful sketch represents the moment when the First Consul and Josephine are visiting the manufactory of the Brothers Sévène. They presented to him an old man who had worked there for fifty years. The First Consul received him kindly, accorded him a pension, and ordered to be admitted to the *Prytanée* military school his grandson, whose father had been killed in the army. This sepia, which unfortunately becomes more and more discolored by the sun, was exhibited in the *Salon* of 1804. It is now in the Versailles collection.—A. D.

"It must be admitted that your Bonaparte, your Napoleon, was a very extraordinary man. We were far from understanding him on the other side of the water. We could not refuse the evidence of his victories and his invasions, it is true ; but Genseric, Attila, Alaric had done as much ; so he made more of an impression of terror on me than of admiration. But when I came here and followed the discussions on the civil code, from that moment I had nothing but profound veneration for him. But where in the world had he learned all that ? And then every day I discovered something new in him. Ah, sir, what a man you had there ! Truly, he was a prodigy."

The modern reader who looks at France and sees how her University, her special schools, her hospitals, her great honorary legion, her treaty with the Catholic Church, her code of laws, her Bank—the vital elements of her life, in short—are as they came from Napoleon's brain, must ask, with De Molleville, How did he do it—he a foreigner, born in a half-civilized island, reared in a military school, without diplomatic or legal training, without the prestige of name or wealth ? How could he make a nation? How could he be other than the barbaric conqueror the English and the *émigrés* first thought him?

Those who look at Napoleon's achievements, and are either dazzled or horrified by them, generally consider his power superhuman. They call it divine or diabolic, according to the feeling he inspires in them; but, in reality, the qualities he showed in his career as a statesman and lawgiver are very human ones. His stout grasp on subjects ; his genius for hard work ; his power of seeing everything that should be done, and doing it himself ; his unparalleled audacity, explain his civil achievements.

The comprehension he had of questions of government was really the result of serious thinking. He had reflected from his first days at Brienne ; and the active interest he had taken in the Revolution of 1789 had made him familiar with many social and political questions. His career in Italy, which was almost as much a diplomatic as a military career, had furnished

BONAPARTE, Iᴱᴿ CONSUL DE LA RÉP. FRANÇ.

"Bonaparte, Iᵉʳ Consul de la Rep. Franc." Engraved in 1801 by Audouin, after a design by Bouillon.

him an experience upon which he had founded many notions. In his dreams of becoming an Oriental lawgiver he had planned a system of government of which he was to be the centre. Thus, before the 18th Brumaire made him the Dictator of France, he had his ideas of centralized government all formed, just as, before he crossed the Great Saint Bernard, he had fought, over and over, the battle of Marengo, with black- and red-headed pins stuck into a great map of Italy spread out on his study floor.

His habit of attending to everything himself explains much of his success. No detail was too small for him, no task too

NAPOLEON IN 1802.

"Buonaparte." Drawn from the life by T. Phillips, Esq., R.A., in 1802. Engraved by Edwards.

they should discuss the opera or the political situation.

The cost of the soldiers' shoes, the kind of box Josephine took at the opera, the style of architecture for the Madeleine, the amount of stock left on hand in the silk factories, the wording of the laws, all was his business.

He thought of the flowers to be scattered daily on the tomb of General Régnier, suggested the idea of a battle hymn to Rouget de l'Isle, told the artists what expression to give him in their portraits, what accessories to use in their battle pieces, ordered everything, verified everything. "Beside him," said those who looked on in amazement, "the most punctilious clerk would have been a bungler."

Without an extraordinary capacity for work, no man could have done this. Napoleon would work until eleven o'clock in the evening, and be up again at three in the morning. Frequently he slept but an hour, and came

menial. If a thing needed attention, no matter whose business it was, he looked after it. Reading letters once before Madame Junot, she said to him that such work must be tiresome, and advised him to give it to a secretary.

"Later, perhaps," he said. "Now it is impossible; I must answer for all. It is not at the beginning of a return to order that I can afford to ignore a need, a demand."

He carried out this policy literally. When he went on a journey, he looked personally after every road, bridge, public building, he passed, and his letters teemed with orders about repairs here, restorations there. He looked after individuals in the same way; ordered a pension to this one, a position to that one, even dictating how the gift should be made known so as to offend the least possible the pride of the recipient.

When it came to foreign policy, he told his diplomats how they should look, whether it should be grave or gay, whether

NAPOLEON.

Engraved by J. B. Massard, after J. H. Point. Below the portrait is printed in French and English the following legend:

"His name will be renowned through all Europe and Egypt for his valor in combat, and yet more so for his wisdom in counsel."

SIGNING OF CONCORDAT.
By Gérard.   The original is at Versailles.

back as fresh as ever. No secretary could keep up to him, and his ministers sometimes went to sleep in the Council, worn out with the length of the session. "Come, citizen ministers," he would cry, "we must earn the money the French nation gives us." The ministers rarely went home from the meetings that they did not find a half-dozen letters from him on their tables to be answered, and the answer must be a clear, exact, exhaustive document. "Get your information so that when you do answer me, there shall be no 'buts,' no 'ifs,' and no 'becauses,'" was the rule Napoleon laid down to his correspondents.

He had audacity. He dared do what he would. He had no conventional notions to tie him, no master to dictate to him. The Revolution had swept out of his way the accumulated experience of centuries—all the habits, the prejudices, the ways of doing things. He commenced nearer the bottom than any man in the history of the civilized world had ever done, worked with imperial self-confidence, with a conviction that he "was not like other men;" that the moral laws, the creeds, the conventions, which applied to them, were not for him. He might listen to others, but in the end he dared do as he would.

CHAPTER IX.

OPPOSITION TO THE CENTRALIZATION OF THE GOVERNMENT.—GENERAL PROSPERITY.

OPPOSITION, AND HOW HE MET IT.

THE centralization of France in Napoleon's hands was not to be allowed to go on without interference. Jacobinism, republicanism, royalism, were deeply-rooted sentiments, and it was not long before they began to struggle for expression.

Early in the Consulate, plots of many descriptions were unearthed. The most serious before 1803 was that known as the "Opera Plot," or "Plot of the 3d Nivose" (December 24, 1800), when a bomb was

MADAME RÉCAMIER. 1800.

By Jacquet, after David. Madame Récamier (Jeanne Françoise Julie Adélaide) was born in Lyons in 1777. Her father, Jean Bernard, afterwards moved to Paris, where he saw much of society and occupied a good position. In 1793 Julie was married to Monsieur Récamier, a rich banker twenty-seven years her senior. During the Directory Madame Récamier became intimate with the members of the Bonaparte family in Paris, and Lucien fell deeply in love with her, an affection she never returned. She first met the First Consul at Lucien's in the winter of 1799-1800, and he noticed her especially. She was much attracted by his simplicity and by his kindness. In 1802 Madame Récamier's father, who was Postmaster-General, was found to be sheltering a royalist correspondence, and was arrested and imprisoned. Through the intercession of Madame Récamier, Bernadotte secured his release from the First Consul. The arrest and trial of Moreau, who was a friend of Madame Récamier, the exile of Madame de Staël, and the execution of the Duc d'Enghien, put her in opposition to the government, though she received both friends and enemies of Napoleon. In 1805 Fouché attempted to persuade her to accept a place at court, which she refused. In 1807 Madame Récamier visited Madame de Staël at Coppet, where she met Prince Augustus of Prussia, who wished to marry her. She seems to have determined once to secure a divorce and marry the Prince, but abandoned the idea because of Monsieur Récamier's distress. In 1811 she was exiled forty leagues from Paris because of her intimacy with Madame de Staël, and she did not return until after the invasion in 1814. In 1817, after Madame de Staël's death, she met Chateaubriand, with whom she remained intimately allied through the rest of her life. In 1830 Monsieur Récamier died. Sixteen years afterwards Chateaubriand became a widower. He wished to marry Madame Récamier, but she refused. She died in Paris in 1849. Of all the women of the period, no one is more interesting than Madame Récamier. Purity of character, independence of spirit, and fidelity to friends distinguished her, as well as remarkable beauty.

placed in the street, to be exploded as the First Consul's carriage passed. By an accident he was saved, and, in spite of the shock, went on to the opera.

Madame Junot, who was there, gives a graphic description of the way the news was received by the house :

"The first thirty measures of the oratorio were scarcely played, when a strong explosion like a cannon was heard.

"'What does that mean?' exclaimed Junot with emotion. He opened the door of the *loge* and looked into the corridor. . . . 'It is strange; how can they be firing the cannon at this hour?' And then, 'I should have known it. Give me my hat; I am going to find out what it is. . . .'

"At this moment the *loge* of the First Consul opened, and he himself appeared with General Lannes, Lauriston, Berthier, and Duroc. Smiling, he saluted the immense crowd, which mingled cries like those of love with its applause. Madame Bonaparte followed him in a few seconds. . . .

"Junot was going to enter the *loge* to see for himself the serene air of the First Consul that I had just remarked, when Duroc came up to us with troubled face.

"'The First Consul has just escaped death,' he said quickly to Junot. 'Go down and see him; he wants to talk to you.' . . . But a dull sound commenced to spread from parterre to orchestra, from orchestra to amphitheatre, and thence to the *loges*.

"'The First Consul has just been attacked in the Rue Saint Nicaise,' it was whispered. Soon the truth was circulated in the *salle*; at the same instant, and as by an electric shock, one and the same acclamation arose, one and the same look enveloped Napoleon, as if in a protecting love.

MADAME DE STAËL (ANNE LOUISE GERMAINE NECKER, BARONNE DE STAËL-HOLSTEIN), 1802.

Engraved in 1818 by Laugier, after Gérard. Madame de Staël was born in Paris in 1766. Her father was the famous banker Necker, and her mother, Suzanne Curchod, the early love of Gibbon. She held a high position in Paris until the Terror obliged her to flee, when she went to Coppet, on Lake Geneva, where a number of her friends gathered about her. She returned to Paris under the Directory, and when Napoleon returned from the Italian campaign she pretended to have the greatest admiration for him, and persisted in putting herself in his way. His dislike was so pronounced that she was irritated, and when, to this personal complaint, she added a more serious one the way he was centralizing power in his hands – she became a noisy and troublesome critic of his policy. In 1803, when she came to Paris from Coppet, she was ordered not to reside within forty leagues of the city. For three years she obeyed, but in 1806 she came too near Paris. In 1807 the publication of "Corinne" called attention to her, and she was sent back to Coppet. For two years she was busy at her work on "Germany," which, when done, she published in Paris : but the whole edition of ten thousand copies was condemned as "not French," and she was forbidden to enter France. When Louis XVIII. was restored, she returned to Paris, but fled to Coppet at the news of Napoleon's return. She died on July 14, 1817.

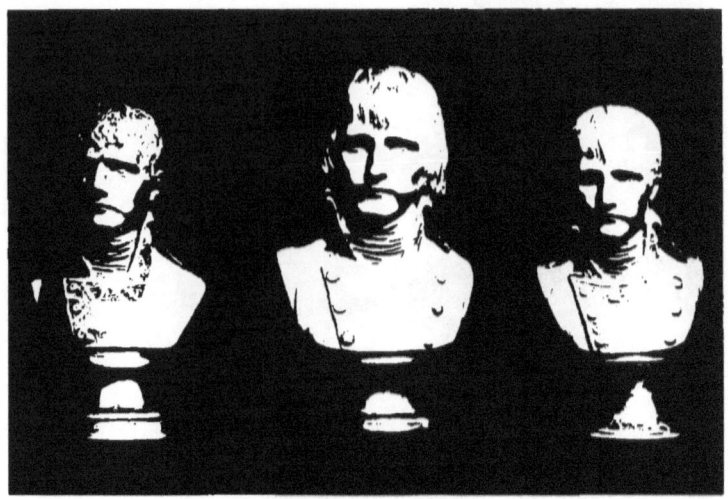

BONAPARTE AS GENERAL, CONSUL, MEMBER OF THE INSTITUTE.

These busts are in Sèvres biscuit. The first, which is much superior to the other two, is attributed to Boizot. The manufactory of Sèvres produced many such busts, especially in the consular period, and Bonaparte, anxious to see his face everywhere, encouraged the production and diffusion of them. I have before me an official document which shows that from the commencement of the year VI. to the end of the year IX. the factory produced more than four hundred busts and thirteen hundred medallions of Bonaparte.—A. D.

"What agitation preceded the explosion of national anger which was represented in that first quarter of an hour, by that crowd whose fury for so black an attack could not be expressed by words! Women sobbed aloud, men shivered with indignation. Whatever the banner they followed, they were united heart and arm in this case to show that differences of opinion did not bring with them differences in understanding honor."

It was such attempts, and suspicion of like ones, that led to the extension of the police service.

One of the ablest and craftiest men of the Revolution became Napoleon's head of police in the Consulate, Fouché. A consummate actor and skilful flatterer, hindered by no conscience other than the duty of keeping in place, he acted a curious and entertaining part. Detective work was for him a game which he played with intense relish. He was a veritable amateur of plots, and never gayer than when tracing them.

Napoleon admired Fouché, but he did not trust him, and, to offset him, formed a private police to spy on his work. He never succeeded in finding anyone sufficiently fine to match the chief, who several times was malicious enough to contrive plots himself, to excite and mislead the private agents.

The system of espionage went so far that letters were regularly opened. It was commonly said that those who did not want their letters read, did not send them by post; and though it was hardly necessary, as in the Revolution, to send them in pies, in coat-linings, or hat-crowns, yet care and prudence had to be exercised in handling all political letters.

It was difficult to get officials for the post-office who could be relied on to intercept the proper letters; and in 1802, the Postmaster-General, Monsieur Bernard, the father of the beautiful Madame Récamier, was found to be concealing an active royalist correspondence, and to be permitting the circulation of a quantity of seditious pamphlets. His arrest and imprisonment made a great commotion in his daughter's circle, which was one of social and intellectual importance. Through the intercessions of Bernadotte, Monsieur Bernard was pardoned by Napoleon. The *cabinet noir*, as the department of the post-office which did this work was called, was in existence when Napoleon came to the

MARIE JOSEPH DE CHÉNIER,
1764–1811.

Anonymous portrait of the celebrated French dramatic author, and brother of the poet André de Chénier, guillotined in 1794. The principal tragedies of Joseph de Chénier are, "Charles IX." and "Henry VIII." but the work above all that makes his name popular and almost the equal of that of Rouget de l'Isle, is the famous revolutionary hymn, "Le Chant du Départ," which Méhul set to music.

Consulate, and he rather restricted than increased its operations. It has never been entirely given up, as many an inoffensive foreigner in France can testify. The theatre and press were also subjected to a strict censorship In 1800 the number of newspapers in Paris was reduced to twelve; and in three years there were but eight left, with a total subscription list of eighteen thousand six hundred and thirty. Napoleon's contempt for journalists and editors equalled that he had for lawyers, whom he called a "heap of babblers and revolutionists." Neither class could, in his judgment, be allowed to go free.

The *salons* were watched, and it is certain that those whose *habitués* criticised Napoleon freely were reported. One serious rupture resulted from the supervision of the *salons*, that with Madame de Staël. She had been an ardent admirer of Napoleon in the beginning of the Consulate, and Bourrienne tells several amusing stories of the disgust Napoleon showed at the letters of admiration and sentiment which she wrote him even so far back as the Italian campaign. If the secretary is to be believed, Madame de Staël told Napoleon, in one of these letters, that they were certainly created for each other, that it was an error in human institutions that the mild and tranquil Josephine was united to his fate, that nature evidently had intended for a hero such as he, her own soul of fire. Napoleon tore the letter to pieces, and he took pains thereafter to announce with great bluntness to Madame de Staël, whenever he met her, his own notions of women, which certainly were anything but "modern."

As the centralization of the government increased, Madame de Staël and her friends criticised Napoleon more freely and sharply than they would have done, no doubt, had

she not been incensed by his personal attitude towards her. This hostility increased until, in 1803, the First Consul ordered her out of France. "The arrival of this woman, like that of a bird of omen," he said in giving the order, "has always been the signal for some trouble. It is not my intention to allow her to remain in France."

In 1807 this order was repeated, and many of Madame de Staël's friends were included in the proscription ;

"I have written to the Minister of Police to send Madame de Staël to Geneva. This woman continues her trade of intriguer. She went near Paris in spite of my orders. She is a veritable plague. Speak seriously to the Minister, for I shall be obliged to have her seized by the *gendarmerie*. Keep an eye upon Benjamin Constant ; if he meddles with anything I shall send him to his wife at Brunswick. I will not tolerate this clique."

But when one compares the policy of restriction during the Consulate with what it had been under the old *régime* and in the Revolution, it certainly was far in advance in liberty, discretion, and humanity. The republican government to-day, in its repression of anarchy and socialism, has acted with less wisdom and less respect for freedom of thought than Napoleon did at this period of his career ; and that, too, in circumstances less complicated and critical.

MÉHUL, 1763–1817.

Celebrated French composer of music. Author of a great number of operas, of which the most celebrated is "Joseph." It is Méhul who composed, to the words of Joseph de Chénier, the music of the "Chant du Départ," the *frère* of "The Marseillaise."

INTERNAL PEACE AND PROSPERITY.

If there were still dull rumors of discontent, a *cabinet noir*, a restricted press, a censorship over the theatre, proscriptions, even imprisonments and executions, on the whole France was happy.

"Not only did the interior wheels of the machine commence to run smoothly," says the Duchesse d'Abrantès, "but the arts themselves, that most peaceful part of the interior administration, gave striking proofs of the returning prosperity of France. The exposition at the *Salon* that year (1800) was remarkably fine. Guérin, David, Gérard, Girodet, a crowd of great talents, spurred on by the emulation which always awakes the fire of genius, produced works which must some time place our school at a high rank."

The art treasures of Europe were pouring into France. Under the direction of Denon, that indefatigable *dilettante* and student, who had collected in the expedition in Egypt more entertaining material than the whole Institute, and had written a report of it which will always be preferred to the "Great Work," the galleries of Paris were reorganized and opened two days of the week to the people. Napoleon inaugurated this practice himself. Not only was Paris supplied with galleries: those department museums which surprise and delight the tourist so in France to-day were then created at Angers, Antwerp, Autun, Bordeaux, Brussels, Caen, Dijon, Geneva, Grenoble, Le Mans, Lille, Lyons, Mayence, Marseilles, Montpellier, Nancy, Nantes, Rennes, Rouen, Strasburg, Toulouse, and Tours.

The *prix de Rome*, for which there had been no money in the treasury for some time, was again reëstablished.

Every effort was made to stimulate scientific research. The case of Volta is one to the point. In 1801 Bonaparte called the eminent physicist to Paris to repeat his experiments before the Institute. He proposed that a medal should be given him, with a sum of money, and in his honor he established a prize of sixty thousand francs, to be awarded to any one who should make a discovery similar in value to Volta's.*

One of our own compatriots—Robert Fulton—was about the same time encouraged by the First Consul. Fulton was experimenting with his submarine torpedo and diving boat, and for four years had been living in Paris and besieging the Directory to grant him attention and funds. Napoleon took the matter up as soon as Fulton brought it to him, ordered a commission appointed to look into the invention, and a grant of ten thousand francs for the necessary experiments.

The Institute was reorganized, and to encourage science and the arts he founded, in 1804, twenty-two prizes, nine of which were of ten thousand francs, and thirteen of five thousand francs. They were to be awarded every ten years by the emperor himself, on the 18th Brumaire. The first distribution of these prizes was to have taken

BERNARDIN DE ST. PIERRE,

1737–1814.

After a portrait by Girodet. Engraved by Wedgewood. Celebrated French writer. His principal works are, "Paul and Virginia," "The Chaumière Indienne," and "Studies from Nature."

FRANÇOIS GÉRARD. 1770–1837.

After a crayon by Girodet. Gérard was one of the best of the portrait painters of Bonaparte, and his "Consul" (collection of the Duc d'Aumale) and his "Empereur" in costume, are two of the principal pieces of the Napoleonic iconography.

* The Volta prize has been awarded only three or four times. An award of particular interest to Americans was that made in 1880 to Dr. Alexander Graham Bell, the inventor of the telephone. The amount of the prize was a little less than ten thousand dollars. Dr. Bell, being already in affluent circumstances, upon receiving this prize, set it apart to be used for the benefit of the deaf, in whose welfare he had for many years taken a great interest. He invested it in another invention of his, which proved to be very profitable, so that the fund came to amount to one hundred thousand dollars. This he termed the Volta Fund. Some of this fund has been applied by Dr. Bell to the organization of the Volta Bureau, which collects all valuable information that can be obtained with reference to not only deaf mutes as a class, but to deaf-mutes individually. Twenty-five thousand dollars has been given to the Association for the Promotion of Teaching Speech to the Deaf. Napoleon is thus indirectly the founder of one of the most interesting and valuable present undertakings of the country.

place in 1809, but the judges could not agree on the laureates; and before a conclusion was reached, the Empire had fallen.

In literature and in music, as in art and science, there was a renewal of activity. A circle of poets and writers gathered about the First Consul. Paisiello was summoned to Paris to direct the opera and conservatory of music. There was a revival of dignity and taste in strong contrast to the license and carelessness of the Revolution. The *incroyable* passed away. The Greek costume disappeared from the street. Men and women began again to dress, to act, to talk, according to conventional forms.

Society recovered its systematic ways of doing things, and soon few signs of the general dissolution which had prevailed for ten years were to be seen.

Once more the traveller crossed France in peace; peasant and laborer went undisturbed about their work, and slept without fear. Again the people danced in the fields and "sang their songs as they had in the days before the Revolution." "France has nothing to ask from Heaven," said Regnault de Saint Jean d'Angely, "but that the sun may continue to shine, the rain to fall on our fields, and the earth to render the seed fruitful."

CHAPTER X.

PREPARATIONS FOR WAR WITH ENGLAND.—FLOTILLA AT BOULOGNE.—SALE OF LOUISIANA.

RUPTURE OF THE TREATY OF AMIENS.

In the spring of 1803 the treaty of Amiens, which a year before had ended the long war with England, was broken. Both countries had many reasons for complaint. Napoleon was angry at the failure to evacuate Malta. The perfect freedom allowed the press in England gave the pamphleteers and caricaturists of the country opportunity to criticise and ridicule him. He complained bitterly to the English ambassadors of this free press, an institution in his eyes impractical and idealistic. He complained, too, of the hostile *émigrés* allowed to collect in Jersey; of the presence in England of such notorious enemies as his as Georges Cadoudal; and of the sympathy and money the Bourbon princes and many nobles of the old *régime* received in London society. Then, too, he regarded the country as his natural and inevitable enemy. England to Napoleon was only a little island which, like Corsica and Elba, naturally belonged to France, and he considered it part of his business to get possession of her.

England, on the other hand, looked with distrust at the extension of Napoleon's in-

MADAME TALLIEN, 1773-1835.

By Quénédey. This picture may be regarded as a faithful portrait of the famous wife of Tallien. It was probably taken when she was about twenty-five years old; a period when she was frequently at Malmaison.

fluence on the Continent. Northern Italy, Switzerland, Holland, Parma, Elba, were under his protectorate. She had been deeply offended by a report published in Paris, on the condition of the Orient, in which the author declared that with six thousand men the French could reconquer Egypt; she resented the violent articles in the official press of Paris in answer to those of the free press of England; her aristocratic spirit was irritated by Napoleon's success; she despised this *parvenu*, this "Corsican scoundrel," as Nelson called him, who had had the hardihood to rise so high by other than the conventional methods for getting on in the world which she sanctioned.

Real and fancied aggressions continued throughout the year of the peace; and when the break finally came, though both nations persisted in declaring that they did not want war, both were in a thoroughly warlike mood.

THE DESCENT ON ENGLAND.

Napoleon's preparations against England form one of the most picturesque military movements in his career. Unable to cope

NAPOLEON IN 1803.

Painted by A. Gérard in 1803. Engraved by Richomme in 1835. This is considered by many the best portrait of Napoleon painted in the consulship.

with his enemy at sea, he conceived the audacious notion of invading the island, and laying siege to London itself. The plan briefly was this—to gather a great army on the north shore of France, and in some port a flotilla sufficient to transport it to Great Britain. In order to prevent interference with this expedition, he would keep the enemy's fleet occupied in the Mediterranean, or in the Atlantic, until the critical moment. Then, leading the English naval commander by stratagem in the wrong direction, he would call his own fleet to the Channel to protect his passage. He counted to be in London, and to have compelled the English to peace, before

JOSEPHINE.

By J. B. Isabey. (Collection of M. Edmond Taigny.) This portrait in crayon, lightly touched with color, was executed at Malmaison, probably in the course of the year 1798. It is very little known. Isabey, whose pencil was quick and sure, must have requested Josephine to pose for a few minutes after a walk in the park. This sketch was given to M. Taigny by Isabey himself. A. D.

Nelson could return from the chase he would have led him.

The preparations began at once. The port chosen for the flotilla was Boulogne; but the whole coast from Antwerp to the mouth of the Seine bristled with iron and bronze. Between Calais and Boulogne, at Cape Gris Nez, where the navigation was the most dangerous, the batteries literally touched one another. Fifty thousand men were put to work at the stupendous excavations necessary to make the ports large enough to receive the flotilla. Large numbers of troops were brought rapidly into the neighborhood: fifty thousand men to Boulogne, under Soult; thirty thousand to Etaples, under Ney ; thirty thousand to Ostend, under Davoust ; reserves to Arras, Amiens, Saint-Omer.

The work of preparing the flat-bottomed boats, or walnut-shells, as the English called them, which were to carry over the army, went on in all the ports of Holland and France, as well as in interior towns situated on rivers leading to the sea. The troops were taught to row, each soldier being obliged to practise two hours a day, so that the rivers of all the north of France were dotted with land-lubbers handling the oar, the most of them for the first time.

In the summer of 1803, Napoleon went to the north to look after the work. His trip was one long ovation. *Le Chemin d'Angleterre* was the inscription the people of Amiens put on the triumphal arch erected to his honor, and town vied with town in showing its joy at the proposed descent on the old-time enemy.

Such was the interest of the people, that a thousand projects were suggested to help on the invasion, some of them most amusing. In a learned and thoroughly serious memorial, one genius proposed that while the flotilla was preparing, the sailors be employed in catching dolphins, which should be shut up in the ports, tamed, and taught to wear a harness, so as to be driven, in the water, of c o u r s e, as horses are on land. This novel cavalry was to transport the French to the opposite side of the Channel.

Napoleon occupied himself not only with the preparations at Boulogne and with keeping Nelson busy elsewhere. Every p r o j e c t which could possibly facilitate his undertaking or discomfit his enemies, he considered. Fulton's diving-boat, the "Nautilus," and his submarine torpedoes, were at that time attracting the attention of the war departments of civilized countries. Already Napoleon had granted ten thousand francs to help the inventor. F r o m the camp at Boulogne he again ordered the matter to be looked into. Fulton promised him a machine w h i c h "would deliver France and the whole world from British oppression."

"I have just read the project of Citizen Fulton, engineer, which you have sent me

J. B. ISABEY AND HIS DAUGHTER.

By Baron Gérard. At the Louvre Isabey was born at Nancy in 1767, and died at Paris in 1855. He made several pictures of Napoleon in pencil and in oil, and many miniatures. The most famous of these are, "Napoleon at Malmaison," "The Consular Review," the thirty-two designs representing "The Coronation of Napoleon," the "Congress of Vienna," and the "Table of Marshals." The latter is executed on Sèvres porcelain, and shows Napoleon surrounded by the illustrious generals of his time.

much too late," he wrote, "since it is one that may change the face of the world. He that as it may, I desire that you immediately confide its examination to a commission of members chosen by you among the different classes of the Institute. There it is that learned Europe would seek for judges to resolve the question under consideration. A great truth, a physical, palpable truth, is before my eyes. It will be for these gentlemen to try and seize it and see it. As soon as their report is made, it will be sent to you, and you will forward it to me. Try and let the whole be determined within eight days, as I am impatient."

He had his eye on every point of the earth where he might be weak, or where he might weaken his enemy. He took possession of Hanover. The Irish were promised aid in their efforts for freedom. "Provided that twenty thousand united Irishmen join the French army on its landing," France is to give them in return twenty-five thousand men, forty thousand muskets, with artillery and ammunition, and a promise that the French government will not make peace with England until the independence of Ireland has been proclaimed. An attack on India was planned, his hope being that the princes of India would welcome an invader who would aid them in throwing off the English yoke. To strengthen himself in the Orient, he sought by letters and envoys to win the confidence, as well as to inspire the awe, of the rulers of Turkey and Persia.

The sale of Louisiana to the United States dates from this time. This transfer, of such tremendous importance to us, was made by Napoleon purely for the sake of hurting England. France had been in possession of Louisiana but three years. She had obtained it from Spain only on the condition that it should "at no time, under no pretext, and in no manner, be alienated or ceded to any other power." The formal

TALMA. 1763-1826.

By Vigneron, after a lithograph by Constans. Throughout his life Napoleon was a warm friend of Talma. He never forgot the time when, disgraced because of his relations with Robespierre, the great actor had been his friend, even aiding him by loans of money.

stipulation of the treaties forbade its sale. But Napoleon was not of a nature to regard a treaty, if the interest of the moment demanded it to be broken. To sell Louisiana now would remove a weak spot from France, upon which England would surely fall in the war. More, it would put a great territory, which he could not control, into the hands of a country which, he believed, would some day be a serious hinderance to English ambition. He sold the colony for the same reason that former French governments had helped the United States in her struggles for independence—to cripple England. It would help the United States, but it would hurt England. That was enough; and with characteristic eagerness he hurried through the negotiations.

"I have just given England a maritime rival which, sooner or later, will humble her pride," he said exultingly, when the convention was signed. The sale brought him twelve million dollars, and the United States assumed the French spoliation claims.

This sale of Louisiana caused one of the first violent quarrels between Lucien Bonaparte and Napoleon. Lucien had negotiated the return of the American territory to France in 1800. He had made a princely fortune out of the treaty, and he was very proud of the transaction; and when his brother Joseph came to him one evening in hot haste, with the information that the General wanted to sell Louisiana, he hurried around to the Tuileries in the morning to remonstrate.

Napoleon was in his bath, but, in the mode of the time, he received his brothers. He broached the subject himself, and asked Lucien what he thought.

"I flatter myself that the Chambers will not give their consent."

THE EMPEROR NAPOLEON I. BESTOWING THE CROWN ON THE EMPRESS JOSEPHINE, DECEMBER 2, 1804.

By David. The emperor advances, holding with both hands a crown which he is about to place on the head of Josephine. Between the emperor and the altar, Pope Pius VII. is seated; near him, Cardinal Fesch; to the right, in front places, are the high dignitaries; behind the empress, the princesses of the Imperial family; to the left, the brothers of the emperor; in a gallery above the marshals, the mother of the emperor. This picture, which has been hanging in the Louvre since 1889, was executed from 1805 to 1807.

NAPOLEON THE GREAT ("NAPOLÉON LE GRAND") IN CORONATION ROBES, 1805.

Painted and engraved by order of the emperor. Engraved by Desnoyers, after portrait painted by Gérard in 1805.

"You flatter yourself?" said Napoleon. "That's good, I declare."

"I have already said the same to the First Consul," cried Joseph.

"And what did I answer?" said Napo-leon, splashing around indignantly in the opaque water.

"That you would do it in spite of the Chambers."

"Precisely. I shall do it without the

consent of anyone whomsoever. Do you understand?"

Joseph, beside himself, rushed to the bathtub, and declared that if Napoleon dared do such a thing he would put himself at the head of an opposition and crush him in spite of their fraternal relations. So hot did the debate grow that the First Consul sprang up shouting: "You are insolent! I ought——" but at that moment he slipped and fell back violently. A great mass of perfumed water drenched Joseph to the skin, and the conference broke up.

An hour later, Lucien met his brother in his library, and the discussion was resumed, only to end in another scene, Napoleon hurling a beautiful snuff-box upon the floor, and shattering it; while he told Lucien that if he did not cease his opposition he would crush him in the same way. These violent scenes were repeated, but to no purpose. Louisiana was sold.

CHAPTER XI.

OPPOSITION TO NAPOLEON.—THE ESTABLISHMENT OF THE EMPIRE.—KING OF ITALY.

PLOT AGAINST THE FIRST CONSUL.

WHILE the preparation for the invasion was going on, the feeling against England was intensified by the discovery of a plot against the life of the First Consul. Georges Cadoudal, a fanatical royalist, who was accused of being connected with the plot of the 3d Nivôse (December 24), and who had since been in England, had formed a gigantic conspiracy, having as its object nothing less than the assassination of Napoleon in broad daylight, in the streets of Paris.

He had secured powerful aid to carry out his plan. The Bourbon princes supported him, and one of them was to land on the north coast to put himself at the head of the royalist sympa-

thizers as soon as the First Consul was killed. In this plot was associated Pichegru, who had been connected with the 18th Fructidor. General Moreau, the hero of Hohenlinden, was suspected of knowing something of it.

It came to light in time, and a general arrest was made of those suspected of being privy to it. The first to be tried and punished was the Duc d'Enghien, who had been seized in Ettenheim, in Baden, a short distance from the French frontier, on the supposition that he had been coming secretly to Paris to be present at the meetings of the conspirators. His trial at Vincennes was short, his execution immediate. There is good reason to believe that Napoleon had no suspicion that the Duc d'Enghien

EMPRESS JOSEPHINE.

From a pencil sketch made by David in the Cathedral of Notre Dame at the time of Josephine's coronation, and presented to his son. The original is now in the Museum of Versailles.

would be executed so soon as he was, and even to suppose that he would have lightened the sentence if the punishment had not been pushed on with an irregularity and inhumanity that recalls the days of the Terror.

The execution was a severe blow to Napoleon's popularity, both at home and abroad. Fouché's cynical remark was just:

members of Napoleon's own household met him with averted faces and sad countenances, and Josephine wept until he called her a child who understood nothing of politics. Abroad there was a revulsion of sympathy, particularly in the cabinets of Russia, Prussia, and Austria.

The trial of Cadoudal and Moreau followed. The former with several of his

NAPOLEON, EMPEROR OF THE FRENCH AND KING OF ITALY ("NAPOLEON, EMPEREUR DES FRANÇAIS, ROI D'ITALIE"). 1805.
Engraved by Audouin, after Charles de Chatillon.

"The death of the Duc d'Enghien is worse than a crime; it is a blunder." Chateaubriand, who had accepted a foreign embassy, resigned at once, and a number of the old aristocracy, such as Pasquier and Molé, who had been saying among themselves that it was their duty to support Napoleon's splendid work of reorganization, went back into obscurity. In society the effect was distressing. The

accomplices was executed. Moreau was exiled for two years. Pichegru committed suicide in the Temple.

EMPEROR OF THE FRENCH.

This plot showed Napoleon and his friends that a Jacobin or royalist fanatic might any day end the life upon which the scheme of reorganization depended. It is

THE EMPEROR NAPOLEON IN STATE COSTUME ("L'EMPEREUR EN GRAND COSTUME"). 1805.

Engraved by Tardieu, after Isabey. Title piece engraved by Malbeste, after Percier. Isabey became intimate with the Bonapartes during the Consulate through Hortense, whose drawing-master he had been. It was then he executed his portraits of Bonaparte at Malmaison, and the Review of the Consular Guard. He enjoyed Napoleon's favor throughout the Empire, and was charged by him to execute a series of thirty-two designs to commemorate his coronation. He was afterwards Marie Louise's drawing-master.

THE EMPRESS JOSEPHINE IN STATE COSTUME ("L'IMPÉRATRICE EN GRAND COSTUME"). 1805.
Engraved by Audouin, after a design by Isabey and Percier.

THE EMPEROR NAPOLEON IN ORDINARY COURT COSTUME ("L'EMPEREUR EN PETIT COSTUME"). 1805.

Engraved by Ribault, after a design by Isabey and Percier.

THE EMPRESS JOSEPHINE IN ORDINARY COURT COSTUME ("L'IMPÉRATRICE EN PETIT COSTUME"). 1805.

Engraved by Ribault, after a design by Isabey and Percier.

JOSEPHINE, EMPRESS OF THE FRENCH AND QUEEN OF ITALY ("JOSEPHINE, IMPÉRATRICE DES FRANÇAIS ET REINE D'ITALIE). 1805.
Designed by Buguet.

true he had already been made First Consul for life by a practically unanimous vote,
but there was need of strengthening his
position and providing a succession. In
March, six days after the death of the
Duc d'Enghien, the Senate proposed to
him that he complete his work and take
the throne. In April the Council of State
and the Tribunate took up the discussion.
The opinion of the majority was voiced by
Regnault de Saint-Jean d'Angély : "It is a
long time since all reasonable men, all true
friends of their country, have wished that
the First Consul would make himself emperor, and reëstablish, in favor of his family,
the old principles of hereditary succession.

It is the only means of securing permanency for his own fortune, and to the men whom merit has raised to high offices. The Republic, which I loved passionately, while I detested the crimes of the Revolution, is now in my eyes a mere Utopia. The First Consul has convinced me that he enjoy the blessings of the present; guarantee to us the future." On the 18th of May, 1804, when thirty-five years old, Napoleon was first addressed as "sire," and congratulated on his elevation to the throne of the French people.

NAPOLEON, 1805,

("Napoleon I. Gall. Imp. Ital. Rex.") Designed and engraved by Longhi.

First Consul has convinced me that he wishes to possess supreme power only to render France great, free, and happy, and to protect her against the fury of factions."

The Senate soon after proceeded in a body to the Tuileries. "You have extricated us from the chaos of the past," said the spokesman; "you enable us to

IMPERIAL HONORS AND ETIQUETTE.

Immediately his household took on the forms of royalty. His mother was Madame Mère; Joseph, Grand-Elector, with the title of Imperial Highness; Louis, Constable, with the same title; his sisters were Imperial Highnesses. Titles were given to

all officials; the ministers were excellencies; Cambacérès and Le-Brun, the Second and Third Consuls, became Arch Chancellor and Arch Treasurer of the Empire. Of his old generals, Berthier, Murat, Moncey Jourdan, Masséna, Augureau, Bernadotte Soult, Brune, Lannes, Mortier, Ney, Davoust, and Bessières were made marshals

NAPOLEON, 1805.

Engraved by Morghen, after Gérard, in 1807. Napoleon wrote a letter thanking Morghen for the beauty of this engraving, and subsequently decorated him with the Legion of Honor.

The red button of the Legion of Honor was scattered in profusion. The title of *citoyen*, which had been consecrated by the Revolution, was dropped, and hereafter everybody was called *monsieur*.

Two of Napoleon's brothers, unhappily, had no part in these honors. Jerome, who had been serving as lieutenant in the navy, had, in 1803, while in the United States, married a Miss Elizabeth Patterson of Baltimore. Napoleon forbade the recording of the marriage, and declared it void. As Jerome had not as yet given up his wife, he had no share in the imperial rewards.

NAPOLEON'S STATE CARRIAGE.

Lucien was likewise omitted, and for a similar reason. His first wife had died in 1801, and much against Napoleon's wishes he had married a Madame Jouberthon, to whom he was deeply attached: nothing could induce him to renounce his wife and take the Queen of Etruria, as Napoleon wished. The result of his refusal was a violent quarrel between the brothers, and Lucien left France.

This rupture was certainly a grief to Napoleon. Madame de Rémusat draws a pathetic little picture of the effect upon him of the last interview with Lucien:

" It was near midnight when Bonaparte came into the room; he was deeply dejected, and, throwing himself into an arm-chair, he exclaimed in a troubled voice, 'It is all over! I have broken with Lucien, and ordered him from my presence.' Madame Bonaparte began to expostulate. 'You are a good woman,' he said, 'to plead for him.' Then he rose from his chair, took his wife in his arms, and laid her head softly on his shoulder, and with his hand still resting on the beautiful head, which formed a contrast to the sad, set countenance so near it, he told us that Lucien had resisted all his entreaties, and that he had resorted equally in vain to both threats and persuasion. 'It is hard, though,' he added, 'to find in one's own family such stubborn opposition to interests of such magnitude. Must I, then, isolate myself from every one? Must I rely on myself alone? Well! I will suffice to myself; and you, Josephine—you will be my comfort always.' "

A fever of etiquette seized on all the inhabitants of the imperial palace of Saint Cloud. The ponderous regulations of Louis XIV. were taken down from the shelves in the library, and from them a code began to be compiled. Madame Campan, who had been First Bedchamber Woman to Marie Antoinette, was summoned to interpret the solemn law, and to describe costumes and customs. Monsieur de Talleyrand, who had been made Grand Chamberlain, was an authority who was consulted on everything.

"We all felt ourselves more or less elevated," says Madame de Rémusat, "Vanity is ingenious in its expectations, and ours were unlimited. Sometimes it was disenchanting, for a moment, to observe the almost ridiculous effect which this agitation produced upon certain classes of society. Those who had nothing to do with our brand new dignities said with Montaigne, 'Let us avenge ourselves by railing at them.' Jests, more or less witty, and puns, more or less ingenious, were lavished on these new-made princes, and somewhat disturbed our brilliant visions; but the number of those who dare to censure success is small, and flattery was much more common than criticism."

No one was more severe in matters of etiquette than Napoleon himself. He studied the subject with the same attention that he did the civil code, and in much the same way. "In concert with Monsieur de Ségur," he wrote De Champagny, "you must write me a report as to the way in which ministers and ambassadors should be received. . . . It will be well for you to enlighten me as to what was the practice at Versailles, and what is done at Vienna and St. Petersburg. Once my regulations adopted, everyone must conform to them. I am master, to establish what rules I like in France."

He had some difficulty with his old comrades-in-arms, who were accustomed to addressing him in the familiar second singular, and calling him Bonaparte, and who persisted, occasionally, even after he was "sire," in using the language of easy intimacy. Lannes was even removed for some time from his place near the emperor for an indiscretion of this kind.

THE FÊTE OF BOULOGNE.

In August, 1804, the new emperor visited Boulogne to receive the congratulations of his army and distribute decorations. His visit was celebrated by a magnificent *fête*. Those who know the locality of Boulogne, remember, north of the town, an amphitheatre-like plain, in the centre of which is a hill. In this plain sixty thousand men were camped. On the elevation was erected a throne. Hereby stood the chair of Dagobert; behind it the armor of Francis I.; and around rose scores of blood-stained, bullet-shot flags, the trophies of Italy and Egypt. Beside the emperor was the helmet of Bayard, filled with the decorations to be distributed. Up and down the coast were the French batteries; in the port lay the flotilla; to the right and left stretched the splendid army.

Just as the ceremonies were finished, a fleet of over a thousand boats came sailing into the harbor to join those already there, while out in the Channel English officers and sailors, with levelled glasses, watched from their vessels the splendid armament,

NAPOLEON, 1808.

Engraved in 1822 by Massard, after Bouillon.

which was celebrating its approaching descent on their shores.

CORONATION OF NAPOLEON AND JOSEPHINE.

On December 1st the Senate presented the emperor the result of the vote taken among the people as to whether hereditary succession should be adopted. There were two thousand five hundred and seventy-nine votes against ; three million five hundred and seventy-five thousand for—a vote more nearly unanimous than that for the life consulate, there being something like nine thousand against him then.

The next day Napoleon was crowned at Notre Dame. The ceremony was prepared with the greatest care. Grand Master of Ceremonies de Ségur, aided by the painter David, drew up the plan and trained the court with great severity in the etiquette of the occasion. He had the widest liberty, it even being provided that "if it be indispensable, in order that the *cortége* arrive at Notre Dame with greater facility, to pull down some houses," it should be done. By a master stroke of diplomacy Napoleon had persuaded Pope Pius VII. to cross the Alps to perform for him the solemn and ancient service of coronation.

Of this ceremony we have no better description than that of Madame Junot :

"Who that saw Notre Dame on that memorable day can ever forget it? I have witnessed in that venerable pile the celebration of sumptuous and solemn festivals ; but never did I see anything at all approximating in splendor the spectacle exhibited at Napoleon's coronation. The vaulted roof reechoed the sacred chanting of the priests, who invoked the blessing of the Almighty on the ceremony about to be celebrated, while they awaited the arrival of the Vicar of Christ, whose throne was prepared near the altar. Along the ancient walls covered with magnificent tapestry were ranged, according to their rank, the different bodies of the state, the deputies from every city ; in short, the representatives of all France assembled to implore the benediction of Heaven on the sovereign of the people's choice. The waving plumes which adorned the hats of the senators, counsellors of state, and tribunes ; the splendid uniforms of the military ; the clergy in all their ecclesiastical pomp ; and the multitude of young and beautiful women, glittering in jewels, and arrayed in that style of grace and elegance which is only seen in Paris ;—altogether presented a picture which has, perhaps, rarely been equalled, and certainly never excelled.

"The Pope arrived first ; and at the moment of his entering the Cathedral, the anthem *Tu es Petrus* was commenced. His Holiness advanced from the door with an air at once majestic and humble. Ere long, the firing of a cannon announced the departure of the procession from the Tuileries. From an early hour in the morning the weather had been exceeding unfavorable. It was cold and rainy, and appearances seemed to indicate that the procession would

be anything but agreeable to those who joined it. But, as if by the especial favor of Providence, of which so many instances are observable in the career of Napoleon, the clouds suddenly dispersed, the sky brightened up, and the multitudes who lined the streets from the Tuileries to the Cathedral, enjoyed the sight of the procession without being, as they had anticipated, drenched by a December rain. Napoleon, as he passed along, was greeted by heartfelt expressions of enthusiastic love and attachment.

"On his arrival at Notre Dame, Napoleon ascended the throne, which was erected in front of the grand altar. Josephine took her place beside him, surrounded by the assembled sovereigns of Europe. Napoleon appeared singularly calm. I watched him narrowly, with a view of discovering whether his heart beat more highly beneath the imperial trappings than under the uniform of the guards ; but I could observe no difference, and yet I was at the distance of only ten paces from him. The length of the ceremony, however, seemed to weary him ; and I saw him several times check a yawn. Nevertheless, he did everything he was required to do, and did it with propriety. When the Pope anointed him with the triple unction on his head and both hands, I fancied, from the direction of his eyes, that he was thinking of wiping off the oil rather than of anything else ; and I was so perfectly acquainted with the workings of his countenance, that I have no hesitation in saying that was really the thought that crossed his mind at that moment. During the ceremony of anointing, the Holy Father delivered that impressive prayer which concluded with these words : 'Diffuse, O Lord, by my hands, the treasures of your grace and benediction on your servant Napoleon, whom, in spite of our personal unworthiness, *we this day anoint emperor, in your name.*' Napoleon listened to this prayer with an air of pious devotion ; but just as the Pope was about to take the crown, *called* the Crown of Charlemagne, from the altar, Napoleon seized it, and placed it on his own head. At that moment he was really handsome, and his countenance was lighted up with an expression of which no words can convey an idea.

"He had removed the wreath of laurel which he wore on entering the church, and which encircles his brow in the fine picture of Gérard. The crown was, perhaps, in itself, less becoming to him ; but the expression excited by the act of putting it on, rendered him perfectly handsome.

"When the moment arrived for Josephine to take an active part in the grand drama, she descended from the throne and advanced towards the altar, where the emperor awaited her, followed by her retinue of court ladies, and having her train borne by the Princesses Caroline, Julie, Eliza, and Louis. One of the chief beauties of the Empress Josephine was not merely her fine figure, but the elegant turn of her neck, and the way in which she carried her head ; indeed, her deportment altogether was conspicuous for dignity and grace. I have had the honor of being presented to many *real princesses*, to use the phrase of the Faubourg Saint-Germain, but I never saw one who, to my eyes, presented so perfect a personification of elegance and majesty. In Napoleon's countenance I could read the conviction of all I have just said. He looked with an air of complacency at the empress as she advanced towards him ; and when she knelt down, when the tears, which she could not repress, fell upon her clasped hands, as they were raised to Heaven, or rather to Napoleon, both then appeared to enjoy one of those fleeting moments of pure felicity which are unique in a lifetime, and serve to fill up a lustrum of years. The emperor performed, with peculiar grace, every

NAPOLEON PRESENTING THE EAGLES TO THE ARMY. (1804).

By David. (At Versailles.) The emperor, surrounded by princes, princesses, dignitaries, ministers, officers, and the chief governing bodies, distributes the eagles to the Grand Army in the Champ de Mars, and addresses to it the following words: "Soldiers, here are your standards; those eagles will always serve you for a rallying point; they will be found everywhere your emperor judges necessary for the defence of his throne and his people. You will swear to sacrifice your lives in their defence, and by your courage to preserve them ever in the path to victory. You swear." "We swear," replies the entire army. The eagles are lowered before the emperor, and the marshals of the Empire raise high their batons. A. D.

action required of him during the ceremony ; but his manner of crowning Josephine was most remarkable : after receiving the small crown, surmounted by the cross, he had first to place it on his own head, and then to transfer it to that of the empress. When the moment arrived for placing the crown on the head of the woman whom popular superstition regarded as his good genius, his manner was almost playful. He took great pains to arrange this little crown, which was placed over Josephine's tiara of diamonds ; he put it on, then took it off, and finally

was of especial interest. The party crossed the Alps by Mont Cenis, and the road was so bad that the carriages had to be taken to pieces and carried over, while the travellers walked. This trip really led to the fine roads which now cross Mont Cenis. At Alessandria Napoleon halted, and on the field of Marengo ordered a review of the manœuvres of the famous battle. At this

NAPOLEON WITH THE IRON CROWN OF LOMBARDY,

Designed and engraved by Longhi, in 1812, for " Vite e Ritratti di illustri Italiani."

put it on again, as if to promise her she should wear it gracefully and lightly."

The fate of France had no sooner been settled, as Napoleon believed, than it became necessary to decide on what should be done with Italy. The crown was offered to Joseph, who refused it. He did not want to renounce his claim to that of France, and finally Napoleon decided to take it himself. A new constitution was prepared for the country by the French Senate, and, when all was arranged, Napoleon started on April 1st for Italy. A great train accompanied him, and the trip

review he even wore the coat and hat he had worn on that famous day four years before.

By the time the imperial party was ready to enter Milan, on May 13, it had increased to a triumphant procession, and the entry was made amidst most enthusiastic demonstrations. On May 26 the coronation took place. The iron crown, used for so long for the coronation of the Lombard kings, had been brought out for the occasion. When the point in the ceremony was reached where the crown was to be placed on Napoleon's head, he seized it, and with his own hands placed it on his head, repeating in a loud voice the words inscribed on

the crown: "God gives it to me; beware who touches it." Josephine was not crowned Queen of Italy, but watched the scene from a gallery above the altar.

Napoleon remained in Italy for another month, engaged in settling the affairs of the country. The order of the Crown of Iron was created, the constitution settled, Prince Eugène was made viceroy, and Genoa was joined to the Empire.

NAPOLEON REVIEWING HIS GUARDS.

Lithographed by Raffet.

CHAPTER XII.

CAMPAIGN OF 1805.—CAMPAIGN OF 1806-1807.—PEACE OF TILSIT.

WAR WITH AUSTRIA.

Austria looked with jealousy on this accession of power, and particularly on the change in the institutions of her neighbor. In assuming control of the Italian and Germanic States, Napoleon gave the people his code and his methods; personal liberty, equality before the law, religious toleration, took the place of the unjust and narrow feudal institutions. These new ideas were quite as hateful to Austria as the disturbance in the balance of power, and more dangerous to her system. Russia and Prussia felt the same suspicion of Napoleon as Austria did. All three powers were constantly incited to action against France by England, who offered unlimited gold if they would but combine with her. In the summer of 1805 Austria joined England and Russia in a coalition against France. Prussia was not yet willing to commit herself.

The great army which for so many months had been gathering around Boulogne, preparing for the descent on England, waited anxiously for the arrival of the French fleet to cover its passage. But the fleet did not come ; and, though hoping until the last that his plan would still be carried out, Napoleon quietly and swiftly made ready to transfer the army of England into the Grand Army, and to turn its march against his continental enemies.

Never was his great war rule, "Time is everything," more thoroughly carried out. "Austria will employ fine phrases in order to gain time," he wrote Talleyrand, "and to prevent me accomplishing anything this year; . . . and in April I shall find one hundred thousand Russians in Poland, fed by England, twenty thousand English at Malta, and fifteen thousand Russians at Corfu. I should then be in a critical position. My mind is made up." His orders flew from Boulogne to Paris, to the German States, to Italy, to his generals, to his naval commanders. By the 28th of

August the whole army had moved. A month later it had crossed the Rhine, and Napoleon was at its head.

The force which he commanded was in every way an extraordinary one. Marmont's enthusiastic description was in no way an exaggeration :

"This army, the most beautiful that was ever seen, was less redoubtable from the number of its soldiers than from their nature. Almost all of them had carried on war and had won victories. There still existed among them something of the enthusiasm and exaltation of the Revolutionary campaigns ; but this enthusiasm was systematized. From the supreme chief down—the chiefs of the army corps, the division commanders, the common officers and soldiers—everybody was hardened to war. The eighteen months in splendid camps had produced a training, an *ensemble*, which has never existed since to the same degree, and a boundless confidence. This army was probably the best and the most redoubtable that modern times have seen."

The force responded to the imperious genius of its commander with a beautiful precision which amazes and dazzles one who follows its march. So perfectly had all been arranged, so exactly did every corps and officer respond, that nine days after the passage of the Rhine, the army was in Bavaria, several marches in the rear of the enemy. The weather was terrible, but nothing checked them. The emperor himself set the example. Day and night he was on horseback in the midst of his troops ; once for a week he did not take off his boots. When they lagged, or the enemy harassed them, he would gather each regiment into a circle, explain to it the position of the enemy, the imminence of a great battle, and his confidence in his troops. These harangues sometimes took place in driving snow-storms, the soldiers standing up to their knees in icy slush. By October 13th, such was the extraordinary march they had made,

the emperor was able to issue this address to the army :

"Soldiers, a month ago we were encamped on the shores of the ocean, opposite England, when an impious league forced us to fly to the Rhine. Not a fortnight ago that river was passed ; and the Alps, the Neckar, the Danube, and the Lech, the celebrated barriers of Germany, have not for a minute delayed our march. . . . The enemy, deceived by our manœuvres and the rapidity of our movements, is entirely turned. . . . But for the army before you, we should be in London to-day, have avenged six centuries of insult, and have liberated the sea.

"Remember to-morrow that you are fighting against the allies of England. . . .

"NAPOLEON."

Four days after this address came the capitulation of Ulm—a "new Caudine Forks," as Marmont called it. It was, as

THE EMPEROR.
By Charlet

NAPOLEON.

Engraved by Cousin, after Lelèvre. Lelèvre probably painted this portrait early in the career of Napoleon. It was engraved by Cousin, a celebrated mezzotint engraver, many years ago, but when finished Napoleon "did not sell." It therefore was laid aside until 1893, when this print was made.

Napoleon said, a victory won by legs, instead of by arms. The great fatigue and the forced marches which the army had undergone had gained them sixty thousand prisoners, one hundred and twenty guns, ninety colors, more than thirty generals, at a cost of but fifteen hundred men, two-thirds of them but slightly wounded.

But there was no rest for the army. Before the middle of November it had so surrounded Vienna that the emperor and his court had fled to Brünn, seventy or eighty miles north of Vienna, to meet the Russians, who, under Alexander I., were coming from Berlin. Thither Napoleon followed them, but the Austrians retreated eastward, joining the Russians at Olmütz. The combined force of the allies was now some ninety thousand men. They had a strong reserve, and it looked as if the Prussian army was about to join them. Napoleon at Brünn had only some seventy or eighty thousand men, and was in the heart of the enemy's country. Alexander, flattered by his aides, and confident that he was able to defeat the French, resolved to leave his strong position at Olmütz and seek battle with Napoleon.

The position the French occupied can be understood if one draws a rough diagram of a right-angled triangle, Brünn being at the right angle formed by two roads, one running south to Vienna, by which Napoleon had come, and the other running eastward to Olmütz. The hypothenuse of this angle, running from northeast to southwest, is formed by Napoleon's army.

When the allies decided to leave Olmütz their plan was to march southwestward, in face of Napoleon's line, get between him and Vienna, and thus cut off what they supposed was his base of supplies (in this they were mistaken, for Napoleon had, unknown to them, changed his base from Vienna to Bohemia), separate him from his Italian army, and drive him, routed, into Bohemia.

THE BATTLE OF AUSTERLITZ.

On the 27th of November the allies advanced, and their first encounter with a small French vanguard was successful. It gave them confidence, and they continued their march on the 28th, 29th, and 30th, gradually extending a long line facing westward and parallel with Napoleon's line. The French emperor, while this movement was going on, was rapidly calling up his reserves and strengthening his position. By the first day of December Napoleon saw clearly what the allies intended to do, and had formed his plan. The events of that day confirmed his ideas. By nine o'clock in the evening he was so certain of the plan of the coming battle that he rode the length of his line, explaining to his troops the tactics of the allies, and what he himself proposed to do.

Napoleon's appearance before the troops, his confident assurance of victory, called out the army. The divisions of infantry raised bundles of blazing straw on the ends of long poles, giving him an illumination as imposing as it was novel. It was a happy thought, for the day was the anniversary of his coronation.

The emperor remained in bivouac all night. At four o'clock of the morning of

THE EMPEROR AT THE BIVOUAC.

After a picture by Philippoteaux.

NAPOLEON AT AUSTERLITZ. 1805.

From a copyrighted etching by Jacquet, after Meissonier. Reproduced by the kind permission of Mr. C. Klackner, owner of the etching. Meissonier constructed his composition from tactical descriptions of the battle. The foreground is occupied by a regiment of cuirassiers, while the emperor and his staff occupy a position in the middle ground. The original picture, which forms part of the collection of the Duc d'Aumale, at Chantilly, is the second upon this subject which Meissonier painted, the first having been accidentally destroyed by fire shortly after it was completed.

THE BATTLE OF AUSTERLITZ, DECEMBER 2, 1805.

Engraved by Godefroy in 1813, after a painting by Gérard, made in 1810. Gérard chose for this picture the moment in the battle when the Russian Imperial Guard fled towards Auster-litz. Rapp, his head bare and forehead bleeding, announces the victory to Napoleon. Behind the emperor are grouped the staff officers, and Russian officers taken prisoners. The picture was painted for the ceiling of the hall of the Council of State in the Tuileries. It was taken from the palace at the Restoration, and went again to Gérard, who refused to sell it to the Duke of Wellington. It is now in the historical gallery of Versailles.

THE RIGHT HONORABLE WILLIAM PITT.

Engraved by Cardon, after Eldridge, 1801. Pitt, born May 28, 1759, was the second son of William Pitt. Earl of Chatham. Before he was fifteen, sent to Cambridge, where he made a remarkable record in mathematics and the classics. He studied law in Lincoln's Inn, and at the age of twenty-one became member of Parliament. His first speech, in favor of economical reform, made a great impression. At twenty-three he was made a member of the cabinet as Chancellor of the Exchequer. At twenty-four he became Premier, with an opposition including Fox, Burke, Sheridan, and North. His courage and determination were such on the East India Company bill, that when Parliament was dissolved, and the country appealed to, he was supported as no minister in England had been for generations. He secured the passage of several important bills, and practically did away with the opposition. When the French Revolution came on, he at first indorsed it, but was revolted by its atrocities. He tried to avoid war with France, and was only driven into it by public opinion ; but his military administration was feeble. The king. George III., refusing to second his plans for Irish relief. Pitt resigned in 1801, after eighteen years of nearly absolute power. When the treaty of Amiens was broken in 1803, he appeared in Parliament again, in favor of war, and the next year was recalled to the premiership. He had great difficulty, however, with his cabinet, and Napoleon's train of victories alarmed him. At last he fell sick from his anxiety. Trafalgar aroused him, but Austerlitz struck him a blow from which he could not rally, and he died January 23, 1806. He was honored with a public funeral, and his remains were placed in Westminster Abbey.

the 2d of December he was in the saddle. When the gray fog lifted he saw the enemy's divisions arranged exactly as he had divined. Three corps faced his right—the southwest part of the hypothenuse. These corps had left a splendid position facing his centre, the heights of Pratzen.

This advance of the enemy had left their centre weak and unprotected, and had separated the body of the army from its right, facing Napoleon's left. The enemy was in exactly the position Napoleon wished for the attack he had planned.

It was eight o'clock in the morning when the emperor galloped up his line, proclaiming to the army that the enemy had exposed himself, and crying out : "Close the campaign with a clap of thunder." The generals rode to their positions, and at once the battle opened. Soult, who commanded the French centre, attacked the allies' centre so unexpectedly that it was driven into retreat. The Emperor Alexander and his headquarters were in

MEETING OF NAPOLEON AND FRANCIS II., EMPEROR OF AUSTRIA, AFTER THE BATTLE OF AUSTERLITZ, DECEMBER, 1805.

Engraved by Delaunay, after Gros. Pointing to the nearest watchfire, Napoleon said: "I must receive your majesty in the only palace I have inhabited for two months." The emperor replied: "You make so good use of it that you must find it very pleasant."

"NAPOLEON BONAPARTE," IN 1812.

Engraved by Lupton, after Robert Lefèvre. Published in London in 1818. Original in the collection
of the Prince Victor. "I prefer this to David's celebrated picture." G. G. H.

MARIE PAULINE, PRINCESS BORGHESE.

By Robert Lefèvre. Versailles gallery. This picture is signed, "Robert Lefèvre fecit, 1806." It was shown in the *Salon* of 1808, and obtained a brilliant success.

this part of the army, and though the young czar did his best to rouse his forces, it was a hopeless task. The Russian centre was defeated and the wings divided. At the same time the allies' left, where the bulk of their army was massed in a marshy country of which they knew little, was engaged and held in check by Davoust, and their right was overcome by Lannes, Murat, and Bernadotte. As soon as the centre and right of the allies had been driven into retreat, Napoleon concentrated his forces on their left, the strongest part of his enemy. In a very short time the allies were driven back into the canals and lakes of the country, and many men and nearly all their artillery lost. Before night the routed enemy had fallen back to Austerlitz.

Of all Napoleon's battles Austerlitz was the one of which he was the proudest. It was here that he showed best the "divine side of war."

The familiar note in which Napoleon an-

Russians and thirty thousand Austrians. I have made forty thousand prisoners, taken forty flags, one hundred guns, and all the standards of the Russian Imperial Guard. . . . Although I have bivouacked in the open air for a week, my health is good. This evening I am in bed in the beautiful castle of Monsieur de Kaunitz, and have changed my shirt for the first time in eight days."

The battle of Austerlitz obliged Austria to make peace (the treaty was signed at Presburg on December 26, 1805), compelled Russia to retire disabled from the field, transformed the haughty Prussian *ultimatum* which had just been presented into humble submission, and changed the rejoicings of England over the magnificent naval victory of Trafalgar (October 21st) into despair. It even killed Pitt. It enabled Napoleon, too, to make enormous strides in establishing a kingdom of the West. Naples was given to Joseph, the Bavarian Republic was made a kingdom for Louis, and the states between the Lahn, the Rhine, and the Upper Danube were formed into a league, called the Confederation of the Rhine, and Napoleon was made Protector.

JEAN LOUIS ERNEST MEISSONIER. 1815–1891.

Sketch by Meissonier himself. The inscription reads: "My dear Chenavard, may this sketch bear witness to our long and good friendship. Meissonier, 1881." Meissonier was one of the most famous *genre* and historical painters of France. He painted a large number of pictures, the greatest of which are the four called the "Napoleon Cycle."

WAR WITH PRUSSIA AND RUSSIA.

At the beginning of 1806 Napoleon was again in Paris. He had been absent but three months. Eight months of this year were spent in fruitless negotiations with England and in an irritating correspondence with Prussia. The latter country had many grievances against Napoleon, the sum of them all being that "French politics had been the scourge of humanity for the last fifteen years," and that an "insatiable ambition was still the ruling passion of France." By the end of September war was declared, and Napoleon, whose preparations had been conducted secretly, it being given out that he was going to

nounced to his brother Joseph the result of the battle, is a curious contrast to the oratorical bulletins which for some days flowed to Paris. His letter is dated Austerlitz, December 3, 1805 :

"After manœuvring for a few days I fought a decisive battle yesterday. I defeated the combined armies commanded by the Emperors of Russia and Germany. Their force consisted of eighty thousand

184. BATTLE OF JENA.

After the picture by Meissonier in the collection of Monsieur Edmond Sienna

Compiègne to hunt, suddenly joined his army.

The first week of October the Grand Army advanced from southern Germany towards the valley of the Saale. This movement brought them on the flanks of the Prussians, who were scattered along the upper Saale. The unexpected appearance of the French army, which was larger and much better organized than the Prussian, caused the latter to retreat towards the Elbe. The retreating army was in two divisions; the first crossing the Saale to Jena, the second falling back towards the Unstrut. As soon as Napoleon understood these movements he despatched part of his force under Davoust and Bernadotte to cut off the retreat of the second Prussian division, while he himself hurried on to Jena to force battle on the first. The Prussians were encamped at the foot of a height known as the Landgrafenberg. To command this height was to command the Prussian forces. By a series of determined and repeated efforts Napoleon reached the position desired, and by the morning of the 14th of October had his foes in his power. Advancing from the Landgrafenberg in three divisions, he turned the Prussian flanks at the same moment that he attacked their centre. The Prussians never fought better, perhaps, than at Jena. The movements of their cavalry awakened even Napoleon's admiration, but they were surrounded and outnumbered, and the army was speedily broken into pieces and driven into a retreat.

While Napoleon was fighting at Jena, to the right at Auerstadt, Davoust was en-

gaging Brunswick and his seventy thousand men with a force of twenty-seven thousand. In spite of the great difference in numbers the Prussians were unable to make any impression on the French; and Brunswick falling, they began to retreat towards Jena, expecting to join the other division of the army, of whose route they were ignorant. The result was frightful. The two flying armies suddenly encountered each other, and, pursued by the French on either side, were driven in confusion towards the Elbe.

HORACE VERNET. 1789-1863.

Portrait by Witkofski in the gallery at Versailles.

THE ENTRY INTO BERLIN—JENA, EYLAU, AND FRIEDLAND.

On October 25th the French were at Berlin. Their entry was one of the great spectacles of the campaign. One particularly touching incident of it was the visit paid to Napoleon by the Protestant and Calvinist French clergy. There were at that time twelve thousand French refugees in Berlin, owing to the revocation of the Edict of Nantes. They were received with kindness by Napoleon, who told them they had good right to protection, and that their privileges and worship would be respected.

Jena brought Napoleon something like one hundred and sixty million francs in money, an enormous number of prisoners, guns, and standards, the glory of the entry of Berlin, and a great number of interesting articles for the Napoleon Museum of Paris, among them the column from the field of Rosbach, the sword, the ribbon of the black eagle, and the general's sash of Frederick the Great, and the flags carried by his guards during the Seven Years' War. But it did not secure him peace. The King of Prussia threw himself into the arms of Rus-

NAPOLEON AT JENA, 1806

After Horace Vernet. This picture of Napoleon is a fragment of a great canvas representing the battle of Jena, found in the Hall of Battles at Versailles. Vernet was commissioned by Louis Philippe to paint the great battles of France when he first conceived the idea of converting the château into an historical museum. This particular picture is one of a series, including the battles of Friedland, Jena, and Wagram. It appeared in the *Salon* of 1836. The moment chosen by Vernet for his picture, is that when the emperor, accompanied by Murat and Berthier, heard in the ranks of the imperial foot-guards the words : " *En avant !* " "What is that ?" said he. "It can only be a beardless boy who thinks he knows what I ought to do. Let him wait until he has commanded in thirty pitched battles before he presumes to give me advice." It was, indeed, one of the conscripts, eager to show his courage.

NAPOLEON, EMPEROR OF THE FRENCH AND KING OF ITALY ("NAPOLÉON, EMPEREUR
DES FRANÇAIS, ROI D'ITALIE"). 1806.

Engraved by Arnold, after Dähling. It was at Berlin, at the time of the entry
of the French army, that Dähling saw the emperor and made his portrait in
colors. Masson says that all the representations of Napoleon from 1806 to 1815
were copied after this design of Dähling.

sia, and Napoleon advanced boldly into Poland to meet his enemy.

The Poles welcomed the French with joy. They hoped to find in Napoleon the liberator of their country, and they poured forth money and soldiers to reënforce him. "Our entry into Varsovia," wrote Napoleon, "was a triumph, and the sentiments that the Poles of all classes show since our arrival cannot be expressed. Love of country and the national sentiment are not only entirely conserved in the heart of the people, but it has been intensified by misfortune. Their first passion, their first desire, is again to become a nation. The rich come from their *châteaux*, praying for the reëstablishment of, the nation, and offering their children, their fortunes, and their influence." Everything was done during the months the French remained in Poland, to flatter and aid the army.

The campaign against the Russians was carried on in Old Prussia, to the southeast of the Gulf of Dantzic. Its first great engagement was the battle of Eylau on February 8, 1807. This was the closest drawn battle Napoleon had ever fought. His loss was enormous, and he was saved only by a hair's-breadth from giving the enemy the field of battle. After Eylau the main army went into winter quarters to repair its losses, while Marshal Lefebvre besieged Dantzic, a siege which military critics declare to be, after Sebastopol, the most celebrated of modern times. Dantzic capitulated in May.

ENTRANCE OF THE FRENCH INTO BERLIN, OCTOBER 27, 1806.

Engraved by Bovinet, after Swebach.

1807.

The simple date that Raffet has given for title to this composition, sums up the great military events : Austerlitz, Jena, Eylau, Friedland - that preceded the treaty of Tilsit. In this picture the artist, with admirable sobriety of method, has succeeded in giving a true characterization of the triumphant attitude of the conqueror sitting erect on his battle-horse, which seems ready to spring forward to fresh victories.—A. D.

On June 14th the battle of Friedland was fought. This battle, the anniversary of Marengo, was won largely by Napoleon's taking advantage of a blunder of his opponent. The French and the Russian armies were on the opposite banks of the Alle. Benningsen, the Russian commander, was marching towards Königsberg by the eastern bank. Napoleon was pursuing by the western bank. The French forces, however, were scattered ; and Benningsen, thinking that he could engage and easily rout a portion of the army by crossing the river at Friedland, suddenly led his army across to the western bank. Napoleon utilized this unwise movement with splendid skill. Calling up his reënforcements he attacked the enemy solidly. As soon as the Russian centre was broken, defeat was inevitable, for the retreating army was driven into the river, and thousands lost. Many were pursued through the streets of Friedland by the French, and slaughtered there. The battle was hardly over when Napoleon wrote to Josephine :

"FRIEDLAND, 15th *June*, 1807.

"MY FRIEND : I write you only a few words, for I am very tired. I have been bivouacking for several days. My children have worthily celebrated the anniversary of Marengo. The battle of Friedland will be just as celebrated and as glorious for my people. The whole Russian army routed, eighty guns captured, thirty thousand men taken prisoners or killed, with twenty-five generals ; the Russian guard annihilated ; it is the worthy sister of Marengo, Austerlitz, and Jena. The bulletin will tell you the rest. My loss is not large. I successfully out-manœuvred the enemy.

"NAPOLEON."

PEACE OF TILSIT.

Friedland ended the war. Directly after the battle Napoleon went to Tilsit, which for the time was made neutral ground, and here he met the Emperor of Russia and the King of Prussia, and the map of Europe was made over.

The relations between the royal parties seem to have been for the most part amiable. Napoleon became very fond of Alexander I. at Tilsit. "Were he a woman I think I should make love to him," he wrote Josephine once. Alexander, young and enthusiastic, had a deep admiration for Napoleon's genius, and the two became good comrades. The King of Prussia, overcome by his losses, was a sorrowful figure in their company. It was their habit at Tilsit to go out every day on horseback, but the king was awkward, always crowding against Napoleon, beside whom he

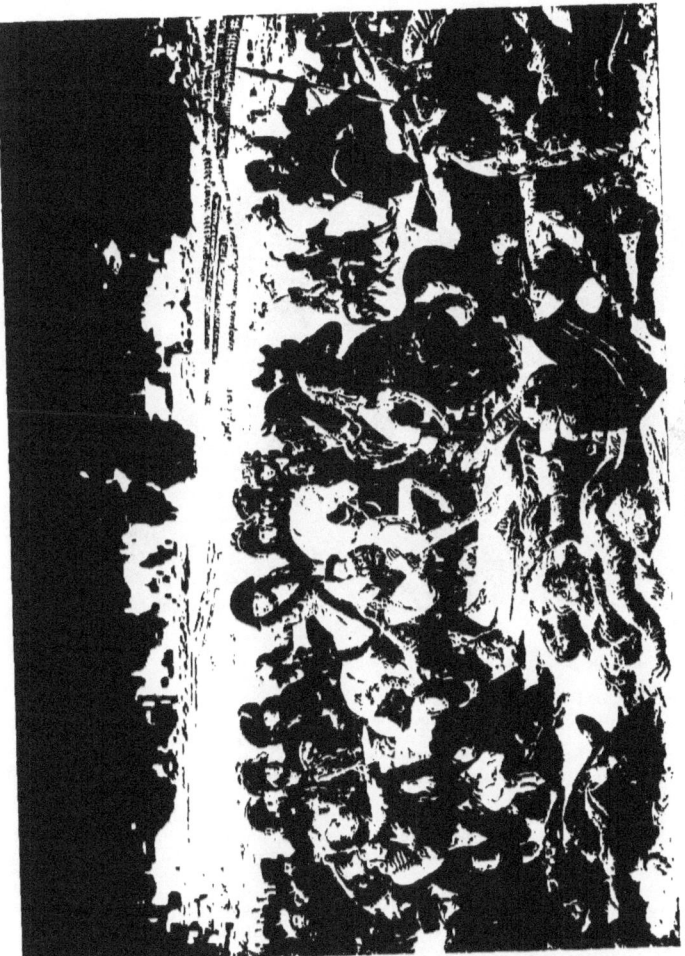

BATTLE OF EYLAU, FEBRUARY 8, 1807.

Etched by Vallot, after Gros. Napoleon appears mounted on a light bay horse, and in the dress he wore on the day of the battle. On the right are Soult, Davoust, and Murat; on the left Berthier, Bessières, and General Caulaincourt. Soon after the battle of Eylau a contest was opened for a picture of Napoleon visiting the battle-field. Gros did not wish to contest, but Denon forced him to it, and his sketch was successful. The order was given him, and the emperor sent him the hat and overcoat which he wore during the battle. This picture was in the *Salon* of 1808, and is now in the Louvre.

BATTLE OF FRIEDLAND, JUNE 14, 1807.

By Horace Vernet. Versailles gallery. Vernet depicts the emperor on the battle-field, giving orders to the general of division, Oudinot, for the pursuit of the enemy.

rode, and making his two companions wait for him to climb from the saddle when they returned.

Their dinners together were dull, and the emperors, very much in the style of two careless, fun-loving youths, bored by a solemn elderly relative, were accustomed after dinner to make excuses to go home early; but later they met at the apartments of one or the other, and often talked together until midnight.

Just before the negotiations were completed, Queen Louise arrived, and tried to use her influence with Napoleon to obtain at least Magdeburg. Napoleon accused the queen to Las Cases of trying to win him at first by a scene of high tragedy, but when they came to meet at dinner, her policy was quite another. "The Queen of Prussia dined with me to-day," wrote Napoleon to the empress on July 7th. "I had to defend myself against being obliged to make some further concessions to her husband; . . ." and the next day, "The Queen of Prussia is really charming; she

is full of *coquetterie* towards me. But do not be jealous; I am an oilcloth, off which all that runs. It would cost me too dear to play the *galant*."

The intercessions of the queen really hurried on the treaty. When she learned that it had been signed, and her wishes not granted, she was indignant, wept bitterly, and refused to go to the second dinner to which Napoleon had invited her. Alexander was obliged to go himself to decide her. After the dinner, when she withdrew, Napoleon accompanied her. On the staircase she stopped.

"Can it be," she said, "that after I have had the happiness of seeing so near me the man of the age and of history, I am not to have the liberty and satisfaction of assuring him that he has attached me for life? . . . "

"Madame, I am to be pitied," said the emperor gravely. "It is my evil star."

By the treaty of Tilsit the face of the continent was transformed. Prussia lost half her territory. Dantzic was made a

"1807." NAPOLEON AFTER FRIEDLAND.

Photographed from the original painting by Meissonier, now in the Metropolitan Museum, New York. The emperor, on a rising ground, is surrounded by his staff, amongst whom are his Marshals Bessières, Duroc, and Berthier. On his left and rear Nansouty is waiting with his division for the signal to defile; farther back are seen the "Old Guard," with their grenadier caps and white breeches. Meissonier is said to have worked upon this picture for fifteen years. He modelled all the horses in wax, and every figure was drawn from the life. The painting was sold to Mr. A. T. Stewart of New York for about three hundred thousand francs (sixty thousand dollars).

MEETING OF FREDERICK WILLIAM III., KING OF PRUSSIA, NAPOLEON, AND ALEXANDER I., EMPEROR OF RUSSIA, AT TILSIT.
THE FIGURE ON THE LEFT IS FREDERICK WILLIAM; THAT ON THE RIGHT IS ALEXANDER.

Engraved by Gügel, after a drawing by Wolff. The meeting occurred June 26, 1807, in the pavilion which had been erected for that purpose on the River Nieman. After Friedland the Russians crossed the Nieman; the French camped on the banks opposite them. The first interview on the raft was between the Emperor Alexander and Napoleon alone on June 25th. The two emperors, accompanied by their staffs, started from the opposite banks at the same time; Napoleon arrived first, passed through the tent and met Alexander. The two embraced warmly in sight of the two armies, who cheered them loudly. A second interview took place the next day, to which the Emperor Alexander brought the King of Prussia. During the time that the sovereigns at Tilsit were negotiating, the two armies kept their positions, and friendly relations grew up between them.

free town. Magdeburg went to France. Hesse-Cassel and the Prussian possessions west of the Elbe went to form the kingdom of Westphalia. The King of Saxony received the grand duchy of Warsaw. Finland and the Danubian principalities were to go to Alexander in exchange for certain Ionian islands and the Gulf of Cattaro in Dalmatia.

Of far more importance than this change of boundaries, was the private understanding which the emperors came to at Tilsit. They agreed that the Ottoman Empire was to remain as it was unless they saw fit to change its boundaries. Russia might occupy the principalities as far as the Danube. Peace was to be made, if possible, with England, and the two powers were to work together to bring it about. If they failed, Russia was to force Sweden to close her ports to Great Britain, and Napoleon was to do the same in Denmark, Portugal, and the States of the Pope. Nothing was to be done about Poland by Napoleon.

According to popular belief, the secret treaty of Tilsit included plans much more startling, it being said that the two emperors pledged themselves to each other for nothing less than driving the Bourbons from Spain and the Braganzas from Portugal, and replacing them by Bonapartes; for giving Russia Turkey in Europe and as much of Asia as she wanted; for ending the temporal power of the Pope; for placing France in Egypt; for shutting the English from the Mediterranean; and for undertaking several other similar enterprises.

NAPOLEON RECEIVING QUEEN LOUISE OF PRUSSIA, JULY 6, 1807.

By Gosse. Versailles gallery. On the arrival of the Queen of Prussia at Königsberg, the emperor descended to the street to meet the brave and beautiful sovereign, and received her at the foot of the steps. The imperial guard were under arms ; the emperor was accompanied by the Grand Duke of Berg, the Marshals Berthier and Ney, General Duroc, and the minister of foreign affairs, Talleyrand, who is represented in this picture standing on the steps.

CHAPTER XIII.

EXTENSION OF NAPOLEON'S EMPIRE.—FAMILY AFFAIRS.

KING OF KINGS.

NAPOLEON's influence in Europe was now at its zenith. He was literally "king of kings," as he was popularly called, and the Bonaparte family was rapidly displacing the Bourbon. Joseph had been made King of Naples in 1806. Eliza was Princess of Lucques and Piombino. Louis, married to Hortense, had been King of Holland since 1806. Pauline had been the Princess Borghese since 1803; Caroline, the wife of Murat, was Grand Duchess of Cleves and Berg; Jerome was King of Westphalia; Eugène de Beauharnais, Viceroy of Italy, was married to a princess of Bavaria.

The members of Napoleon's family were elevated only on condition that they act strictly in accordance with his plans. They must marry so as to cement the ties necessary to his kingdom. They must arrange their time, form their friendships, spend their money, as it best served the interest of his great scheme of conquest. The interior affairs of their kingdoms were in reality centralized in his hands as perfectly as those of France. He watched the private and public conduct of his kings and nobles, and criticised them with absolute frankness and extraordinary common sense. The ground on which he protected them is well explained in the following letter, written in January, 1806, to Count Miot de Mélito:

"You are going to rejoin my brother. You will tell him that I have made him King of Naples; that he will continue to be Grand Elector, and that nothing will be changed as regards his relations with France. But impress upon him that the least hesitation, the slightest wavering, will ruin him entirely. I have another person in my mind who will replace him should he refuse. . . . At present all feelings of affection yield to state reasons. I recognize only those who serve me as relations. My fortune is not attached to the name of Bonaparte, but to that of

FREDERICK WILLIAM III., KING OF PRUSSIA.

Engraved by Dickenson, after a portrait painted in 1798 by Lauer. Frederick William III., born August 3, 1770, was the eldest son of Frederick William II., was trained by his grand-uncle Frederick the Great, and succeeded to his father's throne in 1797. When the treaty of Lunéville ended the war with France in 1801, he was obliged to give up his territory on the left bank of the Rhine. He remained at peace with Napoleon until frightened by the formation of the Confederation of the Rhine in 1806. The war which followed, ending in the treaty of Tilsit, drove him from Berlin, and took away half his kingdom. But he nevertheless continued his efforts to reorganize his state. Frederick joined Napoleon for the Russian campaign, but joined the coalition of 1813. After Waterloo, he continued to improve his kingdom, though he never gave it the liberal constitution he had promised. He died June 7, 1840.

Napoleon. It is with my fingers and with my pen that I make children. To-day I can love only those whom I esteem. Joseph must forget all our ties of childhood. Let him make himself esteemed. Let him acquire glory. Let him have a leg broken in battle. Then I shall esteem him. Let him give up his old ideas. Let him not dread fatigue. Look at me : the campaign I have just terminated, the movement, the excitement, have made me stout. I believe that if all the kings of Europe were to coalesce against me, I should have a ridiculous paunch."

Joseph, bent on being a great king, boasted now and then to Napoleon of his position in Naples. His brother never failed to silence him with the truth, if it was blunt and hard to digest.

"When you talk about the fifty thousand enemies of the queen, you make me laugh. . . . You exaggerate the degree of hatred which the queen has left behind at Naples : you do not know mankind. There are not twenty persons who hate her as you suppose, and there are not twenty persons who would not surrender to one of her smiles. The strongest feeling of hatred on the part of a nation is that inspired by another nation. Your fifty thousand men are the enemies of the French."

With Jerome, Napoleon had been particularly incensed because of his marriage with Miss Patterson. In 1804 he wrote of that affair :

". . . Jerome is wrong to think that he will be able to count upon any weakness on my part, for, not having the rights of a father, I cannot entertain for him the feeling of a father ; a father allows himself to be blinded, and it pleases him to be blinded because he identifies his son with himself. . . . But what am I to Jerome ? Sole instrument of my destiny, I owe nothing to my brothers. They have made an abundant harvest out of what I have accomplished in the way of glory ; but, for all that, they must not abandon the field and deprive me of the aid I have a right to expect from them. They will cease to be anything for me, directly they take a road opposed to mine. If I exact so much from my brothers who have already rendered many services, if I have abandoned the one who, in mature age [Lucien], refused to follow my advice, what must not Jerome, who is still young, and who is known only for his neglect of duty, expect? If he does nothing for me, I shall see in this the decree of destiny, which has decided that I shall do nothing for him. . . ."

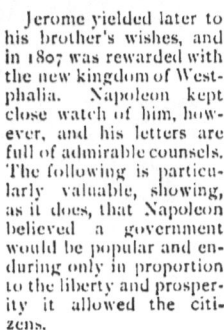

Jerome yielded later to his brother's wishes, and in 1807 was rewarded with the new kingdom of Westphalia. Napoleon kept close watch of him, however, and his letters are full of admirable counsels. The following is particularly valuable, showing, as it does, that Napoleon believed a government would be popular and enduring only in proportion to the liberty and prosperity it allowed the citizens.

LOUISE, QUEEN OF PRUSSIA. 1798.

Engraved by Dickenson, after a portrait painted in 1798 by Lauer. Louise, Queen of Prussia, was born March 10, 1776, in Hanover. Her father was the Duke Charles of Mecklenburg-Strelitz, and her mother a princess of Hesse-Darmstadt. In 1793 she met King Frederick William III. at Frankfort. He was so enamored of her beauty and her nobility of character that he made her his wife. Queen Louise's dignity and sweetness under the reverses her kingdom suffered in the war with France, won her the love and respect of her people, and have given her a place among the most lovable and admirable women of history. She died July 19, 1810, and was buried at Charlottenburg, where a beautiful mausoleum by Rauch has been erected. In 1814 her husband instituted the Order of Louise in her honor. On March 10, 1876, the Prussians celebrated the one hundredth anniversary of her birth.

JOSEPH BONAPARTE IN HIS CORONATION ROBES. 1808.
Engraved by C. S. Pradier in 1813, after Gérard.

"What the German peoples desire with impatience [he told Jerome], is that persons who are not of noble birth, and who have talents, shall have an equal right to your consideration and to public employment (with those who are of noble birth); that every sort of servitude and of intermediate obligations between the sovereign and the lowest class of the people should be entirely abolished. The benefits of the Code Napoleon, the publicity of legal procedure, the establishment of the jury system, will be the distinctive characteristics of your monarchy. . . . I count more on the effect of these benefits for the extension and strengthening of your kingdom, than upon the result of the greatest victories. Your people ought to enjoy a liberty, an equality, a well-being, unknown to the German peoples. . . . What people would wish to return to the arbitrary government of Prussia, when it has tasted the benefits of a wise and liberal administration? The peoples of Germany, France, Italy, Spain, desire equality, and demand that liberal ideas should prevail. . . . Be a constitutional king."

Louis in Holland was never a king to Napoleon's mind. He especially disliked his quarrels with his wife. The two young people had been married for state reasons,

MARIE JULIE CLARY, QUEEN OF NAPLES. 1777-1845.

By Robert Lefèvre. Versailles gallery. Julie Clary married Joseph Bonaparte, the 1st of
August, 1794. Her husband was afterwards King of Naples, then King of Spain. In the canvas of Lefèvre, she holds by the hand her eldest daughter, Zenaïde Charlotte Julie, born in 1801,
afterwards married to Charles, Prince de Canino, son of Lucien Bonaparte.

and were very unhappy. In 1807 Napoleon wrote Louis, apropos of his domestic
relations, a letter which is a good example
of scores of others he sent to one and
another of his kings and princes about
their private affairs.

"You govern that country too much like a Capu-
chin. The goodness of a king should be full of majesty. . . . . A king orders, and asks nothing from

any one. . . . . When people say of a king that he
is good, his reign is a failure. . . . Your quarrels with the queen are known to the public. You
should exhibit at home that paternal and effeminate
character you show in your manner of governing. . .
. . . You treat a young wife as you would command
a regiment. Distrust the people by whom you are
surrounded ; they are nobles. . . . You have the
best and most virtuous of wives, and you render her
miserable. Allow her to dance as much as she likes ;
it is in keeping with her age. I have a wife who is
forty years of age ; from the field of battle I write to

JOSEPH BONAPARTE.

Engraved by S. W. Reynolds after a painting
made in the United States, in 1831, by J. Goubaut.

contempt for the inhabitants, and that your
eyes are unceasingly turned towards Paris.
Although occupied with vast affairs, I nevertheless desire to make known my wishes, and
I hope that you will conform to them.

"Love your husband and his family, be
amiable, accustom yourself to the usages of
Rome, and put this in your head : that if
you follow bad advice you will no longer be
able to count upon me. You may be sure
that you will find no support in Paris, and
that I shall never receive you there without
your husband. If you quarrel with him, it
will be your fault, and France will be closed
to you. You will sacrifice your happiness
and my esteem.

"BONAPARTE."

This supervision of policy, relations, and conduct extended to his
generals. The case of General Berthier is one to the point. Chief of
Napoleon's staff in Italy, he had
fallen in love at Milan with a Madame Visconti, and had never been
able to conquer his passion. In
Egypt Napoleon called him "chief
of the lovers' faction," that part of
the army which, because of their

her to go to balls, and you wish a young
woman of twenty to live in a cloister, or, like
a nurse, to be always washing her children.
. . . Render the mother of your children
happy. You have only one way of doing
so, by showing her esteem and confidence.
Unfortunately you have a wife who is too
virtuous : if you had a coquette, she would
lead you by the nose. But you have a proud
wife, who is offended and grieved at the
mere idea that you can have a bad opinion
of her. You should have had a wife like
some of those whom I know in Paris. She
would have played you false, and you would
have been at her feet. . . . .

"NAPOLEON."

With his sisters he was quite as
positive. While Josephine adapted
herself with grace and tact to her
great position, the Bonaparte sisters, especially Pauline, were constantly irritating somebody by
their vanity and jealousy. The
following letter to Pauline shows
how little Napoleon spared them
when their performances came to
his ears :

"MADAME AND DEAR SISTER : I have
learned with pain that you have not the
good sense to conform to the manners and
customs of the city of Rome ; that you show

ELISA BACCIOCHI, GRAND DUCHESS OF TUSCANY, ELDEST SISTER OF NAPO-
LEON (1777–1820).

Engraved by Morghen in 1814, after Counis.

MARIE PAULINE BONAPARTE, PRINCESS BORGHESE,

This graceful portrait of the most beautiful of Napoleon's sisters, is from the brush of Madame Benoit, and belongs to the Versailles collection.

JOACHIM MURAT (1771-1815).

Engraved by Ruotte, after Gros. Murat was born in 1771, in the department of Lot. He was destined
for the Church, but abandoned the seminary for the army. When Barras called Napoleon to the defence
of the convention, the 13th Vendemiaire, Murat was asked to aid, and for his services he was made an aide-
de-camp of Napoleon in Italy. His valor at Montenotte, Ceva, Dego, and Mondovi, was rewarded by
sending him to Paris with the first flags captured. In 1798 he went to Egypt. He aided in the 18th Brumaire, and was rewarded with the command of the consular guard and the hand of Caroline Bonaparte.
At Marengo he led the French cavalry, and was afterwards made governor of the Cisalpine Republic. In
18 4 he was made a marshal of France, and in 1805 grand admiral, with the title of prince. He commanded
the cavalry of the Grand Army in the campaign of 1805, and after Austerlitz was made grand duke of Berg
and Cleves. Murat led the cavalry at Jena, Eylau, and Friedland, and in 1808 was made general-in-chief
of the French armies in Spain. Soon after he became King of Naples under the title of King Joachim Napoleon. During the retreat from Moscow Napoleon offended him, and he resigned his command and began
to intrigue with Austria. In January, 1814, the alliance with Austria was declared by Murat's seizing
Benevento, while Austria promised him Ancona for thirty thousand men. The alliance was broken by
Murat's declaration that he intended to restore the unity and independence of Italy, and he was defeated by
the Austrians, May 2, 1815, at Tolentino. He escaped to France and offered his sword to Napoleon, who
refused it. After Waterloo he was refused an asylum in England, and, with a few followers, he attempted
to retake Naples, but was deserted, taken prisoner, and shot October 13, 1815.

THE QUEEN OF NAPLES AND MARIE MURAT.

By Madame Vigée-Lebrun. This canvas, executed in 1807, is in the museum of Versailles. Caroline of Naples is represented with her eldest child, Marie Lætitia Joséphe Murat, afterwards Countess Pepoli.

desire to see wives or sweethearts, were constantly revolting against the campaign, and threatening to desert.

In 1804 Berthier had been made marshal, and in 1806 Napoleon wished to give him the princedom of Neufchatel ; but it was only on condition that he give up Madame de Visconti, and marry.

" I exact only one condition, which is that you get married. Your passion has lasted long enough. It has become ridiculous ; and I have the right to hope that the man whom I have called my companion in arms, who will be placed alongside of me by posterity, will no longer abandon himself to a weakness without example. . . . You know that no one likes you better than I do, but you know also that the first condition of my friendship is that it must be made subordinate to my esteem."

JEROME BONAPARTE, 1808.

"Engraved by I. G. Müller, knight, and Frederich Müller, son, engravers to his majesty the King of
Würtemberg. After a design made at Cassel by Madame Kinson." Jerome Bonaparte, youngest brother of
Napoleon, was born in Ajaccio, 1784 ; died near Paris in 1860. Entered the navy at sixteen, and in 1801 was sent
on the expedition to Santo Domingo. On his return went to the United States, where, in 1803, he married
Miss Elizabeth Patterson of Baltimore. Napoleon refused to recognize this marriage, and when Jerome
brought his wife to Europe in 1805, they were forbidden France. Jerome continued in the navy, and his wife
went to England. In 1806 he left naval for military service, was recognized as a French prince, and made
successor to the throne in event of Napoleon's leaving no male heirs. After Tilsit, Jerome was made King of
Westphalia, a new kingdom having its capital at Cassel, and was married to Catherine, daughter of the King
of Würtemberg. The campaign of 1813 drove him to Paris. During the Hundred Days he sat in the chamber
of peers. After the second restoration of Louis XVIII. Jerome lived in various parts of Europe, suffering at
one time serious financial embarrassment, until, in 1847, he was allowed to return to Paris. After the Revolution of 1848 he was made governor of the *Invalides* and marshal. In 1852 he was president of the imperial
senate. Later the right of succession was given him and his son.

Berthier fled to Josephine for help, weeping like a child; but she could do nothing, and he married the woman chosen for him. Three months after the ceremony, the husband of Madame de Visconti died, and Berthier, broken-hearted, wrote to the Prince Borghese:

"You know how often the emperor pressed me to obtain a divorce for Madame de Visconti. But a divorce was always repugnant to the feelings in which I was educated, and therefore I waited. To-day Madame de Visconti is free, and I might have been the happiest of men. But the emperor forced me into a marriage which hinders me from uniting myself to the only woman I ever loved. Ah, my dear prince, all that the emperor has done and may yet do for me, will be no compensation for the eternal misfortune to which he has condemned me."

THE EMPEROR OF THE FRENCH IN 1807.

Never was Napoleon more powerful

JEROME, KING OF WESTPHALIA.

By Kinson. Versailles gallery. This picture ought to be catalogued under the title, "Portrait of King Jerome and his wife, Frédérique Catherine Sophie Dorothée, Princess of Würtemberg."

than at the end of the period we have been tracing so rapidly, never had he so looked the emperor. An observer who watched him through the Te Deum sung at Notre Dame in his honor, on his return from Tilsit, says: "His features, always calm and serious, recalled the cameos which represent the Roman emperors. He was small; still his whole person, in this imposing ceremony, was in harmony with the part he was playing. A sword glittering with precious stones was at his side, and the glittering diamond called the 'Regent' formed its pommel. Its brilliancy did not let us forget that this sword was the sharpest and the most victorious that the world had seen since those of Alexander and Cæsar."

Certainly he never worked more prodigiously. The campaigns of 1805–1807 were, in spite of their rapid movement,—indeed, because of it,—terribly fatiguing for him; that they were possible at all was due mainly to the fact that they had been made on paper so many times in his study. When he was consul the only room opening from his study was filled with enormous maps of all the countries of the world. This room was presided over by a competent cartographer. Frequently these maps were brought to the study and spread upon the floor. Napoleon would get down upon them on all fours, and creep about, compass and red pencil in hand, comparing and measuring distances, and studying the configuration of the land. If he was in doubt about anything, he referred it to his librarian, who was expected to give him the fullest details.

MARRIAGE OF THE PRINCE JEROME BONAPARTE AND THE PRINCESS CATHERINE OF WÜRTEMBERG, AUGUST 22, 1807.

By Regnault. This picture is in the Versailles gallery. The ceremony of contract, here represented by the painter, took place in the *Galerie de Diane* in the Tuileries. Their Majesties were seated on the throne, with the young couple in front of them. Regnault de Saint Jean d'Angély, secretary of state to the imperial family, read the contract of marriage, which was signed by their Majesties. The religious ceremony was afterwards celebrated in the chapel of the Tuileries by the prince primate, on the 23d of August.

Attached to his cabinet were skilful translators, whose business was not only to translate diplomatic correspondence, but to gather from foreign sources full information about the armies of his enemies. Méneval declares that the emperor knew the condition of foreign armies as well as he did his own.

The amount of information he had about other lands was largely due to his ability to ask questions. When he sent to an agent for a report, he rattled at him a volley of questions, always to the point; and the agent knew that it would never do to let one go unanswered.

While carrying on the Austrian and Prus-

ELIZA BONAPARTE.

Drawn by the physionotrace, by Quenèdey. The physionotrace was an instrument invented at the end of the eighteenth century, by the aid of which one could trace portraits mechanically.

sian campaigns of 1805–1807, Napoleon showed, as never before, his extraordinary capacity for attending to everything. The number of despatches he sent out was incredible. In the first three months of 1807, while he was in Poland, he wrote over seventeen hundred letters and despatches.

It was not simply war, the making of kingdoms, the direction of his new-made kings; minor affairs of the greatest variety occupied him. While at Boulogne, tormented by the failure of the English invasion and the war against Austria, he ordered that horse races should be established "in those parts of the empire the most remarkable for the horses they breed ; prizes shall be awarded to the fleetest horses." The very day after the battle of Friedland, he was sending orders to Paris about the form and site of a statue to the memory of the Bishop of Vannes. He criticised from Poland the quarrels of Parisian actresses, ordered canals, planned there for the terior affairs of France. This care of details went, as Pasquier says, to the "point of minuteness, or, to speak plainly, to that of charlatanism ;" but it certainly did produce a deep impression upon France. That he could establish himself five hundred leagues from Paris, in the heart of winter, in a country encircled by his enemies, and yet be in

EMPRESS JOSEPHINE.

Fragment from the picture of the marriage of Jerome Bonaparte and the Princess Catherine.

Bourse and the Odeon Theatre. The newspapers he watched as he did when in Paris, reprimanded this editor, suspended that, forbade the publication of news of disasters to the French navy, censured every item honorable to his enemies. To read the bulletins issued from Jena to Friedland, one would believe that the writer had no business other than that of regulating the interior daily communication with his capital, could direct even its least important affairs as if he were present, could know what every person of influence, from the Secretary of State to the humblest newspaper man, was doing, caused a superstitious feeling to rise in France, and in all Europe, that the emperor of the French people was not only omnipotent, but omnipresent.

LOUIS BONAPARTE, 1778-1846.

King of Holland in 1806. Abdicated in 1810,
taking the title of Comte de St. Leu.

CHAPTER XIV.

THE BERLIN DECREE.—WAR IN
THE PENINSULA. — THE BO-
NAPARTES ON THE SPANISH
THRONE.

THE CONTINENTAL BLOCKADE.

WHEN Napoleon, in 1805, was
obliged to abandon the descent on
England and turn the magnificent
army gathered at Boulogne against
Austria, he by no means gave up the
idea of one day humbling his enemy. Persistently throughout the
campaigns of 1805–1807 his despatches and addresses remind
Frenchmen that vengeance is only
deferred.

In every way he strives to awaken
indignation and hatred against
England. The alliance which has
compelled him to turn his armies
against his neighbors on the Continent, he characterizes as an
"unjust league fomented by the
hatred and gold of England."
He tells the soldiers of the Grand
Army that it is English gold
which has transported the Russian army from the extremities
of the universe to fight them. He
charges the horrors of Austerlitz
upon the English. "May all the
blood shed, may all these misfortunes, fall upon the perfidious
islanders who have caused them!
May the cowardly oligarchies of
London support the conse-
quences of so many woes!"
From now on, all the treaties he
makes are drawn up with a view
to humbling "the eternal enemies of the Continent."

Negotiations for peace went
on, it is true, in 1806, between the
two countries. Napoleon offered
to return Hanover and Malta.
He offered several things which
belonged to other people, but
England refused all of his combinations; and when, a few days

EUGÉNIE HORTENSE DE BEAUHARNAIS, 1783-1837.

Daughter of Josephine, wife of Louis, King of Holland, and mother
of Napoleon III. Engraved by Laugier, after Girodet.

Group in marble, by Monsieur Émile Chatrousse. Gallery at Versailles. The queen has at her side her third son, Charles Louis Napoleon Bonaparte afterwards emperor under the title of Napoleon III.

after Jena, he addressed his army, it was to tell them : "We shall not lay down our arms until we have obliged the English, those eternal enemies of our nation, to renounce their plan of troubling the Continent and their tyranny of the seas."

A month later—November 21, 1806—he proclaimed the famous Decree of Berlin, his future policy towards Great Britain. As she had shut her enemies from the sea, he would shut her from the land. The "continental blockade," as this struggle of land against sea was called, was only using England's own weapon of war ; but it was using it with a sweeping audacity, thoroughly Napoleonic in conception and in the proposed execution. Henceforth, all communication was forbidden between the British Isles and France and her allies. Every Englishman found under French authority—and that was about all Europe as the emperor estimated it—was a prisoner of war. Every dollar's worth of English property found within Napoleon's bounda-

EUGÈNE DE BEAUHARNAIS, NAPOLEON'S STEPSON. ("EUGENIO NAPOLEONE, PRINCE DI FRANCIA, VICE RE D'ITALIA, 1813.")

Engraved by Longhi, after Gérard, Milan, 1813. Eugène de Beauharnais, son of Josephine Tascher de la Pagerie and the Viscount Alexandre de Beauharnais, was born in Paris in 1781. The property of his father having been confiscated. Eugène was apprenticed to a cabinet-maker, but, fortune changing, he was employed on the staff of General Hoche. After the marriage of Josephine and Bonaparte, the latter took his stepson with him into Italy, and sent him on a mission to Corfu. He accompanied General Bonaparte to Egypt, and was wounded at Saint-Jean d'Acre. He rose steadily in military rank, and when the Empire was established was made prince, and in 1805 Archchancellor of State. When Napoleon took the iron crown, Eugène was made Viceroy of Italy. He governed his kingdom with wisdom and fidelity. In 1806 Eugène was married to a daughter of the King of Bavaria, and adopted by Napoleon, who declared that in case he had no direct heir he intended giving him the crown of Italy. When the Austrian war of 1809 broke out, an army invaded Italy, and Eugène was defeated in a first battle, but, rallying, he gained a series of victories, ending with that of Raab, which Napoleon called the "granddaughter of Marengo." It was Eugène and his sister Hortense that Napoleon charged to prepare Josephine for the divorce, and the former explained to the Senate the reasons for the act. He took so distinguished a part in the Russian campaign that Napoleon said : " Eugène is the only one who has not committed blunders in this war." In 1813 and 1814 he fought with great skill against the allies. The final overthrow of Napoleon took his kingdom from him. He retired then to the court of the King of Bavaria, his father-in-law, who made him Duke of Leuchtenberg and Prince of Eichstadt. He died in 1824 at Munich.

ries, whether it belonged to rich trader or inoffensive tourist, was prize of war. If one remembers the extent of the seaboard which Napoleon at that moment commanded, the full peril of this menace to English commerce is clear. From St. Petersburg to Trieste there was not a port, save those of Denmark and Portugal, which would not close at his bidding. At Tilsit he and Alexander had entered into an agreement to complete this seaboard, to close the Baltic, the Channel, the European Atlantic, and the Mediterranean to the English. This was nothing else than asking Continental Europe to destroy her commerce for their sakes.

There were several serious uncertainties in the scheme. What retaliation would England make? Could Napoleon and Alexander agree long enough to succeed in dividing the valuable portions of the continents of Europe, Asia, and Africa? Would the nations cheerfully give up the English cottons and tweeds they had been buying, the boots they had been wearing, the cutlery and dishes they had been using? Would they cheerfully see their own products lie uncalled for in their warehouses, for the sake of aiding a foreign monarch — although the most brilliant and powerful on earth—to carry out a vast plan for crushing an enemy who was not their enemy? It remained to be seen.

In the meantime there was the small part of the coast line remaining independent to be joined to the portion already blockaded to the English. There was no delay in Napoleon's action. Denmark was

BERNADOTTE, ABOUT 1798.

Engraved by Fiesinger, after Guérin. Bernadotte (J. B. Jules) was born at Pau, in 1764; entered the Royal Marine at seventeen years of age, and was sergeant in 1789. In 1792 entered the Army of the North, where he served with honor. He entered the Army of Italy in 1797, and, although suspicious of Bonaparte's ambition, he served him valiantly, and was one of those sent to Paris with captured flags. Was an active supporter of the *coup d'etat* of the 18th Fructidor, and was ambassador at Vienna after the treaty of Campo Formio. Bernadotte married the Désirée Clary, sister-in-law of Joseph Bonaparte, whom Napoleon, in 1795, had thought of making his wife. In 1799 he served in the Rhenish armies. He disapproved of the 18th Brumaire, but after it accepted the command of the Army of the West. In 1804 he was made marshal, and later, Prince of Ponte-Corvo. In the Austrian war of 1805 Bernadotte played an important part, and again in the campaign of 1807. In 1810 the Swedish States proclaimed him prince royal and heir presumptive of Sweden. He was received as a son by Charles XIII., and during the life of that monarch Bernadotte surrounded him by a really filial care. In 1812 he entered the coalition against Bonaparte. At first he tried to act as a mediator, but this failing, he led his army against the French, defeating Ney and Oudinot, and deciding the battle of Leipsic. But he took no part in the invasion of France. In 1818, on the death of Charles XIII., he was proclaimed King of Norway and Sweden, and took the name of Charles Jean IV., though he is usually called Charles XIV. He held the throne for twenty-six years. His son Oscar succeeded him on his death in 1844.

MARIE PAULINE BONAPARTE.

Born at Ajaccio, October 20, 1780; died at Florence, June 9, 1825. She first married General Leclerc, who died during the expedition of Saint Domingo, and afterwards Camillo Borghese.

ordered to choose between war with England and war with France. Portugal was notified that if her ports were not closed in forty days the French and Spanish armies would invade her. England gave a drastic reply to Napoleon's measures. In August she appeared before Copenhagen, seized the Danish fleet, and for three days bombarded the town. This unjustifiable attack on a nation with which she was at peace horrified Europe, and it supported the emperor in pushing to the uttermost the Berlin Decree. He made no secret of his determination. In a diplomatic audience at Fontainebleau, October 14, 1807, he declared:

"Great Britain shall be destroyed. I have the means of doing it, and they shall be employed. I have three hundred thousand men devoted to this object, and an ally who has three hundred thousand to support them. I will permit no nation to receive a minister from Great Britain until she shall have renounced her maritime usages and tyranny; and I desire you, gentlemen, to convey this determination to your respective sovereigns."

Such an alarming extent did the block-

NAPOLEON.

Drawn by John Trumbull. Signed "J. T., 1808." In the "Trumbull Gallery of Revolutionary Sketches," owned by Professor Edward Frossard of Brooklyn, New York. The face is entirely in bold pen-and-ink work, with uniform and background finished in sepia. Under the bust is a locket surrounded by a border of hair work. Set in the frame beneath this is a smaller locket containing a bit of unwoven hair. On the back of the frame is pasted a piece of paper bearing the inscription in ink, written in Trumbull's own hand: "Napoleon at 44 with Parents Hair – his Hair in small case – J. T." The statement of the inscription, "Napoleon at 44," does not agree with the date on the picture, 1808, since Napoleon was not forty four until 1813. The error is undoubtedly in the inscription, and is of a sort into which anybody might fall. It is not unlikely that Trumbull drew a face studied from life, though the production may have been, probably was, from memory. On several occasions he spent some time in Paris, and on one occasion he dined with Talleyrand, and talked with Lucien Bonaparte, who sat beside him at table, "on the subject of his brother's wonderful success." David was his intimate friend. It is not at all unlikely, therefore, that Trumbull had opportunities to study the living features of Napoleon; and, such opportunities occurring, he was not the man to neglect them. But, however produced, the portrait is certainly one of peculiar interest and value.

N. C. OUDINOT, DUC DE REGGIO, 1767-1847.

Engraved by Foster, after Lefèvre. Oudinot, Nicolas Charles, was born at Bar-le-duc, son of a merchant. Left commerce for the army; in 1791 he was made chief of battalion, and three years later general of brigade. The same year he received five wounds and was taken prisoner, remaining captive until 1796. He next served under Moreau, and in 1799 was sent to the army of Helvetia, where he distinguished himself in the battle of Zurich. Oudinot was with Masséna in the siege of Genoa (1800), and in 1803 was commander of a division of the camp of Bruges. In 1805 he received the grand cross of the Legion of Honor. In the campaign of 1805 he greatly distinguished himself at the head of ten thousand grenadiers, called the *grenadiers* Oudinot. For his services in the campaign of 1806-1807 he was made count, and in 1808 governor of Erfurt, where Napoleon presented him to Alexander I, as the *Bayard of the army.* The baton of marshal and the title of Duke of Reggio were given him after Wagram. Oudinot was wounded early in the Russian campaign, but on hearing of the disasters returned to his command, and at the terrible passage of the Beresina he performed prodigies of valor. Throughout the campaign of 1813 and the invasion the next year he was active, and only laid down arms after Napoleon's abdication. He joined Louis XVIII., and refused to leave him during the hundred days. In 1823 he served in the Spanish campaign. He was made governor of the *Invalides* in 1842, a post he held until his death in 1847.

"Since America suffers her vessels to be searched, she adopts the principle that the flag does not cover the goods. Since she recognizes the absurd blockades laid by England, consents to having her vessels incessantly stopped, sent to England, and so turned aside from their course, why should the Americans not suffer the blockade laid by France? Certainly France is no more blockaded by England than England by France. Why should Americans not equally suffer their vessels to be searched by French ships? Certainly France recognizes that these measures are unjust, illegal, and subversive of national sovereignty; but it is the duty of nations to resort to force, and to declare themselves against things which dishonor them and disgrace their independence."

WAR WITH PORTUGAL.

The attempt to force Portugal to close her ports caused war. In all but one particular she had obeyed Napoleon's orders: she had closed her ports, detained all Englishmen in her borders, declared war; but her king refused to confiscate the property of British subjects in Portugal. This evasion furnished Napoleon an excuse for refusing to believe in the sincerity of her pretensions. "Continue your march," he wrote to Junot, who had been ordered into the country a few days before (October 12, 1807). "I have reason to believe that

MARIE ANNA ELSA BONAPARTE.

Born at Ajaccio, January 3, 1777, Princess of Lucques and of Piombino, Grand Duchess of Tuscany, wife of Count Bacciochi. Died at Trieste, August 7, 1820.

ade threaten to take, that even our minister to France, Mr. Armstrong, began to be nervous. His diplomatic acquaintances told him cynically, "You are much favored, but it won't last;" and, in fact, it was not long before it was evident that the United States was not to be allowed to remain neutral. Napoleon's notice to Mr. Armstrong was clear and decisive:

MARSHAL NEY ("LE MARÉCHAL NEY, DUC D'ELCHINGEN, PRINCE DE LA MOSKOWA, PAIR DE FRANCE").

Engraved by Tardieu, after Gérard. Ney (Michel) was born at Sarrelouis in 1769; entered the army at nineteen years of age. In 1792 Ney entered the Army of the North, where he soon attracted attention by his bravery and skill, winning the title of the *Indefatigable*. In 1794 he was made chief of brigade, and two years later general of brigade. He served in the Army of the Rhine and of the Danube until the peace of Lunéville in 1801. Returning to Paris, Napoleon succeeded in attaching him to his fortunes, and sent him to Switzerland as minister plenipotentiary to propose that the Helvetian Republic be placed under the protectorate of France. When, in 1803, war was declared against England. Ney was recalled from Switzerland, where he had succeeded in his negotiations, and sent to the north to command a corps of the Army of Invasion. In 1804 he was named marshal and given the *grand cordon* of the Legion of Honor. In the campaign of 1805 against Austria, Ney played a brilliant part, as well as in those of 1806 and 1807. His audacity, military skill, and bravery won him various titles from his soldiers, such as the "Brave of Braves," the "Red Lion" (Ney's hair was red), and "Peter the Red." When Napoleon instituted his new nobility, after Tilsit, Ney was made Duke of Elchingen. During 1809 and 1810 he served in Spain, but, quarreling with Masséna, his commander-in-chief, he was obliged to return to France. In the Russian campaign no one distinguished himself more than Ney. For his services at the battle of Moskowa he was made Prince of Moskowa. When Louis XVIII. was restored, Ney joined the Bourbons, and was rewarded with high honors, but at court his wife was ridiculed by the ancient nobility, until, deeply wounded, he left Paris. He was in command at Besançon when Napoleon returned from Elba, and was ordered to take his former master prisoner. Ney started, promising to "bring back Bonaparte in an iron cage"; but the enthusiasm over the imperial cause was so great that he made up his mind that the cause of the Bourbons was lost, and went over to Napoleon. He was convicted of treason, and shot in Paris, December 7, 1815.

there is an understanding with England, so as to give the British troops time to arrive from Copenhagen."

Without waiting for the results of the invasion, he and the King of Spain divided up Portugal between them. If their action was premature, Portugal did nothing to gainsay them; for when Junot arrived at Lisbon in December, he found the country without a government, the royal family having fled in fright to Brazil. There was only one thing now to be done: Junot must so establish himself as to hold the country against the English, who naturally would resent the injury done their ally. From St. Petersburg to Trieste, Napoleon now held the seaboard.

THE SPANISH THRONE GIVEN TO A BONAPARTE.

But he was not satisfied. Spain was between him and Portugal. If he was going to rule Western Europe he ought to possess her. There is no space here to trace the intrigues with the weak and vicious factions of the Spanish court, which ended in Napoleon's persuading Charles IV. to cede his rights to the Spanish throne and to become his pensioner, and Ferdinand, the heir apparent, to abdicate; and which placed Joseph Bonaparte, King of Naples, on the Spanish throne, and put Murat, Charlotte Bonaparte's husband, in Joseph's place.

From beginning to end the transfer of the Spanish crown from Bourbon to Bonaparte was dishonorable and unjustifiable. It is true that the government of Spain was corrupt. No greater mismanagement could be conceived, no more scandalous court. Unquestionably the country would have been far better off under Napoleonic institutions. But to despoil Spain was to be false to an ally which had served him for years with fidelity, and at an awful cost to herself. It is true that her service had been through fear, not love. It is true that at one critical moment (when Napoleon was in Poland, in 1807) she had tried to escape; but, nevertheless, it remained a fact that for France Spain had lost colonies, sacrificed men and money, and had seen her fleet go down at Trafalgar. In taking her throne, Napoleon had none of the excuses which had justified him in interfering in Italy, in Germany, in Holland, in Switzerland. This was not a conquest of war, not a confiscation on account of the perfidy of an ally, not an attempt to answer the prayers of a people for a more liberal government.

If Spain had submitted to the change, she would have been purchasing good gov-

GENERAL FOY. ABOUT 1820.

Engraved by Lefèvre, after Horace Vernet. Foy (Maximilien Sébastien), born at Ham in 1775, entered the artillery school at fifteen, and assisted as lieutenant at the battle of Jammapes. Arrested for contra-revolutionary talk, Foy was imprisoned, but was released after the 9th Thermidor. He afterwards served in the Army of the Rhine under Masséna, and made the German campaign of 1800 under Moreau. He voted against the life consulate and the empire, and showed an opposition to the growth of imperialism which hurt his advancement. After the battle of Vimeiro, in 1808, he was named general of brigade, and later general of division. He fought in Spain until the evacuation of the country. Under the restoration Foy served as an inspector-general of artillery; but he joined Napoleon on his return, fought at Waterloo, and went into retirement afterwards. In 1819 he was elected deputy, and almost at once he showed himself an orator of unusual power. He was a pure constitutionalist, and gave all his efforts to holding the Bourbons to the charter. He died in November, 1825.

MARSHAL LEFEBVRE, ABOUT 1798.

Engraved in 1798 by Fiesinger, after Mengelberg. Lefebvre (François Joseph) was born at Ruffach in 1755, son of a miller, destined for the Church, but at eighteen he enrolled in the French guards. When the Revolution broke out he had just reached the grade of sergeant. In 1793 he was made general of brigade under Hoche, and served in the armies of the Rhine with honor until wounded in 1798, when he returned to Paris, where he was named commander of one of the military divisions. On the 18th Brumaire, Lefebvre rendered important service, and in 1800 was named for the Senate by the First Consul. In 1804 he was made a marshal and a grand officer of the Legion of Honor. In 1806 Lefebvre commanded a division of the Grand Army, and at Jena led the Imperial foot-guard. In 1807 he directed the siege of Dantzic, which lasted fifty-one days. For the capture of this town he was made Duke of Dantzic. In 1808 Lefebvre served in Spain, gaining two battles. In the war of 1809 against the Austrians he led the Bavarian army, and in 1812 was commander-in-chief of the Imperial Guard, at whose head he remained during the retreat from Russia. Lefebvre was made a peer of France by the Restoration, and during the Hundred Days he sat in the Imperial Chamber. When Louis XVIII. returned he deposed him, but he was recalled in 1819. He died in 1820. The marshal and his wife are altogether among the most interesting people in the Napoleonic court. Both of them were uneducated and completely impervious to culture, but of such sincerity of thought and speech, and such goodness of heart, that Napoleon valued them highly. The courtiers, however, ridiculed them incessantly, and repeated many of their blunders against etiquette and grammar. Madame Lefebvre, a kind of noble-hearted Mrs. Malaprop, has been made the heroine of several French plays. The latest of these is the "Madame Sans-Gêne" of Victor Sardou, put on at the Vaudeville in Paris in the winter of 1893-94.

THE EMPEROR NAPOLEON IN COSTUME OF CHASSEUR A CHEVAL.

Designed by Charlet, probably about 1834. The costume, save the boots, is the one Napoleon commonly wore in-doors, as well as out.

ernment at the price of national honor. But Spain did not submit. She, as well as all disinterested lookers-on in Europe, was revolted by the baseness of the deed. No one has ever explained better the feeling which the intrigues over the Spanish throne caused than Napoleon himself :

"I confess I embarked badly in the affair [he told Las Cases at St. Helena]. The immorality of it was too patent, the injustice far too cynical, and the whole thing too villanous ; hence I failed. The attempt is seen now only in its hideous nudity, stripped of all that is grand, of all the numerous benefits which I intended. Posterity would have extolled it, however, if I had succeeded, and rightly, perhaps, because of its great and happy results."

It was the Spanish people themselves, not the ruling house, who resented the transfer from Bourbon to Bonaparte.

No sooner was it noised through Spain that the Bourbons had really abdicated, and Joseph Bonaparte had been named king, than an insurrection was organized simultaneously all over the country. Some eighty-four thousand French troops were scattered through the peninsula, but they were powerless before the kind of warfare which now began. Every defile became a battle-ground, every rock hid a peasant, armed and waiting for French stragglers, messengers, supply parties. The remnant of the French fleet escaped from Trafalgar, and now at Cadiz, was forced to surrender. Twenty-five thousand French soldiers laid down their arms at Baylen, but the Spaniards refused to keep their capitulation treaties. The prisoners were tortured by the peasants in the most barbarous fashion, crucified, burned, sawed asunder. Those who escaped the popular vengeance were sent to the Island of Cabrera, where they lived in the most abject fashion. It was only in 1814 that the remnant of this army was released. King Joseph was obliged to flee to Vittoria a week after he reached his capital.

The misfortunes in Spain were followed by greater ones in Portugal. Junot was defeated by an English army at Vimeiro in August, 1808, and capitulated on condition that his army be taken back to France without being disarmed.

CHAPTER XV.

DISASTER IN SPAIN.—ALEXANDER AND NAPOLEON IN COUNCIL.—NAPOLEON AT MADRID.

NAPOLEON PREPARES FOR SPAIN.

NAPOLEON, amazed at this unexpected popular uprising in Spain, and angry that the spell of invincibility under which his armies had fought, was broken, resolved to undertake the Peninsular war himself.

But before a campaign in Spain could be entered upon, it was necessary to know that all the inner and outer wheels of the great machine he had devised for dividing the world and crushing England were working perfectly.

Since the treaty of Tilsit he had done much at home for this machine. The finances were in splendid condition. Public works of great importance were going on all over the kingdom; the court was luxurious and brilliant, and the money it scattered, encouraged the commercial and manufacturing classes. Never had *fêtes* been more brilliant than those which welcomed Napoleon back to Paris in 1807; never had the season at Fontainebleau been gayer or more magnificent than it was that year.

All of those who had been instrumental in

CHARLET. 1792-1845.

This portrait, a perfect likeness, is the work of Charlet himself. Charlet was about twenty-nine years old at the time of Waterloo, and had seen the emperor on several occasions, when he took pains to cover his note book with sketches of Napoleon taken in every attitude. But he never executed a portrait, properly so called, of the hero. Sometimes he enlarged his drawing in the studio, and accentuated the form of his model in a remarkable way in sepia, or occasionally even in color. I know two Napoleons on horseback, by Charlet, one of them an oil-painting, the other a colored lithograph, which are true portraits. But this kind of interpretation of the emperor's face is very rare in the work of Charlet, who was, above all, the painter of the simple soldier. In this he excels. In his numerous lithographs, drawings, and sepias, the emperor only appears by the way, and nearly always in rapid pencil sketch.—A. D.

bringing prosperity and order to France were rewarded in 1807 with splendid gifts from the indemnities levied on the enemies. The marshals of the Grand Army received from eighty thousand to two hundred thousand dollars apiece; twenty-five generals were given forty thousand dollars each; the civil functionaries were not forgotten; thus Monsieur de Ségur received forty thousand dollars as a sign of the emperor's gratification at the way he had administered etiquette to the new court.

It was at this period that Napoleon founded a new nobility as a further means of rewarding those who had rendered brilliant services to France. This institution was designed, too, as a means of reconciling old and new France. It created the titles of prince, duke, count, baron, and knight; and those receiving these titles were at the same time given domains in the conquered provinces, sufficient to permit them to establish themselves in good style.

The drawing up of the rules which were to govern this new order occupied the gravest men of the country, Cam-

NAPOLEON I.

By Carle Vernet. After an unpublished water color in the collection of Monsieur Christophe, ex-Minister of Public Works, Governor of the *Credit-foncier* of France. Carle Vernet, who often had occasion to see the emperor, evidently made this sketch from nature ; then, in the retirement of his studio, copied it in water colors and placed it in a fictitious composition. It may be remarked that the artist has represented his model in the familiar pose rendered by the German painter Dähling, whose well-known portrait is reproduced on page 118.

bacérès, Saint-Martin, d'Hauterive, Portalis, Pasquier. Among other duties they had to prepare the armorial bearings. Napoleon refused to allow the crown to go on the new escutcheons. He wished no one but himself to have a right to use that symbol. A substitute was found in the panache, the number of plumes showing the rank.

Napoleon used the new favors at his command freely, creating in all, after 1807, forty-eight thousand knights, one thousand and ninety barons, three hundred and eighty-eight counts, thirty-one dukes, and three princes. All members of the old nobility who were supporting his government were given titles, but not those which they formerly held. Naturally this often led to great dissatisfaction, the bearers of ancient names preferring a lower rank which had been their family's for centuries to one higher, but unhallowed by time and tradition. Thus Madame de Montmorency rebelled obstinately against being made a countess,—she had been a baroness under the old *régime*,—and, as the Montmorencys claimed the honor of being called the *first Christian barons*, she felt justly that the old title was a far prouder one than any Napoleon could give her. But a countess she had to remain.

In his efforts to win for himself the services of all those whom blood and fortune had made his natural supporters, the emperor tried again to reconcile Lucien. In November, 1807, Napoleon visited Italy, and at Mantua a secret interview took place between the brothers. Lucien, in his "Memoirs," gives a dramatic description of the way in which Napoleon spread the kingdoms of half a world before him and offered him his choice.

"He struck a great blow with his hand in the middle of the immense map of Europe which was extended on the table, by the side of which we were standing. 'Yes, choose,' he said ; 'you see I am not talking in the air. All this is mine, or will soon belong to me ; I can dispose of it already. Do you want Naples? I will take it from Joseph, who, by the by, does not care for it ; he prefers Mortefontaine. Italy —the most beautiful jewel in my imperial crown? Eugène is but viceroy, and, far from despising it, he hopes only that I shall give it to him, or, at least, leave it to him if he survives me ; he is likely to be disappointed in waiting, for I shall live ninety years. I must, for the perfect consolidation of my empire. Besides, Eugène will not suit me in Italy after his mother is divorced. Spain? Do you not see it falling into the hollow of my hand, thanks to the blunders of my dear Bourbons, and to the follies of your friend, the Prince of Peace? Would you not be well pleased to reign there, where you have been only ambassador? Once for all, what do you want? Speak ! Whatever you wish, or can wish, is yours, if your divorce precedes mine.'"

Until midnight the two brothers wrestled with the questions between them. Neither would abandon his position ; and when Lucien finally went away, his face was wet with tears. To Méneval, who conducted him to his inn in the town, he said, in bidding him carry his farewell to the emperor, "It may be forever." It was not. Seven years later the brothers met again, but the map of Europe was forever rolled up for Napoleon.

STATUETTE IN WOOD OF THE EMPEROR NAPOLEON I.

Carved by General Chaugarnier. Collection of the Marquis de Girardin.

THE ERFURT MEETING.

The essential point in carrying out the Tilsit plan was, however, the fidelity of Alexander ; and Napoleon resolved, before going into the Spanish war, to meet the Emperor of Russia. This was the more needful, because Austria had begun to show signs of hostility.

The meeting opened in September, 1807, at Erfurt, in Saxony, and lasted a month. Napoleon acted as host, and prepared a splendid entertainment for his guests. The company he had gathered was most brilliant. Beside the Russian and French emperors, with ambassadors and suites, were the Kings of Saxony, Bavaria, and Würtemberg, the Prince Primate, the Grand Duke and Grand Duchess of Baden, the Dukes of Saxony, and the Princes of the Confederation of the Rhine.

The palaces where the emperors were entertained, were furnished with articles from the *Garde-Meuble* of France. The leading actors of the *Théâtre Français* gave the best French tragedies to a house where there was, as Napoleon had promised Talma, a "parterre full of kings." There was a hare hunt on the battle-field of Jena, to which even Prince William of Prussia was invited, and where the party breakfasted on the spot where Napoleon had bivouacked in 1806, the night before the battle. There were balls where Alexander danced, "but not I," wrote the emperor to Josephine ; "forty years are forty years." Goethe and Wieland were both presented to Napoleon at Erfurt, and the emperor had long conversations with them.

In the midst of the gayeties Napoleon and Alexander found time to renew their Tilsit agreement. They were to make war and peace together. Alexander was to uphold Napoleon in giving Joseph the throne of Spain, and to keep the continent tranquil during the Peninsular war. Napoleon was to support Alexander in getting possession of Finland, Moldavia, and Wallachia. The two emperors were to write and

ALEXANDER I. OF RUSSIA. 1805.

Alexander I. of Russia was born at St. Petersburg in 1777; ascended the throne in 1801, after the murder of his father. His first acts were remarkably liberal. He recalled the banished, opened prisons, abolished the censorship, the torture, the public sale of serfs, founded schools, reformed the code, and did much to put Russia in the line of progress Western Europe was following. He entered into the first coalition against Napoleon in 1805, and suffered a defeat at Austerlitz in December of that year. The next year the battles of Eylau and Friedland drove him to make peace with Napoleon. The negotiations of Tilsit, where this peace was signed, were the beginning of a warm personal friendship between the two emperors, and Alexander consented to aid Napoleon in his vast scheme for conquering England. The fundamental part of this scheme, the continental blockade, at last bore too heavily on the Russians, and Napoleon's occupation of Oldenburg dissatisfied Alexander. The peace was broken in 1812, and Napoleon undertook the invasion of Russia. Alexander refused to come to any terms with his former friend, and in 1813 called Europe to arm itself against France. This coalition was fatal to Napoleon, who was driven to abdicate in 1814: and Alexander, who had pleased the Parisians by his mild treatment of them, was the main instrument in the recall of the Bourbons. At the Congress of Vienna which followed, he succeeded in obtaining assent to his confiscation of Poland. After Waterloo Alexander returned with his troops to Paris, and consented to the rigorous measures taken against the country, but opposed its dismemberment. On leaving Paris he signed the Holy Alliance with Prussia and Austria, which had as its real object opposition to the liberal principles of the Revolution. Alexander fell under new influences afterwards—English and Protestant. He closed the French theatres and opened Bible societies; became, under Madame Krüdener's influence, a devout follower of her mysticism, and received a deputation of Quakers, with whom he prayed and wept. Later he became severe and suspicious. He died in 1825.

sign a letter inviting England to join them in peace negotiations.

This was done promptly ; but when England insisted that representatives of the government which was acting in Spain in the name of Ferdinand VII. should be admitted to the proposed meeting, the peace negotiations a b r u p t l y ended. Under the circumstances Napoleon could not, of course, recognize that government.

NAPOLEON IN SPAIN.

The emperor was ready to conduct the Spanish war. His first move was to send into the country a large body of veterans from Germany. Before this time the army had been made up of young recruits upon whom the Spanish looked with contempt. The men, inexperienced and demoralized by the kind of guerilla warfare which was waged against them, had become discouraged. The worst feature of their case was that they did not believe in the war. That brave story-teller Marbot relates frankly how he felt :

" As a soldier I was bound to fight any one who attacked the French army, but I could not help recognizing in my inmost conscience that our cause was a bad one, and that the Spaniards were quite right in trying to drive out strangers who, after coming among them in the guise of friends, were wishing to dethrone their sovereign and take forcible possession of the kingdom. This war, therefore, seemed to me wicked ; but I was a soldier, and I must march or be charged with cowardice. The greater part of the army thought as I did, and, like me, obeyed orders all the same."

The appearance of the veterans and the presence of the emperor at once put a new face on the war ; the morale of the army was raised, and the respect of the Spaniards inspired.

The emperor speedily made his way to Madrid, though he had to fight three battles to get there, and began at once a work of reorganization. Decree followed decree. Feudal rights were abolished, the inquisition was ended, the number of convents was reduced, the custom-houses between the various provinces were done away with, a political and military programme

UNPUBLISHED PORTRAIT OF NAPOLEON.

Executed on a bonbon-box of straw, by a Chinese artist. Collection of Monsieur le Roux. The fame of Napoleon's exploits, especially after the brilliant triumph of Austerlitz, reached even the extreme Orient ; and at that time the image of Napoleon was reproduced in many and various ways by Chinese and Japanese artists, who had as guide pictures of Napoleon, carried religiously across the sea as relics by the hands of Frenchmen. There even exists a Japanese album, extremely rare, which I have had occasion to handle, and in which the principal facts of Napoleon's reign are depicted in twenty colored plates, in a style at once naïve and picturesque. The portrait here reproduced was made, probably in 1806, by an artist of the Celestial Empire. It is interesting, of course, rather as a rare and curious document than as a work of art.—A. D.

But a flame had been kindled in Spain which no number of even Napoleonic bulletins could quench—a fanatical frenzy inspired by the priests, a blind passion of patriotism. The Spaniards wanted their own, even if it was feudal and oppressive. A constitution which they had been forced to accept, seemed to them odious and shameful, if liberal.

The obstinacy and horror of their resistance was nowhere so tragic and so heroic as at the siege of Saragossa, going on at the time Napoleon, at Madrid, was issuing his decrees and proclamations.

was made out for King Joseph. Many bulletins were sent to the Spanish people. In all of them they are told that it is the English who are their enemies, not their allies ; that they come to the Peninsula not to help, but to inspire to false confidence, and to lead them astray. Napoleon's plan and purpose cannot be mistaken.

"Spaniards [he proclaimed at Madrid], your destinies are in my hands. Reject the poison which the English have spread among you ; let your king be certain of your love and your confidence, and you will be more powerful and happier than ever. I have destroyed all that was opposed to your prosperity and greatness ; I have broken the fetters which weighed upon the people ; a liberal constitution gives you, instead of an absolute, a tempered and constitutional monarchy. It depends upon you that this constitution shall become law. But if all my efforts prove useless, and if you do not respond to my confidence, it will only remain for me to treat you as conquered provinces, and to find my brother another throne. I shall then place the crown of Spain on my own head, and I shall know how to make the wicked tremble ; for God has given me the power and the will necessary to surmount all obstacles."

"JOSÉPHINE, IMPÉRATRICE DES FRANÇAIS."

Reproduction of the model of the marble statue exhibited in the *Salon* of 1857, and executed for the town of St. Pierre (Martinique), the native country of Josephine. This statue is by the sculptor Vital-Dubray. The plaster cast is in the Versailles museum.

Saragossa had been fortified when the insurrection against King Joseph broke out. The town was surrounded by convents, which were turned into forts. Men, women, and children took up arms, and the priests, cross in hand, and dagger at the belt, led them. No word of surrender was tolerated within the walls. At the beginning Napoleon regarded the defence of Saragossa as a small affair, and wished to try persuasion on the people. There was at Paris a well-known Aragon noble whom he urged to go to Saragossa and calm the popular excitement. The man accepted the mission. When he arrived in the town the people hurried forth to meet him, supposing he had come to aid in the resistance. At the first word of submission he spoke he was assailed by the mob, and for nearly a year lay in a dungeon.

The peasants of the vicinity of Saragossa were quartered in the town, each family being given a house to defend. Nothing could drive them from their posts. They took an oath to resist until death, and regarded the probable destruction of themselves and their families with the indifference of stoics. The priests had so aroused their religious exaltation, and were able to sustain it at such a pitch, that they never wavered before the daily horrors they endured.

The French at first tried to drive them from their posts by sallies made into the town, but the inhabitants rained such a murderous fire upon them from towers, roofs, windows, even the cellars, that they were obliged to retire. Exasperated by this stubborn resistance they resolved to blow up the town, inch by inch. The siege was begun in the most terrible and destructive manner, but the people were unmoved by the danger. "While a house was being mined, and the dull sound of the rammers warned them that death was at hand, not one left the house which he had sworn to defend, and we could hear them singing litanies. Then, at the moment the walls flew into the air and fell back with a crash, crushing the greater part of them, those who had escaped would collect about the ruins, and sheltering themselves behind the slightest cover, would recommence their sharpshooting."

Marshal Lannes commanded before Saragossa. Touched by the devotion and the heroism of the defenders, he proposed an honorable capitulation. The besieged scorned the proposition, and the awful process of undermining went on until the town was practically blown to pieces.

For such resistance there was no end but extermination. For the first time in his career Napoleon had met sublime popular patriotism, a passion before which diplomacy, flattery, love of gain, force, lose their power.

It was for but a short time that the emperor could give his personal attention to the Spanish war. Certain wheels in his great machine were not running right. At its very centre, in Paris, there was friction among certain influential persons. The peace of the Continent, necessary to the Peninsular war, and which Alexander had guaranteed, was threatened. Under these circumstances it was impossible to remain in Spain.

A CORNER OF THE NAPOLEON COLLECTION OF THE MARQUIS DE GIRARDIN.

The souvenirs of Napoleon prints must be reckoned by thousands. Paintings, bronzes, snuff-boxes, miniatures, objects of industrial art, symbolic objects, arms, etc.—all figure in the collection of the Marquis de Girardin in Paris. Many of the articles belonged originally to the Duc de Gaëté, father in-law of the Marquis de Girardin, who was Bonaparte's minister of finance from the 18th Brumaire till the abdication at Fontainebleau, and also resumed office during the Hundred Days. He was one of the most faithful followers of the emperor, who loaded him with presents. These form the chief part of the collection of the Marquis de Girardin, to whom our sincere thanks are due for his kind permission to reproduce here one of the most picturesque corners of his veritable museum.—A. D.

CHAPTER XVI.

TALLEYRAND'S TREACHERY.—THE CAMPAIGN OF 1809.—WAGRAM.

PLOTTING OF TALLEYRAND AND FOUCHÉ.

Two unscrupulous and crafty men, both of singular ability, caused the interior trouble which called Napoleon from Spain. These men were Talleyrand and Fouché. The latter we saw during the Consulate as Minister of Police. Since, he had been once dismissed because of his knavery, and restored, largely for the same quality. His cunning was too valuable to dispense with. The former, Talleyrand, made Minister of Foreign Affairs in 1799, had handled his negotiations with the extraordinary skill for which he was famous, until, in 1807, Napoleon's mistrust of his duplicity, and Talleyrand's own dislike of the details of his position, led to the portfolio being taken from him, and he being made Vice-Grand-Elector. He evidently expected, in mak-

TALLEYRAND.

Engraved by Desnoyers, after Gérard. Talleyrand-Périgord (Charles Maurice de) (1754-1838) was educated for the Church, and in 1788 was made Bishop of Autun. He was active in the Revolution, and being struck with Napoleon's talent in Italy, hastened to win his favor. He became Napoleon's most important adviser, but later turned against him, and became his most subtle enemy. After the surrender of Paris, it was Talleyrand who secured from Alexander the declaration that he would treat neither with Napoleon nor with any member of his family. He became Louis XVIII.'s Minister of Foreign Affairs. Soon after Waterloo he lost his position as Minister of Foreign Affairs, but the Revolution of 1830 restored him to favor, and he was sent to London as ambassador. In 1834 he left diplomatic life at his own request, and returned to Paris, where he died in 1838.

ing this change, to remain as influential as ever with Napoleon. The knowledge that the emperor was dispensing with his services made him resentful, and his devotion to the imperial cause fluctuated according to the attention he received.

Now, Napoleon's course in Spain had been undertaken at the advice of Talleyrand, largely, and he had repeated constantly, in the early negotiations, that France ought not to allow a Bourbon to remain enthroned at her borders. Yet, as the affair went on, he began slyly to talk against the enterprise. At Erfurt, where Napoleon had been impolitic enough to take him, he initiated himself into Alexander's good graces, and prevented Napoleon's policy towards Austria being carried out. When Napoleon returned to Spain, Talleyrand and Fouché, who up to this

THE EVE OF THE MASTER.

After Raffet.

time had been enemies, became friendly, and even appeared in public, arm in arm. If Talleyrand and Fouché had made up, said the Parisians, there was mischief brewing.

Napoleon was not long in knowing of their reconciliation. He learned more, that the two crafty plotters had written Murat that in the event of "something happening," that is, of Napoleon's death or overthrow, they should organize a movement to call him to the head of affairs; that, accordingly, he must hold himself ready.

Napoleon returned to Paris immediately, removed Talleyrand from his position at court, and, at a gathering of high officials, treated him to one of those violent harangues with which he was accustomed to flay those whom he would disgrace and dismiss.

"You are a thief, a coward, a man without honor; you do not believe in God; you have all your life been a traitor to your duties; you have deceived and betrayed everybody; nothing is sacred to you; you would sell your own father. I have loaded you down with gifts, and there is nothing you would not undertake against me. For the past ten months you have been shameless enough, because you supposed, rightly or wrongly, that my affairs in Spain were going astray, to say to all who would listen to you that you always blamed my undertakings there; whereas it was you yourself who first put it into my head, and who persistently urged it. And that man, *that unfortunate* [he meant the Duc d'Enghien], by whom was I advised of the place of his residence? Who drove me to deal cruelly with him? What, then, are you aiming at? What do you wish for? What do you hope? Do you dare to say? You deserve that I should smash you like a wine-glass. I can do it, but I despise you too much to take the trouble."

All of this was undoubtedly true, but, after having publicly said it, there was but one safe course for Napoleon—to put Talleyrand where he could no longer continue his plotting. He made the mistake, however, of leaving him at large.

WAR WITH AUSTRIA.

The disturbance of the continental peace came from Austria. Encouraged by Napoleon's absence in Spain, and the withdrawal of troops from Germany, and urged by England to attempt again to repair her losses, Austria had hastily armed herself, hoping to be able to reach the Rhine before Napoleon could collect his forces and meet her. At this moment Napoleon could command about the same number of troops as the Austrians, but they were scattered in all directions, while the enemy's were already consolidated. The question became, then, whether he could get his troops together before the Austrians attacked. From every direction he hurried them across France and Germany towards Ratisbonne. On the 12th of April he heard in Paris that the Austrians had crossed the Inn. On the 17th the emperor was in his headquarters at Donauwörth, his army well in hand. "Neither in ancient or modern times," says Jomini, "will one find anything which equals in celerity and admirable precision the opening of this campaign."

In the next ten days a series of combats broke the Austrian army, drove the Archduke Charles, with his main force, north of the Danube, and opened the road to Vienna to the French. On the 12th of May, one month from the day he left Paris, Napoleon wrote from Schönbrunn, "We are masters of Vienna." The city had been evacuated.

Napoleon lay on the right bank of the Danube ; the Austrian army under the Archduke Charles was coming towards the city by the left bank ; it was to be a hand-to-hand struggle under the walls of Vienna. The emperor was uncertain of the archduke's plans, but he was determined that he should not have a chance to reënforce his army. The battle must be fought at once, and he prepared to go across the river to attack him. The place of crossing he chose was south of Vienna, where the large island Lobau divides the stream. Bridges had to be built for the passage, and it was with the greatest difficulty that the work was accomplished, for the river was high and the current swift, and anchors and boats were scarce. Again and again the boats broke apart. Nevertheless, about thirty thousand of the French got over, and took possession of the villages of Aspern and Essling, where they were attacked on May 21st by some eighty thou-

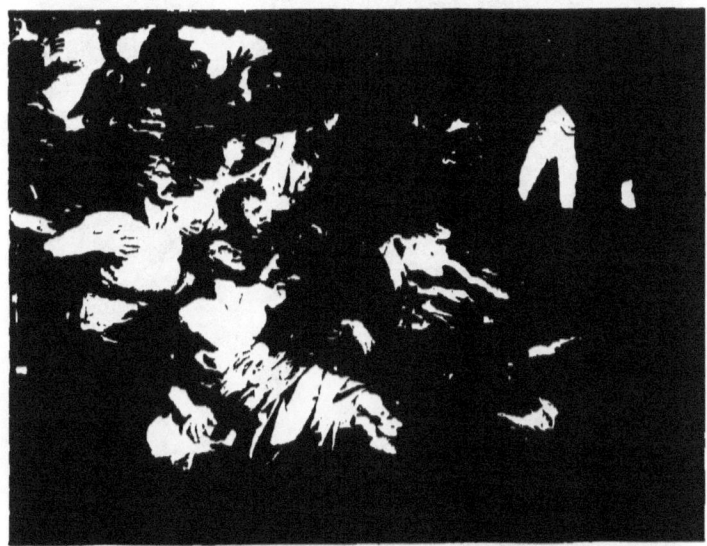

RETURN OF NAPOLEON TO THE ISLAND OF LOBAU, AFTER THE BATTLE OF ESSLING, MAY 23, 1809.

By Charles Meynier. Museum of Versailles. "As the waters of the Danube continued to rise, and the bridges had not been restored during the night, the emperor on the 23d led the army across the narrow arm of the left bank, and took up a position on the island of In-der-Lobau, placing a guard at the ends of the bridge. The numerous wounded on the left bank were brought across the little bridge ; even those who gave only the feeblest sign of life were carried to the island. . . . The greatest precautions were necessary, as our frail pontoons were often displaced by the impetuosity of the Danube. The whole of the general staff were employed in effecting the passage. Nothing was left on the battle-field."—*Tenth Bulletin of the Grand Army.* The emperor, having crossed the Danube, came upon a group of soldiers on the left bank having their wounds dressed. At the sight of him they broke away from the surgeon's hands, and, forgetting their wounds, cheered him in a transport of joy.

sand Austrians. The battle which followed lasted all day, and the French sustained themselves heroically. That night reënforcements were gotten over, so that the next day some fifty-five thousand men were on the French side. Napoleon fought with the greatest obstinacy, hoping that another division would soon succeed in getting over, and would enable him to overcome the superior numbers of the Austrians. Already the battle was becoming a hand-to-hand fight, when the terrible news came that the bridge over the Danube had gone down. The Austrians had sent floating down the swollen river great mills, fire-boats, and masses of timber fastened together in such a way as to become battering-rams of frightful power when carried by the rapid stream. All hope of aid was gone, and, as the news spread, the army resigned itself to perish, but to perish sword in hand. The carnage which followed was horrible. Towards evening one of the bravest of the French marshals, Lannes, was fatally wounded. It seemed as if fortune had determined on the loss of the French, and Napoleon decided to retreat to the island of Lobau, where he felt sure that he could maintain his position, and secure supplies from the army on the right bank, until he had time to build bridges and unite his forces. Communications were

NAPOLEON.

Engraved by Ruotte, after Robert Lefèvre. Probably painted about 1810.

BATTLE OF WAGRAM.

This picture, by Horace Vernet, was first exhibited in the *Salon* of 1836. It now hangs in the Hall of Battles at Versailles. The emperor is watching the effect produced by the battery of one hundred pieces of artillery commanded by the General Comte de Lauriston. At this moment a bullet struck the saddle of the Duc d'Istrie, who was arranging the cavalry attack, slightly bruising him on the thigh and killing his horse.

soon established with the right bank, but the isle of Lobau was not deserted; it was used, in fact, as a camp for the next few weeks, while Napoleon was sending to Italy, to France, and to Germany for new troops. A heavy reënforcement came to him from Italy with news which did much to encourage him. When the war began, an Austrian army had invaded Italy, and at first had success in its engagements against the French under the Viceroy of Italy, Eugène de Beauharnais. The news of the ill-luck of the Austrians at home, and of the march on Vienna, had discouraged the leader, Archduke John, brother of Archduke Charles, and he had retreated, Eugène following. Such were the successes of the French on this retreat, that the Austrians finally retired out of their way, leaving them a free route to Vienna, where Eugène soon united his army to that of the emperor.

With the greatest rapidity the French now secured and strengthened their communications with Italy and with France, and gathered troops about Vienna. The whole month of June was passed in this way, hostile Europe repeating the while that Napoleon was shut in by the Austrians and could not move, and that he was idling his time in luxury at the castle of Schönbrunn, where he had established his headquar-

THE LITTLE CORPORAL.

This statue of Napoleon in the costume of the *Petit Caporal*, from the chisel of Seurre, was placed on the column of the Place Vendome, on July 28, 1835. It succeeded on the pedestal the white flag of the Bourbons, which in its turn had replaced the original statue of "Napoléon en César Romain," by Chaudet. An interesting detail, unknown to most Parisians, is that the equestrian statue of Henri IV. on the Pont Neuf was cast with the bronze of Chaudet's Napoleon. When Napoleon III. ascended the throne, he replaced the "Petit Caporal" of Seurre (whose decorative appearance he did not consider "*assez dynastique*") by a copy of Chaudet's "César," made by the sculptor Drumont. That figure still crowns the summit of the column, which was re-erected after the desecration by the Commune.—A. D.

ters. But this month of apparent inactivity was only a feint. By the 1st of July the French Army had reached one hundred and fifty thousand men. They were in admirable condition, well drilled, fresh, and confident. Their communications were strong, their camps good, and they were eager for a battle.

The Austrians were encamped at Wagram, to the north of the Danube. They had fortified the banks opposite the island of Lobau in a manner which they believed would prevent the French from attempting a passage; but in arranging their fortification they had completely neglected a certain portion of the bank on which Napoleon seemed to have no designs. But this was the point, naturally, which Napoleon had chosen for his passage, and on the night of July 4th he effected it. On the morning of the 5th his whole army of one hundred and fifty thousand men, with four hundred batteries, was on the left bank. In the midst of a terrible storm this great mass of men, with all its equipment, had crossed the main Danube, several islands and channels, had built six bridges, and by daybreak had arranged itself in order. It was an unheard-of feat.

Pushing his corps forward, and easily sweeping out of his way the advance posts, Napoleon soon had his line facing that of the Austrians, which stretched from near the Danube to a point east of Wagram. At seven o'clock on the evening of July 5th the French attacked the left and centre of the enemy, but without driving them from their position. The next morning it was the Archduke Charles who took the offensive, making a movement which changed the whole battle. He attacked the French left, which was nearest the river, with fifty thousand men, intending to get on their line of communication and destroy the bridges across the Danube. The troops on the French centre were obliged to hurry off to prevent this, and the army was weakened for a moment, but not long. Napoleon determined to make the Archduke Charles, who in person commanded this attack on the French left, return, not by following him, but by breaking his centre; and he turned his heavy batteries against this portion of the army, and followed them by a cavalry attack, which routed the enemy. At the same time their left was broken, and the troops which had been engaging it were free to hurry off against the Austrian right, which was trying to reach the bridges, and which were being held in check with difficulty at Essling. As soon as the archduke saw what had happened to his left and centre he retired, preferring to preserve as much as possible of his army in good order. The French did not pursue. The battle had cost them too heavily. But if the Austrians escaped from Wagram with their army, and if their opponents gained little more than the name of a victory, they were too discouraged to continue the war, and the emperor sued for peace.

This peace was concluded in October. Austria was forced to give up Trieste and all her Adriatic possessions, to cede territory to Bavaria and to the Grand Duchy of Warsaw, and to give her consent to the continental system.

THE SETTING UP OF THE COLUMN.

This fine print, of the greatest historical interest as much from the principal subject as from the surrounding details, is due to the talent of Zix, one of the cleverest and most conscientious artists of the period. It has been extremely well engraved by Duplessis-Bertaux. Zix evidently made this drawing in the course of the year 1810, some months before the inauguration of the monument, the erection of which, we know, occupied not more than four years. The weight of the masses of bronze forming the column of Austerlitz, is estimated at two million kilogrammes. The total expense of the column and statue reached the sum of one million nine hundred and ninety-five thousand four hundred and seventeen francs.

THE DIVORCE OF NAPOLEON AND JOSEPHINE.

This interesting composition by Chasselat, engraved by Bosselmann, is a faithful representation of the account of Monsieur de Bausset, prefect of the palace, describing the divorce scene of which he was an eye-witness, and even one of the actors. Here is the fragment of this curious narration which seems to have inspired the painter :

"I was standing near the door when the emperor opened it himself, and, seeing me, said quickly : 'Come in, Bausset, and close the door.' I entered the *salon* and perceived the empress extended on the floor, uttering the most piercing cries and moans. 'No, I shall never survive it,' cried the unfortunate creature. Napoleon addressed me : 'If you are strong enough to raise Josephine, carry her to her apartment by the inner staircase, so that she may receive the care and attention her condition demands.' I obeyed, and lifted the empress, whom I imagined to be suffering from a nervous attack, . . . etc." DE BAUSSET: *Mémoires sur l'intérieur du Palais Impérial.* - A. D.

CHAPTER XVII.

THE DIVORCE.—A NEW WIFE.—AN HEIR TO THE CROWN.

JOSEPHINE DIVORCED.

To further the universal peace he desired, to prevent plots among his subordinates who would aspire to his crown in case of his sudden death, and to assure a succession, Napoleon now decided to take a step long in mind—to divorce Josephine, by whom he no longer hoped to have heirs.

In considering Napoleon's divorce of Josephine, it must be remembered that stability of government was of vital necessity to the permanency of the Napoleonic institutions. Napoleon had turned into practical realities most of the reforms demanded in 1789. True, he had done it by the exercise of despotism, but nothing but the courage, the will, the audacity of a despot could have aroused the nation in 1799. Napoleon felt that these institutions had been so short a time in operation that in case of his death they would easily topple over, and his kingdom go to pieces as Alexander's had. If he could leave an heir, this disaster would, he believed, be averted.

Then, would not a marriage with a foreign princess calm the fears of his continental enemies? Would they not see in such an alliance an effort on the part of new, liberal France to adjust herself harmoniously to the system of government which prevailed on the Continent?

Thus, by a new marriage, he hoped to prevent at his death a series of fresh revo-

IT IS WE ARE LETTERS. NAPOLEON AND JOSEPHINE BEFORE THE DIVORCE. HORTENSE, JOSEPHINE'S DAUGHTER, STANDS BEHIND HER

Etched by Gilli, after Didioni.

lutions, save the splendid organization he had created, and put France in greater harmony with her environment. It is to misunderstand Napoleon's scheme, to attribute this divorce simply to a gigantic egotism. To assure his dynasty, was to assure France of liberal institutions. His glorification was his country's. In reality there were the same reasons for divorcing Josephine that there had been for taking the crown in 1804.

Josephine had long feared a separation. The Bonapartes had never cared for her, and even so far back as the Egyptian campaign had urged Napoleon to seek a divorce. Unwisely, she had not sought in her early married life to win their affection any more than she had to keep Napoleon's; and when the emperor was crowned, they had done their best to prevent her coronation. When, for state reasons, the divorce seemed necessary, Josephine had no supporters where she might have had many.

Her grief was more poignant because she had come to love her husband with a real ardor. The jealousy from which he had once suffered she now felt, and Napoleon certainly gave her ample cause for it. Her anxiety was well known to all the court, the secretaries Bourrienne and Méneval, and Madame de Rémusat being her special confidants. Since 1807 it had been intense, for it was in that year that Fouché, probably at Napoleon's instigation, tried to persuade the empress to suggest her divorce herself as her sacrifice to the country.

After Wagram it became evident to her that at last her fate was sealed; but though she beset Méneval and all the members of her household for information, it was only a fortnight before the public divorce that she knew her fate. It was Josephine's own son and daughter, Eugène and Hortense, who broke the news to her; and it was on the former that the cruel task fell of indorsing the divorce in the Senate in the name of himself and his sister.

Josephine was terribly broken by her disgrace, but she bore it with a sweetness and dignity which does much to make posterity forget her earlier frivolity and insincerity.

"I can never forget [says Pasquier] the evening on which the discarded empress did the honors of her court for the last time. It was the day before the official dissolution. A great throng was present, and supper was served, according to custom, in the gallery of Diana, on a number of little tables. Josephine sat at the centre one, and the men went around her, waiting for that particularly graceful nod which she was in the habit of bestowing on those with whom she was acquainted. I stood at a short distance from her for a few minutes, and I could not help being struck with the perfection of her attitude in the presence of all these people who still did her homage, while knowing full well that it was for the last time; that in an hour she would descend from the throne, and leave the palace never to reënter it. Only women can rise superior to such a situation, but I have my doubts as to whether a second one could have been found to do it with such perfect grace and composure. Napoleon did not show so bold a front as did his victim."

There is no doubt but that Napoleon suffered deeply over the separation. If his love had lost its illusion, he was genuinely attached to Josephine, and in a way she was necessary to his happiness. After the ceremony of separation, he was to go to Saint Cloud, she to Malmaison. While waiting for his carriage, he returned to his study in the palace. For a long time he sat silent and depressed, his head on his hand. When he was summoned he rose, his face distorted with pain, and went into the empress's apartment. Josephine was alone.

When she saw the emperor, she threw herself on his neck, sobbing aloud. He pressed her to his bosom, kissing her again and again, until, overpowered with emotion, she fainted. Leaving her to her women, he hurried to his carriage.

Méneval, who saw this sad parting, remained with Josephine until she became conscious; and when he went, she begged him not to let the emperor forget her, and to see that he wrote her often.

"I left her," that naïve admirer and apologist of Napoleon goes on, "grieved at so deep a sorrow and so sincere an affection. I felt very miserable all along my route, and I could not help deploring that the rigorous exactions of politics should violently break the bonds of an affection which had stood the test of time, to impose another union full of uncertainty."

Josephine returned to Malmaison to live, but Napoleon took care that she should have, in addition, another home, giving her Navarre, a château near Evreux, some fifty miles from Paris. She had an income of some six hundred thousand dollars a year, and the emperor showed rare thoughtfulness in providing her with everything she could want. She was to deny herself nothing, take care of her health, pay no attention to the gossip she heard, and never doubt of his love. Such were the constant recommendations of the frequent letters he wrote her. Sometimes he went to see her, and he told her all the details of his life.

It is certain that he neglected no opportunity of comforting her, and that she, on her side, believed in his affection, and accepted her lot with resignation and kindliness.

MARRIAGE OF NAPOLEON AND MARIE LOUISE.

Over two years before the divorce a list of the marriageable princesses of Europe had been drawn up for Napoleon. This list included eighteen names in all, the two most prominent being Marie Louise of Austria, and Anna Paulowna, sister of Alexander of Russia. At the Erfurt conference the project of a marriage with a Russian princess had been discussed, and Alexander had favored it ; but now that an attempt was made to negotiate the affair, there were numerous delays, and a general

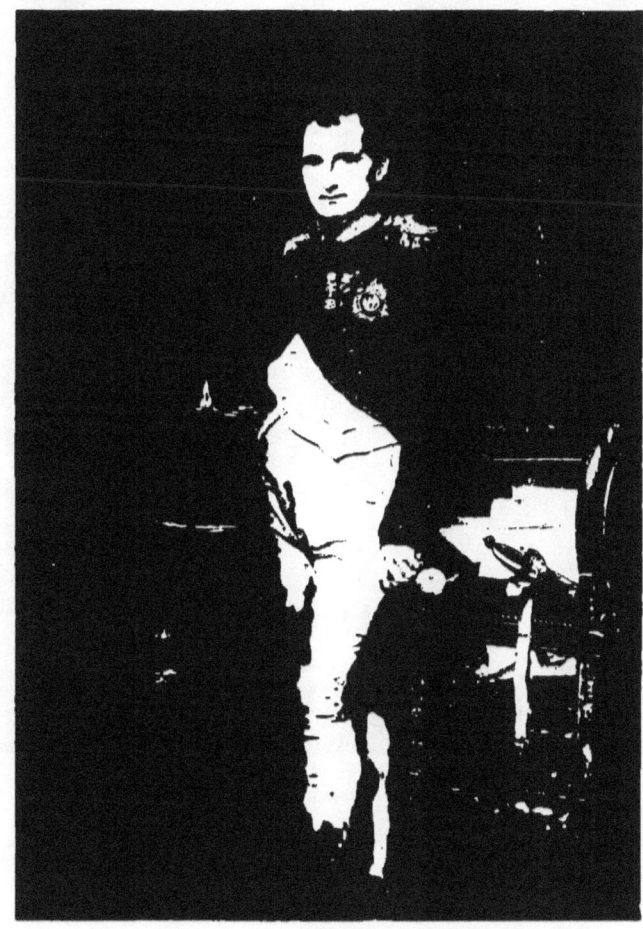

NAPOLEON, 1812.

Engraved by Laugier in 1835, from the etching by Vallot, after portrait painted by David in 1812.

NAPOLEON THE GREAT ("NAPOLÉON LE GRAND"). 1812.

Engraved by Mecou, after a portrait painted in 1812 by Isabey.

lukewarmness which angered Napoleon. Without waiting for the completion of the Russian negotiations, he decided on Marie Louise.

The marriage ceremony was performed in Vienna on March 12, 1810, the Arch- duke Charles acting for Napoleon. The emperor first saw his new wife some days later on the road between Soissons and Compiègne, where he had gone to meet her in most unimperial haste, and in con- tradiction to the pompous and complicated ceremony which had been arranged for their first interview. From the first he was frankly delighted with Marie Louise. In fact, the new empress was a most attractive girl, young, fresh, modest, well-bred, and innocent. She entirely filled Napo-leon's ideal of a wife, and he certainly was happy with her.

Marie Louise in marrying Napoleon had felt that she was a kind of sacrificial offering, for she had naturally a deep horror of the man who had caused her country so

MARIE LOUISE IN ROYAL ROBES, 1810.

"Marie Louise, Archduchesse d'Autriche, Impératrice, Reine, et Régente." Engraved by Mecou, after Isabey.

much woe; but her dread was soon dispelled, and she became very fond of her husband.

Outside of the court the two led an amusingly simple life, riding together informally early in the morning, in a gay Bohemian way; sitting together alone in the empress's little *salon*, she at her needlework, he with a book. They even indulged now and then in quiet little larks of their own, as one day when Marie Louise attempted to make an omelet in her apartments. Just as she was completely engrossed in her work, the emperor came in. The empress tried to conceal her culinary operations, but Napoleon detected the odor.

"What is going on here? There is a singular smell, as if something was being fried. What, you are making an omelet! Bah! you don't know how to do it. I will show you how it is done."

And he set to work to instruct her.

They got on very well until it came to tossing it, an operation Napoleon insisted on performing himself, with the result that he landed it on the floor.

BIRTH OF THE KING OF ROME.

On March 20, 1811, the long-desired heir to the French throne was born. It had been arranged that the birth of the child should be announced to the people by cannon shot; twenty-one if it were a princess, one hundred and one if a prince. The people who thronged the quays and streets about the Tuileries waited with inexpressible anxiety as the cannon boomed forth; one—two—three. As twenty-one died away the city held its breath; then came twenty-two. The thundering peals which followed it were drowned in the wild enthusiasm of the people. For days afterward, enervated by joy and the endless *fêtes* given them, the French drank and sang to the King of Rome.

In all these rejoicings none were so touching as at Navarre, where Josephine, on hearing the cannon, called together her friends and said, "We, too, must have a *fête*. I shall give you a ball, and the whole city of Evreux must come and rejoice with us."

Napoleon was the happiest of men, and he devoted himself to his son with pride. Reports of the boy's condition appear frequently in his letters; he even allowed him to be taken without the empress's knowledge to Josephine, who had begged to see him.

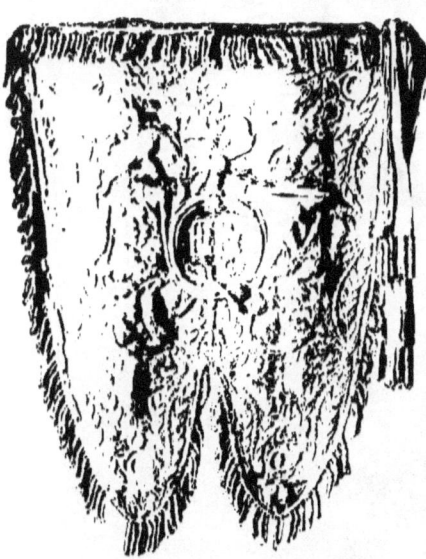

STANDARD OF THE CHASSEURS DE LA GARDE OF NAPOLEON I.

The following is an exact description of this famous standard, for the reproduction of which we are indebted to Prince Victor Napoleon. The foundation of the standard is of green silk, which is embroidered all over with oak and laurel leaves in gold and silver. In the centre is a large hunting-horn in silver, encircling the letters *E. F.*, in gold; above, a scroll with the words: *Chasseurs de la Garde.* The tricolor scarf, fringed with gold, has at the ends, which are embroidered in gold and silver, the inscription: *Vive l'Empereur*, in letters of gold.

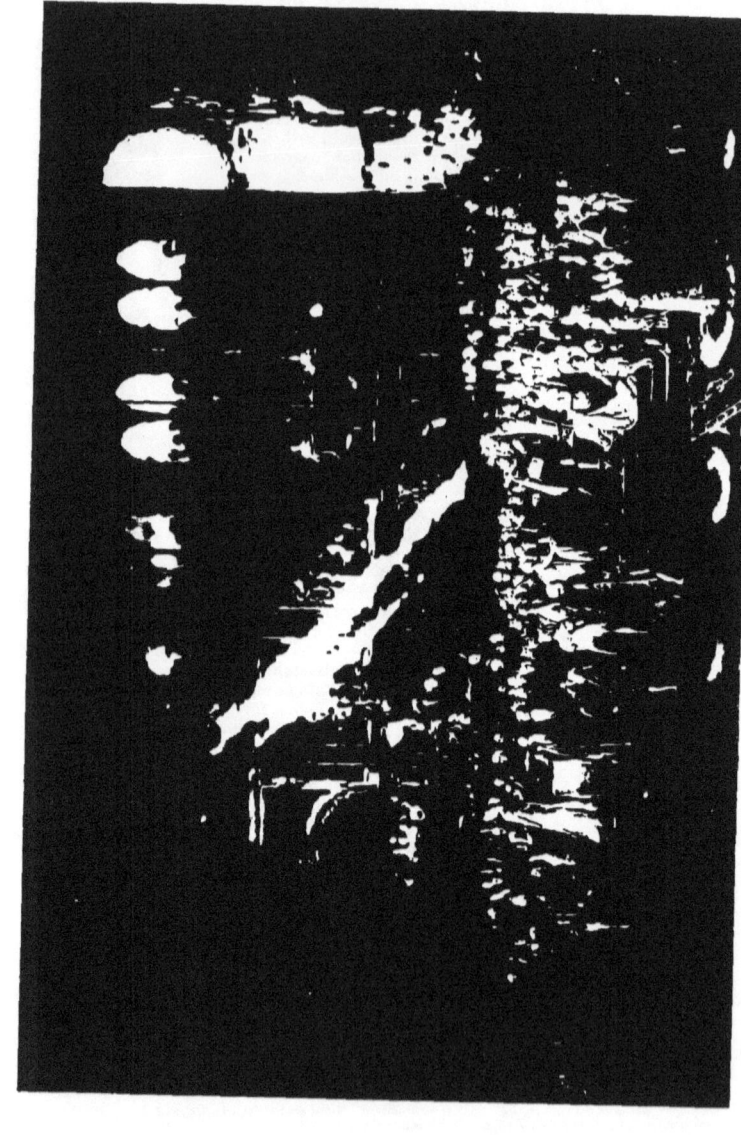

CHRISTENING OF THE KING OF ROME IN THE CHURCH OF NOTRE DAME, JUNE 10, 1811.

This composition, in crayon, crowded with figures, is in the Versailles collection. It is by Goubaut, who made it after a pencil sketch from life. The godfather of the young prince was the Grand Duke of Würzburg, and the godmother Madame Lætitia, mother of the emperor. The Kings of Spain and Westphalia, the Prince Borghese, the Prince Eugène, Viceroy of Italy, the Duke of Parma, and the Prince Arch-chancellor of the Empire witnessed the ceremony.

CHAPTER XVIII.

TROUBLE WITH THE POPE.—THE CONSCRIPTION.—EVASIONS OF THE BLOCKADE.—THE TILSIT AGREEMENT BROKEN.

CAUSES OF DISCONTENT WITHIN FRANCE.

"This child in concert with our Eugène will constitute our happiness and that of France," so Napoleon had written Josephine after the birth of the King of Rome, but it soon became evident that he was wrong. There were causes of uneasiness and discontent in France which had been operating for a long time, and which were only aggravated by the apparent solidity that an heir gave to the Napoleonic dynasty.

First among these was religious disaffection. Towards the end of 1808, being doubtful of the Pope's loyalty, Napoleon had sent French troops to Rome; the spring following, without any plausible excuse, he had annexed four Papal States to the kingdom of Italy; and in 1809 the Pope had been made a prisoner at Savona. When the divorce was asked, it was not the Pope, but the clergy of Paris, who had granted it. When the religious marriage of Marie Louise and Napoleon came to be celebrated, thirteen cardinals refused to appear; the "black cardinals" they were thereafter called, one of their punishments for non-appearance at the wedding being

NAPOLEON, MARIE LOUISE, AND THE KING OF ROME.

Artist unknown.

THE KING OF ROME, 1811.

Engraved by Desnoyers, after Gérard "His Majesty the King of Rome. Dedicated to her Majesty Imperial and Royal, Marie Louise."

that they could no longer wear their red gowns. To the pious all this friction with the fathers of the Church was a deplorable irritation. It was impossible to show contempt for the authority of Pope and cardinals and not wound one of the deepest sentiments of France, and one which ten years before Napoleon had braved most to satisfy.

To the irritation against the emperor's church policy was added bitter resentment against the conscription, that tax of blood and muscle demanded of the country. Napoleon had formulated and attempted to make tolerable the principle born of the Revolution, which declared that every male citizen of age owed the state a service of blood in case it needed him. The wis-

"NAPOLEON IN HIS CABINET." THE CHILD AT HIS SIDE IS HIS SON, THE KING OF ROME.

The manuscript on the floor of the cabinet bears the date "1811." Engraved by Weber, after Steuben.

dom of his management of the conscription had prevented discontent until 1807 ; then the draft on life had begun to be arbitrary and grievous. The laws of exemptions were discarded. The "only son of his mother" no longer remained at her side. The father whose little children were motherless must leave them : aged and helpless parents no longer gave immunity. Those who had bought their exemption by heavy sacrifices were obliged to go. Persons whom the law made subject to conscription in 1807, were called out in 1806 ; those of 1808, in 1807. So far was this

THE DUKE OF REICHSTADT.

Engraved by W. Bromley, after Sir Thomas Lawrence.

premature drafting pushed, that the armies were said to be made up of "boy soldiers," weak, unformed youths, fresh from school, who wilted in a sun like that of Spain, and dropped out in the march.

At the rate at which men had been killed, however, there was no other way of keeping up the army. Between 1804 and 1811 one million seven hundred thousand men had perished in battle. What wonder that now the boys of France were pressed into service ! At the same time the country was overrun with the lame, the blind, the broken-down, who had come back from war to live on their friends or on charity. It was not only the funeral crape on almost every door which made Frenchmen hate the conscription, it was the crippled men whom they met at every corner.

While within, the people fretted over the religious disturbances and the abuses of the conscription, without, the continental blockade was causing serious trouble between Napoleon and the kings he ruled. In spite of all his efforts English merchandise penetrated everywhere. The fair at Rotterdam in 1807 was filled with English goods. They passed into Italy under false

PORTRAIT OF THE KING OF ROME.

Painting by Lawrence. Collection of the Duc de Bassano This portrait of Napoleon II. by Lawrence is an exquisite work of art, a bright and fresh color-harmony. Lawrence must have executed this portrait while travelling in Europe, whither he was sent by his sovereign George IV., and paid at the rate of twenty-five thousand francs a year, in order to paint for the great Windsor gallery the portraits of all the heroes *"du grand hasard de Waterloo."* A. D.

seals. They came into France on pretence that they were for the empress. Napoleon remonstrated and threatened, but he could not check the traffic. The most serious trouble caused by this violation of the Berlin Decree was with Louis the King of Holland. In 1808 Napoleon complained to his brother that more than one hundred ships passed between his kingdom and England every month, and a year later he wrote in desperation, "Holland is an English province."

The relations of the brothers grew more and more bitter. Napoleon resented the half support Louis gave him, and as a punishment he took away his provinces, filled his forts with French troops, threatened him with war if he did not break up the trade. So far did these hostilities go, that in the summer of 1810 King Louis abdicated in favor of his son and retired to Austria. Napoleon tried his best to persuade him at least to return into French territory, but he refused. This break was the sadder because Louis was the brother for whom Napoleon had really done most.

Joseph was not happier than Louis. The Spanish war still went on, and no better than in 1808. Joseph, humbled and unhappy, had even prayed to be freed of the throne.

THE DUKE OF REICHSTADT.

Engraved by Benedetti, after Daffinger.

refusal to enter into French combinations, and pay tribute to carry on French wars, had suppressed his revenues as a French prince —Bernadotte had been created Prince of Ponte-Corvo in 1806 — had refused to communicate with him, and when the King of Rome was born had sent back the Swedish decoration offered. Finally, in January, 1812, French troops invaded certain Swedish possessions, and the country concluded an alliance with England and Russia.

The relations with Sweden were seriously strained. Since 1810 Bernadotte had been by adoption the crown prince of that country. Although he had emphatically refused, in accepting the position, to agree never to take up arms against France, as Napoleon wished him to do, he had later consented to the continental blockade, and had declared war against England; but this declaration both England and Sweden considered simply as a *façon de parler.* Napoleon, conscious that Bernadotte was not carrying out the blockade, and irritated by his persistent

With Russia, the "other half" of the machine, the ally upon whom the great plan of Tilsit and Erfurt depended, there was such a bad state of feeling that, in 1811, it became certain that war would result. Causes had been accumulating upon each side since the Erfurt meeting.

The continental system weighed heavily on the interests of Russia. The people constantly rebelled against it and evaded it in every way. The business depression from which they suffered they charged to Napoleon, and a strong party arose in the kingdom which used every method of showing the czar that

PORTRAIT OF NAPOLEON ON A BILLIARD POCKET.

Collection of Monsieur Paul le Roux. A formidable inventory might be made of the Napoleon images that appeared from 1814 to 1815. Not only are they innumerable, but they assume all kinds of forms. Napoleon became a symbol, a fetish, a household god. He took the form of ink-bottles, knives, flasks, candlesticks, cake moulds, bells, billiard pockets, etc. It would be impossible to enumerate here all the industrial objects invested with Napoleonic shapes by the naïve efforts of the popular imagination. The list would be too long. The collections of certain fervent Bonapartists contain some thousands; that of Monsieur Paul le Roux, among others, who has placed his rich collection at my disposal.—A. D.

NAPOLEON.

Engraved in 1841 by Louis, after a painting made in 1837 by Delaroche, now in the Standish collection, and called the " Snuff-box." Probably the finest engraving ever made of a Napoleon portrait.

the " unnatural alliance," as they called the agreement between Alexander and Napoleon, was unpopular. The czar could not refuse to listen to this party. More, he feared that Napoleon was getting ready to restore Poland. He was offended by the haste with which his ally had dismissed the idea of marriage with his sister and had taken up Marie Louise. He complained of the changes of boundaries in Germany.

NAPOLEON, 1812.

Facsimile of a drawing by Girodet-Trioson, made from life in the emperor's private chapel, March 8, 1812. (" Fac simile d'un Dessin de Girodet-Trioson, fait d'après nature à la chapelle de l'empereur le 8 Mars, 1812.") Engraved by Maile. Published in London in 1827 by R. G. Jones. It is thought to give a more correct delineation of Napoleon than do the paintings by Lefèvre, David, and Isabey, who were the royal painters, and painted, under the instruction of Napoleon, to make him look like the Cæsars. There are other designs by Girodet. Of the one given above, Maile's engraving is the only copy known. Another contains three heads, one of which is a sleeping Napoleon. It was made only a month later, at the theatre of St. Cloud.

Napoleon saw with irritation that English goods were admitted into Russia. He resented the failure of Alexander to join heartily in the wide-sweeping application he had made of the Berlin and Milan Decrees, and to persecute neutral flags of all nations, even of those so far away from the Continent as the United States. He

NAPOLEON READING.

By Girodet. From the collection of Monsieur Cheramy of Paris.

them, and the expression was just, for in the ranks there were Spaniards, Neapolitans, Piedmontese, Slavs, Kroats, Bavarians, Dutchmen, Poles, Romans, and a dozen other nationalities, side by side with Frenchmen. Indeed, nearly one-half the force was said to be foreign. The Grand Army, as the active body was called, numbered, to quote the popular figures, six hundred and seventy-eight thousand men. It is sure that this is an exaggerated number, though certainly over half a million men entered Russia. With reserves, the whole force numbered one million one hundred thousand. The necessity for so large a body of reserves is explained by the length of the line of communication Napoleon had to keep. From the Nieman to Paris the way must be open, supply station guarded, fortified towns equipped. It took nearly as many men to insure the rear of the Grand Army as it did to make up the army itself.

With this imposing force at his command, Napoleon believed that he could compel Alexander to support the continental blockade, for

remembered that Russia had not supported him loyally in 1809. He was suspicious, too, of the good understanding which seemed to be growing between Sweden, Russia, and England.

During many months the two emperors remained in a half-hostile condition, but the strain finally became too great. War was inevitable, and Napoleon set about preparing for the struggle. During the latter months of 1811 and the first of 1812 his attention was given almost entirely to the military and diplomatic preparations necessary before beginning the Russian campaign. By the 1st of May, 1812, he was ready to join his army, which he had centred at Dresden. Accompanied by Marie Louise he arrived at Dresden on the 16th of May, 1812, where he was greeted by the Emperor of Austria, the King of Prussia, and other sovereigns with whom he had formed alliances.

The force Napoleon had brought to the field showed graphically the extension and the character of the France of 1812. The "army of twenty nations," the Russians called the host which was preparing to meet

GIRODET-TRIOSON. 1767-1824.

Portrait by himself. Girodet made several commonplace official portraits of Napoleon, but his rough pencil sketches are of the greatest iconographic value.

EMPEROR NAPOLEON.   1813.

Engraved by Lefèvre, after Steuben ; published December 26, 1826.

come what might that system must succeed. For it the reigning house had been
driven from Portugal, the Pope despoiled
and imprisoned, Louis gone into exile, Bernadotte driven into a new alliance. For it
the Grand Army was led into Russia. It
had become, as its inventor proclaimed, *the
fundamental law of the empire.*

Until he crossed the Nieman, Napoleon
preserved the hope of being able to avoid
war. Numerous letters to the Russian emperor, almost pathetic in their overtures,
exist. But Alexander never replied. He
simply allowed his enemy to advance. The
Grand Army was doomed to make the
Russian campaign.

CHAPTER XIX.

THE RUSSIAN CAMPAIGN.—THE BURNING OF MOSCOW.—A NEW ARMY.

THE ADVANCE OF THE ARMY OF TWENTY NATIONS.

IF one draws a triangle, its base stretching along the Nieman from Tilsit to Grodno, its apex on the Elbe, he will have a rough outline of the "army of twenty nations" as it lay in June, 1812. Napoleon, some two hundred and twenty-five thousand men around him, was at Kowno, hesitating to advance, reluctant to believe that Alexander would not make peace.

When he finally moved, it was not with the precision and swiftness which had characterized his former campaigns. When he began to fight, it was against new odds. He found that his enemies had been studying the Spanish campaigns, and that they had adopted the tactics which had so nearly ruined his armies in the Peninsula : they refused to give him a general battle, retreating constantly before him ; they harassed his separate corps with indecisive contests ; they wasted the country as they went. The people aided their soldiers as the Spaniards had done. "Tell us only the moment, and we will set fire to our dwellings," said the peasants.

By the 12th of August, Napoleon was at Smolensk, the key of Moscow. At a cost of twelve thousand men killed and wounded, he took the town, only to find, instead of the well-victualled shelter he hoped, a smoking ruin. The French army had suffered frightfully from sickness, from scarcity of supplies, and from useless fighting on the march from the Niemen to Smolensk. They had not had the stimulus of a great victory ; they began to feel that this steady retreat of the enemy was only a fatal trap into which they were falling. Every consideration forbade them to march into Russia so late in the year, yet on they went towards Moscow, over ruined fields and through empty villages. This terrible pursuit lasted until September 7th, when the Russians, to content their soldiers, who were complaining loudly because they were not allowed to engage the French, gave battle at Borodino, the battle of the Moskova as the French call it.

THE BATTLE OF BORODINO.

At two o'clock in the morning of this engagement, Napoleon issued one of his stirring bulletins :

ATTENTION! THE EMPEROR HAS HIS EYE ON US.

By Raffet.

THE BRIDGE OVER THE KOLOTSCHA NEAR BORODINO, SEPTEMBER 17, 1812.

From a sketch made at the time by an officer of Napoleon's army. . . . "The bridge behind Borodino, leading over the Kolotscha to Gorki, was, on September 17th, the scene of a terrible fight. This memorable battle began
by the taking of Borodino. The One Hundred and Sixth Regiment of the Fourth Army Corps were charged with
that enterprise, and, carried away by their success, instead of waiting to destroy the Kolotscha bridge, they dashed
on at full gallop towards the heights above Gorki. Here, besides being hemmed in on all sides by the superior numbers of the Russians, they had also to sustain a deadly fire from works thrown up near Gorki, which barred their
passage. Forced back to the bridge with great loss, they would have been utterly destroyed, had it not been for the
efforts of the Ninety-second Regiment, who hastened to their assistance. Although both during and after the battle,
in order to render the bridge practicable, they had cleared away numbers of the dead bodies on it by throwing them
into the river, there still remained only too many heaped up on the banks, affording a terrible evidence of the battle
of Mojaisk that had just taken place."—*Extract from the Diary of an Eye-witness of the Russian Campaign.*

"Soldiers! Here is the battle which you have so
long desired! Henceforth the victory depends upon
you; it is necessary for us. It will give you abun-
dance, good winter quarters, and a speedy return to
your country! Behave as you did at Austerlitz, at
Friedland, at Vitebsk, at Smolensk, and the most
remote posterity will quote with pride your conduct
on this day; let it say of you: *he was at the great
battle under the walls of Moscow.*"

The French gained the battle at Borodino, at a cost of some thirty thousand
men, but they did not destroy the Russian
army. Although the Russians lost fifty
thousand men, they retreated in good
order. Under the circumstances, a victory which allowed the enemy to retire in
order was of little use. It was Napoleon's
fault, the critics said; he was inactive.
But it was not sluggishness which troubled

Napoleon at Borodino. He had a new
enemy—a headache. On the day of the
battle he suffered so that he was obliged
to retire to a ravine to escape the icy wind.
In this sheltered spot he paced up and
down all day, giving his orders from the
reports brought him, for he could see but
a portion of the field.

THE BURNING OF MOSCOW.

Moscow was entered on the 15th of September. Here the French found at last
food and shelter, but only for a few hours.
That night Moscow burst into flames, set
on fire by the authorities, by whom it had
been abandoned. It was three days before
the fire was arrested. It would cost Rus-

ON THE HIGH ROAD FROM MOJAISKA TO KRYMSKOÏE, SEPTEMBER 18, 1812.

From a sketch made at the time by an officer of Napoleon's army. . . . . "It was not uncommon to find in the rooms rows of corpses lying on the floor in the same order they had occupied while yet alive ; while others who had escaped from the flames, but horribly mutilated, sought to prolong their miserable existence by some moments, in a manner pitiable to witness." *Extract from the Diary of an Eye-witness of the Russian Campaign.*]

BIVOUAC NEAR MIKALEWKA, NOVEMBER 7, 1812.

From a sketch made at the time by an officer of Napoleon's army.

BESIDE THE ROAD, NOT FAR FROM PNÉWA, NOVEMBER 8, 1812.

From a sketch made at the time by an officer of Napoleon's army. . . . "At the first milestone, on the left, might be seen a group gathered round a melancholy fire, fed with broken wheels and bits of gun-carriages, by which they were trying to warm their benumbed limbs. Behind this group stand the orderlies, attentive to the smallest sign. Do you know the man in the simple gray overcoat, somewhat disguised by his hat of fur, who had led us like a brilliant meteor to battle and to victory? It is the emperor. Who among us might fathom that mighty soul and read what was passing in it as he gazed at that miserable army? His enemies have insulted him and have sought to trample his glory in the dust. Yet their punishment would be too cruel, were their hearts wrung to-day as his was in that moment. He who beholds true grandeur, abandoned by fortune, forgets his own griefs and suffering ; and half reconciled to our hard fate we defiled past him in mournful silence."— *Extract from the Diary of an Eye-witness of the Russian Campaign.*

sia two hundred years of time, two hundred millions of money, to repair the loss which she had sustained, Napoleon wrote to France.

Suffering, disorganization, pillage, followed the disaster. But Napoleon would not retreat. He hoped to make peace. Moscow was still smoking when he wrote a long description of the conflagration to Alexander. The closing paragraph ran :

"I wage war against your Majesty without animosity ; a note from you before or after the last battle would have stopped my march, and I should even have liked to have sacrificed the advantage of entering Moscow. If your Majesty retains some remains of your former sentiments, you will take this letter in good part. At all events, you will thank me for giving you an account of what is passing at Moscow."

RETREAT FROM MOSCOW.

"I will never sign a peace as long as a single foe remains on Russian ground," the Emperor Alexander had said when he heard that Napoleon had crossed the Nieman.

He kept his word in spite of all Napoleon's overtures. The French position grew worse from day to day. No food, no fresh supplies ; the cold increasing, the army disheartened, the number of Russians around Moscow growing larger. Nothing but a retreat could save the remnant of the French. It began on October 19th, one hundred and fifteen thousand men leaving Moscow. They were followed by forty thousand vehicles loaded with the sick and with what supplies they could get hold of. The route was over the fields devastated a month before. The Cossacks harassed them night and day, and the cruel Russian cold dropped from the skies, cutting them down like a storm of scythes. Before Smolensk was reached, thousands of the retreating army were dead.

Napoleon had ordered that provisions and clothing should be collected at Smolensk. When he reached the city he found that his directions had not been obeyed. The army, exasperated beyond endurance by this disappointment, fell into complete and frightful disorganization, and the rest of the retreat was like the falling back of a conquered mob.

There is no space here for the details of this terrible march and of the frightful passage of the Beresina. The terror of the cold and starvation wrung cries from Napoleon himself.

" Provisions, provisions, provisions," he wrote on November 29th from the right bank of the Beresina. " Without them there is no knowing to what horrors this undisciplined mass will not proceed."

And again : " The army is at its last extremity. It is impossible for it to do anything, even if it were a question of defending Paris."

The army finally reached the Nieman. The last man over was Marshal Ney. " Who are you ? " he was asked. " The rear guard of the Grand Army," was the sombre reply of the noble old soldier.

Some forty thousand men crossed the river, but of these there were many who could do nothing but crawl to the hospitals, asking for " the rooms where people die." It was true, as Desprez said, the Grand Army was dead.

It was on this horrible retreat that Napoleon received word that a curious thing had happened in Paris. A general and an abbé, both political prisoners, had escaped, and actually had succeeded in the preliminaries of a *coup d'état* overturning the empire, and substituting a provisional government.

They had carried out their scheme simply by announcing that Napoleon was dead, and by reading a forged proclamation from the senate to the effect that the imperial government was at an end and a new one begun. The authorities to whom these conspirators had gone had with but little hesitation accepted their orders. They had secured twelve hundred soldiers, had locked up the prefect of police, and had taken possession of the Hôtel de Ville.

The foolhardy enterprise went, of course, only a little way, but far enough to show Paris that the day of easy revolution had not passed, and that an announcement of the death of Napoleon did not bring at once a cry of " Long live the King of Rome ! " The news of the Malet conspiracy was an astonishing revelation to Napoleon himself of the instability of French public sentiment. He saw that the support on which he had depended most to insure his institutions, that is, an heir to his throne, was set aside at the word of a worthless agitator. The impression made on his generals by the news was one of

ON THE ROAD BETWEEN BRAUNSBERG AND ELBING, DECEMBER 21, 1812.

From a sketch made at the time by an officer of Napoleon's army The figure with the sword under the arm is Napoleon in the costume worn in the Russian campaign.

consternation and despair. The emperor read in their faces that they believed his good fortune was waning. He decided to go to Paris as soon as possible.

On December 5th he left the army, and after a perilous journey of twelve days reached the French capital.

gesting that since his good genius had failed him once, it might again.

No one realized the gravity of the position as Napoleon himself, but he met his household, his ministers, the Council of State, the Senate, with an imperial self-confidence and a *sang froid* which are awe-

HOSPITALITY FROM RUSSIAN WOMEN.

From a sketch made at the time by an officer of Napoleon's army.

EXPLAINING THE RETREAT FROM MOSCOW.

It took as great courage to face France now as it had taken audacity to attempt the invasion of Russia. The grandest army the nation had ever sent out was lying behind him dead. His throne had tottered for an instant in sight of all France. Hereafter he could not believe himself invincible. Already his enemies were sug-

inspiring under the circumstances. The horror of the situation of the army was not known in Paris on his arrival, but reports came in daily until the truth was clear to everybody. But Napoleon never lost countenance. The explanations necessary for him to give to the Senate, to his allies, and to his friends, had all the serenity and the plausibility of a victor—a victor who had suffered, to be sure, but not

PASSAGE OF THE BRESINA, NOVEMBER, 1812.

Engraved by Adams, after Langlois. "The greater part of the army had crossed the river; the camp followers and stragglers remained heedless of the commands of Napoleon to retreat, when suddenly the Russian artillery appeared on the hill in the rear, and began firing upon the camp followers. A rush was made for the bridge, and vast numbers were drowned."

NAPOLEON AFTER THE RUSSIAN CAMPAIGN.

In this lithograph Raffet shows Napoleon, just after the Russian campaign, at the head of the young conscripts hastily levied—his *Marie Louises* hardly more than children, but thirsting for war and glory. "Sire," said Ney to the emperor, "give me some of those young and valiant conscripts. I will lead them whither you will. Our old *moustaches* know as much as we do; they understand the ground and the difficulties; but those good children are frightened by no obstacles, they look neither to right nor left, but straight ahead. It is glory they long for."

through his own rashness or mismanagement. The following quotation from a letter to the King of Denmark illustrates well his public attitude towards the invasion and the retreat from Moscow:

" The enemy were always beaten, and captured neither an eagle nor a gun from my army. On the 7th of November the cold became intense; all the roads were found impracticable; thirty thousand horses perished between the 7th and the 16th. A portion of our baggage and artillery wagons was broken and abandoned; our soldiers, little accustomed to such weather, could not endure the cold. They wandered from the ranks in quest of shelter for the night, and, having no cavalry to protect them, several thousands fell into the hands of the enemy's light troops. General Sanson, chief of the topographic corps, was captured by some Cossacks while he was engaged in sketching a position. Other isolated officers shared the same fate. My losses are severe, but the enemy cannot attribute to themselves the honor of having inflicted them. My army has suffered greatly, and suffers still, but this calamity will cease with the cold."

To every one he declared that it was the Russians, not he, who had suffered. It was their great city, not his, which was burnt; their fields, not his, which were devastated. They did not take an eagle, did not win a battle. It was the cold, the Cossacks, which had done the mischief to the Grand Army; and that mischief? Why, it would be soon repaired. " I shall be back on the Nieman in the spring."

But the very man who in public and private calmed and reassured the nation, was sometimes himself so overwhelmed at the thought of the disaster which he had just witnessed, that he let escape a cry which showed that it was only his indomitable will which was carrying him through; that his heart was bleeding. In the midst of a glowing account to the legislative body of his success during the invasion, he suddenly stopped. "In a few nights everything changed. I have suffered great losses. They would have broken my heart if I had been accessible to any other feelings than the interest, the glory, and the future of my people."

In the teeth of the terrible news coming daily to Paris, Napoleon began preparations for another campaign. To every one he talked of victory as certain. Those who argued against the enterprise he silenced peremptorily. "You should say," he wrote Eugène, "and yourself believe, that in the next campaign I shall drive the Russians back across the Nieman." With the first news of the passage of the Beresina chilling them, the Senate voted an army of three hundred and fifty thousand men;

the allies were called upon ; even the marine was obliged to turn men over to the land force.

But something besides men was necessary. An army means muskets and powder and sabres, clothes and boots and headgear, wagons and cannon and caisson ; and all these it was necessary to manufacture afresh. The task was gigantic ; but before the middle of April it was completed, and the emperor was ready to join his army.

The force against which Napoleon went

who commanded a Prussian division, went over to the enemy. It was a dishonorable action from a military point of view, but his explanation that he deserted as "a patriot acting for the welfare of his country" touched Prussia ; and though the king disavowed the act, the people applauded it.

Throughout the German states the feeling against Napoleon was bitter. A veritable crusade had been undertaken against him by such men as Stein, and most of the youth of the country were united in the *Tugendbund*, or League of Virtue, which

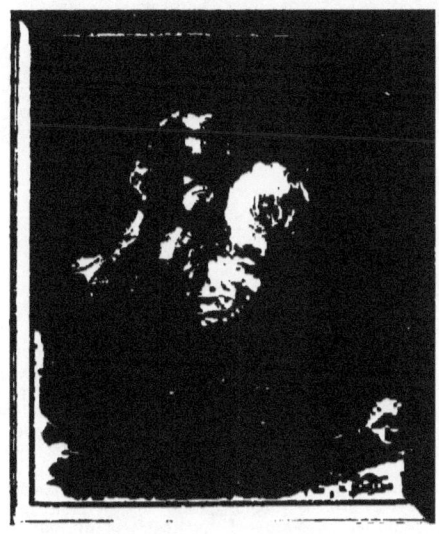

NAPOLEON IN 1814.

After a wash drawing by Charlet, in the collection of Madame Charlet. Hitherto unpublished.

in 1813 was the most formidable, in many respects, he had ever encountered. Its strength was greater. It included Russia, England, Spain, Prussia, and Sweden, and the allies believed Austria would soon join them. An element of this force more powerful than its numbers was its spirit. The allied armies fought Napoleon in 1813 as they would fight an enemy of freedom. Central Europe had come to feel that further French interference was intolerable. The war had become a crusade. The extent of this feeling is illustrated by an incident in the Prussian army. In the war of 1812 Prussia was an ally of the French, but at the end of the year General Yorck,

had sworn to take arms for German freedom.

When Alexander followed the French across the Nieman, announcing that he came bringing "deliverance to Europe," and calling on the people to unite against the "common enemy," he found them quick to understand and respond.

Thus, in 1813 Napoleon did not go against kings and armies, but against *peoples*. No one understood this better than he did himself, and he counselled his allies that it was not against the foreign enemy alone that they had to protect themselves. "There is one more dangerous to be feared—the spirit of revolt and anarchy."

1813. AFTER RAFFET.

CHAPTER XX.

CAMPAIGN OF 1813.—CAMPAIGN OF 1814.—ABDICATION.

THE CAMPAIGN OF 1813.

THE campaign opened May 2, 1813, southwest of Leipsic, with the battle of Lützen. It was Napoleon's victory, though he could not follow it up, as he had no cavalry. The moral effect of Lützen was excellent in the French army. Among the allies there was a return to the old dread of the "monster." By May 8th the French occupied Dresden ; from there they crossed the Elbe, and on the 21st fought the battle of Bautzen, another incomplete victory for Napoleon. The next day, in an engagement with the Russian rear guard, Marshal Duroc, one of Napoleon's warmest and oldest friends, was killed. It was the second marshal lost since the campaign began, Bessières having been killed at Lützen.

The French occupied Breslau on June 1st, and three days later an armistice was signed, lasting until August 10th. It was hoped that peace might be concluded during this armistice. At that moment Austria held the key to the situation. The allies saw that they were defeated if they could not persuade her to join them. Napoleon, his old confidence restored by a series of victories, hoped to keep his Austrian father-in-law quiet until he had crushed the Prussians and driven the Russians across the Nieman. Austria saw her power, and determined to use it to regain territory lost in 1805 and 1809, and Metternich came to Dresden to see Napoleon. Austria would keep peace with France, he said, if Napoleon would restore Illyria and the Polish provinces, would send the Pope back to Rome, give up the protectorate of the Confederation of the Rhine, restore Naples and Spain. Napoleon's amazement and indignation were boundless.

"How much has England given you for playing this *rôle* against me, Metternich ? " he asked.

A semblance of a congress was held at Prague soon after, but it was only a mock-

NAPOLEON AND POPE PIUS VII. IN CONFERENCE AT FONTAINEBLEAU.
Engraved by Robinson, after a painting made in 1836 by Wilkie.

ery. Such was the exasperation and suffering of Central Europe, that peace could only be reached by large sacrifices on Napoleon's part. These he refused to make. There is no doubt but that France and his allies begged him to compromise; that his wisest counsellors advised him to do so. But he repulsed with irritation all such suggestions. "You bore me continually about the necessity of peace," he wrote Savary. "I know the situation of my empire better than you do; no one is more interested in concluding peace than myself, but I shall not make a dishonorable peace, or one that would see us at war again in six months. . . . These things do not concern you."

By the middle of August the campaign

began. The French had in the field some three hundred and sixty thousand men. This force was surrounded by a circle of armies, Swedish, Russian, Prussian, and Austrian, in all some eight hundred thousand men. The leaders of this hostile force included, besides the natural enemies of France, Bernadotte, heir-apparent to the throne of Sweden, who had fought with Napoleon in Italy, and General Moreau, the hero of Hohenlinden. Moreau was on Alexander's staff. He had reached the army the night that the armistice expired, having sailed from the United States on the 21st of June, at the invitation of the Russian emperor, to aid in the campaign against France. He had been greeted by the allies with every mark of distinction. Another deserter on the allies' staff was the eminent military critic Jomini. In the ranks were stragglers from all the French corps, and the Saxons were threatening to leave the French in a body, and go over to the allies.

The second campaign of 1813 opened brilliantly for Napoleon, for at Dresden he took twenty thousand prisoners, and captured sixty cannon. The victory turned the anxiety of Paris to hopefulness, and their faith in Napoleon's star was further revived by the report that Moreau had fallen, both legs carried off by a French bullet. Moreau himself felt that fate was friendly to the emperor. "That rascal Bonaparte is always lucky," he wrote his wife, just after the amputation of his legs.

But there was something stronger than luck at work: the allies were animated by a spirit of nationality, indomitable in its force, and they were following a plan which was sure to crush Napoleon in the long run. It was one laid out by Moreau; a general battle was not to be risked, but the corps of the French were to be engaged one by one, until the parts of the army were disabled. This plan was carried out. In turn Vandamme, Oudinot, Macdonald, Ney, were defeated, and in October the remnants of the French fell back to Leipsic. Here the horde that surrounded them was suddenly enlarged. The Bavarians had gone over to the allies.

The three days' battle of Leipsic exhausted the French, and they were obliged to make a disastrous retreat to the Rhine, which they crossed November 1st. Ten days later the emperor was in Paris.

The situation of France at the end of 1813 was deplorable. The allies lay on the right bank of the Rhine. The battle of Vittoria had given the Spanish boundary to Wellington, and the English and Spanish armies were on the frontier. The allies which remained with the French were not to be trusted. "All Europe was marching with us a year ago," Napoleon said; "to-day all Europe is marching against us." There was despair among his generals, alarm in Paris. Besides, there seemed no human means of gathering up a new army. Where were the men to come from? France was bled to death. She could give no more. Her veins were empty.

"This is the truth, the exact truth, and such is the secret and the explanation of all that has since occurred," says Pasquier. "With these successive levies of conscriptions, past, present, and to come; with the Guards of Honor; with the brevet of sub-lieutenant forced on the young men appertaining to the best families, after they had escaped the conscript lot, or had supplied substitutes in conformity with the provisions of the law, there did not remain a single family which was not in anxiety or in mourning."

Yet hedged in as he was by enemies, threatened by anarchy, supported by a fainting people, Napoleon dallied over the peace the allies offered. The terms were not dishonorable. France was to retire, as the other nations, within her natural boundaries, which they designated as the Rhine, the Alps, and the Pyrenees. But the emperor could not believe that Europe, whom he had defeated so often, had power to confine him within such limits. He could not believe that such a peace would be stable, and he began preparations for resistance. Fresh levies of troops were made. The Spanish frontier he attempted to secure by making peace with Ferdinand, recognizing him as King of Spain. He tried to settle his trouble with the Pope.

While he struggled to simplify the situation, to arouse national spirit, and to gather reënforcements, hostile forces multiplied and closed in upon him. The allies crossed the Rhine. The *corps législatif* took advantage of his necessity to demand the restoration of certain rights which he had taken from them. In his anger at their audacity, the emperor alienated public sympathy by dissolving the body. "I stood in need of something to console me," he told them, "and you have sought to dishonor me. I was expecting that you would unite in mind and deed to drive out the foreigner; you have bid him come. Indeed, had I lost two battles, it would not have done France any greater evil." To crown his evil day, Murat, Caroline's husband, now King of Naples, abandoned him. This betrayal

THEY GRUMBLED, BUT THEY FOLLOWED ALWAYS.

Reflet shows us a Napoleon worn out by the disastrous success even of his victories, marching under a sad, rainy sky, at the head of his little army; which, although hopeful, decreased daily in numbers after repeated fights all of them victorious. The legend chosen by the artist sums up the state of mind of these old *grognards* always discontented, and yet always ready, in spite of wearing fatigue and increasing discouragements, to run even to death on a sign from their emperor. Meissonier meditated long and earnestly before this beautiful picture, inspired by the campaign of France, previous to painting his immortal canvas, "1814."   A. D.

1814.

Etched by Ruet, after Meissonier. Original in Walters's gallery, Baltimore. Meissonier was fond of short titles, and very often in his historical works made choice of only a simple date. Among such titles are, 1806, 1807, 1814, which might very well be replaced by, Battle of Jena, Friedland, and Campaign of France. This last subject he treated twice under different aspects. First, in the famous canvas, his great masterpiece, where we see a gloomy, silent Napoleon, with face contracted by anguish, slowly riding at the head of his discouraged staff across the snowy plains of Champagne. This important work forms part of the collection of Monsieur Chauchard of Paris, who bought it for eight hundred thousand francs. The second picture is the one reproduced here, in which Napoleon is represented at the same period, but only at the outset of this terrible campaign—the last act but one of the Napoleonic tragedy. The carefully studied face shows as yet no expression of discouragement, but rather a determined hope of success. Napoleon wears the traditional gray overcoat over the costume of the *Chasseurs de la Garde*, and rides his faithful little mare *Marie*, painted with a living, nervous effect that cannot be too much admired. Meissonier, inaccessible to the poetic seductions of symbolism, has nevertheless indicated here in a superb manner the gloomy future of the hero, by surrounding his luminous form with darkness, and casting on his brow the shadow of a stormy, threatening sky.—A. D.

"1814."

Engraved by Jules Jacquet, after Meissonier. In his preparation for this picture, we are told that "Meissonier, dressed in an old coat of the emperor's, and seated in a saddle on a house-top, in the falling snow of a gloomy winter's day, studied himself in a mirror, and therefrom painted in the sombre tints laid by the winter atmosphere on the flesh of the face, and the flakes of snow fallen on the coat-sleeve."

was the more bitter because his sister her-self was the cause of it. Fearful of losing her little glory as Queen of Naples, Caroline watched the course of events until she was certain that her brother was lost, and then urged Murat to conclude a peace with England and Austria.

This accumulation of reverses, coming upon him as he tried to prepare for battle, drove Napoleon to approach the allies with proposals of peace. It was too late. The idea had taken root that France, with Napoleon at her head, would never remain in her natural limits ; that the only hope for Europe was to crush him completely. This hatred of Napoleon had become al-most fanatical, and made any terms of peace with him impossible.

CAMPAIGN OF 1814.

By the end of January, 1814, the em-peror was ready to renew the struggle. The day before he left Paris, he led the empress and the King of Rome to the court of the Tuileries, and presented them to the National Guard. He was leaving them what he held dearest in the world, he told them. The enemy were closing around ; they might reach Paris ; they might even destroy the city. While he fought without to shield France from this calamity, he prayed them to protect the priceless trust left within. The nobility and sincerity of the feeling that stirred the emperor were unquestionable ; tears flowed down the cheeks of the men to whom he spoke, and for a moment every heart was animated by the old emotion, and they took with eagerness the oath he asked.

The next day he left Paris. The army he commanded did not number more than sixty thousand men. He led it against a force which, counting only those who had crossed the Rhine, numbered nearly six hundred thousand.

In the campaign of two months which followed, Napoleon several times defeated the allies. In spite of the terrible disad-vantages under which he fought, he nearly drove them from the country. In every way the campaign was worthy of his genius. But the odds against him were too tre-mendous. The saddest phase of his situa-tion was that he was not seconded. The people, the generals, the legislative bodies, everybody not under his personal influence seemed paralyzed. Augereau, who was at Lyons, did absolutely nothing, and the following letter to him shows with what energy and indignation Napoleon tried to arouse his stupefied followers.

> "NOGENT, 21st *February*, 1814.

" . . . What ! six hours after having received the first troops coming from Spain you were not in the field ! Six hours' repose was sufficient. I won the action of Nangis with a brigade of dragoons coming from Spain, which, since it left Bayonne, had not unbridled its horses. The six battalions of the division of Nismes want clothes, equipment, and drilling, say you. What poor reasons you give me there, Augereau ! I have destroyed eighty thousand enemies with conscripts having nothing but knap-sacks ! The National Guards, say you, are pitiable. I have four thousand here, in round hats, without knapsacks, in wooden shoes, but with good muskets, and I get a great deal out of them. There is no money, you continue ; and where do you hope to draw money from ? You want wagons ; take them wherever you can. You have no magazines ; this is too ridiculous. I order you, twelve hours after the reception of this letter, to take the field. If you are still Augereau of Castiglione, keep the command ; but if your sixty years weigh upon you, hand over the command to your senior general. The country is in danger, and can be saved by boldness and good will alone. . . .

> "NAPOLEON."

The terror and apathy of Paris exasper-ated him beyond measure. To his great disgust, the court and some of the coun-sellors had taken to public prayers for his safety. "I see that instead of sustaining the empress," he wrote Cambacérès, " you discourage her. Why do you lose your head like that ? What are these *misereres* and these prayers forty hours long at the chapel ? Have people in Paris gone mad ?"

The most serious concern of Napoleon in this campaign was that the empress and the King of Rome should not be captured. He realized that the allies might reach Paris at any time, and repeatedly he in-structed Joseph, who had been appointed lieutenant-general in his absence, what to do if the city was threatened.

" Never allow the empress or the King of Rome to fall into the hands of the enemy. . . . As far as I am concerned, I would rather see my son slain than brought up at Vienna as an Austrian prince ; and I have a sufficiently good opinion of the empress to feel persuaded that she thinks in the same way, as far as it is possible for a woman and a mother to do so. I never saw Andromaque represented without pitying Astyanax surviving his family, and without regarding it as a piece of good fortune that he did not survive his father."

Throughout the two months there were negotiations for peace. They varied ac-cording to the success or failure of the emperor or the allies. Napoleon had reached a point where he would gladly have accepted the terms offered at the close of 1813. But those were withdrawn. France

NAPOLEON AT FONTAINEBLEAU THE EVENING AFTER HIS ABDICATION, APRIL 11, 1814.

François, after Delaroche, 1845.

must come down to her limits in 1789.
"What!" cried Napoleon, "leave France
smaller than I found her? Never."

The frightful combination of forces
closed about him steadily, with the deadly
precision of the chamber of torture, whose
adjustable walls imperceptibly, but surely,
draw together, day by day, until the victim
is crushed. On the 30th of March Paris
capitulated. The day before, the Regent
Marie Louise with the King of Rome and
her suite had left the city for Blois. The
allied sovereigns entered Paris on the 1st
of April. As they passed through the
streets, they saw multiplying, as they advanced, the white cockades which the
grandes dames of the Faubourg St. Germain
had been making in anticipation of the
entrance of the foreigner, and the only cries

which greeted them as they passed up the
boulevards were, "*Long live the Bourbons!
Long live the sovereigns! Long live the Emperor Alexander.*"

NAPOLEON AT FONTAINEBLEAU.

The allies were in Paris, but Napoleon
was not crushed. Encamped at Fontainebleau, his army about him, the soldiers
everywhere faithful to him, he had still a
large chance of victory, and the allies looked
with uneasiness to see what move he would
make. It was due largely to the wit of
Talleyrand that the standing ground which
remained to the emperor was undermined.
That wily diplomat, whose place it was to
have gone with the empress to Blois, had
succeeded in getting himself shut into Paris.

ADIEUX DE FONTAINEBLEAU, APRIL 20, 1814.

In this beautiful canvas of Horace Vernet. now in the Versailles gallery, the personages depicted are all faithful
portraits ; and here lies the chief merit of this historic composition. General Petit, commander of the *Grenadiers de
la Garde*, overcome by emotion, clasps the emperor in his arms. Behind Napoleon stands the Duc de Bassano ; then
a compact group composed of Baron Fain, Generals Belliard, Corbineau, Ornano, and Kosakowski. To the right, in
the corner of the picture, is another important group where figure the commissioners of the coalition General Koller
(Austrian). Colonel Campbell (English), General Schouwaloff (Russian). Colonel Campbell, impressed by the touching grandeur of the scene, raises his hat with a fine gesture of enthusiasm. General Bertrand (who looks round on
Campbell's movement), General Drouot, and Colonel Gourgaud stand in the front row before the group of foreign-
ers. Colonel Gourgaud occupies the foreground, in an attitude perhaps rather theatrical. Horace Vernet, in painting the picture, was evidently inspired by the dramatic account given of the scene by Baron Fain, the emperor's
private secretary. The passage that might serve as legend is as follows : ". . . Farewell, my children ! I would
clasp you all to my heart ; let me at least kiss your flag !"

and, on the entry of the allies, had joined Alexander, whom he had persuaded to announce that the allied powers would not treat with Napoleon nor with any member of his family. This was eliminating the most difficult factor from the problem. By his fine tact Talleyrand brought over the legislative bodies to this view.

From the populace Alexander and Talleyrand feared nothing; it was too exhausted to ask anything but peace. Their most serious difficulty was the army. All over the country the cry of the common soldiers was, "Let us go to the emperor."

"The army," declared Alexander, "is always the army; as long as it is not with you, gentlemen, you can boast of nothing. The army represents the French nation; if it is not won over, what can you accomplish that will endure?"

Every influence of persuasion, of bribery, of intimidation, was used with soldiers and generals. They were told in phrases which could not but flatter them: "You are the most noble of the children of the country, and you cannot belong to the man who has laid it waste. . . . You are no longer the soldiers of Napoleon; the Senate and all France release you from your oaths." The older officers on Napoleon's staff at Fontainebleau were unsettled by adroit communications sent from Paris. They were made to believe that they were fighting against the will of the nation and of their comrades. When this disaffection had become serious, one of Napoleon's oldest and most trusted associates, Marmont, suddenly deserted. He led the vanguard of the army. This treachery took away the last hope of the imperial cause, and on April 11, 1814, Napoleon signed the act of abdication at Fontainebleau. The act ran:

"The allied powers having proclaimed that the Emperor Napoleon Bonaparte is the only obstacle to the reestablishment of peace in Europe, the Emperor Napoleon, faithful to his oath, declares that he renounces, for himself and his heirs, the thrones of France and of Italy, and that there is no personal sacrifice, even that of his life, which he is not ready to make in the interest of France."

For only a moment did the gigantic will waver under the shock of defeat, of treachery, and of abandonment. Uncertain of the fate of his wife and child, himself and his family denounced by the allies, his army scattered, he braved everything until Marmont deserted him, and he saw one after another of his trusted officers join his enemies; then for a moment he gave up the fight and tried to end his life. The poison he took had lost its full force, and he recovered from its effects. Even death would have none of him, he groaned.

But this discouragement was brief. No sooner was it decided that his future home should be the island of Elba, and that its affairs should be under his control, than he began to prepare for the journey to his little kingdom with the same energy and zest which had characterized him as emperor. On the 20th of April he left the palace of Fontainebleau.

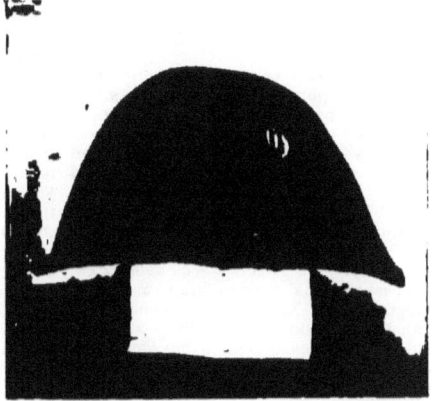

HAT WORN BY NAPOLEON DURING THE CAMPAIGN OF RUSSIA.

During nearly the whole of the Russian campaign Napoleon wore a toque reaching down over the ears, made of Siberian sable. This protected him better than his *petit chapeau* against the icy wind of the steppes. However, he was often observed to forsake it and return to the already legendary headgear, especially on the occasion of victorious entries into captured towns. I have seen lately one of the hats worn by Napoleon at this period. The parchment document that accompanies it says: "This is the manner the hat came into my hands. At the time of that terrible campaign my wife was employed in the imperial laundry. She addressed herself by chance to M. Gervais, keeper of the emperor's wardrobe, and asked for some old hats to serve as iron-holders such as laundresses used then. He gave her two hats that had belonged to the emperor; this one, which I have preserved, had been in use during the campaign. She gave the other to someone who had expressed a desire for it. This is the truth.

[Signed] "J. Delio."

This hat, here reproduced for the first time, is the property of Monsieur Georges Thierry of Paris.—A. D.

CHAPTER XXI.

RULER OF THE ISLAND OF ELBA.—RETURN TO PARIS.—THE HUNDRED DAYS.— THE SECOND ABDICATION.

A WEEK after bidding his Guard farewell, Napoleon sent from Frejus his first address to the inhabitants of Elba:

"Circumstances having induced me to renounce the throne of France, sacrificing my rights to the interests of the country, I reserved for myself the sovereignty of the island of Elba, which has met with the consent of all the powers. I therefore send you General Drouot, so that you may hand over to him the said island, with the military stores and provisions, and the property which belongs to my imperial domain. Be good enough to make known this new state of affairs to the inhabitants, and the choice which I have made of their island for my sojourn in consideration of the mildness of their manners and the excellence of their climate. I shall take the greatest interest in their welfare.

"NAPOLEON."

The Elbans received their new ruler with all the pomp which their means and experience permitted. The entire population celebrated his arrival as a *fête.* The new flag which the emperor had chosen—white ground with red bar and three yellow bees—was unfurled, and saluted by the forts of the nation and by the foreign vessels in port. The keys of the chief town of the island were presented to him, a *Te Deum* was celebrated. If these honors seemed poor and contemptible to Napoleon in comparison with the splendor of the *fêtes* to which he had become accustomed, he gave no sign, and played his part with the same seriousness as he had when he received his crown.

His life at Elba was immediately arranged methodically, and he worked as hard and seemingly with as much interest as he had in Paris. The affairs of his new state were his chief concern, and he set about at once to familiarize himself with all their details. He travelled over the island in all directions, to acquaint himself with its resources and needs. At one time he made the circuit of his domain, entering every port, and examining its condition and fortifications. Everywhere that he went he planned and began works which he pushed with energy. Fine roads were laid out; rocks were levelled; a palace and barracks were begun. From his arrival his influence was beneficial. There

was a new atmosphere at Elba, the islanders said.

The budget of Elba was administered as rigidly as that of France had been, and the little army was drilled with as great care as the Guards themselves. After the daily review of his troops, he rode on horseback, and this promenade became a species of reception, the islanders who wanted to consult him stopping him on his route. It is said that he invariably listened to their appeals.

Elba was enlivened constantly during Napoleon's residence by tourists who went out of their way to see him. The majority of these curious persons were Englishmen; with many of them he talked freely, receiving them at his house, and letting them carry off bits of stone or of brick from the premises as souvenirs.

His stay was made more tolerable by the arrival of Madame *mère* and of the Princess Pauline and the coming of twenty-six members of the National Guard who had crossed France to join him. But his great desire that Marie Louise and the King of Rome should come to him was never gratified. It is told by one of his companions on the island, that he kept carefully throughout his stay a stock of fireworks which had fallen into his possession, planning to use them when his wife and boy should arrive, but, sadly enough, he never had an occasion to celebrate that event.

FROM ELBA TO PARIS.

While to all appearances engrossed with the little affairs of Elba, Napoleon was, in fact, planning the most dramatic act of his life. On the 26th of February, 1815, the guard received an order to leave the island. With a force of eleven hundred men, the emperor passed the foreign ships guarding Elba, and on the afternoon of the 1st of March landed at Cannes on the Gulf of Juan. At eleven o'clock that night he started towards Paris. He was trusting himself to the people and the army. If there never was an example of such audacious confidence, certainly there never was such a response. The people of the South received him joyfully, offering to sound the

AN 2. LA SERVIEUK.

Lithograph by Hippolyte Bellangé.

tocsin and follow him *en masse*. But Napoleon refused ; it was the soldiers upon whom he called.

"We have not been conquered [he told the army]. Come and range yourselves under the standard of your chief ; his existence is composed of yours ; his interests, his honor, and his glory are yours. Victory will march at double-quick time. The eagle with the national colors will fly from steeple to steeple to the towers of Notre Dame. Then you will be able to show your scars with honor ; then you will be able to boast of what you have done ; you will be the liberators of the country."

At Grenoble there was a show of resistance. Napoleon went directly to the soldiers, followed by his guard.

"Here I am ; you know me. If there is a soldier among you who wishes to kill his emperor, let him do it."

"Long live the emperor ! " was the answer ; and in a twinkle the six thousand men had torn off their white cockades and replaced them by old and soiled tricolors. They drew them from the inside of their caps, where they had been concealing them since the exile of their hero. "It is the same that I wore at Austerlitz," said one another, "I had at Marengo."

From Grenoble the emperor marched to Lyons, where the soldiers and officers went over to him in regiments. The royalist leaders who had deigned to go to Lyons to exhort the army found themselves ignored; and Ney, who had been ordered from Besançon to stop the emperor's advance, and who started out promising to "bring back Napoleon in an iron cage," surrendered his entire division. It was impossible to resist the force of popular opinion, he said.

From Lyons the emperor, at the head of what was now the French army, passed by Dijon, Autun, Avallon, and Auxerre, to Fontainebleau, which he reached on March 19th. The same day Louis XVIII. fled from Paris.

The change of sentiment in these few days was well illustrated in a French paper

NAPOLEON'S RETURN FROM THE ISLAND OF ELBA, MARCH, 1815.

Engraved by George Sanders, after Steuben. Soon after landing in France, Napoleon met a battalion sent from Grenoble to arrest his march. He approached within a few paces of the troop, and throwing up his surtout, exclaimed : "If there be amongst you a soldier who would kill his general, his emperor, let him do it now! Here I am !" The cry "Vive l'Empereur!" burst from every lip. Napoleon threw himself among them, and taking a veteran private, covered with chevrons and medals, by the whiskers, said, "Speak honestly, old moustache ; couldst thou have had the heart to kill thy emperor ?" The man dropped his ramrod into his piece to show that it was uncharged, and answered, "Judge if I could have done thee much harm : all the rest are the same." One of the soldiers is showing the emperor the eagle he had preserved in his knapsack.

DEFEAT OF THE SACRED BATTALION AT WATERLOO.

One of the finest and most tragic of Raffet's compositions. Showing the last moments of the square of the Old Guard. In the middle stands out the silhouette of the emperor mounted on his white mare. In this tiny lithograph, Raffet has been able to express one of the most gigantic dramas of history.

FLÜCHER.

Gebhard Leberecht von Blücher, Prince of Wahlstadt, was born in 1742, and died in 1819. He distinguished himself as a cavalry officer in the wars against the French, and was made major-general. In 1813 he was appointed commander in-chief of the Prussian army, and defeated Marshal Macdonald, and, later, Marshal Marmont. He was made field marshal in 1813, and he led the Prussian army which, sixty thousand strong, invaded France in 1814. On the renewal of the war in 1815 he commanded the Prussian army, was defeated at Ligny, June 16th, but reached Waterloo in time to decide the victory.

which, after Napoleon's return, published the following calendar gathered from the royalist press.

February 25.—" The *exterminator* has signed a treaty offensive and defensive. It is not known with whom."

February 26.—" The *Corsican* has left the island of Elba."

March 1.—" *Bonaparte* has debarked at Cannes with eleven hundred men."

March 7.—" *General Bonaparte* has taken possession of Grenoble."

March 10.—" *Napoleon* has entered Lyons."

March 19.—" *The emperor* reached Fontainebleau to-day."

March 19.—" *His Imperial Majesty* is expected at the Tuileries to-morrow, the anniversary of the birth of the King of Rome."

Two days before the flight of the Bourbons, the following notice appeared on the door of the Tuileries :

" *The emperor begs the king to send him no more soldiers ; he has enough.*"

" What was the happiest period of your life as emperor?" O'Meara asked Napoleon once at St. Helena.

" The march from Cannes to Paris," he replied immediately.

His happiness was short-lived. The

WATERLOO, JUNE 18, 1815.

In this composition, the centre of which is the heroic figure of Napoleon, Raffet depicts the last *débris* of the Old Guard, shattered by the cannon of Wellington, and soon to be crushed entirely by the arrival of Blücher's army. The emperor feels that all is over; that fortune has forsaken him. The generals surround him and prevent him from putting his fatal design into execution.

THE DUKE OF WELLINGTON.

Engraved by Forster in 1818, after Gérard. 1814.

overpowering enthusiasm which had made that march possible could not endure. The bewildered factions which had been silenced or driven out by Napoleon's reappearance recovered from their stupor. The royalists, exasperated by their own flight, reorganized. Strong opposition developed among the liberals. It was only a short time before a reaction followed the delirium which Napoleon's return had caused in the nation. Disaffection, coldness, and plots succeeded. In face of this revulsion of feeling, the emperor himself underwent a change. The buoyant courage, the amazing audacity which had induced him to return from Elba, seemed to leave him. He became sad and preoccupied. No doubt much of this sadness was due to the refusal of Austria to restore his wife and child, and to the bitter knowledge that Marie Louise had succumbed to foreign influences and had promised never again to see her husband.

If the allies had allowed the French to manage their affairs in their own way, it is

PORTRAIT OF THE CZAR ALEXANDER I.

This portrait is from a sketch from life made by Carle Vernet in 1815, at Paris. After an unpublished water color forming part of the collection of Monsieur Albert Christophle, ex-Minister of Public Works, governor of the *Crédit-foncier* of France.

probable that Napoleon would have mastered the situation, difficult as it was. But this they did not do. In spite of his promise to observe the treaties made after his abdication, to accept the boundaries fixed, to abide by the Congress of Vienna, the coalition treated him with scorn, affecting to mistrust him. He was the disturber of the peace of the world, a public enemy; he must be put beyond the pale of society, and they took up arms, not against France, but against Napoleon. France, as it appeared, was not to be allowed to choose her own rulers.

The position in which Napoleon found himself on the declaration of war was of exceeding difficulty, but he mastered the opposition with all his old genius and re-

sources. Three months after the landing at Cannes he had an army of two hundred thousand men ready to march. He led it against at least five hundred thousand men.

On June 15th, Napoleon's army met a portion of the enemy in Belgium, near Brussels, and on June 16th, 17th, and 18th were fought the battles of Ligny, Quatre Bras, and Waterloo, in the last of which he was completely defeated. The limits and nature of this sketch do not permit a description of the engagement at Waterloo. The literature on the subject is perhaps richer than that on any other subject in military science. Thousands of books discuss the battle, and each succeeding generation takes it up as if nothing had been written on it. But while Waterloo cannot be discussed here, it is not out of place to notice that among the reasons for its loss are certain ones which interest us because they are personal to Napoleon. He whose great rule in war was, "Time is everything," lost time at Waterloo. He who had looked after everything which he wanted well done, neglected to assure himself of such an important matter as the exact position of a portion of his enemy. He who once had been able to go a week without sleep, was ill. Again, if one will compare carefully the Bonaparte of Guérin (page 55) with the Napoleon of David (page 167), he will understand, at least partially, why the battle of Waterloo was lost.

The defeat was complete; and when the emperor saw it, he threw himself into the battle in search of death. As eagerly as he had sought victory at Arcola, Marengo, Austerlitz, he sought death at Waterloo. "I ought to have died at Waterloo," he said afterwards; "but the misfortune is that when a man seeks death most he cannot find it. Men were killed around me, before, behind—everywhere. But there was no bullet for me."

He returned immediately to Paris. There was still force for resistance in France. There were many to urge him to return to the struggle, but such was the condition of public sentiment that he refused. The country was divided in its allegiance to him; the legislative body was frightened and quarrelling; Talleyrand and Fouché were plotting. Besides, the allies proclaimed to the nation that it was against Napoleon alone that they waged war. Under these circumstances Napoleon felt that loyalty to the best interest of France required his abdication; and he signed the act anew, pro-

claiming his son emperor under the title of Napoleon II.

EFFORTS TO REACH THE UNITED STATES.

Leaving Paris, the fallen emperor went to Malmaison, where Josephine had died only thirteen months before. A few friends joined him—Queen Hortense, the Duc de

BEFORE WATERLOO.
After a lithograph by Charlet.

Rovigo, Bertrand, Las Cases, and Méneval. He remained there only a few days. The allies were approaching Paris, and the environs were in danger. Napoleon offered his services to the provisional government, which had taken his place, as leader in the campaign against the invader, promising to retire as soon as the enemy was repulsed, but he was refused. The government feared him, in fact, more than it did the allies, and urged him to leave France as quickly as possible. In his disaster he turned to America as a refuge, and gave his family rendezvous there.

Various plans were suggested for getting to the United States. Among the offers of aid to carry out his desire which were made to Napoleon, Las Cases speaks of one coming from an American in Paris, who wrote :

" While you were at the head of a nation you could perform any miracle, you might conceive any hopes ; but now you can do nothing more in Europe. Fly to the United States ! I know the hearts of the leading men and the sentiments of the people of America. You will there find a second country and every source of consolation."

Mr. S. V. S. Wilder, an American shipping merchant who lived in France during the time of Napoleon's power, and who had been much impressed by the changes brought about in society and politics under his rule, offered to help him to escape. He proposed that the emperor disguise himself as a valet for whom he had a passport. On board the ship the emperor was to conceal himself in a hogshead until the danger-line was crossed. This hogshead was to have a false compartment in it. From the end in view, water was to drip incessantly. Mr. Wilder proposed to take Napoleon to his own home in Bolton, Massachusetts, when they arrived in America. It is said that the

emperor seriously considered this scheme, but finally declined, because he would leave his friends behind him, and for them Mr. Wilder could not possibly provide. Napoleon explained one day to Las Cases at St. Helena what he intended to do if he had reached America. He would have collected all his relatives around him, and thus would have formed the nucleus of a national union, a second France. Such were the sums of money he had given them that he thought they might have realized at least forty millions of francs. Before the conclusion of a year, the events of Europe would have drawn to him a hundred millions of francs and sixty thousand individuals, most of them possessing wealth, talent, and information.

"America [he said] was, in all respects, our proper asylum. It is an immense continent, possessing the advantage of a peculiar system of freedom. If a man is troubled with melancholy, he may get into a coach and drive a thousand leagues, enjoying all the way the pleasures of a common traveller. In America you may be on a footing of equality with everyone ; you may, if you please, mingle with the crowd without inconvenience, retaining your own manners, your own language, your own religion."

On June 29th, a week after his return to Paris from Waterloo, Napoleon left Malmaison for Rochefort, hoping to reach a vessel which would carry him to the United States ; but the coast was so guarded by the English that there was no escape.

MALMAISON.
(See note on page 40.)

CHAPTER XXII.

ENGLAND'S DECISION.

WHEN it became evident that it was impossible to escape to the United States, Napoleon considered two courses—to call upon the country and renew the conflict, or seek an asylum in England. The former was not only to perpetuate the foreign war, it was to plunge France into civil war; for a large part of the country had come to the conclusion of the enemy—that as long as Napoleon was at large, peace was impossible. Rather than involve France in such a disaster, the emperor resolved at last to give himself up to the English, and sent the following note to the regent:

"ROYAL HIGHNESS: Exposed to the factions which divide my country and to the hostility of the greatest powers of Europe, I have closed my political career. I have come, like Themistocles, to seek the hospitality of the British nation. I place myself under the protection of their laws, which I claim from your Royal Highness as the most powerful, the most constant, and the most generous of my enemies.

"NAPOLEON."

On the 15th of July he embarked on the English ship, the "Bellerophon," and a week later he was in Plymouth.

Napoleon's surrender to the English was made, as he says, with full confidence in their hospitality. Certainly *hospitality* was the last thing to expect of England under the circumstances, and there was something theatrical in the demand for it. The "Bellerophon" was no sooner in the harbor of Plymouth than it became evident that he was regarded not as a guest, but as a prisoner. Armed vessels surrounded the ship he was on; extraordinary messages were hurried to and fro; sinister rumors ran among the crew. The Tower of London, a desert isle, the ends of the earth, were talked of as the hospitality England was preparing.

But if there was something theatrical, even humorous, in the idea of expecting a friendly welcome from England, there was every reason to suppose that she would

NAPOLEON EMBARKING ON THE "BELLEROPHON,"
Designed and engraved by Baugeau.

NAPOLEON AT PLYMOUTH.

In 1815, while Eastlake was employed painting portraits in his native town (Plymouth), Napoleon arrived there on board the "Bellerophon," and the young artist took advantage of every glimpse he could obtain of the ex-emperor to make studies of him, by the aid of which he made a life-size picture of Napoleon standing in the gangway of the ship, attended by his officers.

receive him with dignity and considera-tion. Napoleon had been an enemy worthy of English metal. He had been defeated only after years of struggle. Now that he was at her feet, her own self-respect demanded that she treat him as became his genius and his position. To leave him at large was, of course, out of the ques-tion; but surely he could have been made a royal prisoner and been made to feel that if he was detained it was because of his might.

NAPOLEON ON BOARD THE "NORTHUMBERLAND."

Engraved by Steele, after Orchardson.

The British government no sooner realized that it had its hands on Napoleon than it was seized with a species of panic. All sense of dignity, all notions of what was due a foe who had surrendered, were drowned in hysterical resentment. The English people as a whole did not share the government's terror. The general feeling seems to have been similar to that which Charles Lamb expressed to Southey : " After all, Bonaparte is a fine fellow, as my barber says, and I should not mind

standing bare-head-
ed at his table to do
him service in his
fall. They should
have given him
Hampton Court or
Kensington, with a
tether extending
forty miles round
London."

But the govern-
ment could see
nothing but danger
in keeping such a
force as Napoleon
within its limits. It
evidently took
Lamb's whimsical
suggestion, that if
Napoleon were at
Hampton the people
might some day
eject the Brunswick
in his favor, in pro-
found seriousness.
On July 30th it
sent a communica-
tion to *General* Bonaparte—the English
henceforth refused him the title of emperor, though permitting him that of general, not reflecting, probably, that if one was
spurious the other was, since both had been
conferred by the same authority—notify-
ing him that as it was necessary that he
should not be allowed to disturb the repose of England any longer, the British
government had chosen the island of St.
Helena as his future residence, and that

CHAIR USED BY NAPOLEON AT ST. HELENA.

three persons with a
surgeon would be
allowed to accom-
pany him. A week
later he was trans-
ferred from the
" Bellerophon " to
the " Northumber-
land," and was *en
route* for St. Helena,
where he arrived in
October, 1815.

The manner in
which the British
carried out their de-
cision was irritating
and unworthy.
They seemed to feel
that guarding a
prisoner meant hu-
miliating him, and
offensive and un-
necessary restric-
tions were made
which wounded and
enraged Napo-
leon.

The effect of this treatment on his character is one of the most interesting studies
in connection with the man, and, on the
whole, it leaves one with increased respect and admiration for him. He received
the announcement of his exile in indignation. He was not a prisoner, he was the
guest of England, he said. It was an outrage against the laws of hospitality to
send him into exile, and he would never
submit voluntarily. When he became con-

LONGWOOD.

From a recent photograph.

vinced that the British were inflexible in their decision, he thought of suicide, and even discussed it with Las Cases. It was the most convenient solution of his dilemma. It would injure no one, and his friends would not be forced then to leave their families. It was the easier because he had no scruples which opposed it. The idea was finally given up. A man ought to

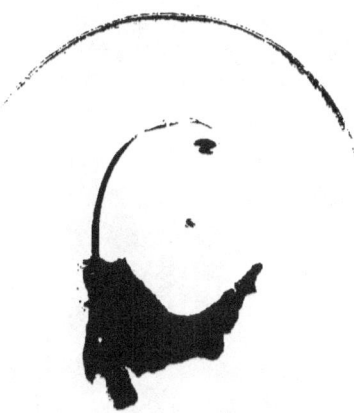

STRAW HAT WORN BY NAPOLEON AT ST. HELENA.

From the collection of Prince Victor Napoleon

live out his destiny, he said, and he decided that his should be fulfilled.

The most serious concern Napoleon felt in facing his new life was that he would have no occupation. He saw at once that St. Helena would not be an Elba. But he resolutely made occupations. He sought conversation, studied English, played games, began to dictate his memoirs. It is to this admir-

THE EIGHT EPOCHS OF THE LIFE OF NAPOLEON.

This original series of hats presented in different significant positions is from the pencil of Steuben, one of the most fertile painters of the First Empire, and symbolizes the eight principal epochs in Napoleon's career.

1. Vendémiaire.   4. Austerlitz.   7. Waterloo.
2. Consulate.   5. Wagram.   8. St. Helena.
3. Empire.   6. Moscow.

NAPOLEON AT ST. HELENA.

Dictating to young Las Cases the notes which were used in compiling the "Memorial."
After a steel engraving in the collection of the Cabinet des Estampes at Paris.

able determination to find something to do, that we owe his clear, logical commentaries, his essays on Cæsar, Turenne, and Frederick, his sketch of the Republic, and the vast amount of information in the journals of his devoted comrades, O'Meara, Las Cases, Montholon.

But no amount of forced occupation could hide the desolation of his position. The island of St. Helena is a mass of jagged, gloomy rocks; the nearest land is six hundred miles away. Isolated and inaccessible as it is, the English placed Napoleon on its most sombre and remote part—a place called Longwood, at the summit of a mountain, and to the windward. The houses at Longwood were damp and unhealthy. There was no shade. Water had to be carried some three miles.

The governor, Sir Hudson Lowe, was a tactless man, with a propensity for bullying those whom he ruled. He was haunted by the idea that Napoleon was trying to escape, and he adopted a policy which was more like that of a jailer than of an officer. In his first interview with the emperor he so antagonized him that Napoleon soon refused to see him. Napoleon's antipathy was almost superstitious. "I never saw such a horrid countenance," he told

O'Meara. " He sat on a chair opposite to my sofa, and on the little table between us there was a cup of coffee. His physiognomy made such an unfavorable impression upon me that I thought his evil eye had poisoned the coffee, and I ordered Marchand to throw it out of the window. I could not have swallowed it for the world."

Aggravated by Napoleon's refusal to see him, Sir Hudson Lowe became more annoying and petty in his regulations. All free communication between Longwood and the inhabitants of the island was cut off. The newspapers sent Napoleon were mutilated; certain books were refused; his letters were opened. A bust of his son brought to the island by a sailor was withheld for weeks. There was incessant haggling over the expenses of his establishment. His friends were subjected to constant annoyance. All news of Marie Louise and of his son was kept from him.

It is scarcely to be wondered at that Napoleon was often peevish and obstinate under this treatment, or that frequently, when he allowed himself to discuss the governor's policy with the members of his suite, his temper rose, as Montholon said, " to thirty-six degrees of fury." His situation was made more miserable by his ill-health. His promenades were so guarded by sentinels and restricted to such limits that he finally refused to take exercise, and after that his disease made rapid marches.

His fretfulness, his unreasonable determination to house himself, his childish resentment at Sir Hudson Lowe's conduct, have led to the idea that Napoleon spent his time at St. Helena in fuming and complaining. But if one will take into consideration the work that the fallen emperor did in his exile, he will have a quite different impression of this period of his life. He

SKETCHES OF NAPOLEON AT VARIOUS EPOCHS.

By Charlet.

NAPOLEON AT ST. HELENA.

By Delaroche.

lived at St. Helena from October, 1815, to May, 1821. In this period of five and a half years he wrote or dictated enough matter to fill the four good-sized volumes which complete the bulky correspondence published by the order of Napoleon III., and he furnished the great collection of conversations embodied in the memorials published by his companions.

This means a great amount of thinking and planning; for if one will go over these dictations and writings to see how they were made, he will see that they are not slovenly in arrangement or loose in style. On the contrary, they are concise, logical, and frequently vivid. They are full of errors, it is true, but that is due to the fact that Napoleon had not at hand any official documents for making history. He depended almost entirely on his memory. The books and maps he had, he used diligently, but his supply was limited and unsatisfactory.

It must be remembered, too, that this work was done under great physical difficulties. He was suffering keenly much of the time after he reached the island. Even for a well man, working under favorable circumstances, the literary output of Napoleon at St. Helena would be creditable. For one in his circumstances it was extraordinary. A look at it is the best possible refutation of the common notion that he spent his time at St. Helena fuming at Sir Hudson Lowe and "stewing himself in hot water," to use the expression of the governor.

DEATH IN MAY, 1821.

Before the end of 1820 it was certain that he could not live long. In December of that year the death of his sister Eliza was announced to him. "You see, Eliza has just shown me the way. Death, which had forgotten my family, has begun to strike it. My turn cannot be far off." Nor was it. On May 5, 1821, he died.

His preparations for death were methodical and complete. During the last fortnight of April all his strength was spent in dictating to Montholon his last wishes. He even dictated, ten days before the end, the note which he wished sent to Sir Hudson Lowe to announce his death. The articles he had in his possession at Longwood he had wrapped up and ticketed with the names of the persons to whom he wished to leave them. His will remem-

NAPOLEON'S LAST DAYS.

From a sculpture by Véla. This superb statue was exhibited in Paris at the Exhibition Universelle of 1867 (Italian section), and obtained the gold medal. It was purchased by the French Government, and is now at Versailles.

NAPOLEON AS HE LAY IN DEATH. ("NAPOLEON UT IN MORTE RECUMBIT.")

Dedicated, "with permission, to the Countess Bertrand, by her obliged and most obedient servant, William Rubidge. Taken at St Helena in presence of Countess Bertrand, Count Montholon, etc." Engraved by H. Meyer, London, after W. Rubidge, and published August, 1821.

bered numbers of those whom he had loved or who had served him. Even the Chinese laborers then employed about the place were remembered. "Do not let them be forgotten. Let them have a few score of napoleons."

The will included a final word on certain questions on which he felt posterity ought distinctly to understand his position. He died, he said, in the apostolical Roman religion. He declared that he had always been pleased with Marie Louise, whom he be-

NAPOLEON LYING DEAD.

"From the original drawing of Captain Crockatt, taken the morning after Napoleon's decease." Published July 18, 1821, in London.

sought to watch over his son. To this son, whose name recurs repeatedly in the will, he gave a motto—*All for the French people.* He died prematurely, he said, assassinated by the English oligarchy. The unfortunate results of the invasion of France he attributed to the treason of Marmont, Augereau, Talleyrand, and Lafayette. He defended the death of the Duc d'Enghien. "Under similar circumstance I should act in the same way." This will is sufficient evidence that he died as he had lived, courageously and proudly, and inspired by a profound conviction of the justice of his own cause. In 1822 the French courts declared the will void.

They buried him in a valley beside a spring he loved, and though no monument but a willow marked the spot, perhaps no other grave in history is so well known. Certainly the magnificent mausoleum which marks his present resting place in Paris has never touched the imagination and the heart as did the humble willow-shaded mound in St. Helena.

NAPOLEON'S CHARACTER.

The peace of the world was insured. Napoleon was dead. But though he was dead, the echo of his deeds was so loud in the ears of France and England that they tried every device to turn it into discord or to drown it by another and a newer sound. The ignoble attempt was never entirely successful, and the day will come when personal and partisan considerations will cease to influence judgments on this mighty man. For he was a mighty man. One may be convinced that the fundamental principles of his life were despotic ; that he used the noble ideas of personal liberty, of equality, and of fraternity, as a tyrant ; that the whole tendency of his civil and military system was to concentrate power in a single pair of hands, never to distribute it where it belonged, among the people ; one may feel that he frequently sacrificed personal dignity to a theatrical desire to impose on the crowd as a hero of classic proportions, a god from Olympus ;

DEATH MASK OF NAPOLEON, MADE BY DR. ANTOMMARCHI AT ST. HELENA, 1821.

Calamatta, 1834. Calamatta produced the mask from the cast taken by Dr. Antommarchi, the physician of Napoleon at St. Helena, in 1834, grouping around it portraits (chiefly from Ingres's drawings) of Madame Dudevant and others.

one may groan over the blood he spilt. But he cannot refuse to acknowledge that no man ever comprehended more clearly the splendid science of war; he cannot fail to bow to the genius which conceived and executed the Italian campaign, which fought the classic battles of Austerlitz, Jena, and Wagram. These deeds are great epics. They move in noble, measured lines, and stir us by their might and perfection. It is only a genius of the most magnificent order which could handle men and materials as Napoleon did.

He is even more imposing as a statesman. When one confronts the France of 1799, corrupt, crushed, hopeless, false to the great ideas she had wasted herself for, and watches Napoleon firmly and steadily bring order into this chaos, give the country work and bread, build up her broken walls and homes, put money into her pocket and restore her credit, bind up her wounds and call back her scattered children, set her again to painting pictures and reading books, to smiling and singing, he has a Napoleon greater than the warrior.

Nor were these civil deeds transient. France to-day is largely what Napoleon made her, and the most liberal institutions of continental Europe bear his impress. It is only a mind of noble proportions which can grasp the needs of a people, and a hand of mighty force which can supply them.

But he was greater as a man than as a warrior or statesman ; greater in that rare and subtile personal quality which made men love him. Men went down on their knees and wept at sight of him when he came home from Elba—rough men whose hearts were untrained, and who loved naturally and spontaneously the thing which was lovable. It was only selfish, warped, abnormal natures, which had been stifled by etiquette and diplomacy and self-interest, who abandoned him. Where nature lived in a heart, Napoleon's sway was absolute. It was not strange. He was in everything a natural man ; his imagination, his will, his intellect, his heart, were native, untrained. They appealed to unworldly men in all their rude, often brutal, strength and sweetness. If they awed them, they won them.

This native force of Napoleon explains, at least partially, his hold on men ; it explains, too, the contrasts of his character. Never was there a life lived so full of lights and shades, of majors and minors. It was

FUNERAL PROCESSION OF NAPOLEON.

Drawn by Captain Marryat. "As the procession proceeded from old Longwood along the edge of Rupert's Valley, the troops stood drawn up with arms reversed, and after it had passed, followed up in the rear."

a kaleidoscope, changing at every moment. Beside the most practical and commonplace qualities are the most idealistic. No man ever did more drudgery, ever followed details more slavishly ; yet who ever dared so divinely, ever played such hazardous games of chance ? No man ever planned more for his fellows, yet who ever broke so many hearts ? No man ever made practical realities of so many of liberty's dreams, yet it was by despotism that he gave liberal and beneficent laws. No man was more gentle, none more severe. Never was there a more chivalrous lover until he was disillusioned ; a more affectionate husband, even when faith had left him; yet no man ever trampled more rudely on womanly delicacy and reserve.

He was valorous as a god in danger, loved it, played with it ; yet he would turn pale at a broken mirror, cross himself if he stumbled, fancy the coffee poisoned at which an enemy had looked.

He was the greatest genius of his time, perhaps of all time, yet he lacked the crown of greatness—that high wisdom born of reflection and introspection which knows its own powers and limitations, and never abuses them ; that fine sense of proportion which holds the rights of others in the same solemn reverence which it demands for its own.

CHAPTER XXIII.

THE SECOND FUNERAL OF NAPOLEON.—REMOVAL OF NAPOLEON'S REMAINS FROM ST. HELENA TO THE BANKS OF THE SEINE IN 1840.

It is my wish that my ashes may repose on the banks of the Seine, in the midst of the French people, whom I have loved so well.—TESTAMENT OF NAPOLEON, 2d Clause.

He wants not this ; but France shall feel the want
Of this last consolation, though so scant ;
Her honor, fame, and faith demand his bones,
To rear above a pyramid of thrones ;
Or carried onward, in the battle's van,
To form, like Guesclin's dust, her talisman.
But be it as it is, the time may come,
His name shall beat the alarm like Ziska's drum.
—BYRON, in *The Age of Bronze.*

ON May 12, 1840, Louis Philippe being king of the French people, the Chamber of Deputies was busy with a discussion on sugar tariffs. It had been dragging somewhat, and the members were showing signs of restlessness. Suddenly the Count de Rémusat, then Minister of the Interior, appeared, and asked a hearing for a communication from the government.

"Gentlemen," he said, "the king has ordered his Royal Highness Monseigneur the Prince de Joinville* to go with his frigate to the island of St. Helena, there to collect the remains of the Emperor Napoleon."

A tremor ran over the House. The announcement was utterly unexpected. Napoleon to come back ! The body seemed electrified, and the voice of the minister was drowned for a moment in applause. When he went on, it was to say :

"We have come to ask for an appropri-

* The Prince de Joinville was the third son of Louis Philippe.

ation which shall enable us to receive the remains in a fitting manner, and to raise an enduring tomb to Napoleon."

"*Très bien ! Très bien !*" cried the House.

"The government, anxious to discharge a great national duty, asked England for the precious treasure which fortune had put into her hands.

"The thought of France was welcomed as soon as expressed. Listen to the reply of our magnanimous ally:

"'The government of her Majesty hopes that the promptness of her response will be considered in France as a proof of her desire to efface the last traces of those national animosities which armed France and England against each other in the life of the emperor. The government of her Majesty dares to hope that if such sentiments still exist in certain quarters, they will be buried in the tomb where the remains of Napoleon are to be deposited.'"

The reading of this generous and dignified communication caused a profound sensation, and cries of "*Bravo ! bravo !*" re-

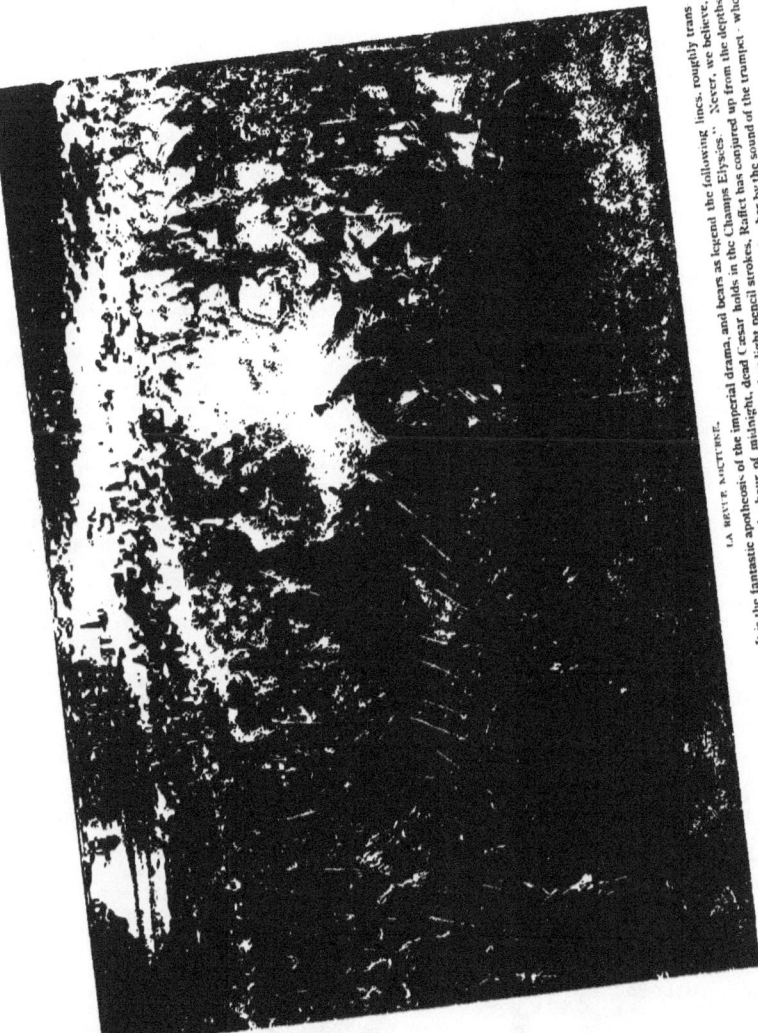

LA BELLE NUICTURE.

This is considered one of Raffet's finest works. It is the fantastic apotheosis of the imperial drama, and bears as legend the following lines, roughly trans-lated from the German poet Seidlitz: "It is the grand review which, at the hour of midnight, dead Cæsar holds in the Champs Elysées. Never, we believe, has greater perfection than in this work, by a few light pencil strokes, Raffet has conjured up from the depths has bibliographic art manifested itself with a whole army of horsemen—spectres aroused for one night from eternal slumber by the sound of the trumpet - who of night, faintly illumined by a clouded moon, a whole army of horsemen, a whole army of horsemen, who pass by like the whirlwind, and salute with their swords Cæsar on his white charger.—A. D.

echoed through the hall. The minister, so well received, grew eloquent.

" England is right, gentlemen ; the noble way in which restitution has been made will knit the bonds which unite us. It will wipe out all traces of a sorrowful past. The time has come when the two nations should remember only their glory. The frigate freighted with the mortal remains of Napoleon will return to the mouth of the Seine. They will be placed in the Invalides. A solemn celebration and grand religious and military ceremonies will consecrate the tomb which must guard them forever.

" It is important, gentlemen, that this august sepulchre should not remain exposed in a public place, in the midst of a noisy and inappreciative populace. It should be in a silent and sacred spot, where all those who honor glory and genius, grandeur and misfortune, can visit it and meditate.

" He was emperor and king. He was the legitimate sovereign of our country. He is entitled to burial at Saint-Denis. But the ordinary royal sepulchre is not enough for Napoleon. He should reign and command forever in the spot where the country's soldiers repose, and where those who are called to defend it will seek their inspiration. His sword will be placed on his tomb.

" Art will raise beneath the dome of the temple consecrated to the god of battles, a tomb worthy, if that be possible, of the name which shall be engraved upon it. This monument must have a simple beauty, grand outlines, and that appearance of eternal strength which defies the action of time. Napoleon must have a monument lasting as his memory, . . .

" Hereafter France, and France alone, will possess all that remains of Napoleon. His tomb, like his fame, will belong to no one but his country. The monarchy of 1830 is the only and the legitimate heir of the past of which France is so proud. It is the duty of this monarchy, which was the first to rally all the forces and to conciliate all the aspirations of the French Revolution, fearlessly to raise and honor the statue and the tomb of the popular hero. There is one thing, one only, which does not fear comparison with glory—that is liberty."

Throughout this speech, every word of which was an astonishment to the Chamber, sincere and deep emotion prevailed. At intervals enthusiastic applause burst forth. For a moment all party distinctions were forgotten. The whole House was under the sway of that strange and powerful emotion which Napoleon, as no other leader who ever lived, was able to inspire.

When the minister followed his speech by the draft of a law for a special credit of one million francs, a member, beside himself with excitement, moved that rules be laid aside and the law voted without the legal preliminaries. The president refused to put so irregular a motion, but the House would not be quiet. The deputies left their places, formed in groups in the hemicycle, surrounded the minister, congratulating him with fervor. They walked up and down, ges-

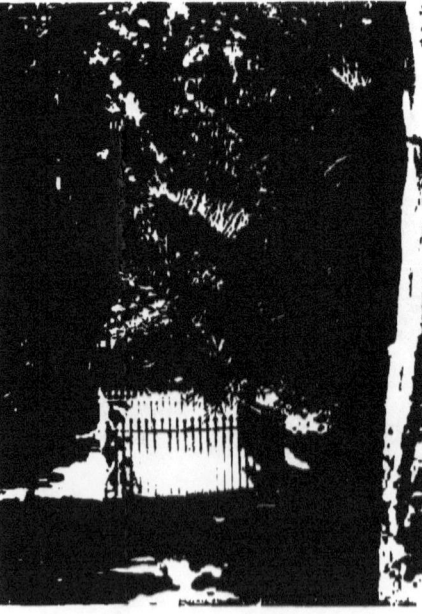

NAPOLEON'S TOMB AT ST. HELENA.

From a recent photograph.

RECEIVING NAPOLEON'S BODY ON THE "BELLE POULE," AT ST. HELENA, OCTOBER 15, 1840.

ticulating and shouting. It was fully half
an hour before the president was able to
bring them to order, and then they were in
anything but a working mood.

"The president must close the session,"
cried an agitated member; "the law which
has just been proposed has caused too
great emotion for us to return now to discussing sugar."

But the president replied very properly,
and a little sententiously, that the Chamber owed its time to the country's business,
and that it must give it. And, in spite of
their excitement, the members had to go
back to their sugar.

THE AUTHOR OF THE "GRANDE PENSÉE."

But how had it come about that the
French government had dared burst upon
the country with so astounding a communication?

There were many explanations offered.
A curious story which went abroad took
the credit from the king and gave it to
O'Connell, the Irish agitator.

As the story went, O'Connell had warned
Lord Palmerston that he proposed to pre-
sent a bill in the Commons for returning
Napoleon's remains to France.

"Take care," said Lord Palmerston.
"Instead of pleasing the French government, you may embarrass it seriously."

"That is not the question," answered
O'Connell. "The question for me is what
I ought to do. Now, my duty is to propose
to the Commons to return the emperor's
bones. England's duty is to welcome the
motion. I shall make my propositions,
then, without disturbing myself about
whom it will flatter or wound."

"So be it," said Lord Palmerston.
"Only give me fifteen days."

"Very well," answered O'Connell.

Immediately Lord Palmerston wrote to
Monsieur Thiers, then at the head of the
French Ministry, that he was about to be
forced to tell the country that England had
never refused to return the remains of Napoleon to France, because France had never
asked that they be returned. As the story
goes, Monsieur Thiers advised Louis Philippe to forestall O'Connell, and thus it
came about that Napoleon's remains were
returned to France.

The *grande pensée*, as the idea was immediately called, seems, however, to have
originated with Monsieur Thiers, who saw
in it a means of reawakening interest in
Louis Philippe. He believed that the very
audacity of the act would create admiration

and applause. Then, too, it was in harmony with the claim of the *régime*; that
is, that the government of 1830 united all
that was best in all the past governments of
France, and so was stronger than any one
of them. The mania of both king and
minister for collecting and restoring made
them think favorably of the idea. Already
Louis Philippe had inaugurated galleries
at Versailles, and hung them with miles of
canvas, celebrating the victories of all his
predecessors. In the gallery of portraits
he had placed Marie Antoinette and Louis
XVI. beside Madame Roland, Charlotte
Corday, Robespierre, and Napoleon and
his marshals.

He had already replaced the statue
of Napoleon on the top of the Column
Vendôme. He had restored cathedrals,
churches, and *châteaux*, put up statues
and monuments, and all this he had done
with studied indifference to the politics of
the individuals honored.

Yet while so many little important personages were being exalted, the remains
of the greatest leader France had ever
known, were lying in a far-away island.
Louis Philippe felt that no monument he
could build to the heroes of the past would
equal restoring Napoleon's remains.

The matter was simpler, because it was
almost certain that England would not
block the path. The *entente cordiale*, whose
base had been laid by Talleyrand nearly
ten years earlier, had become a compara-
tively solid peace, and either nation was
willing to go out of the way, if necessary,
to do the other a neighborly kindness.
France was so full of good will that she
was even willing to ask a favor. Her confidence was well placed. Two days after
Guizot, then the French minister to England, had explained the project to Lord
Palmerston, and made his request, he had
his reply.

The remains of the "emperor" were at
the disposition of the French. Of the "emperor," notice! After twenty-five years
England recalled the act of her ministers
in 1815, and recognized that France made
Napoleon emperor as well as general.

EFFECT ON THE COUNTRY.

The announcement that Napoleon's remains were to be brought back, produced
the same effect upon the country at large
that it had upon the Chamber—a moment
of acute emotion, of all-forgetting enthusiasm. But in the Chamber and the
country the feeling was short-lived. The

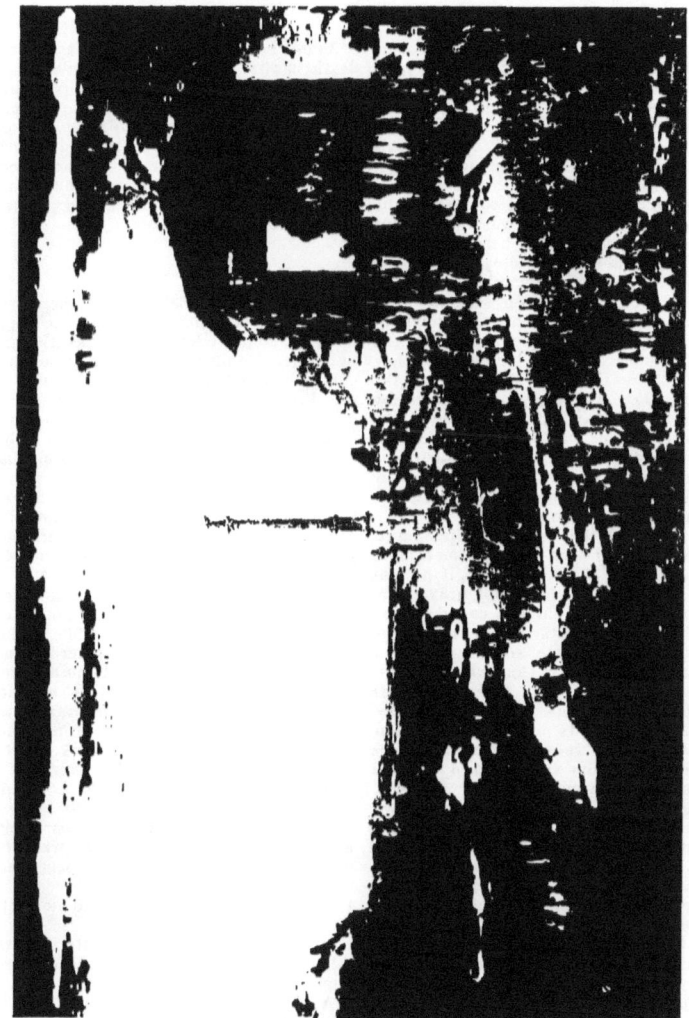

TRANSFER OF NAPOLEON'S BODY FROM THE VESSEL TO THE FUNERAL CAR AT CHERBOURG, DECEMBER 15, 1840.

political aspects of the bold movement were too conspicuous. A chorus of criticisms and forebodings arose. It was more of Monsieur Thiers' clap-trap, said those opposed to the English policy of the government. What particularly angered this party, was the words "magnanimous ally" in the minister's address.

The Bonapartes feigned to despise the proposed ceremony. It was insufficient for the greatness of their hero. One million francs could not possibly produce the display the object demanded. Another point of theirs was more serious. The emperor was the legitimate sovereign of the country, they said, quoting from the minister's speech to the Chamber, and they added : "His title was founded on the *senatus consultum* of the year 12, which, by an equal number of suffrages, secured the succession to his brother Joseph. It was then unquestionably Joseph Bonaparte who was proclaimed emperor of the French by the Minister of the Interior, and amid the applause of the deputies."

Scoffers said that Louis Philippe must have discovered that his soft mantle of popularity was about worn out, if he was going to make one of the old gray redingote of a man whom he had called a monster. The Legitimists denied that Napoleon was a legitimate sovereign with a right to sleep at Saint-Denis like a Bourbon or a Valois. The Orleanists were wounded by the hopes they saw inspired in the Bonapartists by this declaration. The Republicans resented the honor done to the man whom they held up as the greatest of all despots.

There was a conviction among many that the restoration was premature, and probably would bring on the country an agitation which would endanger the stability of the throne. It was tempting the Bonaparte pretensions certainly, and perhaps arousing a tremendous popular sentiment to support them.

While the press and government, the clubs and *cafés*, discussed the political side of the question, the populace quietly revived the Napoleon legend. Within two days after the government had announced its intentions, commerce had begun to take advantage of the financial possibilities in the approaching ceremony. New editions of the "Lives" of Napoleon which Vernet and Raffet had illustrated, were advertised. Dumas' "Life" and Thiers' "Consulate and Empire" were announced. Memoirs of the period, like those of the Duchesse d'Abrantès and of Marmont, were revived.

As on the announcement of Napoleon's death in 1821, there was an inundation of pamphlets in verse and prose ; of portraits and war compositions, lithographs, engravings, and wood-cuts ; of thousands of little objects such as the French know so well how to make. The shops and street carts were heaped with every conceivable article *à la Napoléon.* The legend grew as the people gazed.

TO ST. HELENA AND BACK.

On July 7th the "Belle Poule," the vessel which was to conduct the Prince de Joinville, the commander of the expedition, to St. Helena, sailed from Toulon accompanied by the "Favorite." In the suite of the Prince were several old friends of Napoleon : the Baron las Cases, General Gourgaud, Count Bertrand, and four of his former servants. All of these persons had been with him at St. Helena.

The Prince de Joinville had not received his orders to go on the expedition with great pleasure. Two of his brothers had just been sent to Africa to fight, and he envied them their opportunities for adventures and glory ; and, besides, he was sick of a most plebeian complaint, the measles. "One day as I lay in high fever," he says in his "Memoirs," " I saw my father appear, followed by Monsieur de Rémusat, then Minister of the Interior. This unusual visit filled me with astonishment, and my surprise increased when my father said, 'Joinville, you are to go out to St. Helena and bring back Napoleon's coffin.' If I had not been in bed already I should have fallen down flat, and at first blush I felt no wise flattered when I compared the warlike campaign my brothers were on with the undertaker's job I was being sent to perform in the other hemisphere. But I served my country, and I had no right to discuss my orders."

If the young prince was privately a little ashamed of his task, publicly he adapted himself admirably to the occasion.

A voyage of sixty-six days brought the "Belle Poule," on October 8th, to St. Helena, where she was welcomed by the English with every honor. Indeed, throughout the affair the attitude of the English was dignified and generous. They showed plainly their desire to satisfy and flatter the pride and sentiment of the French.

It had been decided that the exhumation of the body and its transfer to the French should take place on the twenty-fifth anniversary of the arrival of Napoleon at the

THE FUNERAL PROCESSION IN PARIS. FUNERAL CAR PASSING UNDER THE ARC DE TRIOMPHE.

island. The disinterment was begun at mid-night on October 15th, the English conduct-ing the work, and a number of the French, including those of the party who had been with Napoleon at his death, being present. The work was one of extraordinary diffi-culty, for the same remarkable precautions against escape were taken in Napoleon's death as had been in his life.

The grave in the Valley of Napoleon, as the place had come to be called, was sur-rounded by an iron railing set in a heavy stone curb. Over the grave was a cover-ing of six-inch stone which admitted to a vault eleven feet deep, eight feet long, and four feet eight inches broad. The vault was apparently filled with earth, but digging down some seven feet a layer of Roman cement was found ; this broken, laid bare a layer of rough-hewn stone ten inches thick, and fastened together by iron clamps. It took four and one-half hours to remove this layer. The stone up, the slab forming the lid of the interior sarcophagus was ex-posed, enclosed in a border of Roman cement strongly attached to the walls of the vault. So stoutly had all these various coverings been sealed with cement and bound by iron bands, that it took the large party of laborers ten hours to reach the coffin.

As soon as exposed the coffin was puri-fied, sprinkled with holy water, consecrated by a *De Profundis*, and then raised with the greatest care, and carried into a tent which had been prepared for it. After the re-ligious ceremonies, the inner coffins were opened. "The outermost coffin was slightly injured," says an eye-witness; "then came one of lead, which was in good condition, and enclosed two others—one of tin and one of wood. The last coffin was lined inside with white satin, which, having be-come detached by the effect of time, had fallen upon the body and enveloped it like a winding-sheet, and had become slightly attached to it.

" It is difficult to describe with what anx-iety and emotion those who were present waited for the moment which was to expose to them all that was left of the Emperor Napoleon. Notwithstanding the singular state of preservation of the tomb and cof-fins, we could scarcely hope to find any-thing but some misshapen remains of the least perishable part of the costume to evi-dence the identity of the body. But when Dr. Guillard raised the sheet of satin, an indescribable feeling of surprise and affec-tion was expressed by the spectators, many of whom burst into tears. The emperor

himself was before their eyes ! The feat-ures of the face, though changed, were per-fectly recognizable ; the hands extremely beautiful ; his well-known costume had suf-fered but little, and the colors were easily distinguished. The attitude itself was full of ease, and but for the fragments of satin lining which covered, as with fine gauze, several parts of the uniform, we might have believed we still saw Napoleon lying on his bed of state."

A solemn procession was now formed, and the coffin borne over the rugged hills of St. Helena to the quay. "We were all deeply impressed," says the Prince de Join-ville, "when the coffin was seen coming slowly down the mountain side to the fir-ing of cannon, escorted by British infantry with arms reversed, the band playing, to the dull rolling accompaniment of the drums, that splendid funeral march which English people call the *Dead March in Saul.*"

At the head of the quay, the Prince de Joinville, attended by the officers of the French vessels, was waiting to receive the remains of the emperor. In the midst of the most solemn military funeral rites the French embarked with their precious charge. "The scene at that moment was very fine," continues the prince. "A mag-nificent sunset had been succeeded by a twilight of the deepest calm. The British authorities and the troops stood motionless on the beach, while our ship's guns fired a royal salute. I stood in the stern of my long-boat, over which floated a magnificent tricolor flag, worked by the ladies of St. Helena. Beside me were the generals and superior officers. The pick of my topmen, all in white, with crape on their arms, and bareheaded like ourselves, rowed the boat in silence, and with the most admirable precision. We advanced with majestic slowness, escorted by the boats bearing the staff. It was very touching, and a deep national sentiment seemed to hover over the whole scene."

But no sooner did the coffin reach the French cutter than mourning was changed to triumph. Flags were unfurled, masts squared, drums set a-beating, and *salvos* poured from forts and vessels. The em-peror had come back to his own !

Three days later the "Belle Poule" was *en route* for France. One incident alone marked her return. A passing vessel brought the news that war had been de-clared between France and England. The Prince de Joinville was only twenty-two, a hot-headed youth, and the news of war

THE FUNERAL PROCESSION IN PARIS. FUNERAL CAR PASSING DOWN THE CHAMPS ELYSÉES.

immediately convinced him that England had her fleet out watching for him, ready to carry off Napoleon again. He rose to the height of his fears. The elegant furnishings of the saloons of his vessel were torn out and thrown overboard to make room to put in batteries; the men were made ready for fighting, and everybody on board was compelled to take an oath to sink the vessel before allowing the remains to be taken. This done, the "Belle Poule" went her way peacefully to Cherbourg, where she arrived on November 30th, forty-three days after leaving St. Helena.

The town of Cherbourg owes much to Napoleon—her splendid harbors, and great tracts of land rescued from the sea—and she honored the return of his remains with every pomp. Even the poor of the town were made to rejoice by lavish gifts in the emperor's honor; and one of the chief squares—one he had redeemed from the sea—became the Place Napoleon.

The vessels lay eight days at Cherbourg, for the arrival had been a fortnight earlier than was anticipated, and nothing was ready for the celebration in Paris; but the time was none too long for the thousands who flocked in interminable processions to the vessels. When the vessels left for Havre, Cherbourg was so excited that she did what must have seemed to the nervous inhabitants an extravagance, even in Napoleon's honor. She fired a *thousand* guns!

FROM CHERBOURG TO PARIS.

The passage of the flotilla from Cherbourg to Paris took seven days. At almost every town and hamlet elaborate demonstrations were made. At Havre and Rouen they were especially magnificent.

A striking feature of the river *cortége* was the ceremonies at the various bridges under which the vessels passed. The most elaborate of these was at Rouen, where the central arch of the suspension bridge had been formed into an immense arch of triumph. The decorations were the exclusive work of wounded legionary officers and soldiers of the Empire. When the vessel bearing the coffin passed under, the veterans showered down upon it wreaths of flowers and branches of laurel.

These elaborate and grandiose ceremonies were not, however, the really touching feature of the passage. The hill-sides and river-banks were crowded with people from all the surrounding country, who sometimes even pressed into the river in order better to see the vessels. Those on the flotilla saw aged peasants firing salutes with ancient muskets, old men kneeling with uncovered heads on the sod, and others, their heads in their hands weeping —these men were veterans of the Empire paying homage to the passage of their hero.

It was on the afternoon of December 14th, just as the sun was setting radiantly behind Mt. Valerian, that the flotilla reached Courbevoie, a few miles from Paris, where Napoleon's body was first to touch French soil. The bridge at Courbevoie, the islands of Neuilly, the hills which rise from the Seine, were crowded, far as the eye could reach, with a throng drawn from the entire country around.

The flotilla as it approached was a brilliant sight. At the head was the "Dorade," a cross at her prow, and, behind, the coffin. It was dressed in purple velvet, surrounded by flags and garlands of oak and cypress, surmounted by a canopy of black velvet ornamented with silver and masses of floating black plumes. Between cross and coffin stood the Prince de Joinville in full uniform, and behind him Generals Bertrand and Gourgaud and the Abbé Coquereau, almoner of the expedition. The vessels following the "Dorade" bore the crews of the "Belle Poule" and the "Favorite" and the military bands. A magnificent funeral boat, on whose deck there was a temple of bronzed wood, hung with splendid draperies of purple and gold, brought up the official procession. Behind followed numberless craft of all descriptions. Majestic funeral marches and *salvos* of artillery accompanied the advance.

At Courbevoie the flotilla anchored. Notwithstanding the intense cold, thousands of people camped all night on the hill-sides and shores, their bivouac fires illuminating the landscape.

DECEMBER 15, 1840.

Only those who have seen Paris on the day of a great *fête* or ceremony can picture to themselves the 15th of December, 1840. The day was intensely cold, eight degrees below the freezing point, but at five o'clock in the morning, when the drums began beating, and the guns booming, the populace poured forth, taking up their positions along the line of the expected procession. This line was fully three miles in length,

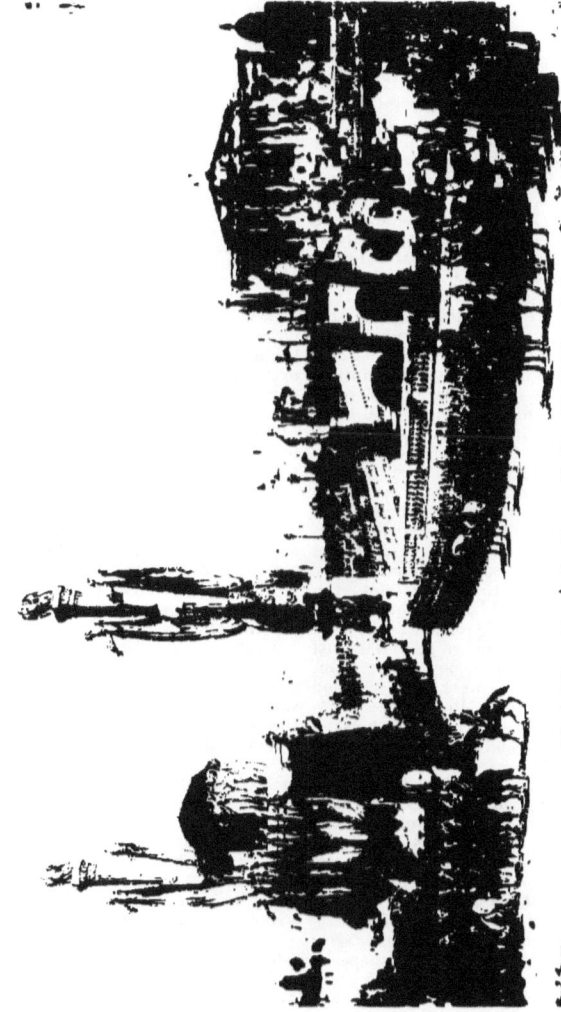

THE FUNERAL PROCESSION IN PARIS. FUNERAL CAR CROSSING THE PONT DE LA CONCORDE.

and ran from Courbevoie to the Arc de Triomphe by way of Neuilly, thence down the Champs Elysées, across the Place and Bridge de la Concorde, and along the *quai* to the Esplanade des Invalides. From one end to the other it was packed on either side a hundred deep, before nine o'clock. The journals of the day compute the number of visitors expected in Paris as about half a million. Inside and outside of the Hôtel des Invalides alone, thirty-six thousand places were given to the Minister of the Interior, and that did not cover *one-tenth* of the requests he received. It is certain that nearly a million persons saw the entry of Napoleon's remains. The people hung from the trees, crowded the roofs, stood on ladders of every description, filled the windows, and literally swarmed over the walks and grass plots. A brisk business went on in elevated positions. A ladder rung cost five francs ($1.00); the man who had a cart across which he had laid boards, rented standing-room at from five to ten francs. As for windows and balconies—they sold for fabulous prices, in spite of the fact that the placard *fenêtres et balcons à louer* appeared in almost every house from Neuilly to the Invalides, even in many a magnificent hotel of the Champs Elysées. Fifty francs ($10.00) was the price of the meanest window ; a good one cost one hundred francs ($20.00); three thousand francs ($600.00) were paid for good balconies. One speculator rented a vacant house for the day for five thousand francs ($1,000.00), and made money on his investment.

The crowd made every preparation to keep warm ; some of them carried foot-stoves filled with live coals, others little hand-warmers. At intervals along the procession great masses of the spectators danced to keep up their circulation. Venders of all sorts of articles did a thriving business. Every article was, of course, Napoleonized ; one even bought *gauffrettes* and *Madeleines* cut out in the shape of Napoleons. There were badges of every form—imperial eagles, bees, crowns, even the *petit chapeau*. Many pamphlets in prose and verse had a great sale, especially those of Casimir Delavigne, Victor Hugo, and Barthélemy ; though all these stately odes were far outstripped by one song, thousands upon thousands of copies of which were sold. It ran :

" Premier capitaine du monde
Depuis le siége de Toulon,
Tant sur la terre que sur l'onde
Tout redoutait Napoleon.

Du Nil au nord de la Tamise !
Devant lui l'ennemi fuyait,
Avant de combattre, il tremblait
Voyant sa redingote grise." *

The *cortége* which had brought this crowd together was magnificent in the extreme. A brilliant military display formed the first portion : *gendarmerie*, municipal guards, officers, infantry, cavalry, artillery, cadets from the important schools, national guards. But this had little effect on the crowd. The genuine interest began when Marengo, Napoleon's famous battle-horse, appeared—it was not Marengo, but it looked like him, which for spectacular purposes was just as well ; and the saddle and bridle were genuine—the defile now became exciting. The commission of St. Helena appeared in carriages, then the Marshals of France, the Prince de Joinville, the crews of the vessels which had been to St. Helena, finally the funeral car, a magnificent creation over thirty feet high, its design and ornaments symbolic. Sixteen black horses in splendid trappings drew the car, whose funeral pall was held by a marshal and an admiral of France, by the Duc de Reggio and General Bertrand.

The passing of the car was everywhere greeted with sincere emotion, profound reverence.

Even the opposition recognized the genuineness of the feeling ; many of them owned to sharing it for one moment of self-forgetfulness, and they began to ask themselves, as Lamartine had asked the Chamber six months before, what they had been thinking to allow the French heart and imagination to be so fired ? Even cynical Englishmen who looked on with stern or contemptuous countenances, said to themselves meditatively that night, as they sat by their fire resting, " Something good must have been in this man, something loving and kindly, that has kept his name so cherished in the popular memory and gained him such lasting reverence and affection."

Following the car came those who had been intimately associated with the emperor in his life—his aides-de-camp and civil and military officers. Many of them had been with him in famous battles ; some were at Fontainebleau in 1814, others at Malmaison in 1815. The veterans of the

---

* The greatest captain, all agree,
Since the siege of Toulon ;
On the earth as on the sea,
All yielded to Napoleon.
His enemies fled, full of dismay,
Beyond the Thames from off the Nile,
Before the fight, trembling the while
If they but saw his redingote gray.

THE FUNERAL PROCESSION IN PARIS. TRANSFERRING THE COFFIN INTO THE COACH OF THE HÔTEL DES INVALIDES.

Imperial Guard followed ; behind them a deputation from Ajaccio.

From Courbevoie to the Hôtel des Invalides, one walked through a hedge of elaborate decorations—of bees, eagles, crowns, N's; of bucklers, banners, and wreaths bearing the names of famous victories ; of urns blazing with incense ; of rostral columns ; masts bearing trophies of arms and clusters of flags ; flaming tripods ; allegorical statues ; triumphal arches ; great banks of seats draped in imperial purple and packed with spectators, and phalanges of soldiers.

On the top of the Arc de Triomphe was an imposing apotheosis of Napoleon. Each side of the Pont de la Concorde was adorned with huge statues. On the Esplanade des Invalides the car passed between an avenue of thirty-two statues of great French kings, heroes, and heroines—Charles Martel, Charlemagne, Clovis, Bayard, Jean d'Arc, Latour d'Auvergne, Ney. The chivalry and valor of France welcomed Napoleon home. Oddly enough, this hedge of statues ended in one of Napoleon himself ; the incongruity of the arrangement struck even the *gamins.* "Tiens," cried one urchin, " voilà comme l'empereur fait la queue à lui-même." (" Hello, see there how the emperor brings up his own procession.")

The procession passed quietly from one end to the other of the route, to the great relief of the authorities. Difficulty was anticipated from several sources : from the Anglophobes, the Revolutionists, the Legitimists, the Bonapartists, and the great mass of dissatisfied, who, no matter what form of rule they are under, are always against the government. The greatest fear seems to have been on the part of the English. Thackeray, who was in town at the time, gives an amusing picture of his own nervousness on the morning of the 15th.

" Did the French nation, or did they not, intend to offer up some of us English over the imperial grave ? And were the games to be concluded by a massacre ? It was said in the newspapers that Lord Granville had despatched circulars to all the English residents in Paris, begging them to keep their homes. The French journals announced this news, and warned us charitably of the fate intended for us. Had Lord Granville written ? Certainly not to me. Or had he written to all *except me?* And was I *the victim*—the doomed one ?—to be seized directly I showed my face in the Champs Elysées, and torn in pieces by French patriotism to the frantic chorus of the Marseillaise? Depend on it, Madame, that high and low in this city on Tuesday were not altogether at their ease, and that the bravest felt no small tremor. And be sure of this, that as his Majesty Louis Philippe took his nightcap off his royal head

that morning, he prayed heartily that he might at night put it on in safety."

Fortunately Thackeray's courage conquered, and so we have the entertaining " Second Funeral of Napoleon," by " Michael Angelo Titmarsh."

In spite of all forebodings, the hostile displays were nothing more than occasional cries of "*A bas les Anglais,*" a few attempts to promenade the tricolor flag and drown *Le Premier Capitaine du Monde* by the Marseillaise, and a strong indignation when it was learned that the representatives of the allies had refused to be present at the final ceremony.

Most of the observers of the funeral attributed the good order of the crowd to the cold. A correspondent of the "National Intelligence " of that date says :

" If this business had fallen in the month of June or July, with all its excitements, spontaneous and elaborate, I should have deemed a sanguinary struggle between the government and the mob certain or highly probable. The present military array might answer for an approaching army of Cossacks. Forty or fifty thousand troops remain in the barracks within and camps without, besides the regular soldiery and National Guards in the field, ready to act against the domestic enemy.

" *Providentially* the cold increased to the utmost keenness ; the genial currents of the insurrectionary and revolutionary soul were frozen."

The climax of the pageant was the temple of the Invalides. The spacious church was draped in the most magnificent and lavish fashion, and adorned with a perfect bewilderment of imperial emblems. The light was shut out by hangings of violet velvet ; tripods blazing with colored flames, and thousands upon thousands of waxen candles in brilliant candelabra lighted the temple. Under the dome, in the place of the altar, stood the catafalque which was to receive the coffin.

From early in the morning the galleries, choir, and tribunes of the Invalides were packed by a distinguished company. There were the Chambers of Deputies and Lords —neither of which had been represented in the *cortège*—the judicial and educational bodies, the officers of army and navy, the ambassadors and representatives of foreign governments, the king, and the court.

But none of these dignitaries were of more than passing interest that day. The centre of attention, until the coffin entered, was the few old soldiers of the Empire to be seen in the company ; most prominent of these was Marshal Moncey, the decrepit governor of the Invalides.

THE FUNERAL MASS IN THE CHURCH OF THE HÔTEL DES INVALIDES. THE CATAFALQUE ON WHICH THE COFFIN RESTS IS SEEN IN THE DISTANCE.

It was two o'clock in the afternoon when the Archbishop of Paris, preceded by a splendid cross-bearer, and followed by sixteen incense boys and long rows of white-clad priests, left the church to meet the procession. They returned soon. Following them were the Prince de Joinville and a select few from the grand *cortège* without; in their midst, Napoleon's coffin.

As it passed, the great assemblage was swayed by an extraordinary emotion. There is no one of those who have described the day who does not speak of the sudden, intense agitation which thrilled the company, whether he refers to it half-

NAPOLEON'S TOMB IN THE CHURCH OF THE HÔTEL DES INVALIDES AS IT APPEARS AT THE PRESENT DAY.

humorously as Thackeray, who told how "everybody's heart was thumping as hard as possible," or cries with Victor Hugo :

"Sire: En ce moment-là, vouz aurez pour royaume,
　Tous les fronts, tous les cœurs qui battront sous
　　le ciel,
　Les nations feront asseoir votre fantôme,
　　Au trone universel." *

* Sire, in that moment your kingdom will be on every brow, in every heart which beats under heaven. The nations will seat your phantom on a universal throne.

The king descended from his throne and advanced to meet the *cortège*. "Sire," said the Prince de Joinville, "I present to you the body of Napoleon, which, in accordance with your commands, I have brought back to France."

"I receive it in the name of France," replied Louis Philippe.

Such at least is what the "Moniteur" affirms was said, but the "Moniteur" is an official journal whose business is, not to tell what really happened, but what would have happened if the government had had its way. The Prince de Joinville gives a different version: "The king received the body at the entrance to the nave, and there rather a comical scene took place. It appears that a little speech which I was to have delivered when I met my father, and also the answer he was to give me, had been drawn up in council, only the authorities had omitted to inform me concerning it. So when I arrived I simply saluted with my sword, and then stood aside. I saw, indeed, that this silent salute, followed by retreat, had thrown something out; but my father, after a moment's hesitation, improvised some appropriate sentence, and the matter was arranged in the 'Moniteur.'"

Beside the king stood an officer, bearing a cushion; on it lay the sword of Austerlitz. Marshal Soult handed it to the king, who, turning to Bertrand, said:

"General, I commission you to place the emperor's glorious sword on the bier."

And Bertrand, trembling with emotion, laid the sword reverently on his idol's coffin. The great company watched the scene in deepest silence. The only sound which broke the stillness was the half-stifled sobs of the gray-haired soldiers of the Invalides, who stood in places of honor near the catafalque.

The king and the procession returned to their places, and then followed a majestic funeral mass. The *Requiem* of Mozart, as rendered that day by all the great singers of Paris, is one of the historic musical performances of France. The archbishop then sprinkled the coffin with holy water, the king taking the brush from him for the same sacred duty.

The funeral was over. Napoleon lay at last "on the banks of the Seine, among the people whom he had so loved."

AFTER THE FUNERAL.

For eight days after the ceremony the church remained open to the public, and in spite of the terrible cold thousands stood from morning until night waiting patiently their turn to enter. After hours of waiting, they frequently were sent away, only to come back earlier the next day. In this company were numbers of veterans of the imperial army who had made the journey to Paris from distant parts of the kingdom. In the delegation from Belgium were many who had walked part of the way, not being able to pay full coach fare.

Banquets and dinners followed the funeral. At one of these, a "sacred toast to the immortal memory" was drunk *kneeling*. In a dozen theatres of Paris the translation of the remains was dramatized. At the Porte Saint-Martin, the actor who took the part of Sir Hudson Lowe had a season of terror, he being in constant danger of violence from the wrought-up audience.

The advertising columns of the newspapers of the day blazed for weeks with announcements of Napoleonized articles; the holiday gifts prepared for the booths of the boulevards and squares, and for the magnificent shops of the Palais Royal and the fashionable streets, whatever their nature—to eat, to wear, to look at—were made up as memorials. Paris seemed to be Napoleon-mad.

In the February following the funeral, the coffin of Napoleon was transferred from the catafalque in the centre of the church to a *chapelle ardente* in the basement at one side. The chapel was richly draped in silk and gold, and hung with trophies. On the coffin lay the imperial crown, the emperor's sword, and the hat which he had worn at Eylau, and which he had given to Gros when he ordered the battle of Eylau painted. Over the coffin waved the flags taken at Austerlitz.

Here Napoleon's body lay until the mausoleum was finished. This magnificent structure was designed by Visconti, the eminent architect, who had also planned the entire decorations of the 15th of December. Visconti utterly ignored the appropriations in executing the monument, ordering what he wanted, regardless of its cost. For the marble from which Pradier made the twelve colossal figures around the tomb, he sent to Carrara; the porphyry which was used to inclose the coffin, he obtained in Finland.

In this magnificent sepulchre Napoleon still sleeps. Duroc and Bertrand lie on either side of the entrance to the chamber, guarding him in death as in life; and to the right and left of the entrance to the church are the tombs of his brothers Jerome and Joseph. On the stones about him are inscribed the names he made glorious; over him are draped scores of trophies; attending him are the veterans of the Invalides.

" Qu'il dorme en paix sous cette voûte !
C'est un casque bien fait, sans doute,
Pour cette tête de géant." *

* "Let him rest in peace beneath this dome. It is a helmet made for a giant's head."

CHARLES BONAPARTE.

(1746-1785.)

MARRIED

From this

---

1. *Joseph* (1768-1844), married in 1794 to Marie Julie Clary.

   From this marriage:

   (1) Zénaïde Charlotte (1801-1854), married in 1832 to her cousin, Charles Bonaparte, Prince de Canino.

   (2) Charlotte (1802-1839), married in 1831 Napoleon Louis, her cousin, second son of Louis.

2d. NAPOLEON I. (1769-1821), married:

   (1) Marie Josephine Rose Tascher de la Pagerie in 1796.

   (2) Marie Louise, Archduchess of Austria, in 1810.

   Adopted the first wife's two children:

   (1) Eugène (1781-1824), who married the Princess Augusta Amelia, daughter of the King of Bavaria.

   From this marriage:

   (a) Maximilian Joseph, Duke of Leuchtenberg, who married in 1839 a daughter of the Czar Nicholas.

   (b) Josephine, married in 1823 to Oscar Bernadotte, since King of Sweden under the name of Charles XIV.

   (c) Eugénie Hortense, married in 1826 to Prince Frederick of Hohenzollern Hechingen.

   (d) Amélie Augusta, married in 1829 to Dom Pedro, Emperor of Brazil.

   (e) Auguste Charles, married in 1835 to Donna Maria, Queen of Portugal.

   (f) Théodeline Louise, married in 1841 to William, Count of Würtemberg.

   (2) Eugénie Hortense (1783-1827), married to Louis Bonaparte. (See Louis.)

   From second marriage:

   François Charles Joseph (NAPOLEON II.), King of Rome, afterwards Duke of Reichstadt (1811-1832).

3d. *Lucien* (1775-1840), married:

   (1) in 1794, Christine Eleonore Boyer.

   (2) in 1802, Madame Jouberthon.

   From first marriage:

   (1) Charlotte, married in 1815 to Prince Mario Gabrielli.

   (2) Christine Egypta, married in 1818 to Count Avred Posse, a Swede, and in 1824 to Lord Dudley Coutts Stuart.

   From second marriage:

   (1) Charles Lucien Jules Laurent, Prince of Canino, married to elder daughter of Joseph Bonaparte. (Charles Lucien had eight children: Joseph, who died young; Lucien, a cardinal in 1868; Napoleon, served in French army; Julie, married to the Marquis de Boccagiovine; Charlotte, who became the Countess of Primoli; Augusta, afterwards the Princess Gabrielli; Marie, married to Count Campello; Bathilde, married to Count Cambacérès.)

   (2) Lætitia, married to Sir Thomas Wyse.

   (3) Paul, killed in 1826.

   (4) Jeanne, died in 1828.

   (5) Louis Lucien, known as Prince Lucien, and distinguished as a writer.

   (6) Pierre Napoleon, known as Prince Pierre, married to a sempstress, and refused to give her up. The oldest son of Prince Pierre is the Prince Roland Bonaparte. He would now be the chief of the House of Bonaparte, if Lucien had not been cut off from the succession.

   (7) Antoine.

   (8) Marie, married to the Viscount Valentini.

   (9) Constance, who took the veil.

4th. *Marie Anne Elisa* (1777-1820), married to Felix Bacciochi in 1797.

   From this marriage:

   (1) Charles Jerome Bacciochi (1810-1830).

   (2) Napoleone Elisa, married to Count Camerata.

BONAPARTE FAMILY.

MARIE LÆTITIA RAMOLINO.

(1750–1836.)

IN 1765.

marriage :

5th. *Louis* (1778–1846), married in 1802 to Eugénie Hortense de Beauharnais, daughter of Josephine.

From this marriage :

(1) Napoleon Charles, heir-presumptive to the throne of Holland, died in 1807.
(2) Charles Napoleon Louis, married his cousin Charlotte, daughter of Joseph; died in 1831.
(3) Charles Louis Napoleon, Emperor of the French in 1852, under the title of NAPOLEON III., married in 1853 to Eugénie de Montijo de Guzman, Countess of Teba.

From this marriage :

Napoleon Eugène Louis Jean Joseph, Prince Imperial, born in 1856, killed in Zululand in 1879.

6th. *Marie Pauline* (1780–1825), married :
(1) in 1801 to General Leclerc.
(2) in 1803 to Prince Camille Borghese. No children.

7th. *Caroline Marie Annonciade* (1782–1819), married Joachim Murat in 1800.

From this marriage :

(1) Napoleon Achille Charles Louis Murat (1801–1847), went to Florida, where he married a grandniece of George Washington.
(2) Lætitia Josèphe, married to the Marquis of Pepoli.
(3) Lucien Charles Joseph François Napoleon Murat, married an American, a Miss Fraser, in 1827. From this marriage there were five children.
(4) Louise Julie Caroline, married Count Rospoli.

8th. *Jerome* (1784–1860), married :
(1) in 1803 to Miss Eliza Patterson of Baltimore ; and
(2) in 1807 to the Princess Catherine of Würtemberg.

From first marriage :

Jerome Napoleon Bonaparte-Patterson (1805–1870) married in 1829 to Miss Suzanne Gay. Two children were born from this marriage :
(1) Jerome Napoleon Bonaparte (1832–1893).
(2) Charles Bonaparte, at present a resident of Baltimore.

From second marriage :

(1) Jerome Napoleon Charles, who died in 1847.
(2) Mathilde Lætitia Wilhelmine, married in 1840 to a Russian, Prince Demidoff, but separated from him ; known as the Princess Mathilde.
(3) Napoleon Joseph Charles Paul, called Prince Napoleon, also known as Plon-Plon, married in 1859 the Princess Clotilde, daughter of King Victor Emmanuel of Italy. On the death of the Prince Imperial, in 1879, became chief of the Bonapartist party. Died in 1891. Prince Napoleon had three children :
(a) Napoleon Victor Jerome Frederick, born in 1862, called Prince Victor, and the present Head of the House of Bonaparte.
(b) Napoleon Louis Joseph Jerome.
(c) Marie Lætitia Eugénie Catherine Adelaide.

V

CHRONOLOGY OF THE LIFE OF NAPOLEON BONAPARTE.

Age.	Date.	Event.
	1769.	Aug. 15.—Napoleon Bonaparte born at Ajaccio, in Corsica. Fourth child of Charles Bonaparte and of Lætitia, née Ramolino.
9.	1778.	Dec. 15.—Napoleon embarks for France with his father, his brother Joseph, and his uncle Fesch.
9.	1779.	Jan. 1.—Napoleon enters the College of Autun.
9.	1779.	April 25.—Napoleon enters the Royal Military School of Brienne.
15.	1784.	Oct. 23.—Napoleon enters the Royal Military School of Paris.
16.	1785.	Sept. 1.—Napoleon appointed Second Lieutenant in the Artillery Regiment de la Fère.
16.	1785.	Oct. 29.—Napoleon leaves the Military School of Paris.
16.	1785.	Nov. 5 to Aug. 11, 1786.—Napoleon at Valence with his regiment.
17.	1786.	Aug. 15 to Sept. 20.—Napoleon at Lyons with regiment.
17.	1786.	Oct. 17 to Feb. 1, 1787.—Napoleon at Douai with regiment.
17.	1787.	Feb. 1 to Oct. 14.—Napoleon on leave to Corsica.
18.	1787.	Oct. 15 to Dec. 24.—Napoleon quits Corsica, arrives in Paris, obtains fresh leave.
18.	1787.	Dec. 25 to May, 1788.—Napoleon proceeds to Corsica and returns early in May.
18-19.	1788.	May to April 4, 1789.—Napoleon at Auxonne with regiment.
19.	1789.	April 5 to April 30.—Napoleon at Seurre in command of a detachment.
19-20.	1789.	May 1 to Sept. 15.—Napoleon at Auxonne with regiment.
20-21.	1789.	Sept. 16 to June 1, 1791.—Napoleon in Corsica.
21-22.	1791.	June 2 to Aug. 29.—Napoleon joins the Fourth Regiment of Artillery at Valence as First Lieutenant.
22.	1791.	Aug. 30.—Napoleon starts for Corsica on leave for three months; quits Corsica May 2, 1792, for France, where he has been dismissed for absence without leave.
23.	1792.	Aug. 30.—Napoleon reinstated.
23.	1792.	Sept. 14 to June 11, 1793.—Napoleon in Corsica engaged in revolutionary attempts; having declared against Paoli, he and his family have to quit Corsica.
23.	1793.	June 13 to July 14.—Napoleon with his company at Nice.
24.	1793.	Oct. 9 to Dec. 19.—Napoleon placed in command of part of artillery of army of Carteaux before Toulon, 19th Oct.; Toulon taken 19th Dec.
24.	1793.	Dec. 22.—Napoleon nominated provisionally General of Brigade; approved later; receives commission, 16th Feb., 1794.
24.	1793.	Dec. 26 to April 1, 1794.—Napoleon appointed inspector of the coast from the Rhone to the Var, on inspection duty.
24.	1794.	April 1 to Aug. 5.—Napoleon with army of Italy; at Genoa 15th-21st July.
24-25.	1794.	Aug. 6 to Aug. 20, 1794.—Napoleon in arrest after fall of Robespierre.
25.	1794.	Sept. 14 to March 29, 1795.—Napoleon commanding artillery of an intended maritime expedition to Corsica.
25.	1795.	March 27 to May 10.—Napoleon ordered from the south to join the army in La Vendée to command its artillery; arrives in Paris, 10th May.
25-26.	1795.	June 13.—Napoleon ordered to join Hoche's army at Brest, to command a brigade of infantry; remains in Paris; 21st Aug., attached to Comité de Salut Public as one of four advisers; 15th Sept., struck off list of employed generals for disobedience of orders in not proceeding to the west.
26.	1795.	Oct. 5 (13th Vendémiaire, Jour des Sections).—Napoleon defends the Convention from the revolt of the Sections.
26.	1795.	Oct. 16.—Napoleon appointed provisionally General of Division.
26.	1795.	Oct. 26.—Napoleon appointed General of Division and Commander of the Army of the Interior (i.e., of Paris).
26.	1796.	March 2.—Napoleon appointed Commander-in-Chief of the Army of Italy; 9th March, marries Josephine Tascher de la Pagerie.

Age.	Date.	Event.
26.	1796.	March 11, leaves Paris for Italy.
26.	1796.	First Italian campaign of Napoleon against Austrians under Beaulieu, and Sardinians under Colli. Battle of Montenotte, 12th April; Millesimo, 14th April; Dego, 14th and 15th April; Mondovi, 22d April; Armistice of Cherasco with Sardinians, 28th April; Battle of Lodi, 10th May; Austrians beaten out of Lombardy, and Mantua besieged.
26.	1796.	July and Aug.—First attempt of Austrians to relieve Mantua; battle of Lonato, 31st July; Lonato and Castiglione, 3d Aug.; and, again, Castiglione, 5th and 6th Aug.; Wurmser beaten off, and Mantua again invested.
27.	1796.	Sept.—Second attempt of Austrians to relieve Mantua; battle of Calliano, 4th Sept.; Primolano, 7th Sept.; Bassano, 8th Sept.; St. Georges, 15th Sept.; Wurmser driven into Mantua and invested there.
27.	1796.	Nov.—Third attempt of Austrians to relieve Mantua; battles of Caldiero, 11th Nov., and Arcola, 15th, 16th, and 17th Nov.; Alvinzi driven off.
27.	1797.	Jan.—Fourth attempt to relieve Mantua; battles of Rivoli, 14th Jan., and Favorita, 16th Jan.; Alvinzi again driven off.
27.	1797.	Feb. 2.—Wurmser surrenders Mantua with eighteen thousand men.
27.	1797.	March 10.—Napoleon commences his advance on the Archduke Charles; beats him at the Tagliamento, 16th March; 18th April, provisional treaty of Leoben with Austria.
28.	1797.	Oct. 17.—Treaty of Campo Formio between France and Austria to replace that of Leoben; Venice partitioned, and itself now falls to Austria.
28.	1798.	Egyptian expedition. Napoleon sails from Toulon, 19th May; takes Malta, 12th June; lands near Alexandria, 1st July; Alexandria taken, 2d July; battle of the Pyramids, 21st July; Cairo entered, 23d July.
28.	1798.	Aug. 1.—Battle of the Nile.
29.	1799.	March 3.—Napoleon starts for Syria; 7th March, takes Jaffa; 18th March, invests St. Jean d'Acre; 16th April, battle of Mount Tabor; 22d May, siege of Acre raised; Napoleon reaches Cairo, 14th June.
29.	1799.	July 25.—Battle of Aboukir; Turks defeated.
30.	1799.	Aug. 22.—Napoleon sails from Egypt; lands at Fréjus, 6th Oct.
30.	1799.	Nov. 9 and 10 (18th and 19th Brumaire).—Napoleon seizes power.
30.	1799.	Dec. 25.—Napoleon, First Consul; Cambacérès, Second Consul; Lebrun, Third Consul.
30.	1800.	May and June.—Marengo campaign. 14th June, battle of Marengo; armistice signed by Napoleon with Melas, 15th June.
31.	1800.	Dec. 24 (3d Nivôse).—Attempt to assassinate Napoleon by infernal machine.
31.	1801.	Feb. 9.—Treaty of Lunéville between France and Germany.
31.	1801.	July 15.—*Concordat* with Rome.
32.	1801.	Oct. 1.—Preliminaries of peace between France and England signed at London.
32.	1802.	Jan. 26.—Napoleon Vice-President of Italian Republic.
32.	1802.	March 27.—Treaty of Amiens.
32.	1802.	May 19.—Legion of Honor instituted; carried out, 14th July, 1814.
32.	1802.	Aug. 4.—Napoleon First Consul for life.
33.	1803.	May.—War between France and England.
33.	1803.	March 5.—Civil Code (later, Code Napoleon) decreed.
34.	1804.	March 21.—Duc d'Enghien shot at Vincennes.
34-35.	1804.	May 18.—Napoleon, Empereur des Français; crowned, 2d Dec.
36.	1805.	Ulm campaign. 25th Sept., Napoleon crosses the Rhine; 14th Oct., battle of Elchingen; 20th Oct., Mack surrenders Ulm.
36.	1805.	Oct. 21.—Battle of Trafalgar.
36.	1805.	Dec. 2.—Russians and Austrians defeated at Austerlitz.
36.	1805.	Dec. 26.—Treaty of Presburg.
36.	1806.	July 1.—Confederation of the Rhine formed; Napoleon protector.
37.	1806.	Jena campaign with Prussia. Battles of Jena and of Auerstadt, 14th Oct.; Berlin occupied, 25th Oct.
37.	1806.	Nov. 21.—Berlin decrees issued.
37.	1807.	Feb. 8.—Battle of Eylau with Russians, indecisive; 14th June, battle of Friedland, decisive.
37.	1807.	July 7.—Treaty of Tilsit.
38.	1807.	Oct. 27.—Secret treaty of Fontainebleau between France and Spain for the partition of Portugal.
38.	1808.	March. — French gradually occupy Spain; Joseph Bonaparte transferred from Naples to Spain; replaced at Naples by Murat.
39.	1808.	Sept. 27 to Oct. 14.—Conferences at Erfurt between Napoleon, Alexander, and German sovereigns.
39.	1808.	Nov. and Dec.—Napoleon beats the Spanish armies; enters Madrid; marches against Moore, but suddenly returns to France to prepare for Austrian campaign.

AGE.	DATE.	EVENT.
39.	1809.	Campaign of Wagram. Austrians advance, 10th April ; Napoleon occupies Vienna, 13th May ; beaten back at Essling, 22d May ; finally crosses Danube, 4th July, and defeats Austrians at Wagram, 6th July.
40.	1809.	Oct. 14.—Treaty of Schönbrunn or of Vienna.
40.	1809.	Dec. 15-16.—Josephine divorced.
40.	1810.	April 1 and 2.—Marriage of Napoleon, aged 40, with Marie Louise, aged 18 years 3 months.
41.	1810.	Dec. 13.—Hanseatic towns and all northern coast of Germany annexed to French Empire.
41.	1811.	March 20.—The King of Rome, son of Napoleon, born.
42-43.	1812.	June 23.—War with Russia ; Napoleon crosses the Niemen ; 7th Sept., battle of Moskwa or Borodino ; Napoleon enters Moscow, 15th Sept.; commences his retreat, 19th Oct.
43.	1812.	Oct. 22-23.—Conspiration of General Malet at Paris.
43.	1812.	Nov. 26-28.—Passage of the Beresina ; 5th Dec., Napoleon leaves his army ; arrives at Paris, 18th Dec.
43-44.	1813.	Leipsic campaign. 2d May, Napoleon defeats Russians and Prussians at Lützen ; and again, on 20th-21st May, at Bautzen ; 26th June, interview of Napoleon and Metternich at Dresden ; 10th Aug., midnight, Austria joins the allies ; 26th-27th Aug., Napoleon defeats allies at Dresden, but Vandamme is routed at Kulm on 30th Aug., and on 16th-19th Oct., Napoleon is beaten at Leipsic.
44.	1814.	Allies advance into France ; 29th Jan., battle of Brienne ; 1st Feb., battle of La Rothière.
44.	1814.	Feb. 5 to March 18.—Conferences of Chatillon (sur Seine).
44.	1814.	Feb. 11.—Battle of Montmirail ; 14th Feb., of Vauchamps ; 18th Feb., of Montereau.

AGE.	DATE.	EVENT.
44.	1814.	March 7.—Battle of Craon ; 9th-10th March, Laon ; 20th March, Arcis sur l'Aube.
44.	1814.	March 21.—Napoleon commences his march to throw himself on the communications of the allies ; 25th March, allies commence their march on Paris ; battle of La Fère Champenoise, Marmont and Mortier beaten ; 28th March, Napoleon turns back at St. Dizier to follow allies ; 29th March, empress and court leave Paris.
44.	1814.	March 30.—Paris capitulates ; allied sovereigns enter on 1st April.
44.	1814.	April 2.—Senate declares the dethronement of Napoleon, who abdicates, conditionally, on 4th April, in favor of his son, and unconditionally on 6th April ; Marmont's corps marches into the enemy's lines on 5th April ; on 11th April, Napoleon signs the treaty giving him Elba for life ; 20th April, Napoleon takes leave of the Guard at Fontainebleau ; 3d May, Louis XVIII. enters Paris ; 4th May, Napoleon lands in Elba.
45.	1814.	Oct. 3.—Congress of Vienna meets for settlement of Europe ; actually opens 3d Nov.
45.	1815.	Feb. 26.—Napoleon quits Elba ; lands near Cannes, 1st March ; 19th March, Louis XVIII. leaves Paris ; 20th March, Napoleon enters Paris.
45.	1815.	June 16.—Battle of Ligny and Quatre Bras ; 18th June, battle of Waterloo.
45-46.	1815.	June 29.—Napoleon leaves Malmaison for Rochefort ; surrenders to English, 15th July ; sails for St. Helena, 8th Aug.; arrives at St. Helena, 15th Oct.
51 yrs. 8 mos.	1821.	May 5.—Napoleon dies, 5.45 P.M.; buried, 8th May.
	1840.	Oct. 15.—Body of Napoleon disentombed ; embarked in the "Belle Poule," commanded by the Prince de Joinville, son of Louis Philippe, on 16th Oct.; placed in the Invalides, 15th Dec., 1840.

THE END.